DATE DUE		
FEB 6 '70	MAR 21 '72	
MAR 6 '70	MAR 13 '74	
MAR 1 4 '70	JAN 27 '75	
MAR 2 1 '70	R	
APR 7 '70	OCT 29 '76	
APR 1 5 '70		
JUN 17 '70	FEB 16 77	
JUN 26 '70	DEC 9 77	
JUL 10 '70		
APR 2 '71		
MAR 18 '72		

SANCTUARY V

BY BUDD SCHULBERG

Fiction

WHAT MAKES SAMMY RUN?

THE HARDER THEY FALL

THE DISENCHANTED

WATERFRONT

SOME FACES IN THE CROWD

SANCTUARY V

Plays and Screenplays

ON THE WATERFRONT

WIND ACROSS THE EVERGLADES

A FACE IN THE CROWD

THE DISENCHANTED
  (*with Harvey Breit*)

WHAT MAKES SAMMY RUN?
  (*Libretto with Stuart Schulberg*)

Anthology

FROM THE ASHES—VOICES OF WATTS
  (*Edited, with an Introduction*)

SANCTUARY V

BUDD SCHULBERG

Sch

AN **NAL** BOOK | THE WORLD PUBLISHING COMPANY

New York and Cleveland

The author and publisher gratefully acknowledge permission to reprint the Italian lyrics of "Volare" (Nel Blu,
Dipinto di Blu); Italian text by D. Mudugno–F. Migliacci;
music by Domenico Modugno; © Copyright 1958
Edizioni Curci, Milan, Italy; rights for U.S. and Canada
controlled by Robbins Music Corp.; used by permission.

On pp. 338 and 339, the excerpt from "Como el toro"
by Miguel Hernandez is adapted from *The Penguin Book
of Spanish Verse,* edited by J. M. Cohen.

First Printing—1969

Published by The New American Library, Inc.
in association with The World Publishing Company,
2231 West 110th Street, Cleveland, Ohio 44102

Library of Congress Catalog Card Number: 71-93470
Printed in the United States of America

WORLD PUBLISHING
TIMES MIRROR

To Ad

For her years of counsel and devotion

With special thanks to G.B.S. and S.O'S.
for editorial services above and beyond the call
of family duty.

And to *Joaquín Godoy*

whose own experience and that of his friends
provided the key unlocking the doors of diplomatic
asylums similar to the composite sanctuary
described in these pages.

ARTICLE V

Asylum may not be granted except in urgent cases and for the period of time strictly necessary for the asylee to depart from the country with the guarantees granted by the government of the territorial state, to the end that his life, liberty, or personal integrity may not be endangered, or that the asylee's safety is ensured in some other way . . .

. . . Urgent cases are understood to be those, among others, in which the individual is being sought by persons or mobs over whom the authorities have lost control, or by the authorities themselves, and is in danger of being deprived of his life or liberty because of political persecution and cannot, without risk, ensure his safety in any other way.

—PAN AMERICAN CONVENTION
ON DIPLOMATIC ASYLUM
Caracas, March 1–28, 1954

"One does not show one's greatness by being at one extreme, but by touching both at once." PASCAL

PROLOGUE

Now that I am here, waiting, I try to remember. What curious chain of circumstances brought me here? How did I, me, the precious but vulnerable little vessel that contains Justo Moreno Suárez, achieve this predicament? Justo Moreno Suárez, a civilized man, a keeper of the peace.

My old friends, my colleagues (almost but not quite my comrades) of the Revolution are being kind to me. They provide solitary confinement, but with sufficient paper and pencils to keep myself amused. When I say they are being kind to me in this fashion, it is the new fashion of expediency. If God has been pulled down from his high fence—and all the good Pope Johns in the world may not be able to put that Humpty-Dumpty together again—then expediency is the next best thing in this modern world that rushes us forward to—to what? Those who say they know are mostly liars and those who think they know are mostly fools. So I sit and write to some expedient purpose of my captors. They know I am one of those tormented Gutenberg souls who live words as fishermen live fish, soccer players live goals and archaeologists live ruins. I will read philosophy, novels, newspapers, telephone books. And in my deprivation I write in order to have something to read. And that is where my old friends of the Angel Bello Revolution know their expediency. Whatever they are saving me for, whatever role I may be called on to play in our country's People's Republic, role to play or sacrifice to make, be it forced or voluntary, I must be sane to perform it usefully. And so I write to preserve my sanity. Here Angel Bello and I are partnered strangely once again.

For different reasons, Angel Bello and I share concern for the state of my mental health. So I write this not merely to amuse myself but to satisfy myself that there was some purpose beyond whim, bad luck, happenstance, that has brought me so close to the wall: *El Paredón* we call it, that angry rifle rain of lead that leaves of what had been a man a crumpled heap of dead flesh and murdered desires. It is not the pain I fear most—though I was never a brave man—no, not the pain but the humiliation. To be led in as a manacled slave. To be carried out as slaughtered meat. And not even to have the force or fortune to die the exalted death of martyred heroes. For I am no longer either hero or martyr to my friends or my enemies. Yes, I write this with a paranoiac sense of isolation: everybody is against me, from the First Colonel of the Revolution, as Angel Bello calls himself, to my beloved wife, Marta, who never answers my letters. Do they ever reach her? Or is she unable to forgive me? Have you ever called long distance to someone who hangs up on you? The rage is constipating, not cathartic. You shout, you threaten, you commit the violence of tearing out the wires only to realize you are committing a form of communicational suicide. But I have not given up. Every week I am here I write my long letter to Marta. If they do not take me to the wall—and I am inclined to think Angel Bello will keep me rotting here in this island prison to live out the absurdity of my existence—I will keep up the weekly letters. I know my Marta. She is strong and pigheaded and prideful, but she is also loving and emotional and unpredictable, and one of these weeks she may be holding my letter in her hand, knowing so well the handwriting that kept our courtship alive in the days when she was in Washington with her father—ambassador for the self-elected President Zamora—and I was a strange Latin fish-out-of-water on scholarship at Columbia University. Yes, she will see that erratic handwriting with the t's never crossed and printed words, for no clear reason, exploding into the script and she will think, that is my Justo, whom I fought my formidable father to marry, with whom I sobbed and groaned and laughed with pleasure, with whom I had a life that was so much more than your typical Latin society marriage of convenience. That is my Justo calling out to me from his solitary cell within rifle sound of the wall. And she will read my words and hurry to answer and her words will touch even the heart of the censor and Celestino the guard who is not a bad fellow, merely venal and haphazardly cruel and rather good-natured. Celestino will be in on the miracle and it will be like one of those scenes in a Hollywood movie, with the mustachioed guard, a gringo with an exaggerated Latin accent, saying, "Today I have the beeg surprise for you, Señor Presidente."

Dreams, I wrote as a trusting schoolboy poet, are the bread of the soul. When Dostoevski was at the stake prepared for execution, was he not dreaming still? When the nails of the Cross were drawing the last blood from Christ, did he not take refuge in his strange theories of love?

And so I wait, and I daydream that Marta will answer me, that this island prison will open, that Angel Bello will revert to the youthful dreams of democracy he indulged in, back in student days when everything was theory and future, when everything was soft mañana, before the hard reality, the nails of now.

PART ONE

1

Late one afternoon I was sitting at my elliptical leather desk in the big office in the old palace that had been the administrative nerve center of the country since the early Spanish days. I was working on a speech to be delivered at graduation exercises at the University, commemorating the Bello Revolution. As the hand-picked—local humorists sometimes called me hand-plucked—Provisional President of our People's Republic, I was preparing the rousing text the University boys were expecting of me, glorifying Angel Bello and the Revolution that had given us our first taste of independence in nearly five hundred years. I would castigate the American carpet-baggers who had swarmed in and stolen from us our own War of Independence in the late nineties. I was thinking of the cheers from the gringo-hating student body and the smiles and applause of the new Communist rector. The rector worried me, as did a number of the recent appointments. Old-line Communists who had dismissed our movement as "adventurism" in the days of the Zamora dictatorship were replacing left-wing nationalists who had been Angel Bello's first supporters in the dangerous days of the rebellion.

Of course I would be careful to omit these doubts from my speech. Revolution feeds on unabated enthusiasm. I would dwell on the familiar enemies that had plagued us, the Zamora millionaires and their North American partners, their secret police and their campaign to keep our country both illiterate and intimidated. I would not be lying. I simply would be repressing recent qualms.

The intercom brought the voice of my plump, pretty-faced secretary, Señorita Naranja: Claude Lewison of the London *Observer* was on the phone. I had met Lewison in the early days of the Bello victory. Better informed and more simpático than most American journalists who came to perform their hatchet jobs, Lewison had written a useful series on the positive changes our Revolution was making in a country drained by the colonialism of the dollar.

"Hello, old boy. Lewison here. On my way to the Press Club for a hard-earned daiquiri. Thought you might like to join me."

I always enjoyed the International Press Club, with its comfortable mahogany bar, the rack of newspapers and magazines, ranging from the Communist *Política* to the London *Economist,* the books written by club members, and the veteran bartender Gonzalo who seemed to keep a card-file in his mind of everybody's order. And Lewison was a congenial drinking companion who would bring interesting news of the outside world. I said I was on my way to the family beach house but would stop in for a few minutes.

He was waiting for me at a small table on the outside terrace of the club, overlooking the sun-baked orange tile rooftops and the narrow streets of the old town, the bell towers of the sixteenth-century cathedral and the historic harbor guarded by Spanish fortresses. It was pleasing to the eye in a way that the glass cities of North America would never be. Centuries of cruelty, avarice and colonial aggrandizement were hidden behind a facade of aesthetic antiquity.

"Welcome, old boy. Let me order you a double. British fair play. Two ahead of you." Claude Lewison was in his early thirties, tall, unusually handsome for a correspondent, urbane, intelligent. A Cambridgeman, always dressed impeccably, but with individual flair, he was wearing a double-breasted blue blazer with old military silver buttons and his club emblem on the breast pocket.

Gonzalo brought my double daiquiri made with the finest of our light and our dark rums, a national triumph rivaling Hemingway's celebrated Floridita. We touched glasses, toasted each other's health and drifted into discussion of our impending soccer match against Wales. Lewison had been a respectable amateur player who began his journalistic career as a sports writer. Conversation flowed from soccer to bullfighting to a comparison of the current pocketsized boxers with some of the gifted champions of the past.

"I've seen most of the great ones," I said, warming to a subject free of anxieties. "Back to Kid Chocolate, Sixto Escobar . . . But I wish you had seen Willie Pep. The manly art—classic ballet. Years ago he came here to box our local star, Baby Bando—when it was over the Baby said to me, 'Imagine, for ten rounds he dances in front of me and everytime I try to hit him *whiff* like magic he disappears.' "

Lewison laughed and with a *ssssst* attracted Gonzalo's attention: another round. The cathedral bells were banging out the hour. Other chimes across the city answered them, like dogs barking at each other across great distances to prove that they are there.

"Baby Bando." Lewison enjoyed the sound of the name. "I saw him box, back in Zamora days, my first visit here. Haven't heard of him in years."

"He's still fighting once in a while. In Miami now."

"I gather most of your name fighters have defected."

I nodded. "I was sorry to see them leave but—a man should have a right to decide his own life."

"I drink to that. And may your quaint notion come back into style again."

Tropical night was dropping a purple curtain over the city. Lewison lowered his glass and studied me for a moment. "Moreno Suárez, let me ask you a question. More or less the same one I asked when I was here ten months ago. But one of the reasons this country is so fascinating is that it seems to be constantly changing. You are still in a unique position. After all, when Angel was on trial—"

"The heroic citizen judge who saved his life," I said with a mocking bow.

"Well, it was a bloody brave thing to do, old boy," Lewison insisted. "How many people were inviting the fury of Zamora—in public?"

In the time of Zamora the death penalty required the verdict of three judges, two professional and one citizen chosen specifically for that case. As a professor of political science, walking a tightrope but trusted because my wife Marta was the daughter of a Zamora ambassador, I had been given the honor of helping to tighten the noose around Angel's neck. But I had caused a national *escándalo* by voting not guilty, on the basis that Angel Bello was attempting to overthrow a regime that was itself illegal since it had seized power in breach of the Constitution. Of course, Zamora had not known that I was a member of Angel's underground.

"With that decision," Lewison went on, "you put your life on the line—"

"You make me sound heroic. Actually I was frightened, almost out of my mind."

"Mmm. I think I understand you, to some extent. But with all the things that seem to be happening, if you went back to that trial, knowing what you know now, would you do it again?"

I drained the last drops of the second daiquiri. "Yes. Yes! Of course I would do it again. If I had voted with those two corrupted pigs, Angel would be dead today . . ."

"And you prefer to have him alive, and in total control?"

"One question at a time," I said. "Those two Zamora bastards could hardly wait to drop the noose around his throat. Then where would we be? Back in the same old trough we had lived in so long. No, it was a time for revolution. I had no choice. I had to vote to save the neck of the only man who could lead it."

Lewison nodded and signaled again for Gonzalo.

"Thank you, Claude, but I have a long drive to the beach and Marta is waiting. And two of Gonzalo's doubles is one more than enough."

Lewison smiled. "One final 'Gonzalón' for the road to the beach— to the pugilistic balletics of Willie Pep."

On the third daiquiri I was trying to explain our revolutionary accomplishments. "Take this hotel—it was full of American gang-sters running the casinos and splitting the profits with Zamora and Romano. All gone now. The mansions of the sugar barons—more than half of them gringos—turned into kindergartens, schools for the poor, hospitals. The telephone company owned by our rich cousins to the north charging whatever they wanted and paying off Zamora. Now it's nationalized and—"

"And the service is godawful," Lewison interrupted with a smile.

"True, true, we still lack the famous North American efficiency. But Angel is right—how will our people ever learn to handle their

own affairs if our utilities and natural resources are left in the hands
of foreign profiteers?"

"In other words," Lewison said over the rim of his daiquiri glass,
"you still think of Angel Bello as you did when I was here last—as
the Second Coming?"

"My friend, I admire the brilliance and the stamina and many of
the new ideas. But after all, Angel is mortal. And although he may
not be quite the god-figure he seems to millions of our people, he
does have an uncanny knack for knowing how to lead them." I hesitated. "But sometimes I ask myself—is it our fate to jump from the
Wall Street pot into the Communist fire? We start with a humanist
revolution born with noble promises. Now—" There was still a
jiggerful of good rum in the glass. I drank from it and heard myself
saying, "Communists who never stood up with us against the old
regime—getting more and more of the key positions—I begin to
worry—"

"—that your fellow 'humanist' is turning his coat inside out and
handing you over to the—"

"You speak too fast, Lewison. I am still an Angelista. When the
gringos use Somoza in Nicaragua—Trujillo in Hispaniola, Batista,
Zamora, Armas—the whole bloody parade of hatchet men from
Guatemala on down, I stand with Angel. But there is also the need
to be a free man in a free country. Nobody's satellite. Nobody's
trained monkey on a string."

"I drink to that," Lewison said and drained his glass.

So did I. Our own rum with our own juicy little limes and our
own sugar—no wonder we made the best daiquiris in the world.

The cathedral bells were clanging again, that raucous bong-bong
bonging before the ceremonial tolling of the hours. I looked out
across the tile rooftop that had become a darkening mosaic as the
dying light of the sun moved on into the western sea.

"—must be off," I said, pushing my chair back and rising, not
unsteadily but with a sense of accomplishment at being able to stand
so firmly. "Gonzalo—" I waved for the check.

"My treat," Lewison insisted. "Not that I am being all that generous. I sign the chit and send the bill to the *Observer*. Which is

why you see so many of my colleagues getting themselves gloriously whiffled."

I smiled. Already a group of Anglo-Saxon correspondents were on their way to a long evening at the bar.

"We must do this again," Lewison said, with his debonair charm. "Enjoyed every minute of it."

Marta's greeting at the door had been blunt but deserved, as usual. I should have been home thirty minutes earlier. Especially when she was preparing red snapper poached in hot tomato and green chili sauce, her own adaptation of a Mexican recipe. We washed it down with a cold bottle of our country's underrated white wine, followed by a ripe mango for dessert and rich black coffee that was a mixture of native beans ground in our kitchen just before serving. When I complimented Marta on the meal, she told me how Chino, the little one-eyed fisherman, had brought the red snapper still alive to the door.

"The secret of cooking fish," Marta said, "is to get them so fresh the meat still flinches from the lime juice."

I asked Marta to spare me these delicate details. She knew I was squeamish about pain—an odd schizo who enjoyed fishing and prize-fighting and yet always felt a tendency to nausea at the sight of blood. Marta laughed. She was a hearty woman who was still strikingly handsome at forty-five, although the slim ballet dancer she had been long ago was now trapped in hard flesh. Her ankles had thickened, as had her waist and her buttocks. With the years her legs had grown heavy too and she had a bad knee, arthritic, that made her favor her right leg on rainy days. But it would be misleading to dwell on Marta's age or physical deterioration. Great beauty may thicken and age but never loses its essence. Dark eyebrows directed you to laughing, loving, evil eyes. A large mouth laughed and whispered outrageous promises. That was Marta—still the most vigorous Latin lady I have ever known. She had an Irish ancestor who fought with Bolívar and although I am never sure you can put that much faith in heredity, there did seem to be something in her that was oddly "Irish." If it was not that accident of blood, there was something fiercely unconventional about her for a lady of high Latin society. She had been not only a ballet dancer but a tomboy and she was an extrovert with strong opinions on practically everything. Marta was enthusiastically, uninhibitedly female. She loved to cook and to make clothes and to make love with a man. For a Latin matron she was shockingly rowdy and coarse-spoken. The coarse speech had begun as something of an affectation in her late teens when it had seemed startling and charming for a dainty and beautiful highborn ballerina to call a rival *cursi,* still one of her favorite words, or to describe a man she didn't like as a *pendejo.* Now her friends and I were used to it. Her violent one-sentence assassinations, her own *cursi*-ness, were simply part of her character.

She could say to one of her friends, "What a lovely dress, you should give it to your daughter, she has the figure for it," and the friend would laugh because that was the sort of thing one expected from Marta. The conventional ladies of Latin society accepted her as a bold original. She was much closer in spirit to the liberated women of North America. There were those who thought it was refreshing and those who thought it was overbearing. But whatever it was, it was distinctly Marta. You either take it or reject it. I had taken it for nearly all of my adult life and on the whole I enjoyed it. I had been in love with her twenty-five years ago and although the heat of passion had cooled to strong affection, we had the only marriage I knew of that was still alive. In North America it seemed to me that marriage was seventy-five percent fraud and in our Latin society at least ninety-five percent convenience.

There were times when I envied men their young mistresses, and at restaurant lunches I might find myself glancing at attractive women and enjoying the silken legs that passed my table. But I was one of the few men in our society who did not maintain a *casa chica*, that convenient second home where most of my friends enjoyed illegal but socially accepted bliss. I would not say that I had been completely faithful to Marta. But there had been no serious or damaging affairs. Over the marriage span I had been content to be man to Marta's woman and at an age when these things tend to cool and drop off like the ash of a smoked-out cigar, Marta and I still had a life together behind the drawn shades.

That night at dinner I kept trying to call to mind what I had said to Lewison, while Marta was gossiping about someone's affair with our good friend Alejandro Castillo, the cultural attaché of one of the few Latin countries still maintaining diplomatic relations with our regime. "Suzi and I happened to be having lunch at El Gato just across the street from Alejandro's apartment when who do we see but Alejandro driving up to the door in his Mercedes and who do you think is with him—Tina Alonso—of course they had no idea we were watching. You know, Justo, I suspected that something special was happening in Tina's life. She has been looking so well lately. That husband of hers takes her out to dinner once a week—a big favor—and meanwhile everybody in town knows that he and that *cursi* nightclub singer are—"

"Marta, must I hear all this silly gossip?"

When Marta gossiped there was so much emotion in it that it made me wonder. Had she ever been unfaithful to me? Or was this passion for the illicit trysts of her friends the sublimation of boredom with her own fidelity?

"I know you think your pal Alejandro is a *maricón*. But my theory is he's a secret *macho*—so chic he wants everyone to believe he is *maricón*. Because if I know Tina—"

"Marta, who gives a damn if Alejandro spends his afternoons with five girls wound up in all the Arabian delights!" I slammed my napkin down. "I am going for a walk on the beach."

"Justo, is something wrong?"

"No, no, I just want a little peace."

"You had too much to drink. And you know you can't drink as you did before you were forty."

"Please, Marta. No lectures."

"Something is bothering you. It always comes out when you drink. I can read you like—the lines in your balls."

"The expression is—the lines in your hand."

"I know the other better."

"Marta, you are a disgusting woman. Now I *am* going for a walk."

I had to be careful not to underrate Marta: like the time when the Angel Bello trial was nearing its end. Angel was fighting back in his own defense: "Can a government that seized power illegally, as did the regime of General Zamora, invoke the powers of the Constitution it had violated?" I had not discussed with Marta the legal conclusions I was searching. I only told her the case was going to be a crucial one for us. I thought it might be wise if she were out of the country when the decision came down.

"Will you be in danger, Justo?" she had asked.

"I hope not. But I may be in more danger if you and the family are here. It will be easier for me if the Tigers of Romano do not threaten you."

"What about you?"

"I will feel my way. With friends in high places—I think I can manage."

She had come over and kissed me on the mouth.

"That Zamora is a *pendejo*. Do what you have to do. But be careful."

Now, as I turned away from Marta and headed for the screen door leading out to the beach, I heard the small waves of the bay rushing in, flowing out, repeating their endless challenge: *do what you have to do.* I would always think of this bay as a special friend. For the night the Tigers of Romano were hunting me after the Angel Bello verdict, I had taken refuge in Chino's fishing shack, where he had disguised me as a fellow-fisherman and sneaked me aboard his cousin's shrimp boat. Fifty miles out to sea, I had been lowered into a dinghy and pointed toward the far shore, and safety, if I could make it there alone in the dark. I had done what I had to do. So had Marta, and reunited in Mexico we survived. But unlike Angel Bello I was not a man of action. I never enjoyed daring as I had seen Angel exalt in his. He inhaled and exhaled extreme danger as if it were some hallucinatory drug. Guided by an automatic pilot, my course was decided for me by a conscience I was unable to control. In the Bello case I had rendered a brave verdict. But with a coward's anxiety. Now the ghost of that old anxiety followed me to the screen door that opened on the beach. Near the threshold I stumbled and heard a screech. It was our ever-pregnant tramp of a cat, Dolores.

"Justo, look where you are going!" Marta scolded. "Dolores is getting ready to have her babies. It is not easy for her to move out of the way."

I did not answer. But I was careful to step over the swollen and indignant Dolores. We had raised her from a sickly kitten and I was as attached to her as were the rest of the family. On the steps outside the screen door I almost tripped over another sleeping form, that of my potbellied guard, Rosendo. He staggered to his feet and managed to utter a "Buenas noches, Señor Presidente." Rosendo was an illiterate corporal left over from the bottom of Zamora's military barrel and tolerated by the revolutionary army boys as a harmless innocent, an old reliable who didn't really care for whom he was soldiering so long as he got his rations of black beans and rice and enough pesos in his pocket to enjoy a good drunk on Saturday night.

It was only when I had left my redoubtable guard behind me and stepped out onto the beach that I felt peacefully alone and out of the way of Marta and her gossip and her tough concern, of Dolores and her perpetual kittens, of Claude Lewison and his casual way of asking pointed questions, of Angel Bello, whom I admired and feared . . .

The edge of the sea was good. I loved this old beach house with its ocean sea without end as primordial front yard. How calm it was that evening. Sometimes the waves pounded up toward the fence, but that night they were reduced to ripples that made a liquid sound as they rolled up the beach over the little shells and the rounded pebbles. Often I carried a flashlight to hunt for crabs in the shallows, but that night the moon did a better job. In the glow of the almost round white moon I followed the familiar crescent of the beach to the long arm of coral rocks that divided our beach, the Playa de los Papagayos, from the next crescent of sand on our

magnificent Bay of the Pirates. Behind this pink beach that grew
rosy and sometimes theatrically vermilion in the glow of the falling
sun were the coconut palms where a flock of mynah birds kept up
their noisy chatter until nightfall, and where the green parrots that
gave our beach its name went soaring over the treetops.

I called out to one that had become a wild, free-flying pet, "Mano
—Mano?" but my parrot friend would not venture forth at night.
Apparently he was sleeping as any sensible *papagayo* should. It was
in the first light of morning that he always responded. I was an early
riser with some puritan sense of misgiving if I slept beyond half-past
seven. Rising while Marta was still asleep, dressing quickly and
going out into the tropical morning gave me an almost religious
sense of rebirth—the comforting coo of the mourning doves and the
busy mynahs beginning their day. I liked to carry bread out for
the seabirds. It was good to stand at the edge of the sea and watch
the athletic gulls swoop down. And the quick-legged sandpipers.
On the point of rocks there was an old white-crowned pelican so
lazy he would no longer fish for himself. He had taught the surf-
casters to drop the shivering fish down his throat. *El Viejo*, we
called him, the old one. Old and spoiled. Quite mean, really. I was
fond of him. But my true compañero was Mano, the parrot. Mano
had his own independent but quietly outgoing personality. When he
saw me he would fly down and walk his funny bowlegged walk
along the fence railing. He had learned to say "Buenos días." Sometimes he would fly off and land ahead of me and then walk back
toward me to greet me with another "Buenos días." I discovered
that Mano had a sweet tooth and I would feed him pieces of cake.
For a wild creature of the tropics he had a strange gentleness. His
predatory beak would take the piece of cake from my fingers with
delicate care.

That night when I called out "Mano" I did not really expect him
to come to me in the dark. But I enjoyed the conceit that I had a
personal friend in that wild aviary of coconut palms. I walked to the
end of the beach and stood on a rock platform rising above the
sand. The sea that was sometimes violent in the autumn months
lap-lapped gently at the rocks. The sea was eternal and the sky was
eternal and the rocks and the shore were eternal and the renewal of

the life of the palm jungles was eternal—if not without a beginning
and an end, at least resistant to change. Slowly, slowly the water
wore away the rock; from century to century there were changes in
topography and changes in the flora and fauna, but standing on the
rock under the stars and hearing, seeing and smelling the sea I felt
the consistency of nature. How much of its beauty was its reassurance that it would be there tomorrow and tomorrow while man
struggles to find himself in this consistency. Someday, and all too
quickly, the little speck that was so important to me, called Justo
Moreno Suárez, would be gone, vanished, forgotten, and the sea
would wash against the rocks and roll up upon the shore, inces-
santly saying, who cares, who cares? Put your ear to the sea some-
time and see if that is not its haughty question. Who cares? Who
cares . . . ? It does not mean this harshly, merely impersonally, but
just the same you must stand up to the sea, you must stand up to all
these eternal elements and tell them, *I* care . . . That they will not
hear you does not matter. You will hear yourself telling them and
that will matter. If you care about yourself, only then will you be
able to care about the living things that are related to your existence—from your hearty and loyal old wife to your children and
your friends and your cats and your parrots and your principles.

A swell larger than those before rose, crested and broke against
the rock. I tried to jump back, but the spent wave splashed me and
soaked one of my shoes. Even the sea of my own crescent of beach
was not to be trusted. It broke my reverie, my momentary trust in
nature. I turned and walked slowly up the beach toward the lights
of my house, my right foot damp and cold.

At the white picket gate opening on my front yard, Rosendo was
now playing the on-the-ready military guard ever awake and un-
blinking. He snapped to attention and gave me a smart "El Señor
Presidente."

"*Buenas noches, Rosendo, duerme bien,* sleep well," I said.

"I stand here awake so that you may sleep well, my Presidente,"
Rosendo said, suppressing a yawn.

Life is like an old-fashioned morality play in our Latin culture.
When people are in love they sing out their joys or suffer their sor-
rows in public. What we are is half real, half the part we are playing. Rosendo, for instance, was half mercenary revolutionary soldier,

half dreamer and dramatist, hamming up the part of presidential guard. He took extreme advantage of me because he knew that I would never report him for any minor dereliction of duty. Should I have done so to the wrong superior officer whose mood was sour that day, Rosendo might be shot. The Revolution had been fought in the name of campesinos like Rosendo, but the actual living Rosendo was a meaningless cipher who could be swatted dead with as little thought as one swats a mosquito.

At the kitchen door, I thought of the refrigerator and the cold seafood and wine left over from dinner, and when I switched on the light I discovered another kitchen snoop, our daughter Clarita. In her nightgown with a blue robe thrown over it, she was at the cake box, preparing to slice herself a slab of chocolate fudge cake.

At fifteen Clarita still had not lost her baby fat. Her strong, straight nose should have been attractive but it was not yet in proportion to her apple-round face. Of course, Marta was convinced that she would be the most stunning of her classmates if only we could slim her down.

"A-ha," I said, "caught in the act."

She giggled. "Popee, when you were my age, did homework always make you hungry? I started to draw a triangle and it looked like a slice of chocolate cake."

"Clarita, everything reminds you of chocolate cake. You're picking up my bad habits. But, if we have a secret feast, we must go on a strict diet together mañana."

"Yes, Popee," Clarita said, taking a large mouthful of cake from her fingers, "tomorrow we will both start getting very thin." And then, again using that name I thought it time for her to outgrow, she said, "Popee, read to me a little while. Read me *The Little Prince.*"

I had begun to read *The Little Prince* when she was still too small to understand its hidden meanings and subtle colors. I had turned to it out of boredom with the inane, repetitious, patronizing books that were all I could find for five-year-olds in Spanish. She had fallen in love with the "extraordinary small person" with golden hair and yellow scarf who came from a planet no bigger than a little house.

"Piggyback me to my room."

"Clarita, you're too old for that now."

While I was protesting she had jumped on a kitchen chair and flung herself on my back.

I was off balance, she was heavy, and I almost went to my knees.

"Giddyap, horsie." I carried her unsteadily through the dining room.

"Faster, horsie!" She dug her knees hard into my sides. Inside our plump fifteen-year-old was the small girl she still wanted to be.

"Clara, I have to put you down."

She clung to my neck, and for a moment it changed from a game to a duel as I had to pry her hands loose. At the foot of the steps in the hallway she hopped the first two steps on one leg and challenged, "Bet me five pesos I can hop all the way to the top?"

"And wake up the whole household? Walk up quietly. Behave yourself or no story."

Compared with her classmates, rapidly growing into boy-crazy coquettes, Clarita had seemed so backward that it troubled me.

"Give her time," Marta had said. "Not every avocado on the tree ripens on the same day."

Clarita remembered exactly where I had left off in our story of the lost aviator and the Little Prince in the African desert. It was no longer just a story but a ritual we both could have recited by heart:

"And at night you will look up at the stars . . . I am going to make you a present . . . It will be as if, in place of the stars, I had given you a great number of little bells that knew how to laugh!"

Sometimes when we took walks together along our crescent beach in the moonlight, Clarita would look up at the stars and say, "Can you hear them, Popee? Millions of little bells. A hundred trillion little bells."

Now I read on until her eyes grew heavy, just as they had when she was small enough to be carried easily on my shoulders. When I tucked her in and reached down to kiss her, she moved her head out of range at the last moment and I kissed the pillow. In spite of my concern that she was not maturing as normally or at least as rapidly as her classmates, selfishly I enjoyed these silly moments of little girlhood in our overgrown fifteen-year-old.

From her room I went to the bar, poured myself a rum-soda, lit a cigar and carried my highball up the stairs.

"Justo?" It was Marta calling out from her dressing room where she seemed to be serving as interior sentry to our master bedroom.

"Marta, dear," I called up to her. She turned as I entered. She was wearing a satin peignoir. Removing the last of the combs that had held her hair tightly in place, she looked at me and her eyes were soft.

"I'm sorry if I was talking foolish woman chatter about Alejandro. You are fond of Alejandro. And I know you have serious things on your mind."

I went close to Marta and she put her arms around me and held me against her. We had been married so long that we knew without ever having to say when we were going to make love. I kissed her. "I'll be there in a moment."

"Te quiero."

"Yo también."

In the bathroom as I made those last-minute ablutions to our lovemaking, the brushing of teeth, the lilac toilet water to sweeten and freshen the flesh, I thought how good it was that after all these years, when neither of us was so young nor so pretty as we had been in our thirties, how good it was that there were still the lingering fires.

Naked, I put on a silk dressing gown, enjoying the feel of it against my skin, thinking of Marta, amply spread on the ample bed with its massive headboard and carved footposts. Once again I would feel the interior pleasure and passionate writhe of my long known, much loved woman.

I admired myself in the full-length mirror. I was not unduly vain, but because Marta had loved me a long time, she had made me conscious of my physical self. Only the overweight, that bay window, marred Marta's image of the ideal man. I sucked in my breath to pull in my waist and expand my chest and it helped to conceal the soft places and the excesses, and I enjoyed thinking to myself, Justo, old friend, Marta is right, with your big chest and muscular legs you are indeed what she calls "a meal."

It was not romantic but neither was it irreverent to wonder how many times had I made love to Marta? Maybe three thousand times. How obscene to think quantitatively of such a singular act. I treasured each one of those *ay-vengo's*—long ones and quick ones, Irish simple ones and Oriental elaborations.

At this moment Eros was interrupted by the sound of automobile motors racing into the driveway, loud voices and heavy boots on the gravel, the bell ringing—impatiently, and rapid pounding on the door. As I hurried into the dressing room between our bedroom and the bath, Marta was there in her nightgown.

"My God, who comes after midnight? Justo—another revolution!"

Moments later a frightened Don Pepe, in the striped woolen bathrobe we had given him two Christmases ago, was at the dressing-room door. The old man had been in Marta's family for forty years. He was not a "Don," of course, but over the years the joking title had grown comfortably on him. In his regalia, his tuxedo when serving at evening, his white jacket and small black bow tie by day, he had an elegance, a sense of position that went with "Don." But now the midnight intrusion had called him from his bed so quickly he had not bothered to insert his teeth, and so had lost all claim to public dignity. "Thee-yor!—Thee-yor!" is how his startled cry of "Señor" emerged. "Here is Angel!"

In his gummy mouth it sounded more like "Ah-hell," but it did not matter. I knew the habits of my caller well enough. He was a manic night worker and night prowler with uncanny energy and a total absence of sense of time.

I grabbed my pajama pants from a hook on the wall, pulled them on under my robe and prepared myself to walk down the long stairway.

3

"Tu madre—you gringo-loving son of a whore! I just read the cable!"

"What are you talking about?"

"Your fellow-conspirator, Lewison. Twenty minutes after that foreign saboteur filed his filthy story it was on my desk. *Gusano!* We ought to give you a trial and shoot you!"

I had come down the circular stairs to find Angel waiting for me in the entranceway. His threat was fortified by a brace of .45 revolvers on his hips, with cartridge belts strung at the familiar revolutionary angle. He wore an unpressed green jungle fatigue uniform, and sported his guns and ammunition as a silk-tuxedoed playboy of the old regime showed off his emerald-and-diamond studs and cuff links. Behind Angel were a squad of his Angelitos Verdes, his Little Green Angels, have-nothing boys who had followed Angel all the way from his jungle redoubt, small and scrawny but lithe and fierce and trigger-quick, ready to die for Angel and their Revolution. They carried with them enough pistols, rifles, automatics and small machine guns to arm a regiment rather than a motley dozen, and the way they looked out of their young eyes at me made it difficult for me to look back.

Angel ordered his boys to wait in the vestibule and they stretched out on the floor, some of them propping themselves against the walls and closing their eyes, their bulbous revolvers resting uncomfortably against their thighs, others talking, whispering, laughing together, all of them prepared to wait ten minutes, ten hours, ten days, for they knew their leader, knew him and adored him, feared him, revered him, did not try to understand him, accepted and exulted in him as their Revolution, personified in the selfless, demanding, sentimental, loving, unforgiving, dangerous, superhuman Angel.

"Whore! Liar! Enemy of the People—" With epithets and insults laced with fevered justification of the Revolution, Angel Bello pursued me into the living room. As he paced he loosened his holster belts, tossing those pet revolvers on one of the silk-embroidered eighteenth-century chairs that Marta had inherited and that I always thought inappropriate for a beach house. Angel did not pace in an orderly way, say five steps in each direction in even rhythm. No, he would take four rapid strides, stop suddenly, wheel, then rapidly step off the entire room, then without warning turn again and head straight for me as if he were going to strike me with his fist. A foot away from me he would execute an about-face and shout at me over his shoulder as he stalked out of the living room into the vestibule where some of his Angelitos were now dozing with their heads cushioned on their submachine guns. It was all in a night's work to the Little Green Angels.

"The Revolution made you the Provisional President because it trusted you. And now you throw shit on the Revolution, you traitor!"

"I say no, never!"

"You accuse the Revolution of selling out our old comrades to the Communists. Anybody who tries to do anything for the campesinos—to the gringos they are all Communists. So I say, Yes I am proud to be called a Communist, call me anything you like as long as you let me run the Yankees and the whoremongers and the generals and all the rest of that Zamora-gringo *mierda* out of our country."

"You oversimplify, Angel, I never defended the gringos. And you know how I feel about Zamora. But when—"

"*Puto,* this is a revolution! The people had nothing and now— they begin to live—for the first time in our miserable history—get that through your stupid bourgeois head. And you prattle about Communists. When a man is drowning, who does he turn to—the fellow trying to hit him on the head with an oar or the one who throws him a rope? Well, my friend the President, who threw us that rope? Who sent us oil and bought our sugar when Uncle Sam was helping us drown? In the milk of their mothers! Twenty years ago when they would have gone under if Stalin hadn't saved their asses, were they letting people say 'You must be Communists because you are all fighting on the same side'? The Yankees were all patting themselves on the back for their brilliant statesmanship. But when our Revolution accepts the same help, then the whole 'free' capitalist press screams, 'Look at Angel Bello, look at his Revolution, hand-in-hand with Moscow!' If we are hand-in-hand, what other hand did we have to grab, you syphilitic excuse for a President?"

"*Calma*, Angel, I never betrayed the Revolution. What I told Lewison was—"

"Liar! I saw the cable. In the first line you accuse me of deceiving my guerrilla comrades and filling the ministries with old-line Communists! What do you call that? I call it selling out to the enemy."

Angel wheeled and snatched up one of his .45's. He spun it around his index finger the way cowboys do in Western movies. I thought—or I think I thought, for the mind in panic is hardly a trustworthy instrument—he is going to shoot me now, on Marta's expensive carpet. When he pointed the gun at me, my legs felt numb. At the same time something in my head was saying, "This is not the moment."

Angel was an emotional show-off, but he was also a canny politician and as impulsive as he seemed, his final acts had definition and significance. To barge in at midnight and personally assassinate me made little sense. If he wanted to get rid of his personal choice for President, I would be more useful on public display, exposed as a dupe of Wall Street trying to restore the discredited Zamora regime. No, I was frightened, but reasonably hopeful that Angel had not come to blow my brains out. Not yet.

"Remember, I am not judging you," he was shouting. "The Revolution is judging you. Personally, you are my friend. But the Revolution accuses you of selling out to our enemies."

"Angel, selling out implies taking money, bribes—I have my conscience. Because of it you happen to be alive today. Zamora sold out to the Yankees, yes. But no matter what you do to me, you cannot call me a Zamorista. In my way I fought him as hard as you did."

"Your way! In a penthouse apartment in Mexico City. That is where you went soft in the head, my friend. Too much tequila and enchiladas. In the days when we were surrounded, fighting for our lives, you were fighting the revolution of the cocktail lounge."

"Angel, as always you remember only what you choose to remember. There was no cocktail lounge in the Cessna that flew me to your secret headquarters in the jungle. And what did you tell me? 'Bravo. You took your life in your hands. You are now the Provisional President.' "

"You live in the past!"

"You said, 'Go back and unite all the anti-Zamora exiles into a single front. Get them to contribute to our war-chest.' How many factions there were, all fighting each other! It wasn't easy, Angel, but I did it."

"The Revolution never looks back."

"Maybe it should. Flying in a little crate over Zamora territory with a price on my head—floodlights, antiaircraft guns . . ."

"*Mierda!* In a plane with two engines, one of our best pilots, a mile in the air. What courage!"

"So I am not bravado-brave like you. But I did fly in twice. I did what I had to do. While your Communists were still playing games with Zamora."

"Imbecile! You think I am going to let the Communists swallow the Revolution? Give me a little time and the Revolution will swallow the Communists. At least the middle-aged Communists who grew up sucking on Stalin's hind tit. We will raise our own young Communists on coconut milk. You do not see that, you miserable informer?"

"I see one newspaper where there used to be eight. One paper in the entire capital—yours. I see Ismael, a hero of the Revolution, one of the earliest of the guerrilla fighters, serving life on the Isla de las Barricudas for daring to criticize the Communist hacks taking over the rebel army—"

I had touched a nerve. Ismael had been one of his closest friends and most dedicated comrades of the early days. Angel brought his body so close to mine that I thought this time he is going to hit me with his fist and if he does and I hit him back, Little Green Hornets will be swarming all over me. But instead of hitting me with his hand he unleashed an angry flow of words that rattled from his mouth like machine-gun bullets.

"Bourgeois pig! If I was not so fond of you I would turn you over to my Little Angels right now. They have no use for your democracy, individual rights, free elections . . . All they know is, their man is in the saddle now, not some thieving lackey like Zamora. When Zamora and Romano and the rest of them stole two hundred million dollars of the people's money while campesino babies died from hunger, did your great Democracy cry out? No, the gringo ambassador threw his arms around Zamora and pinned a beautiful North American medal on him and welcomed him into the family of freedom-loving nations. I say *mierda* to that freedom. I say if General Zamora is a proud soldier of Western civilization, as that stinking hypocrite gringo ambassador called him—then I say *chinga* Western civilization—we will take our chances with some other civilizations. Yes, we have to make concessions, but we are going to hang on to our Revolution. The first time we haven't been like a ripe papaya hanging down from a tree for the imperialists to pick off and suck out and throw the rinds away. The first time the campesinos can talk about *our* government and not *their* government, *our* schools, *our* hospitals, *our* sugar fields, and yes, *our* courts and *our* firing squads. The first time things are being done *our* way and not the gringo way. And when you give out a statement bleating about your disappointments, how I do not keep my promises, I do not hold free elections, I fill the cabinet with veteran Communists, I say you would screw your own mother. Maybe you think you are not with Zamora and Romano and all the exploiters, but anything you do to hurt us helps them. There is a time for hair-splitting and a time for head-splitting. Revolution is a time for head-splitting. When we have beaten back the counterrevolution, then we can enjoy the democratic luxury of hair-splitting. But when the Zamora bastards and the gringo sons-of-bitches are still trying to wipe us off the map, if you think you can be for the Revolution Monday through Friday but take Saturday off to throw shit at it, then you are even a bigger fool than I thought you were when I made you Provisional President."

"Provisional President. Well, Angel. Your personal Provisional President hereby tenders his resignation."

Angel stopped pacing and planted himself in front of me. I remember his eyes. They were so black that you could not distinguish the pupil from the iris. They were like a mask you could not see behind. No, that still does not describe them because they could also be eyes that moved you. Whether or not they were feeling deeply, they had the power to make you feel deeply and to respond, to think, "That man is suffering, that man is driven, that man is dying for us all." Christ eyes. Think about Christ eyes in the paintings of Michelangelo and Da Vinci and you have some idea of the eyes of Angel Bello.

"You will resign when I tell you to resign, you son of a two-peso gringo-sucking whore. You will resign when it serves the Revolution for you to resign, you *sinvergüenza*. Not one second before and not one second later. When the Revolution commands, you will obey. No more statements. No more interviews. I do not wish the Revolution to lose face by sending its first President to the wall. If the Revolution shoots you it proclaims its own mistakes. The Revolution does not make mistakes."

"All right, Señor Revolution!" I said. "If I am not allowed to resign, I say this: I know you call me one but I am not a fool. I realize that the ego of Angel Bello and the mystique of the Revolution are one. You are the First Colonel and the Secretary of Defense, and that is where the power lies. I am only the Provisional President. But dignity is a big word in our country. Every night people kill each other for personal reasons in the name of dignity. There is a difference between being a figurehead, a dignified promise of what is yet to come, and being a puppet only able to speak when you put the words in his mouth."

Angel laughed. "Okay. Okay, Bigshot!" Unexpectedly he said this in English. He was proud of his gringo slang borrowed from old Humphrey Bogart movies. Often, after a night of political prowling such as this, he would start a favorite film at four o'clock and run it until dawn. His English was better than he pretended. One of his complaints against the gringos was that they rarely learned our language. It was typical of their arrogance, he insisted, to force you

to learn theirs. Often I had watched him pretending not to understand when every English word was clear to him. But there was a
childish streak that could not resist "Okay, Bigshot," or "Drop the
gat, Bigboy."

He went around to the different chairs collecting his weapons. It
should have been funny, a touch of opéra bouffe. But those pistols
were real and the lead they fired was real and the man behind them
for all his bravura was as real as revolution and as difficult to control.

As he adjusted his holster belts and buttoned his tunic, the Angelitos, anticipating their leader, roused themselves, stretched,
yawned, blinked, joked, spat, farted, adjusted weapons and got
ready to surround the Revolution. They followed him out to the
drowsing peasant chauffeur whose comic book had fallen into his
lap behind the wheel of a big black Sputnik, the limousine the Russians had presented to the Revolution on his last trip to the Kremlin.
There were rumors that Angel had been reluctant to give up the
custom-built bulletproof Cadillac he had inherited from General
Zamora, who had received it as a gift from the American ambassador.

Suddenly, inexplicably, and I might add, typically, Angel paused
on the front steps, turned, and embraced me, his barrel chest pressing hard against mine.

"Okay, Bigshot," he said again. "So you flew over enemy territory and risked your precious democratic skin. If we set up a home
for burned-out revolutionaries, we may send you there—with tape
over your mouth so you never again slander the Revolution in the
name of some romantic ideal that you and I once believed in—but
that this country is not ready for. Meanwhile, I am for the dignity
of everyone. As long as he does nothing to hurt the Revolution. It
is ours now, Justo, my boy. And we must hold it. If it means shooting every *hijo* in the country we must hold it. I would shoot my own
mother to hold it." He took a few rapid steps toward his car, then
half-turned and said over his shoulder, *"Cuidado!* Watch your step!"

Angel awakened his young chauffeur by tapping him on the elbow. The youth opened his eyes with a sleepy grin but did not
bother to jump out and open the door for his leader. Nor did Angel
expect him to. He flung the door open and shouldered his way into

the rear compartment of the limousine. Sometimes he was known to shove the driver aside and handle the car himself. But this time there was a woman waiting for him in the back seat. I thought I recognized Angel's secretary and constant companion, Elena Concepción. The lead jeep roared off, followed by Angel's limousine and two more jeeps full of Angelitos.

I stood in the driveway and watched them power off into the moonlight. From the front of the house I could hear the muffled sound of the surf, the rustle of palm trees and jacarandas. The reassuring sounds of my peaceful Playa de los Papagayos came home to me now that the storm of Angel Bello had blown over. I felt becalmed.

I believed in this Revolution. It was difficult to argue with Angel when so much of what he said was true. He jumped off from truth. By the time he got to his own lies he had you by the truth. Zamora had been everything crawling in the cesspools of Latin American political life. A thief. A pig. A sadist. A tool who served the Colossus of the North not for its democratic pronouncements but simply for the gold with which it bought him.

I had shared Angel's dream of pulling down all the statues erected to the glory of Victoriano Zamora. There had been at least three thousand of them and when they literally had come tumbling down, the people had cried, *Viva la Revolución! Viva Angel! Viva Libertad!* Well, they had their Revolución and their Angel but that last one, that Libertad, that was still the joker in the pack. I could distinguish between reaction and rebellion all right and as I had told Lewison, if I had to do it again I would still thumb up for Angel and thumb down for Zamora. But I was on a lonely search for the revolution that was not there, a socialism without Lubiankas, without political informers, without one-man rule and one-party arrogance and one-newspaper blinders.

Meanwhile, fate had played on me the nasty little trick of appointing me President and as such I felt a sense of responsibility even if I were permitted none. We are a great country for jokes and I had heard some of them on the absurdity of my position. I was called "the President in charge of the First Colonel's spittoons," and if the President did not happen to have one ready the First Colonel would spit into the cupped hands of the President and the President would say, "Thank you, my Colonel, for honoring me with the true spittle of the Revolution." That was only one of the cleaner and milder of the *chistes* at the expense of *El Presidente de Nada*.

In Mexican exile I had been a hero to the Angelistas. Refugees from Zamora would make secret pilgrimages to my door. An old leftist who had mellowed as a moderate revolutionary, I found my true character swallowed up in the myth of the Fearless Citizen Judge who had given the lie to the murder trial stage-managed by Victoriano Zamora. When Zamora saw the bloody message on the wall he took off for Miami in his hundred-foot yacht while I flew home from exile with honor and fanfare and a bear-hug *abrazo* from Angel himself.

Standing there in the doorway it seemed unreal. There was a sound like human laughter in the coconut trees. Probably a parrot cawking for his roost in the pecking order. "Shut up, Mano," I said. It was momentary therapy to give orders to something. I am surprised that no one had thought to call me *El Presidente de los Papagayos*.

"Justo, come back into the house. Tomorrow you will be complaining of a sore throat and I will not be feeling sorry for you."

Marta had come to the foot of the stairs in a woolen robe she had put on over her nightgown. The anticipation of lovemaking that had softened her features was gone from her now and she looked formidable.

"I suppose you heard it all?"

Instinctively we moved into the small bar-den, paneled in white cypress and lined with books. When we were discussing Clarita, our friends, the servants, our occasional emotional differences or our political predicaments, we invariably turned to this warm room where there was an illusion of privacy and safety.

I poured us each a Scotch and only then became aware of how my hand was trembling.

"I tried to listen," Marta said. "Of course, I didn't hear it all. But I heard enough. That *pendejo!* I don't blame the others because they are campesinos who never saw the inside of a school. But he comes from a good family and went to the University. He knows better. He's only pretending to be a savage—this business of catching people by surprise in the middle of the night—Hitler did it—Zamora did it—now *this pendejo* does it. Well, up his mother, he isn't going to do it to us."

"Marta, I think it's all a bluff. You know how Angel is—"

"A *pendejo!*" Marta always spoke the word with a special zest. "No matter what the colors of his flag, he'll always be a *pendejo*. I never trusted him even when he was a young poet writing sonnets. Bad sonnets. We should always be on guard against the perpetrators of bad adolescent poetry. In their frustration they turn into *pendejos.*"

"Ridiculous, Marta. No matter what Angel is turning into, you have to admit that he's a dedicated—"

"*Pendejo,*" Marta said. She slugged down her whiskey and poured herself another. "You know what I think we ought to do."

I stared into my glass. I knew.

"*Vámanos*. Pronto. Before this dedicated poet of yours lines us up against the wall. Because after tonight, it is only a question of time. We will be sitting here like pigs in a barrel."

"Fish in a barrel," I reminded her. I was never sure whether she mixed her idioms accidentally or to be different, to be a character.

"So correct me, Señor Professor," Marta said. "What difference does it make—pigs—fish—a dead amoeba is just as dead as a dead whale."

"Now Marta, I know Angel can be ruthless, but—"

"There is no such thing as 'ruthless—but.' There is ruthless and there is ruthful. There is no such thing as half merciful."

I poured another whiskey. The surf pounding on the beach made the house shudder a little.

"You are an idealist," Marta said accusingly. "The most impractical people in the world. They see life only in terms of what it should be. It is not bad enough that you speak out publicly against Communism. Angel was already resenting you for saving his life. You could have sentenced him to death—he did lead an attack on the Presidential Palace."

"But Marta, his self-defense had a strong legal foundation. Zamora had seized the state power illegally . . ."

"Please," Marta had said, "I know the case by heart. I am not interested in the fine points of international law. I'm interested in the fine points of the survival of the Justo Moreno Suárez family. We had to escape from Zamora or he would have shot you in Angel's place. And now the *pendejo* you risked your neck for is going to shoot you because he resents you for saving his life. I tell you, Justo dear, that is human nature. The virtues of man come as an afterthought. The first things they think of to do are usually rotten and *cursi*."

I was accustomed to Marta's cynicism—what she called realism. But I found it galling to be constantly accused of idealism. Marta made it sound dirty, almost in a class with Angel's *"puto."*

"Anything that interferes with Angel's image of himself is a major crime. If you cannot see that, Justo, you are a hopeless fool."

It was the second time in a single evening that I had been accused of being a hopeless fool. "I would say—hopeful fool."

"Joke." Marta glared. "I say, do your joking in Miami or Mexico City. I say it's time to phone Alejandro."

Alejandro Castillo had promised to arrange political asylum for us in his embassy whenever we gave the signal.

"But my God, I am the President." I tried to make my voice sound clearer and stronger than I felt. "Hand-picked but still, constitutionally, the President, the last link between a constitutional government and the Bello Revolution. I took an oath of office."

"To serve the whole country. Not just the personal whims of that *pendejo*—"

"Marta—wait—even if Angel doesn't permit me to function as a president should, you know what holds me here. The plague of Latin politics is—no orderly succession. Orderly succession—ever since my University days my dream—sometimes you call it my obsession—"

"Surely you do not want the whole family to die on your cross of orderly succession!"

"Marta, you exaggerate. Even now I still believe in the Revolution. If only I could—I must—influence Angel to—"

"If—if. If your grandmother had wheels you would be a trolley car!"

A rooster crowed. Though it was still several hours before dawn. For some reason Latin roosters are not clock-watchers like their North American cousins. They crow at two A.M. or at three A.M. or whenever they feel like crowing.

"Justo, I know all about that beloved stability theory of yours," Marta was saying. No matter how hard they try, husbands and wives invariably begin to bore each other. She had heard my theory a hundred times, in Spanish at the National University, in English at the New School for Social Research in New York City, in articles for liberal weeklies and at cocktail parties after too many highballs: the Latin American political thinkers were more brilliant, more sensate, more human than the North American políticos but nearly all of them suffered the deep flaw of instability. The best of the Latin politicians were artists. The best of the North Americans were like engineers.

Now another cock was crowing, a louder, younger fellow, not an erratic night prowler but a true heralder of dawn.

"Justo, I know how you feel about responsibility." She gave the word *responsabilidad* a mocking sound. It became another accusation. She had an almost *cursi* way of taking ideas which basically we shared and saddling me with them as if they were my weakness alone. "It is a gringo word. A gringo abstraction—responsibility to an idea. What about your responsibility to Clarita? To me? And to Justo Moreno Suárez? That is what I call *responsabilidad*. Who will care about the responsibility to an empty presidency after you're dead?"

My stomach cramped. I had a pounding headache. Marta always put things a little too bluntly.

"Marta," the courage in me, like sweat, seeped through the layers of fear, "I am not ready. I am not ready to go." But at the crowing of the next cock I was urging Marta to fly to Mexico City with Clarita. As she had done before, Marta could make the escape seem like a casual journey, a holiday visit with friends and relatives. She would have to travel light and leave most of her possessions behind to make it convincing, but as long as I remained I thought we could carry it off.

"No! He's smart. That's the trouble with him, so much smarter than the gringos give him credit for. Before Clarita and I are away three weeks he will know exactly what we are up to—and it will be—" With her forefinger she made that gesture of knife across throat with appropriate sound.

"Ni modo," I said. "You and Clarita go for a visit. Then we can talk on the telephone, using our code and if it begins to look as though—"

"It will be too late," Marta said. "While we are going through our code, that *pendejo* will be oiling his revolver. If you are an idiot then I will be the wife of an idiot and stay with you."

I moved along the bar to Marta and opened my arms to her and she came to me and held herself against me. We stood that way for a moment and, breaking the silence, the advance guard of the roosters of Playa de los Papagayos completed their pre-dawn program. Now the late risers who waited until the sun was almost ready to give light to the tropic sky would join in, the me-too's, me-too's of the dirt roads of the jungle clearing of the servant-poor behind the great beach castles of the rich. I had belonged to that monied society largely through my marriage. But it was a class to which I had never sacrificed my convictions, in fact in Marta's world I always had felt something of an impostor.

"We stay?"

"We stay."

We kissed as if to make a shaky bargain stronger. Marta went to the window still heavily curtained against the night, peered through the green vine-patterned draperies and said, "My God, daylight. And I have to get Clarita ready for a *Quinceañera* party. I'm going with her so we older ladies have a chance to gossip. If I hurry I can still find six hours sleep before noon."

How could she think of sleep? How could she worry about Clarita's *Quinceañera* and the idle gossip of the afternoon?

She touched my cheek and moved toward the door, casually.

"Sleep well, *querida*," I said.

"Do not stay here and drink and brood and have a bad headache and a bad conscience this afternoon," she said.

"How often do I do that?"

"More often than you should. But do as you please." And she was gone.

Alone in the protective darkness of the den I cursed Marta gently and poured myself another drink. Then I went to the kitchen and picked out a sweet roll from the breadbox. Everyone was sleeping, Dolores the cat, Don Pepe the butler, María Magdalena the cook, Daphne and Chloe the canaries . . . I walked through the quiet house and out onto the beach.

The air was still cool. The color of morning was gray-blue. Small breakers gathered and curled and broke lazily upon the sand. I threw some bread into the air and the gulls came screaming and jostling down to snatch the little pieces. I chose the sandy road that curved in from the shore and ran behind the luxurious beach houses. One of the most magnificent had belonged to General Carlos Romano, whose secret police, *Los Tigres,* had been the scourge of the country until Angel's boys swooped down and drove him into diplomatic asylum. Now the gates of the Romano beach palace were padlocked and the windows were boarded up. No one had inhabited the place since El Gordo Romano, with his wife Adriana, had fled their weekend mansion in the middle of the night. They had escaped a few minutes ahead of the Little Green Angels, bent on doing to Romano what he had done to students and doctors and taxi drivers and sugar farmers at the rate of at least a thousand a month in the peak years of bloodshed before the Angelistas caught up with him—figuratively. Literally, Carlos (El Gordo) Romano was said to be enjoying asylum in the embassy with enough money to satisfy even his sybaritic tastes. Good old Article V had saved Romano's size seventeen neck.

I remembered what I had seen and heard: the taxi driver who inadvertently picked up an Angelista terrorist. The old man had been tortured to force from him the confession of the name of the underground revolutionary he had driven through the capital. While *Los Tigres de Romano* held his writhing body on what they called their "massage table," one by one his teeth had been extracted. But the driver could not tell the name for the simple reason that he did not know it. When all of his teeth were gone he slumped to the floor where the Tigers kicked at him with their boots until his jaw was smashed. After the night of the overthrow, when Zamora made for Miami in his floating palace and the Romanos took refuge in embassy asylum, I talked with the celebrated taxi driver. Somehow he had survived. In fact, in the Roman holiday trials staged in the bullring at night, he had pointed out his tormentors. "That last night I drove my cab I was not political," he testified through ill-fitting store teeth. "But by the time those *hijos* pulled out my first tooth, I was a diehard Angelista."

The audience jammed into the bullring had howled with dangerous laughter and the once terrifying secret policemen were listless with fear. As one of the ranking members of the new order, I was privileged to attend all the trials. Like most of our countrymen I had been shaken by the atrocities and felt hatred for the Tigers and police officers who had taken part in the bloodbath. I had read Camus and Koestler on capital punishment and shared their revulsion for this relic of the law of revenge, in principle, but what I had seen of the inhuman work of El Gordo Romano and his Tigers aroused a more primitive sense of justice in me. Yes, I agreed sadly, those who directed the pulling of teeth and the squeezing of testicles and the repeated bayonet stabs that left a man leaking red tears from a score of wounds had to suffer for their crimes.

But there was a savagery to the retribution that shocked me al-

most as much as the original brutality. Former police captain Ol-
meda in an unpressed blue Zamora uniform stripped of epaulets and
medals sat, quaking and sunken-eyed, in the middle of the garishly
illuminated bullring as the mutilated taxi driver pointed at him and
repeated to the revolutionary tribunal his terrible story. The fallen
police captain, the vacant look of death already in his eyes, tried
feebly to answer the charges. There was no doubt in my mind that
he was a scoundrel, a cog in the system of organized sadism that had
bled and terrorized the tropical paradise our country was meant to
be. But when twenty thousand voices drowned out his half-whis-
pered defense with their hyena cries of *"Paredón! Paredón!"* I felt
ashamed of having to be a witness to old bestiality parading as new
justice.

Now, as the sun rose with brilliant haste, the gilt spires of the
elaborate Romano mansion were alive with light. I walked up to the
high padlocked gates and stared in. A disheveled guard was dozing
on the top step. The lovely gardens were overgrown, the hibiscus,
the camellia and gardenia bushes once cared for by a team of highly
skilled gardeners had lost their shape and vitality. Romano had
been a man of great sensibility and selectivity when it came to
flowers, wines, ladies . . . a connoisseur.

The soldier roused himself and came forward. Behind his beard
he was very young.

"Buenos días, Señor Presidente," he said. "You wish something?"

"Buenos días, joven," I said. "No, just taking my early-morning
constitutional, thank you."

"Viva Angel," he said automatically.

"Viva—" I nodded and turned away and walked on down the
sandy road between the great rows of houses and the palm jungle. I
was thinking of the unique character of Carlos Romano. He was in
all his obsessions and excesses so much one of ours. He was not to
be found in North American society, nor in European. No, like Angel Bello, he was a true son of our land, from the thin wisps of
Napoleonic hair strategically combed around his balding dome to the
elegantly pedicured toenails, toenails Angel Bello would have happily extracted one by one if he had caught him—just as El Gordo

would have returned the compliment if only he had been able to trap Angel and deliver him in chains to Victoriano Zamora.

Pausing to look back at the padlocked Romano home, my eyes were drawn to one turret higher than all the rest. This tower room of circular windows was popularly known as the *"Vista Hermosa de Adriana,"* the view from the vantage point of Adriana Ponce de Romano, the mysterious wife of El Gordo.

Before she was eighteen, Adriana had married a rich sugar-family playboy, Lalo Monti. At first it was private gossip, then public knowledge, that she had become El Gordo's mistress. Cruising on his yacht, Lalo Monti was said to have fallen overboard during a storm. His brother Memo was convinced that the drowning was not accidental. A member of the crew had heard that a fellow-crewman was being paid off by El Gordo. Without visible means of support, the crewman had bought a large house well stocked with women and rum. Memo never had a chance to prove his case because he was shot on a country road at night on the way to the family sugar plantation. After that it was considered unhealthy to express an interest in the fate of the Monti brothers. A year or so later El Gordo married Adriana in a gala ceremony, presided over by the Archbishop and General Zamora.

Marta and I were struck by the classic beauty of Adriana in the published wedding photographs. High cheekbones gave form and shadow to her face. Her dark green eyes were exaggerated as if by the deliberate choice of a portrait painter who knows the features that will make his painting, and to heighten the effect they were cut into her head at an unexpected angle. Connoisseurs of beauty were reminded of the Egyptian queen Nefertiti, with her look of a smoldering fawn. Only the nose, long and finely shaped but for an incongruous bump, suggested an earthiness that the rest of her smoothly chiseled face might have concealed.

Her skin was ivory white. In a country where there was a thin creamy band at the top, plunging quickly to swarthy *mestizo*, Indian red-brown, and finally African black, Adriana's complexion (Marta's friends said she worked with imported Parisian creams to achieve that glowing patina) was both an aphrodisiac and a social virtue. Zamora was dark-skinned and pockmarked. Romano was the true mestizo. In him, the Indian and the conquering Spaniard tipped back and forth in neurotic balance. But the aristocrats they gathered around them were mostly white. There was an unspoken understanding that white was the preferential color of human epidermis. One was a member of the aristocracy by the possession of this simple attribute alone. Zamora, Romano and the rest of the bottom dogs who had clawed their way up could only achieve the aristocratic heights by working hard at it, stealing hard, murdering hard.

Our paths rarely crossed with the Romanos. Only at the great parties Zamora liked to give for the diplomatic set would I catch fleeting glimpses of Adriana. She seemed haughty, aloof, removed —and in a gathering of four hundred I could sense her approach in the hunger of masculine eyes. But the combination of the dread with which her husband was regarded and her own tantalizing reserve made her seem unattainable.

Then she dropped out of sight. El Gordo Romano began appearing alone at the diplomatic balls, apologizing for the Señora's illness. The busy tongues of local society soon had their story which grew richer with each telling, though in this case even the most ardent exaggerators insisted on the truth of the terrible secret.

It seemed that El Gordo had caught his cool Adriana *in flagrante delicto* with a certain Captain Maldonado, a plainclothes officer in his own *Tigres*. He was said to have put more horns on more husbands than any other *macho* in the land. His feats or the gossip about them had built him into something of a folk hero. One time he and a squad of *Tigres* had broken into the home of a University student suspected of being a member of the underground. The boy's older sister had cried and begged for her brother's release. But Maldonado had taken the young man to the woods outside of the city, tortured him until he revealed the names of fellow-conspirators and finally shot him. Then Maldonado had returned to the sister, and while she was pleading with him to tell her what they had done to her brother, had managed to arouse her and take her. That was one of a hundred stories.

The Maldonado-Adriana affair had begun with El Gordo kissing his wife good-bye and saying he would be spending the weekend in Ocampo, the capital of our southernmost state, almost a thousand miles away. That afternoon Captain Maldonado went to the Romano home on official business. There are many versions of what happened. Some were sure the liaison was of long standing. Others believed that Maldonado had achieved another of his lightning conquests. At any rate, nearly everybody who participated in the high-keyed gossip that swept our city agreed that the master had returned home unexpectedly. They were convinced that El Gordo had set the trap, announcing his own departure and ordering the captain to their home. This conviction was reinforced by the fact that he had brought a couple of bodyguards with him, including the notorious Búfalo de Sa. Maldonado was no longer seen in polite or impolite circles. The story of the price he paid for his afternoon, or afternoons, the horror of his punishment was something dredged up from the native netherworld that most of us, thank God, had never seen, but was as real to us as were the flaming levels of the Inferno to the people who read Dante in the original in the so-called centuries of darkness.

Earlier, when Carlos Romano had accompanied Zamora on a state visit to the Dominican Republic, Trujillo had shown off the special section maintained by the secret police as a gentle persuader for political opposition. They called it the Blood Pit. It was here that the old spider of the Dominicans introduced his guests to his pet dwarf, El Caníbal. El Caníbal had been brought to the prison originally as a degenerate freak whose passion it was to attack male genitals with his teeth. It occurred to El Benefactor, as Trujillo was affectionately known, that the strange passion of El Caníbal could be useful to the Motherland. Political enemies were threatened with intimate exposure to the voracious jaws of El Caníbal and it was said that the threat alone was more effective than twenty-four hours of more conventional maltreatment. Once El Gordo met El Caníbal, Romano's keen sense of competition gave him no rest until he had a prison dwarf of his own. He sent his scouts ranging through the Caribbean and South America until they discovered a true Caliban barely risen from the mud, a dwarf who came from a long inbred line of giant-headed cretins who inhabited a small tropical island. We consider ourselves more imaginative than Dominicans and so

Romano's cannibal quickly acquired a different sort of nickname. He was called El Amante. The lover.

To strip and bind and lock a prisoner in a soundproof room with El Amante became the Tigers' ultimate weapon. Captain Maldonado paid this price, or so it was widely reported. It was also believed that after the deed had been committed, a package had been dispatched to Señora Adriana de Romano and that when El Gordo's lady opened the brown paper wrapper and lifted the lid from the long black box inside, a felt-covered silk-lined container that usually displayed an expensive necklace, she fainted at what she saw. We heard she was in bed for weeks under extreme sedation. And once she rose, she did not reenter the social life of the capital with her loving husband. Some thought he had forbidden her to leave the house. But friends who had known Adriana insisted it was she who refused to be seen with her husband publicly after the Maldonado incident.

In those years, before my trouble with Zamora, I would take my beach walk and then circle back along the sandy road behind the beach houses. My eyes would be drawn to that tower room and I would see Adriana standing at one of her seven windows, staring out in a kind of fixed, sightless trance. Sometimes I would pause near the gate—no one came too close because it was always heavily guarded by Tiger thugs—and look up until it seemed we were in communion with each other. Of course, I had to guard against my own romantic turn of mind, a streak of sentimentalism that misled me into going wet-eyed at bathetic scenes in *cursi* films. Her friends said she was intensely nearsighted and yet too vain to wear glasses and that the hypnotic beauty of her eyes was due to this malfunction. To Marta I never mentioned those brief conversations of the eye I thought I was having with the captive or self-imprisoned Adriana. Certainly no extramarital conspiracy was intended. It was what a Chinese poet called "the slight shadow of a faint fragment of an imagined moment in time."

"Señor"—an unexpected voice startled me—"you are looking for something?"

My first impulse was that an alert *Tigre de Romano* was on the prowl. Then I realized it was not two years ago but now and that my questioner was another bearded young son of the Revolution, probably coming on guard to take over the morning shift from the drowsy young man I had awakened. This new guard, with a rifle slung carelessly over his shoulder, looked sleepy-eyed too, as if he had just tumbled out of his bed of straw.

He did not recognize his President, which was hardly surprising as these young Angelitos Verdes, recruited from the sugar country to the south, were often familiar only with the militant heroes of the Revolution.

"Chamaco," I said, "young man, I am your President, Justo Moreno Suárez."

"Sí Señor, como no?" he said, taking cover in the familiar native answer that is something like "why not" in English, only with a Latin twist of duplicity, "Corporal Julio Bustamente at your service."

"Thank you, Corporal," I said and walked on in the direction of my house up the beach.

"Viva Angel," the now awake sugarcane corporal called after me, pointedly.

"Viva." Viva me, Justo Moreno Suárez. Gone was the image that had been staring down at me from the tower room, vanished, not as the actual past folds away but as a dream recedes until we think we have forgotten it: the presence of the unnoticed moon in a tropical daylight sky.

When I reached the house Marta was sleeping soundly. Things were settled, for the moment. I would shower and dress and drive into the city to sit at my big desk in the office of the President, in the opposite wing of the palace from the littered suite where Angel Bello and his motley array of sincere Communists, chameleon opportunists and existentialist rebels did their erratic, bureaucratic and contradictory best to build the new society.

6

There was a cabinet meeting that day—we always met on Monday though the hours varied according to Angel's whim. For the first time I was not invited. I learned of my new déclassé status from Señorita Naranja, my overly solicitous butterball of a secretary. There were many like her in government offices, lonely girls who automatically fell in love with their bosses. For me, Señorita Naranja's overardent concern, expressed not in terms of romance but in intense professional dedication, was a source of embarrassment. Being adored is a responsibility. If you cannot adore back it seems inhuman not to reciprocate at least a little kindness and special attention. I was always saying, "Thank you, it was thoughtful of you to arrange the flowers on my desk," when what I really wanted to say was, "For God's sake, just stay at your desk and take care of the typing and the phone calls."

This time she brought me some routine mail with an anxious face. "Señor Presidente, you are not going to the meeting?"

I looked up from a double-talk agricultural report I was trying to understand. "Meeting?"

"The cabinet is meeting in Angel's office." It was one of the charming aspects of the regime that everyone down to the lowliest office worker or field hand did not call Bello the Duce or the Führer, or even El Benefactor, but simply "Angel." "Lola phoned me about it a few minutes ago." Her friend, Lola, was secretary to our security chief, Juan del Campo. "She said—" Señorita Naranja paused and her small dark eyes sought mine in an effort to bind us together in a conspiracy of self-pity.

"Yes, Señorita—?" She was a good soul but I was tense enough already without having to cope with her oversecretion of sentiment.

"—Lola said Señor del Campo told her that you—"

"Jesus and Mary, say it, Señorita, say it!"

She flushed slightly. "Señor del Campo says he has heard it from Angel that you are no longer to preside over or even attend the meetings of the cabinet, Señor Presidente—" My secretary produced a tiny handkerchief from her silk pleated blouse and dabbed at her eyes.

"Señorita, have you finished typing my University speech for the graduating class?" Señorita Naranja retreated to the reception room.

I went to the ornate window and looked down into the courtyard of the Spanish colonial palace. There were confident young girls in militia uniforms and petty spies, and sugarcane workers who had walked hundreds of miles to thank Angel for giving them the oligarchical land they had been promised. There were anxious parents who had come to plead for sons who had disappeared as their brothers had disappeared into the secret chambers of the previous regime.

As I turned from the window and paced my walnut-paneled office with its Empire furniture, crystal chandeliers and bronze candelabras, I became aware of the silence. My phone had ceased to ring. On an ordinary day even a figurehead is interrupted by the constant ringing. My tasks had been almost entirely ritualistic, presiding over lunches and making speeches written for me by the propaganda ministry. Sometimes I had even taken Angel's place at diplomatic functions, especially those involving countries he wished to snub politely. No one was truly interested in my opinions, but there would be questions from the press. I would make my pat answers full of the correct revolutionary militancy. I would be called upon to place a wreath on the tomb of a martyr to independence on the anniversary of his death. We were a country rich in fallen heroes. They had fallen in the war against Spain, and in the countless abortive revolutions of the nineteenth century and in our Constitutional Revolution of 1900. They had fallen in the Corporals' Revolution of 1935 and in our Green Revolution of the sixties. Were our hibiscus, our carnations and our gladiolas so red because our dark earth had been irrigated with blood for four hundred years?

The silence began to oppress me. In desperation I flipped on the intercom and said sharply to Señorita Naranja, "Tell Tony I want to see him right away."

Special presidential assistant Antonio Cruz was a twenty-six-year-old dandy with a quick mind and a swarthy, handsome face, a real on-the-make *capitalino*. I was sure that he had been placed at my right hand to report any suspicious visits or phone calls to his real superiors.

"Señor Cruz is not in his office."

"How do you know? Have you tried?"

"I saw him go down the corridor twenty minutes ago, Señor Presidente."

"Then find him and tell him I want to see him immediately."

There was a pause.

"Señorita?—Are you still there?"

"*Sí*, Señor Presidente."

"What is the matter with you today?"

"I—nothing, Señor Presidente. I will leave word for Señor Cruz to report to you as soon as he returns."

"Thank you, Señorita."

"*Por nada,* Señor."

I was surrounded by silence. And frustration. I knew very well where Tony Cruz was. At the cabinet meeting in Angel's office.

An hour later I was getting ready to be driven home in my official limousine when he breezed in, dapper in his tight-fitting Italian suit. His manner could not have been more correct. But there was something mocking about his flawless courtesy. "You sent for me, my President?"

"An hour ago, Tony. Where the devil have you been?"

There was a hesitation, a canny pause.

"I—was at the Ministry of Information, going over the list of Arab guests for the Middle Eastern Conference next month."

The eyes of this impertinent and confident young man looked at me steadily.

"You have something you wish me to do for you?"

"I wanted to find out when you would have the draft of my speech to the UN Assembly," I said. "I will need time to polish it."

"You will have time, my President," Tony Cruz said. "You are not scheduled to represent us there until after the first of the year. More than ten weeks."

I had introduced the subject of the UN speech as a test of my new status. If Angel thought I was planning to defect, he might fear the New York visit as an ideal escape hatch. So, if he decided to move against me, he would time it to deprive me of that strategic platform. If so, there was a good chance that Tony Cruz was in on the secret. But if in the mind of the Revolution I already had been separated from my presidency, like a chicken that has lost its head to the sharp ax and flops around unaware of its loss, I read no trace of my sentence in the suave composure of my young assistant. He bowed, *"A sus órdenes,* Señor Presidente," and turned to leave. With his impeccable manners he would assist me right to the wall. I could see him coming forward with a correct smile, bringing his feet together smartly and tying the blindfold around my head, then stepping back, politely, out of range of the fusillade. "At your service, my President."

In the days to follow, there was a subtle change in the attitude of Señorita Naranja. She no longer greeted me as she had been accustomed to, or asked if I would like my *café con leche* and *pan dulce,* which had been a coffee-break ritual. I could imagine her discussing her strange predicament with her parents and her numerous brothers and sisters and being sternly advised not to appear too close to me: the watchful Tony Cruz might report her for being overzealous in her loyalty. She could control her voice, her behavior but she seemed to be trying to express some silent apology for the distance she had been obliged to put between us.

When this happened I would find some way to get her moist, anxious presence out of my office. I would say, "Señorita, will you call the Señora and advise her that I will be home early this afternoon?" *"Muy bien,* Señor Presidente," she would say and escape the office like a frightened bird. Or I would ask her to call the Hilton barbershop and make an appointment for half-past three. "And tell him I will require a full hour of the Maestro's time." In my state of quarantine I was becoming more vain, partly to fill the vacuum of inactivity, partly to impress people that I was not slipping into physi-

cal decline through discouragement or moral depression. But mostly
these orders to Señorita Naranja were the kindest way of getting rid
of her so that I would not have to be exposed to her compassion.

Often after she returned to her lonely reception room, I would
spread on my desk the official newspaper, *La Verdad*. The independent *El Sol*, after fighting off the censors of the previous regime,
had managed to survive only the first year of the Bello Revolution.
Then the editor, who had been jailed and harassed by Zamora, disappeared into a Bello forced-labor camp.

Leafing through *La Verdad*, I read of Angel's achievements in
raising the sugar output, and of the success of the Revolution in
decreasing illiteracy by forty-seven percent, and of a new state cattle
ranch that Angel was dedicating in the long-deprived southern plains
of Ocampo. As I turned the pages I became aware of a total absence
of my name or any reference to the office of the presidency. A
speech that I had made at the dedication of a new park named for
José Martí had dropped from sight like a small stone in a deep lake.
My father, a poor schoolteacher, had been an admirer of Martí, the
Cuban poet-apostle of freedom and the dedication of this new city
park had special meaning for me. I had said that we owed it to his
memory not to be smaller or meaner or more narrowly partisan than
he. The editor of *La Verdad* had caught the point and had telephoned me to suggest that this reference be dropped, in the interest
of brevity. But that was last week. Now, not only the offending sentence but the entire speech was omitted. The words of lesser officials
spoken at the Martí monument were reported, but so far as readers
of *La Verdad* would know, the Provisional President had not been
present in the park.

In the past months, Señorita Naranja was accustomed to mark
the headlines and the columns noting my activities in gay red pencil.
Sometimes she would comment on a news photo. *"Muy bien, muy
guapo,"* she would flatter me and take an extra copy home to show
off her illustrious boss to her proud family. Now she handed me the
papers in silence. Like two flies trapped together under glass, we
were too frustrated even to buzz any longer.

One day, just to break the monotony, I had flipped the intercom
and said, "Get Angel for me. Make clear it is important that I talk

to him." In a few minutes the mechanical voice replied, "Señor Presidente, they say Angel is in the interior. They have no idea when he will be back." God knows, that could have been true—it was said that Angel ran the country out of his pocket. And his sudden dropping out of sight here and popping up there had the virtue of keeping his subordinates on their toes.

"Well, leave word I want him to phone me as soon as he returns. This is an order."

I could imagine Señorita Naranja on the other end of the wire, thinking, this will do it—this will take the old man to the wall. And I could hear Tony Cruz and his inner circle laughing and making nasty *chistes* about the suicidal arrogance of the silent President.

One afternoon as I was about to leave for the Playa de los Papagayos, the office was startled by the ring of the telephone. Señorita Naranja lowered her voice as if doing so made it a little safer to announce that Claude Lewison of the *Observer* was on the line.

Lewison? My first reaction was to say I was not in. Still, I wavered. One of the best-informed foreign correspondents, he must be aware of the risks. Perhaps he had some inside information. Curiosity was gnawing at my fears. And also a hunger for communication.

"*Bueno?* Hello? Is this Lewison?"

"Yes, Mr. President," he said in his clipped English. "Claude Lewison here. I'm flying back to London in a day or so. Would you mind if I popped over to your office for a moment? A few details to go over with you."

He was calling from the Foreign Press Club Bar, an easy fifteen minutes' walk to the palace. I agreed to wait for him in my office.

Fifteen minutes passed, and another fifteen. I thumbed through a new book on Mayan archaeology but soon became too restless even to study the pictures of a new stele recently discovered at an eighth-century religious center in Central Mexico. Ordinarily this would have intrigued me. But now I slammed the book shut and pushed it away impatiently. The chimes of the cathedral bonged noisily, each heavy note resounding ominously over the old city. Five o'clock. The hour of Lorca. Five o'clock in the afternoon.

My troubled Señorita Naranja entered. She was no longer used to seeing me at my desk after official office hours. If there was nothing more I wished, she said in a half voice, she would be leaving for the evening. Yes, there was something. I wanted her to call the Press Club and ask if Señor Lewison was still there—or when he had left. She made a sound somewhere between a sigh and a sob. Claude Lewison had become a dangerous name. But in a few moments she reported that Señor Lewison had left the club almost an hour ago. Now, she begged, could she please leave.

"Go—go—I am sorry to keep you so late. Hasta mañana, Señorita."

"Tomorrow is Saturday, Señor Presidente."

"Of course, I have lost track of time I have been so busy lately," I said.

My failure of a joke seemed only to increase her panic.

"Hasta luego," she said, and left the office so quickly that one might have said she fled.

"One more thing," I called after her. "Leave word with the night guard at the gate that I am still expecting Señor Lewison."

I followed her into the reception room, but she must have grabbed her bag on the run, for she was already gone. It was a most unprepossessing farewell.

Now I dialed the Hilton and asked for Lewison's room. After a short delay, an impersonal voice informed me, "I am sorry, Señor Lewison has checked out."

"But that is impossible." I tried to make my voice sound positive and authoritative. "I know for a fact that Claude Lewison is there. Will you page him in the Press Club? This is Justo Moreno Suárez. I insist that you check again."

There was a long delay and then the impersonal voice, "I am very sorry, Señor Presidente, but Lewison does not answer the page. And he is no longer registered."

It took almost an hour to drive to the beach and when I arrived Marta was outside waiting on the front steps. *"Cariño,"* she said, "I am glad you are back. I was afraid."

She waited until we were inside, beyond earshot of the chauffeur Ramón whom she no longer trusted.

"Your Claude Lewison has been arrested."

"How do you know?"

"Suzi phoned me an hour ago."

Suzi Cisneros was a friend of Marta's and also of our security chief, Juan del Campo.

"I was talking to Claude before I left the office. That's why I'm late. I was waiting for him there."

"Suzi says he is being held on suspicion of being an agent for British Intelligence."

"Insane. Revolutionary paranoia."

"At least he has the British government to worry about him. Who's going to worry about us?"

"Are you sure Suzi knows what she is talking about?"

"Of course not. But at least sometimes she's right."

I was afraid it was true. Although the daily gossip of Tina Alonso and Suzi Cisneros and their friends was highly spiced by their obsession with sex, their informal network operated as an oddly effective counterespionage.

As a matter of habit I walked to the glass windows to look out at the sea.

There at the gate, instead of my sleepy-eyed guard, Rosendo, were two smartly uniformed members of Angel's new Special Force. I would miss Rosendo and his relaxed colleague Diego. They were like personal friends.

"Look at those *cabrones*," Marta said. She had come up behind me. "Justo, you stubborn idiot, you would not listen when I tried to tell you."

I was silent.

"I think it is time we went to a movie with Alejandro," Marta said, as if she had been reading my mind.

If ever we were to require asylum in the embassy where he served as cultural attaché, we were to mention the film playing at the Theater Diana and ask what time he would like to see it with us. He in turn was to answer, "Why not pick me up at home?"

From that moment Alejandro would be expecting us and would set in motion the complicated mechanism for achieving asylum, while we would make a run to his house.

"Maybe you're right, Marta," I said. "Maybe it is time."

"Maybe," Marta said. "When they stand us all against the wall will you still be saying 'maybe'?"

I went to the phone and dialed. I spoke to a maid for a few moments and then I slowly put the instrument back on the cradle. "Alejandro had to fly home for the funeral of his uncle. He returns in five days."

Marta cursed Alejandro's uncle.

"I doubt that anything will happen in five days," I said. "For one thing if we were in immediate danger I am certain Elena would warn us."

Angel's devoted Elena Concepción had been one of our closest friends, an unpredictable society girl who had attached herself to Angel's cause. We had known her before the Revolution, in artistic circles, but had come to know her bettter when she served as a courier between the guerrilla headquarters and our civic underground.

"Elena Concepción," Marta dismissed her. "When Angel catches cold, Elena sneezes for him."

"People are more than one thing, Marta."

"*Vamos a ver*," Marta said. "I believe it when I see it."

I walked toward the large picture window looking out on the beach. Beyond the erect guards was the evening sea, my eternal sea.

7

Next morning I was lying in our luxurious triple-sized bed late into the day. The wooden shutters were still closed but from the broad windows facing the sea we could sense the winter sunshine. I had awakened first and had found Marta in a familiar position with her back curved in against me. The anxieties of my weeks in quarantine had affected my desires. But that morning—I remember it in titillating detail because it was to be the last of home-bed pleasures—I had felt maleness rising and thrusting forward with a life of its own. I had not begun by playing tentatively and seductively with Marta's breasts, barely touching the nipples and then moving my hand slowly down to the center of her as I usually did when I wanted to bring her to me. I had cupped her breast firmly and had drawn her closer not asking her but insisting, as the poor campesinos took their women on the mats of their dirt-floor huts. In half sleep she had responded and at first we had begun slowly, moaning the plea-sure of it together as she reached her hand between her legs and mine until her fingers touched and encouraged my testicles. Then we were turning together, still together, and still able to rotate around and around in a kaleidoscope delirium, sheets and blankets impatiently kicked away and no longer a hindrance to our horizontal dance. Marta had begun to strain toward me and to slap me lustily—the wellborn lady so naturally turned jungle primitive. When the final flare of passion was sweetly gone, sweetly spent, we lay together and spoke in another, softer language: an animal moan, a catching of breath, a renewal of life. Marta reached down to rearrange the blankets. The sheets had been twisted and pushed out of reach. The woolen immediacy of the blankets felt warmly reassuring. I remem-ber slipping off to sleep again with my legs entwined in Marta's. Outside, faintly, I could hear the spent waves rolling lazily to the waterline. In the sweet torpor of satiety, there were no Angel Bellos and Tony Cruzes and elite guards in German boots.

I had not realized I was sleeping or that Marta had left my side until I heard the ringing of the telephone and turned to see her com-ing from the dressing room to answer it. In a burnt-orange smock, her hair up with a yellow hibiscus as a coiffured exclamation point, she looked especially fresh that late morning—brisk, attractive and girlish.

"Elena darling," she was saying, "how good to hear your voice. Of course we'd love to see you. Come for lunch. I'm doing my paella Valenciana. Chino just brought me the most marvelous *camarones* and *langostinos* that are still swimming—"

"Marta," I muttered. "You're not going to prepare the entire paella on the telephone?"

She signaled me to be silent. "Ah—well, then another time. But one o'clock will be perfect. *Ciao,* darling."

"Ciao, darling." The irony of that international phrase of sophisticated social grace pierced and stuck in my consciousness like *banderillas.* With *"Ciao,* darling," I was thinking, Angel Bello's Elena Concepción must be coming to alert me that the ceremonial sacrifice of the Provisional President was near at hand.

"You had better shower and shave—Elena will be here around one—she's down the beach visiting friends and thought she would drop in for a few minutes."

It was one of Marta's gifts that she could make this sound so casual. Soaping myself under the hard spray of hot water, I was unable to enjoy the steaming ritual bath because—like white corpuscles overwhelming the red and polluting the blood—the pleasure cells were being routed by the cells of unease. In the old days a visit from Elena Concepción Bravo y Del Rio brought innocent joy and stimulation. Elena was young enough to be Marta's daughter—actually they were distantly related, as Marta's mother was a blueblood Del Rio—but they were good friends, drawn to each other by intellect; although where Marta was bright, *lista,* quick-and-ready, Elena was thoughtful and poetic. She was not so much a beautiful girl as one of those of whom it is asked, "Hasn't she a lovely quality?"

Her *Poems for Two Guitars* was pleasing lyrical verse and we had enjoyed many evenings together as, light-headed on two sherries, Elena would provide guitar accompaniment for her elegant songs of tragic love.

I turned the shower knob from hot to cold and let the icy water beat on me as long as I could stand it, giving myself totally to its pleasure-pain. It was not until I had reached for the towel that I found myself thinking again of Elena Concepción. Most of the young ladies from her stratum of society had been automatic Zamoristas because their fathers enjoyed the profitable fruit of the root-rotten Zamora tree. But from the beginning Elena had been one of a small group of debutantes who had followed Angel Bello ardently and dangerously. The attraction was undoubtedly more sexual than idealistic or political—Angel was a magnet for women of all ages and classes. He had the sexual power essential to every political catalyst and it drew to him not only a passionate following of women, but also of men.

Turning to the sink to lather my face, my mind reached back to Hitler and Mussolini, highly charged symbols of sex to the millions who adored them for their cruelties and their madness. Heil! Doo-chay! Mouths by the millions eager to commit political fellatio. For better reasons, we were drawn to Bolívar whose revolutionary courage and sexual impact were a single force.

I was a cipher in our political life because I appealed to reason and justice in a country that responded to violence and emotion, religion and myth. Angel Bello was turning the power structure up-side down; in a convulsive paraphrase of Christ some of the last were indeed going first. As a symbol of power his sexual force pro-vided dynamic energy for the Revolution. Sex, economy and poli-tics became a single mighty phallus. On the great plantations that were like autonomous sugar states, when a field hand was betrothed to a local maiden, the master rather than the groom enjoyed the privilege of the first night. "Congratulations, Juan," he would say to his peon. "In your behalf I have subjected your *novia* to the test of truth and I am happy to report that she was a virgin just as her father claimed." And the young peon was expected to turn his straw hat around in his hands and say, "Thank you, master, for using your valuable time to prove this to our mutual satisfaction."

Yes, to the end of the Zamora rule that feudal rite persisted on the vast holdings of our more primitive states. From the days of the Spanish conquest, the people were accustomed to being led—no, not just led but pulled like their burros, beaten and kicked like their pack animals. And in the unloving sense of that word—which has become its contemporary meaning—fucked. The Mexican poet Octavio Paz divided the Latin world into the *hijos de chingada,* the sons of the fucked, and the *gran chingón,* the master fucker who does it to the others. When we say, *"Vete a la chingada,"* we are say-ing literally, "Go to the fucked," to the defeated country of the fucked, the despised country of the weak, of those who are unable to defend themselves against the *gran chingón.*

The Maximum Leader, the *Jefe,* the Strongman, the First Colonel, call him what you will, remains the *gran chingón.* Even when there is revolution and the old *chingones* are overthrown, the *hijos de la chingada,* the children of the fucked, the little brown brothers of the fucked, seem unable to march into the capital under the flag of equality, of justice under republican law. They still need to be led by a new *gran chingón* of their own.

Shaving was always a good time for thinking and as I stared impersonally at the familiar face in my mirror, I wondered if Elena Concepción was coming for some specific purpose of Angel Bello's or to warn us. Was Marta right that for Elena the end was Angel and that she was dedicated to that end despite the means? Certainly she had the power to turn our lives upside down as the hand of the gambler spins the revolving dice cage.

Under the Zamora tyranny she had been the link between Angel in his fluid jungle headquarters and the head of his city underground, identified to the Angelistas only as "Garbo." The disguises Elena had used to elude the secret police and paid informers had given her name a legendary shine. She had found her way to Garbo's underground center passing as a young man with her long hair piled under her cap. She had fooled the Romano Tigers by posing as a priest. Dressed as a fat old woman she had carried small arms and money to Garbo in a pillow under her ample shirt. Elena Concepción became the highborn Joan of Arc who risked her life and the torture of the Tigers a hundred times because as Angel boasted, "Her heart beats as one with the heart of the people."

The plainer truth was that her heart beat with the heart of Angel Bello, or to put it even more accurately, her heart raced after his but always a beat or two behind because it was impossible to keep pace with the trip-hammer instrument that propelled him. Elena had shared many intimacies with Marta, had cried on Marta's shoulder about the unusual demands involved in loving an unstoppable locomotive like Angel Bello. Of course Marta had promised not to tell anyone and of course I had heard it all. In the beginning their affair had followed the conventional pattern, the passionate give-and-take of love. But grudgingly she had come to realize that he was too restless, too busy, too complicated for individual love. He was on the fly, on the move, and took his honey like a bee from whatever flower he found himself near. At first, the jealousy in Elena had been bitter. But in time she had come to accept Angel as he was and

to carve a new role for herself. There was something Oriental about
her evolution from passionate lover to head wife, to whom sooner or
later he would return for support and stability. Sometimes he would
appear at her home at three o'clock in the morning, discuss his
problems with rice production or the floundering industrialization,
make love to her and leave by dawn. And with her Oriental attitude
providing peace of mind, she would be grateful. Sad that he could
not be hers alone, regretful that she could only have him to herself
for a sporadic few hours at his impulse once or twice a week, but
grateful that she possessed more of him than any other single person.
As his number one mistress and confidante, Elena could rationalize
that she had no personal rival—on one side were the assorted young
chicas who threw themselves at Angel wherever he went. On the
other side was his super-mistress, the Revolution. For Elena Concepción it was a new form of revolutionary marriage. All of her female
energy and emotions channeled into Angel and the Revolution.
Without him, she had confessed to Marta, she would have been
merely a wealthy dilettante dabbling in poetry and finally making
the proper *boda*, the family-prescribed marriage of advantage that
would link her family fortune with that of some other "respectable"
lineage.

"So," Elena had said to Marta many times in different ways,
"thank God for Angel. Angel—not my poor romantic poetry—gives
my life meaning." It was for this that she had been born, she now
believed, to serve him as a handmaiden to the Revolution. Elena
was no Communist. In fact she feared the growing strength of the
hard core around Angel. But she had vowed to follow Angelismo
wherever it might lead and if the road veered toward Communism
all she could do was try to temper it a little here and there, intercede
with Angel carefully for certain friends of goodwill caught in the
tightening discipline. This was what the gringo press seemed unable
to understand. There had been a sensational magazine spread on
"Angel Bello's Red Mistress-Secretary" suggesting that she might
emerge as the Eva Perón of our Revolution. Oversimplification. We
never doubted that within the limits of her subservience she would
try to protect Angel against the professional party-liners closing in
around him. But what Elena was able to accomplish was only—

"Justo—Justo—are you still in there?" It was Marta at the

bathroom door. "*Chihuahua*—you take longer at the mirror than I do. Elena will be here any moment."

"I was thinking about something and I cut myself," I said.

"Is it bad? Why do you always cut yourself?"

"Marta, please. Go downstairs and be ready for Elena. I will be there in five minutes."

"Maybe she isn't coming for what we think at all. Maybe it's only to complain about some new lady love of Angel's. I hear rumors that the wife of the French naval attaché—"

"Ay!" In my haste and nervousness I had nicked myself again. "Marta, dammit, if you don't close that door I will never finish shaving. *Vete, vete, por favor.*"

I was still doctoring my tiny wounds when I heard the sound of chimes at the front door. A few minutes later I joined Marta and Elena on the sun porch where they were sipping cream sherry and laughing together as if these were the carefree days of old. I greeted Elena with an affectionate *abrazo*. She looked elegant in a black riding habit with a white ruffled shirt. Tailored trousers tapered into suede boots and her long dark hair was drawn back and held in place with a large tortoise-shell barrette. Her lean, athletic figure suggested a stylish lady bullfighter, a Conchita Cintron, rather than an official messenger dispatched from the roving headquarters of Angel Bello.

I toasted her health and tried to enter into the spirit of their congenial small talk. But underneath the chatter my mind was crouched on its marks like a sprinter poised for the starter's gun. Marta was a model of animated composure: "Elena darling, I'm disappointed in you. I was hoping you would bring me the latest gossip from the city. I've been working in the garden this month and being such a perfect wife and mother that I am going crazy with boredom."

I wanted to cry out, "*Basta!* That's enough! Let's get to the point. *Basta* with this idiotic charade."

Elena responded as if I had said it aloud. "I wish I could stay but I have to meet Angel at the palace. There's a reception for the winners of the young militia competition."

"Elena," I said, "we have known each other a long time. What have you come to tell us?"

Her answer was both surprising and anticlimactic. "Angel is inviting reporters from all over the world to spend two weeks here as
guests of the Revolution. Even from the United States. They will be
free to travel anywhere they like and then to ask questions at a
press conference in the People's Auditorium. Angel feels the time
has come to counteract the lies being spread about our Revolution
in the bourgeois press."

"Justo is against dishonest journalism everywhere," Marta said
lightly.

"We know," Elena Concepción conceded. "That is what makes
him such a lonely man. Angel respects your integrity, Justo. Which
is why he sent me to ask if you would be willing to preside over the
press conference."

"Tell Angel—I will be delighted to preside."

Elena rose and placed her hands affectionately on my shoulder.
"Justo, it does my heart good to see that you are still with us. To
speak frankly, as an old friend, I was afraid this past month might
have embittered you."

She embraced us both warmly and hurried out to her waiting
limousine.

"Well, Señora of the x-ray eye, what do you make of it?" I asked
Marta, after seeing Elena to the door.

"Won't you come into my parlor?" said Marta with a cynical
bow.

"No, there is no need for Angel to set a trap. He could send a
squad of Angelitos right now and pack us off to Las Barricudas."

"I still think we should get away from that *hijo* the moment
Alejandro gets back—"

"We are certainly safe till the end of the press conference," I
said. "As long as he keeps Claude Lewison in jail he needs me to
counteract the bad effect on the press. If there are embarrassing
questions about Lewison, he can say this is not a question of freedom of the press—here is President Justo Moreno Suárez himself
presiding over the conference. Lewison is not in jail for what he
wrote in the London *Observer* but because he is suspected of being
a British agent."

"And do you want to be a party to that *cursi* lie?"

"Marta, with Alejandro out of the country, do we have any choice?"

"Maybe not. But I wonder if you really want to make the choice."

I wondered too. Through the window I could see the businesslike guards posted at our front gate.

"Oh my God!" Marta jumped to her feet. "I forgot the paella. I hope María Magdalena had enough sense to take it out of the oven."

"In this household we go from crisis to crisis," I said as Marta, favoring her bad leg, hurriedly disappeared into the kitchen.

As in a muddled dream I see myself sitting at the long green felt table on the stage of the auditorium facing several hundred foreign correspondents. On my left was Angel and beside him Elena Concepción looking solemn and appropriately proletarian in her gray tweed suit. Seated next to her was "Garbo," now Secretary of the Interior and able to acknowledge his identity as Dr. Luis Levy. Tall, thin and almost totally bald, he stared coldly through rimless glasses with pale blue eyes. Only a man with his scientific detachment could have gone through the Revolution serving the twin posts as director of the government hospital and also of the underground network in the capital. To my right was Juan del Campo, Angel's useful Lord High Executioner, and next to him my unnerving little fashion-plate, Tony Cruz. I listened and I did not listen. I was there and I was not there. I felt like a disembodied spirit called back to a séance but not given the gift of speech. Meanwhile the hoarse voice of Angel Bello droned on. He had made a speech to the graduating class of the new Air Force Academy that morning and he had spent an hour and a

half at a cocktail reception at the Foreign Press Club talking all the
while the foreign guests were freeloading and now he had been
talking almost steadily for two more hours. He had been brilliant,
informative, argumentative, arrogant, humble, charming, insulting,
repetitious, disingenuous—which is to say he had been Angel Bello.
But if this was to be just another one-man show, what had been his
purpose in sending Elena Concepción to urge me to attend? Merely
to demonstrate to the world that the Provisional President was still
alive and intact? Was it wise to go to the trouble and expense of
inviting the press of the world to witness the humiliation of a silenced
President exhibited like a cowed circus lion?

A pudgy, beetle-browed Englishman who identified himself as a
writer for *The Manchester Guardian* rose to ask a question of the
Provisional President. "I understand that you were an early advocate
of collective farms for your country on the model of the Israeli
kibbutz. But we have heard nothing from you on the subject of
establishing much larger farm units run by outside administrators on
the model of the Soviet state farms. Informed critics are calling this
'bureaucratized anarchy' and I . . ."

I nodded, hesitated because the subject was so delicate, and was
about to speak when I heard Angel answering for me. He was warming to the newfound virtues of state farm centralization rather than
smaller unit fragmentation when *The Manchester Guardian* somehow
managed to slip in a second question. "Sir, I was asking the opinion
of President Moreno Suárez. Is he not to be permitted to respond?"

Angel's defense of my absent presence was typically aggressive:
"What you people overlook is that we are still in the throes of a
revolution. You Anglo-Saxons have not had a revolution in so long
that you have forgotten what it is like. The guerrilla activities may
be over but the fighting goes on. So we hold the power in trust for
the President. The office of the presidency is the promise of the democracy of the future, toward which our Revolution is moving.
Later the voice of the President will be heard."

"And how long will it be before this democratic miracle takes
place?" asked a half-sympathetic, half-cynical Italian reporter.

I looked up. I felt the impulse to cry out, "My question exactly!
How long, Angel, how long? Remember, I said 'A figurehead—not

a puppet.' All those people who lived in darkness, yes you teach them how to spell. But when will you teach them the most important lesson of all, how to run their own lives without Angel Bello leading them step by step? You want a country of happy children with a stern but loving Papa. But what if Papa dies, or changes his mind? Your President wants the same reforms. But not handed down to them like lollipops."

Instead I leaned my elbow on the green felt table and rested my forehead in my palm. I glanced across at Garbo. He was staring straight ahead, reserved and enigmatic as always. From our first meeting at a secret rendezvous at his villa in the early days of the Revolution I had wondered how a man who seemed so disinterested in his fellowman could involve himself in our left-wing politics. Perhaps the reorganization of society was a chess game to him, as was his brilliant management of the underground. The Angel Bello oratory rolled on like a shoreless sea. "My mandate comes from the brotherhood of the poorest of the peasants . . ." I sat there vulnerable and violated, thinking—brotherhood, that mirage, that shadow flag of a hollow Christianity and a hollow Marxism, that key to the secular religion that Angel and I both shared and disputed. Except Angel's side was powerful, muscular and demoniac, while my side— if I still had one—was diffident, self-doubting and permissive. I had permitted Angel Bello to live. My decision had been an act of faith in an open society. Do we fail that society when we permit agents of certainty to override us? Are we limited to a magnetized field where our choice is unchoice? To cling to right-wing tyrant or left-wing god?

I had thought Angel would turn to me for some formal closing remarks, as a token gesture of my existence. But suddenly he brought his press conference to a close. He thanked his inquiring reporters for their interest in our Revolution. He assured them that they could travel freely and seek out any information they wished. Then as if he had not consumed hours to answer half a dozen questions, he suddenly consulted his watch—wags claimed it was a watch that told him only what day of the month it was—announced that he was sorry he had to bring this informative question-and-answer period to a close due to an emergency cabinet meeting, and dismissed them by extending his hands toward them palms inward like a triumphant matador.

A group of the more conscientious of the foreign press were ready to move forward and intercept me. Their eyes were full of questions that Angel had reached across to snag from me like an overzealous tennis player who constantly crosses into the terrain of his doubles partner. But at that moment Angel "rescued" me again by hurrying toward me and walking me off with that friendly chimpanzee-arm clasped around my shoulder. In that eloquent embrace I was led directly to my waiting limousine. There Angel bowed me politely into its comfortable interior.

"Good-bye, my friend," he said. *"Que vayas bien.* That you go well."

He slammed the door, stepped back and turned to rejoin Elena Concepción, Juan del Campo and his adoring Angelitos.

I leaned my head against the upholstered seat. In my right eyelid I felt a twitch I could not control. Why had I said nothing? Because I was not Martí forsaking his family and charging forward to meet the first bullet for the sacred cause. I was merely citizen Moreno Suárez with a portfolio of principles but a mind full of fear.

When I reached the beach house I went straight through the hall-way to the bar-den and poured myself a double rum. I was having my second when Marta came in.

"So it went badly," she said.

"It went badly. He let me say nothing. Nothing! Why did he want me there? For what purpose?"

"You know what I think?" Marta said.

"You think we should already be in Miami. With the chronic complainers and the counterrevolutionists."

"Yes," Marta said. "Exiles are a bore. They squabble. They stew in their own juice. But I would rather stew in my own juice than die in my own blood."

"Marta, I want to live as much as you do."

The accusation of martyrdom always riled me. It was true that commitment moved me in that direction, just as Marta's instinct was to devote herself to our selfish interests and immediate needs. But hers was a total dedication. To call me martyr was not to praise but

to demean me. I knew my feeling of self-preservation and family
loyalty flawed the purity of the true religious or political martyr
ready and sometimes eager to die for his cause. Is a reluctant martyr
not a contradiction in terms? Because the dichotomy disturbed me,
I was always quick to deny Marta's charge that I was pursuing an
uneasy courtship with the wall.

Our argument was interrupted by an unexpected arrival. Don
Pepe came to announce that Señora Cisneros had sent her maid with
a message. Then, bossy as he always was with servants he considered
beneath him, the old major domo ordered the maid to come forward. She reached into her small bosom and produced a sealed
envelope which she handed to Marta with a mumbled "At your
service." I offered her a few pesos and told her to wait in the
kitchen in case the note required an answer. As soon as we were
alone Marta tore it open. We read it together. "Destroy this as soon
as you read it. Juan called after the emergency cabinet meeting—he
has taken over Garbo's post. Garbo has been arrested. Your Tony
Cruz moves up to Juan's job. There will be a roundup of leaders of
the non-Communist Left before dawn. Hurry." I took the note and
crumpled it in my hand and burned it in a large ashtray.

"Good old Suzi," I said. "I always thought she was just a vain
little bitch but—"

"But thank God for vain little bitches—rather than noble, dedicated Elenas. What time is it?"

I glanced at my watch. "Almost six-thirty."

"Those *pendejos* like to do their work between midnight and
dawn. When the streets are deserted. That gives us five or six hours
—if we are lucky."

I nodded. The unreality of the afternoon and now the reality of
Suzi's note had convinced me that there was no ground left to stand
firm on. It was all quicksand. Now I must stop thinking, dreaming,
hoping, generalizing, rationalizing and simply act. It was time for
Article V—the rights of asylum and safe passage to anyone endangered for political reasons. It made nice reading, but between the
fine print of international law there was an urgent law of the jungle.
There was nothing automatic about political refuge. Between us and
safe harbor in the embassy compound stood Angel's crack militiamen, under orders to shoot anyone seeking to escape.

I went to the phone and called Alejandro, whom we had heard was back in the country. His butler answered. He would see if the master was at home. A stab of panic. What if he were out for the evening? Where could we hide until he returned?

The wait was agony although it could not have been more than a minute before Alejandro picked up the phone. His voice was cultivated and high-pitched—some thought effeminate—and his way of speaking was a Spanish imitation of the delicate lilt he had assumed at Oxford.

"Justo old boy!" Alejandro began with his usual élan. "Sorry I was away for that dreary funeral when you called. Barbaric affairs, funerals. Unless you do them like those New Orleans Negroes. March them into the grave with a rousing jazz number."

"Alejandro," I said, self-consciously using the code. "You remember that film we talked about? Marta and I would like to meet you—at the Diana at eleven. There will just be time to catch the last show."

I must say this for Alejandro, his tone never changed. He was one of those effete playboys steady as a rock behind the facade. "Perfecto," he made a happy little song of it. "We have a date. Eleven o'clock it is. Ciao." Which meant he would get in touch with his embassy at once. Meanwhile he would hide us until the Ambassador agreed to accept us. There were only two ways to achieve embassy asylum. Either you scaled the wall and broke in by force or the embassy agreed in advance to accept you.

I looked around the den for the last time. Marta was saying that we must pack quickly, taking only what we could carry without arousing suspicion. She would use her oversized handbag and I would put a few essentials into the largest of the fish boxes I used for surf-casting. I would wear my old fishing pants and a windbreaker. Marta would wear blue jeans and a heavy sweater as if she were accompanying me on an impromptu bit of surf-fishing down the beach.

I looked lovingly over my shelves of books. They were like old friends I was leaving behind, deserting. I picked a few that might fit into my fish box. *Ismaelillo* by Martí—*The Plague* by Camus— *Bolívar as Seen by His Contemporaries*—two volumes of his *Letters* were too large for the box—I would ask Alejandro to send them later—now what else—I must carry along something by Stendhal and—*The Ballads of Lorca* came to hand—yes, they would just fit.

"Justo, you idiot. Forget your books. There will be plenty of books in the embassy—if we make it. Now vámanos. Pronto!" She seemed to have forgotten her arthritic knee as she hurried up the stairs.

I could not help noticing the pictures along the wall, the Orozco sketch for a mural I had bought directly from the proud, crippled little Mexican when he was close to starving in New York. And a primitive painting I had purchased for a few pesos from an old man with black skin in the hot country of the south. My books, my paintings, my bed, my shower, my garden, my beach, my parrot, the familiar faces of my friends, my servants, people like Chino the fisherman, people you barely know but who have become an inextricable part of your *ambiente*.

"Justo, hurry. Hurry," Marta said over her shoulder as she reached the landing.

"I am," I said. "I was just thinking—"

"I told you—there is no time to think. Just move, pack, get ready. Take only what you absolutely need. And as many valuable small things as you can stuff into your pockets—watches, cuff links, lighters—things that are useful as bribes. But don't lose time picking anything out. Hurry. Hurry."

In the bathroom I took the essential toilet articles. I folded the lightest dressing gown that I could stuff into the fish box. But I couldn't stop thinking, what a century, the century of gas chambers and genocide, of refugees streaming from burning cities, the century of move, hurry and take only what you need. I paused at the night stand. A new book on Pre-Columbian art I was halfway through. And *The Making of the President 1960*—on which I had been making notes in the loose-leaf diary I often wrote in before turning off the light. Our version might be *The Making of the Dictator:* Was there something in our social climate that turned so many young democratic heroes into aging tyrants? A Porfirio Díaz Complex. . . ?

"Justo, I am going to leave you behind."

"But I must have the notebook. We have no idea how long they will hold us. If I have nothing to do I will go crazy. At least the notebook—"

"Idiot, you are not playing the game of choosing the favorite things to take with you on a tropical island."

"Marta, you are a very tough lady."

But I knew she was right.

Down to essentials in two small bags. Marta came over and put her hand on my shoulder. "We'll have all these things again. Not the same things. But the same kinds of things."

She was wearing her old blue jeans that she filled to the splitting point. She had never been better than she was that night. I put on my old fishing cap that completed my surf-casting costume. "Vámanos," I said. "Let's go, old girl."

"How should we handle Clarita?" Marta said.

"I think we should tell her."

"No. Only to join us down the beach, at the cottage, in twenty minutes. Not why."

"But she will ask. You know Clarita."

"Not this time. This time she will understand not to ask. I'll take care of Clarita. You take care of the servants."

I walked down the wide circular stairway for the last time, feeling sluggish with too much sentiment. Are women less sentimental than men? Or were they given a supplemental infusion of practicality necessary to childbearing? At the basic center of life woman was able to suffer the pain and force out the child alone, somehow manage the cord and carry it home from the field as our primitive campesinas did when there was no other way. Whatever the reason, I found it harder than Marta to endure the cruelty of walking out on the servants. Of having to betray them deliberately.

I went into the kitchen and partly from force of habit opened the icebox and stared into it. It was well stocked. There were the baby shrimp that María Magdalena was planning for tomorrow's seafood salad. The sight of it made me linger, unaccountably sad, not just for myself and Marta and Clarita but for the trusting María Magdalena, for the helpless shrimp.

"*Sí*, Señor? Can I get you anything, Señor?"

"Oh—tell María Magdalena we have changed our minds. We

will—be dining with some friends down the beach. So—good night, Don Pepe. There is no need for anything further."

Don Pepe looked pleased to have the evening off.

"Very well. Until tomorrow, Señor Presidente."

It pained me to think of old Don Pepe going to his room, removing his uniform and his teeth and dropping weary into his bed with faith that he would resume his life as he had left it the night before. The hard truth of it was that Marta and I had no choice but to conspire to destroy that faith. Our security depended on our ability to betray or at least deceive our servants and friends. To betray or risk betrayal. I dwell on this out of guilt because Don Pepe and María Magdalena's years of service were paid off in abandonment. Instead of rising to the security of the accustomed chores of an affectionate household there would be the frightening interrogation of Juan del Campo's security police. I could see my toothless Don Pepe blinking into the oversized light. "You have been with the Moreno Suárez family over twenty years? Then surely they would have confided in you. So come on now, be a good fellow. Tell us where they went, where are they hiding?"

When we slipped out on Don Pepe that night without a word of forewarning it was the beginning of the slow, gradual, tortuous process of demoralization that every seeker of asylum must suffer as the price of admission to the exclusive club of survival. I had left some cash in an envelope in the pantry, in the hope that it might help him through the hard days to which we must abandon him. But I could not afford even the luxury of a parting note.

As I turned away from the sideboard where I had placed the envelope for Don Pepe, I saw Dolores in her box contentedly nursing her week-old kittens. There were six of them, all black and white but no two in the same proportion. Each one was an individualist and although they barely had their eyes open, we already had names for them suggested by their special characteristics, the fat one, the sleepy one, the growler, the bright one, the greedy one, the runt. I kneeled down. Dolores meowed a greeting. She was unusually trusting for a new mother cat and instead of resisting seemed to welcome our interest in her family. Dolores is as trusting and secure as Don Pepe and María Magdalena, I thought, hopeful, while hopelessly ignorant of their impending desertion. I felt my eyes tear for the purring mother cat and the kittens and the people of the household who would soon be curled peacefully into sleep. These are the details of political asylum one doesn't read about in the whole literature of refugee travail from Latvia to Spain and from Haiti to Tibet —a hunted man's pausing to weep over a cat and her squirming brood of kittens.

"Justo—I am waiting for you!"

Marta had thrown open the door to the kitchen.

"I was just saying good-bye to Dolores."

"Oh my God," Marta said. "And on the way out I suppose we are going to take leave of all the parrots, the mynah birds and the pelicans, one by one!"

"All right, Marta, that's enough. Maybe it is not so hard for you but—"

"It is hard enough."

Then I felt badly because now that I looked at her more closely I could see that she meant it. "Now vámanos, Saint Francis, vámanos," she said.

She was right to taunt me . . . kittens and parrots and doves that came quietly to the garden every morning for a handout. I would be thinking of Mano betrayed and abandoned next time he flew down to visit. All these uncomplicated relationships that add to the enjoyment of being human had to be left behind.

"Do not look around. Think of nothing but getting past the guards and walking down that beach."

Suddenly it was real. The guards. The secret police. The wall.

"Clarita?" I said.

"She will meet us at the cottage in fifteen minutes."

For the last time in our lives we walked through the house to the sun porch and from the screen door stepped out onto the beach. I did not need Marta to instruct me not to look back. All my senses were straining forward now.

"Venga lo que venga," I said—that which comes, comes.

"Shh," Marta warned.

"But we should be talking to each other. It will look more natural."

"Bravo!" Marta said. "The first sensible thing you have said all day."

The weather was against us. The night was dark and a strong wind was blowing in from the sea, hardly the sort of night one chooses to go fishing. As we came closer to the fence I was surprised to see a familiar silhouette, the human barrel that encased my old guard, Rosendo. Where were the elite guards who had replaced him? What sort of game of cat and mouse had brought Rosendo back to me?

He was half asleep against the fence as we approached. "Buenas noches, Rosendo, cómo te va?"

"Bien, bien, Señor Presidente," Rosendo said, rousing himself with that always humorous effort to stay awake.

"And how is your wife feeling? Is she fully recovered from the colic?"

"Yes, thank you, my President. Only now the baby has caught it."

"*Que lástima!*" Marta said. "When you go off duty in the morning, perhaps you can take home a bowl of hot garlic broth from our kitchen."

"A thousand thank you's, Señora," said our beer-fat, guileless soldier of the Revolution.

Another betrayal, I thought. There will be no garlic broth. Instead there will be the security police.

"Well, I see we have the beach all to ourselves tonight." I tried to maintain a casual tone.

"Sí, Señor. The wind is blowing hard. You are a brave man to go fishing on a night like this."

"Not brave, clever. The fish will not be expecting us."

Rosendo chuckled, accommodatingly. "Como no, mi Presidente. Buena suerte."

"*Gracias. Hasta luego*—until later," I said. I wasn't carrying it off casually at all. But my lack of talent was not detected by Rosendo. What I had gambled on was not his stupidity, for he had the canniness of the true *guajiro* jungle cat, but his simple friendliness. I pulled my old fishing hat further down my forehead against the wind and waved Rosendo a friendly, treacherous good-bye.

Together Marta and I bent into the wind. It was an impossible night for fishing all right. A plug cast into this gale would have hooked only the fisherman. It was a night for hugging one's hearth, not for fighting the wind along the beach. What if good old Rosendo suspected our charade? With his own unwashed and precious neck to protect, he might be already in the house phoning his superiors. The fear was an instant goiter of anxiety that made it difficult to swallow or breathe. I quickly glanced at Marta. Head straight, lips pressed, she was walking on. The arm of coral rocks was only fifty yards down the beach. Slowed by the wind and with sense of time befuddled by tension it could have been half an hour until we reached that familiar landmark at the far corner of the crescent beach. Behind the rock formation there was high ground, rising half a dozen feet above the beach, a promontory protected by sea grape trees and the hardy Australian pines. Tucked into this scraggly grove was Marta's makeshift studio, a cozy unprepossessing shack looking out on the sea. It was there that Marta filled canvases with seascapes that I thought atrocious and that her friends pretended to admire.

There was no electricity in the shack but Marta lit a hurricane lamp which filled the cluttered, primitive room with an intense white light. There we waited for Clarita. Marta had instructed her to wait ten minutes and then come looking for us, as if she had an important telephone message for me. She was to ask Rosendo if he had seen us, and then go hurriedly down the beach. Marta stood at the front window looking out at the fretful night. I paced, glanced at my watch, opened a large book on the bare wood table that simply said *Picasso*. I thumbed impatiently, the pink circus boy with his horse, the early cubist guitars, a two-page spread of modern terror from the sky: "Guérnica." I slammed the book shut. "She should be here by now."

Marta stamped out her cigarette. "It's not even five minutes."

"What if Rosendo doesn't let her pass?"

I paced again. The wind grew angrier. The flimsy shack shuddered. Its windows rattled. Marta stood at the window smoking.

"*Calma*. The pacing makes me nervous," she said.

There was a knock on the door. I hurried to open it. When I slid the bar back and turned the latch, it flew open and the sand swept in, and a dry bush the wind had torn from the sandbank. I stood on the threshold and stared into the darkness. No Clarita. I called her name.

"Calling upwind, *tonto!* You expect her to hear you?"

I turned and looked at Marta, exasperated. It is sentimental nonsense that adversity brings people closer together. Pressures pry them apart.

I stepped back into the shack and with some effort shut the door again. "You didn't tell Clarita anything of what we are doing?"

"No. Only what I told you."

"What if—because of the storm—she doesn't come? If she thinks it isn't that important?"

"She knows it is important."

"How? How does she know? If she fails to meet us in the next few minutes, our whole plan—"

"Her intuition will tell her. Woman's intuition. Clarita's is especially well-developed."

"Intuition! Well, if she isn't here in five more minutes I'm going back for her."

"No—Justo—I am the one to go back. If you are gone they may question us but I hardly think they will shoot us. You are the one that *pendejo* is after. If I am not back in fifteen minutes, take the little car and go on to Alejandro's without us."

Behind Marta's studio shack was a carport in which she kept her Volkswagen.

"Marta, the three of us leave together or not at all."

"But since we are women, and not political—"

"Together or not at all."

"You are being noble. This is no time for 'attitudes,' Justo. You have to survive."

The wind blew hard around the shack and made the walls and

rafters groan. The door rattled. Or was it a knocking? I hurried to open it and this time it was not the wind but Clarita. She was wearing an old cloth coat over tight toreador pants, which I resented even in this moment of escape. She had tied a kerchief over her thick hair.

"Clarita! You had no trouble with the guard?"

"Why should I have trouble, except when he tries to kiss me, Popee?"

Seeing how Clarita accepted this improbable night, perhaps there was something to female intuition.

I blew out the hurricane lamp and we groped through the darkness to the door. Marta led the way around the shack to the open carport, holding my left hand with Clarita behind holding hard to my right. The wind was blowing so fiercely that we had to lean forward and force ourselves through it. Fortunately the little black Volkswagen was not too far away. It had been Marta's way of escaping the official life of long black limousines that reminded her of funerals. "If the government had provided us with something sporty like a Ferrari . . ."

The dirt road led directly from the shack to the main road. Marta drove, with Clarita beside her. I hunched down in the back seat with my fishing cap pulled down over my eyes and the collar of my heavy windbreaker up around my chin. As we turned onto the highway, hard rain cracked against the windshield. Let it pour! It no longer looked suspicious to huddle into coats, mufflers and head covers for protection. And Marta could throttle the little car to the floor, barreling along at one hundred kilometers an hour with the logical excuse that she was speeding home to avoid being caught in a possible hurricane. In the final year of Zamora, the mere fact of cruising open roads after dark had been equated with rebellion, and trigger-happy Zamora soldiers had fired on impulse and suspicion. Angelitos may not have been as bloodthirsty as the Tigers of Romano but once again night roamers were looked on with distrust.

With the wind and stinging rain of this hurricane night as our allies, we drove for half an hour without seeing a single car. Then the headlights of two vehicles speeding toward us flashed by at about fifteen-minute intervals. From the small back window I

84 BUDD SCHULBERG

watched the first one become a disappearing red dot. The second
one slowed up and its headlights swung around until they were
almost facing in our direction again.

"Por Dios," I said. "They seem to be—"

"Popee—if they catch us, what will they do?" Clarita asked
gravely.

I felt ashamed for putting anxiety in this child who was con-
trolling herself so well.

"They are not going to catch us," Marta said. It sounded like a
positive threat to the motorized militia. The lights behind us veered
off to the left and disappeared.

I huddled into my fishing gear as if trying to hide from myself.
Marta hunched over the steering wheel like a bulky, overweight
racing driver, while Clarita sat as straight as an obedient child on
her first day in school, not knowing what she was escaping from or
to but carrying out her assignment with unexpected poise.

Occasionally the wind would seem to swing out and sideswipe us
and Marta would have to grip the wheel more firmly against its
force. Rain battered the windshield and the small rubber wipers
could not work fast enough to keep ahead of the violence of the
downpour. Marta leaned forward until her face was almost pressed
against the glass and I wondered how she could follow the road.
The butt of a cigarette flickered in her mouth and when it threatened to burn her lip she quickly stuffed it into the ashtray and asked
me over her shoulder to light another one. Clarita handed one back
to me and I lit it and passed it on to Marta. The tobacco was dark
and strong and the smoke filled the confining interior of the Volkswagen.

"Clarita dear," I spoke up to the stiff back of our uprooted daughter, "would you pass me one of Mama's *Delicados*?"

"Justo?" Marta's voice came back to me sharply, a mixture of
concern and accusation. "Are you all right?"

"Of course I'm all right. I simply thought I would launch a
counteroffensive."

"Is my smoke bothering you?"

"No, I am enjoying it. Truly. It gives me something to watch in
the dark."

Clarita also spoke. "But Popee, you always say you hate cigarettes."

"It is true, *querida*. Now will you please hand me the hated cigarette."

"Papa is a little nervous," Marta explained to Clarita condescendingly, as if running the gantlet of the Bello militia was a daily occurrence for them.

"I am fine," I defended myself against these two strong-willed ladies. "I am cold, miserable and terrified. Other than that, I feel absolutely fine."

"You should not talk like that, Popee. You are supposed to say things that will make me feel safer and more secure."

"*Claro, chica, claro,*" I said. "Actually I am sure everything will be fine. Uncle Alejandro will be waiting for us and very soon we will be safe in the United States."

"Are we going to fly there or go by boat?" Clarita wanted to know.

"Boat—plane—*no importa,*" I said. "Either way, we are going to get there."

"Are we going to Miami first, and then New York and then Mexico City, just like last time?" Clarita made it sound like a vacation we had booked at the travel bureau.

I noticed a light far ahead on the road. Any moment a checkpoint guard or a militia highway patrol could put an end to our journey. "*Vamos a ver, vamos a ver,*" I mumbled. "Now, *chiquita*, let us be quiet for a moment, shall we? Mama is trying to drive."

The highway was beginning to rise and fall, gently, like a tamed roller coaster, and I realized we were approaching the fashionable suburb of Lomas Lindas where Alejandro lived. The single light loomed larger, from a roadside booth. Marta began to check our momentum. "Pretend to be asleep," she said to me over her shoulder.

"Mama, shall I pretend to be asleep, too?" Clarita said obligingly.

"No, little one. You and I are going to flirt with the guard."

"Even if he is very ugly?"

"Especially if he is very ugly," Marta said emphatically and braked the car to a stop.

I leaned my head against the corner of the back seat and pulled the fishing cap down over my eyes. The guard moved reluctantly from his narrow shelter. He was wearing a black rubber coat and floppy rain hat and his voice was deep and hoarse, a giant bullfrog in the rain.

"Where are you going?"

"Home, Señor Sargento, where else on a night like this?"

"And from where do you come?"

"We drove down to do some surf-fishing near Papagayos. But the storm came up."

"I think you are very brave to stand outside in this hurricane all by yourself," Clarita spoke up.

"Well, it is not quite a hurricane, Señorita." His husky voice sounded a little less harsh now that he had swallowed Clarita's over-generous honey.

"And after all," Marta volunteered, "we must guard our Revolution twenty-four hours a day."

"*Como no,* Señora, you speak the truth," said the cold, wet, proud militiaman.

"You wish to see my driver's license?" Marta asked.

The guard sounded apologetic. "It is the regulation."

While Marta was searching her large bag, she seemed to fish out a pack of cigarettes accidentally. "I know I have my license somewhere here in this mess—meanwhile, if you care for a cigarette . . ."

The corporal, whom she had promoted to sergeant, hesitated. "Well . . . perhaps for later in the booth."

As he selected one, Marta said casually, "Keep the pack. We have more."

The corporal-sergeant tucked them through his rubber greatcoat into an inside pocket. Then he peered over the car window to glance at the license in the uncertain light of a small plastic flashlight that seemed to be running low on power. All this I could see from my simulated sleep under the broad brim of my fishing cap. For a moment I wondered if the license would give us away. But Latin ladies are the original Lucy Stoners—they do not surrender their

surnames in marriage. They simply tack on the first part of their
husband's name. Thus Marta's legal name was Señora Marta Bravo
y Del Rio de Moreno. "Bravo y Del Rio," the militiaman struggled
with it. "It is very familiar."

"Perhaps you are thinking of my niece, Elena Concepción
Bravo, the personal secretary of Angel."

The guard snapped to attention. He hoped he had not delayed
us too long.

Marta pressed her advantage. "Shall I wake my husband? You
wish to see his papers also?"

"No, no, it will not be necessary. Be careful driving home. The
road is very slick. Buenas noches, Señora, Señorita."

"Viva Angel," Marta nodded.

"Viva Angel, Viva!" the checkpoint guard echoed her fervently
as we drove on.

I turned and watched the poor fellow through the rain pattern on
the rear window. I say "poor fellow" because the next morning, as
soon as it was realized that the Provisional President had flown his
Papagayos coop and slipped through this highway checkpoint into
the capital, the frog-voiced militiaman would be drowning like a
fly that had fallen accidentally into the counter-revolutionary soup.
The wind and the rain and the sweet talk of my ladies had jammed
the efficient machine our militiaman might have been on a clear
night when the stars are fixed and the mind is ready.

Now the open highway had led into the garden-divided parkway
of the prosperous Lomas Lindas and we were passing large houses
blazing with lights. Marta swung the car violently to the left onto a
narrow street, the front wheels splashed into a puddle and she momentarily lost control. The Volkswagen became a drunken campesino staggering out of the *cantina* with a bellyful of the cheapest
rum, lurching from one side of the street to the other. A lamp ca-
reened toward us at a surrealist angle, a parked car threatened to
plunge into us head on. I had visions of sirens, *transito* police, and
the fear that the ordinary traffic cops whom everybody laughed off as
stupid and grafting would have the honor of intercepting the fugitive
President only a block and a half from his hiding place.

A narrow stone bridge over a deep barranca was a welcome land-

mark. Beyond the bridge the road rose steeply to the hilltop residence of Alejandro Castillo. There were the graceful posts with their
elegant coach lamps lighting the gate between the thick walls. But
most welcome of all was the sight of the gates already open to
receive us, like arms stretched out to us. Wise Alejandro to leave
them open. There is nothing more suspicious than a lonely midnight
call on a friendly Latin diplomat.

Marta aimed the Volkswagen at the narrow carriage port and
gunned the little car through. I thought I saw the blurred face of
the surprised portero as we shot past him. She skidded to a stop,
flung open the door and, with hard rain pelting our faces, we ran
across the driveway and up the stone steps of the rear entrance.
The door was unlocked. From inside we could hear footsteps approaching. At least the first stage had gone according to plan.

10

Alejandro Castillo was walking toward us from the library game
room. In his late thirties, his slender, stylish figure and the crew-cut
he affected made him look younger by ten years. A dandy, a
fashion-plate in mahogany cashmere, from turtleneck sweater to
soft crushed handmade Gucci boots, Alejandro might have been
described as handsomely homely in the traditional Castillian manner, his aristocratic hook nose accentuating his long, thin, sensu-
ously lidded face.

Setting down an oversized brandy snifter, he threw his arms
around me in an intense *abrazo*, then turned quickly to kiss the
hands of Marta and Clarita. I must have glanced toward the doors
leading from the billiard room, for Alejandro said, "No fears. The
servants are out. And I told the portero to leave the gates open as I

was expecting a visit from a lady friend who did not want to wait at the entrance for fear of being recognized."

He gave a twisted smile. "Fortunately a wicked reputation is excellent cover."

"Noble Alejandro! Now I understand why you are always so busy," Marta said. "In the interest of humanity."

"It is kind of you to put it that way," Alejandro said with a mocking little bow. "Now—a splash of cognac, Señora?"

"For tonight a double splash," Marta said, and we all laughed.

Alejandro turned gallantly to Clara. "And for you, my little bird, I have a chilled bottle of—Pepsi Cola *Grande*."

She blushed and looked at him adoringly.

Behind the face of social butterfly, Alejandro was unexpectedly brave. He had dared to criticize publicly the feudal conditions in which hundreds of thousands of his countrymen were forced to work themselves to early deaths for their absentee landlords. He had described it as a tragic anachronism for the Three Hundred Families to control eighty percent of the land and an even more disproportionate share of the national wealth. It was an unusual statement to come from a Castillo, one of the most influential of the Three Hundred. "I am not a radical," Alejandro had protested. "I am not even political. I am simply tired of feudalism." The army generals, who tolerated civilian rule as long as it did not swing too far to the left, thought that Alejandro needed a few years in their steaming jungle prison to remind him of his loyalties to God and Country and the Three Hundred Families. But Alejandro's father, brother of a previous president and a power in the National Bank, had intervened with the suggestion that Alejandro be politely exiled from the country as a cultural attaché. Thus he had come to our capital, a sort of silk-shirt political refugee. Yes, he was adjusted to crises, but just the same I worried that he might be a little too cool where our physical safety was concerned.

"Alejandro, we must get to the embassy before they learn what we're up to."

Alejandro offered Marta one of the Dunhill cigarettes flown in specially for him from London via diplomatic pouch.

"Believe me, Justo, I understand the urgency. But I have not been able to talk to the Ambassador. By curious coincidence he is giving a dinner for your friend Angel at the embassy. I have sent a note asking him for an audience as soon as the dinner party is over."

"And you explained the reason for the meeting?"

"You mean did I mention you by name? No, amigo, I carefully did not. You will remember that I have had a bit of experience with these cases. When I first came here—a graduate student who had risked his life with Angel in that attack on the Presidential Palace—"

"Tacho Flores," I interrupted, remembering the secretary of the Students Resistance League.

"Yes, poor boy," Alejandro continued. "When he came to me for help, like an idiot I spoke to one of the personal secretaries to the Ambassador who told me to keep him here until one o'clock in the morning and then drive him into the embassy compound."

He could never erase that memory. Tacho had been there at midnight like a sitting duck when the security police broke in. Even though Alejandro was on the embassy staff, his residence was not considered extraterritorial. He had had to stand there helplessly and watch young Flores dragged away.

Tacho had been one of the first of the student revolutionaries close to Angel to die for resisting the forced merger of his socialist youth movement with the Young Communists. The thought of that incorruptible young man snatched from Alejandro's own castle and dragged to the wall made my eyelid twitch again.

"Yes," Alejandro went on, "I felt I had betrayed him. God help me, I had. Inadvertently. I should have known better. But I was still young at this *asilo diplomático* business and believe me it is a business. A thriving and lucrative business."

"I think I am ready for another cognac," I said.

"Of course," said Alejandro. "I am not reminding you of poor Flores to alarm you but rather to assure you that now I know what I am doing. As long as you are certain nobody saw you on the way, you will be safe here. I will show you to the guest room. I have already taken the precaution of drawing all the blinds. You and Marta and Clara can make yourselves comfortable there until I return from the embassy." Alejandro was a man of sensitivity to language; a wrong word from his lips would give off the hollow sound of a counterfeit coin. "I mean, of course, as comfortable as possible under these ridiculous circumstances."

He reached into his humidor and scooped out a handful of Corona Especiales. "For later," he said, dropping his voice to a whisper. I reached out my hand for them and I was grateful. It is a bitter thing to record that I was grateful. Because the asylee—the asilado, the protected fugitive, is of necessity a beggar. Something less than a living man, he is a thing in suspension waiting to be born again in a new land. Meanwhile he puts out his hand and takes what is given him. It is surprising how quickly the man of possession adopts the psychology of the supplicant. Already there was no time to be bitter, to think: if fates had reversed our circumstances I might have been handing out largesse to Alejandro Castillo. No, in these few minutes I had made that first adjustment to the status of the have-nothing, grateful for small favors.

In this new, grateful state of mind, I followed the bouncing and practiced conspirator Alejandro to our next hiding place. Up the classical stairway he led us to the colonial guest room that was as large as the master bedroom we had enjoyed at Papagayos. Like everything else in Alejandro's home, it was a room without a single jarring detail—except for the television set which intruded its twentieth-century glass screen on surroundings that had known two hundred years of quiet antiquity. Alejandro ushered us in with a courtly bow.

"Whiskey and brandy, here," he said, indicating a silver tray on a rectangular leather table. "The bathroom, *thataway*"—giving a British inflection to his affected Americanese. Out of old habit, Marta and I smiled at each other. "My house is your house," he said, turning toward the door. "Now try to relax, my loves. All the doors will be locked. As soon as I get back with the *permiso* from Don Ernesto we will make the run for the embassy. *Ciao.*"

The run for the embassy. Alejandro, bless his effete and daring soul, had tried to make it sound casual, like dropping over to our favorite open-air bar for daiquiris at the leisure end of a busy day. From the corridor his high voice added a final instruction, "Bolt the door from inside. When I come back, I will knock. Everything is going to pour like honey water, believe me." Again we heard

"*Ciao*" and then we were left alone to our luxuriously appointed prison.

I reached my hand slowly toward the doorknob but Clarita was already there. She slammed the door and bolted it quickly. Marta walked to the high-canopied four-poster bed where she took off her old tennis shoes, the ones she had used when we went crabbing on the arm of coral rock at the end of our beach. She was limping more than usual, from the dampness and the prolonged tension of her foot against the floorboard. "Justo dear, will you bring me a towel?"

As I knelt down and dried her feet for her I thought how slim and dainty they had been. Now they were broadened and toughened from years of going barefoot on the beach, disfigured with calluses and the red welts from high-heeled shoes that were vanity-tight. I dried them carefully because they were dear to me. When I stood up, Marta reached out her hand and squeezed mine in our tactile code of reassurance.

"Alejandro has a beautiful tub in there," I said. "Why don't you run a hot bath? It will help fill the time until he comes back."

"Splendid idea," Marta said. "This could be the last hot bath until we get to Miami!"

All this time Clarita had been sitting silently on the window seat. Now that we could hear Marta running her bath, she came over to me thoughtfully, and full of questions. She was always more relaxed when the strong figure of her mother was removed.

"How long will we stay in Alejandro's embassy?"

"Two weeks, three weeks. As political refugees we are supposed to get our safe-conduct *permisos* 'without undue delay.' That is the official language, *querida*, 'without undue delay.' "

"Where are we going to live?"

"In the rooms the embassy sets aside for us. Alejandro will explain as soon as he gets back."

"Will I have my own room?"

"I don't know, Clarita. I don't think so. If we are lucky the three of us will have a room together. There are at least a hundred people in there already, Alejandro tells me. So it may be a little crowded."

"I cannot fall asleep if I do not have my own room," Clarita said. She returned to the window seat. "Tell Alejandro I must have my own room."

"Clarita, I know this is difficult for you, and strange. But please, one step at a time."

She turned her head abruptly away from me, the same gesture she used when she was told she couldn't look at television until she had finished her homework.

"I'm sorry you have to go through all this. I know it is hard for you to understand."

"I understand," she said. "If we do not get safely into the embassy, we will all go to the wall—Poof! Poof! Poof!"

"Clarita, my imagination is vivid enough without the sound effects."

She giggled. She had succeeded in making an adult uncomfortable. "Oh well, at least I don't have to study for my algebra test tomorrow morning."

"Ah my silly *chiquita*. Who else would think to welcome asylum to avoid an algebra test!"

"Is it so stupid to act stupid when everything is crazy?"

I stared at her. Fifteen-year-olds are a defeating lot. Behind the bathroom door I could hear the sloshing sound of the hot water in Marta's bath. I went over to the leather table in the middle of the room and poured myself another snifter of Rémy Martin. But I could not really taste the cognac. So the hunted fox must feel when he passes his favorite chicken farm with the hounds too close behind.

"Popee, is it all right if I turn on the television?"

"Of course, of course." I remembered I had planned to watch our soccer match against Wales. National games are always played with the intensity of the struggle for life against death. All games, it occurred to me now, are merely stylized versions of the effort of one side to break through the lines of the other. Only in the Pre-Columbian ball games of Mexico was the playful mask sometimes removed: then the captain of the losing team would forfeit his life as a sacrifice to the offended gods. It was for those kinds of stakes that we were racing across our ball court, with *asilo diplomático* at one end of our field and *el paredón* at the other.

I heard a familiar male voice and turned around to see Clark

Gable speaking Spanish to Joan Crawford. He was a South American rancher and she was the mistress of a rich old man who was hoping to divorce his wife and marry her. It was one of the favorite tearjerkers of late-evening television. Despite the boycott of Yankee culture, Angel did not quite have the courage to banish Clark Gable and Joan Crawford from the little screens in the homes of the people. Russian films were replacing their American rivals but we were intense movie fans and Angel was smart enough to know that to deprive the people of their Joans and Clarks was only a little less serious than depriving them of their staple black beans and yellow rice with *barbacoa* on the holidays.

This particular movie was a local staple because it followed the pattern of romantic tragedy. Joan loves Clark but she feels duty-bound to return to her aging millionaire who is sacrificing his family for her. So she conceals her true feelings behind the mask of a coquette who tells Clark their involvement was merely a passing fancy. Of course Clark comes to New York and meets her accidentally. He treats her with brusque casualness to hide his wound. Meanwhile her heart is breaking as she prepares for marriage to her pale protector. If it had been made in our country, Joan would have committed suicide in some attractive manner in her white wedding gown, the old lover would have gone back to his wife, and a sadder and wiser Clark Gable would have gone back to his ranch and his horse. But the gringos like to sweeten their tears with happy endings and so the understanding protector sees through her sacrificial gesture and sends her back to Clark and South America with his blessings. If only life could be like those movies, with a good cry in the middle and a triumphant laugh at the end.

Clarita had seen the film before but she was watching it intensely. I turned away and sipped my brandy and tried to picture Alejandro with his distinguished ambassador Don Ernesto de San Martín. People often have a way of looking their parts, or growing into them, and everything about the Ambassador was theatrical perfection: his blood-ties to the illustrious General San Martín who fought great battles for independence from Spain, his semi-bald head with its circle of pomaded black hair, his carefully trimmed Vandyke beard, his air of a great man of the world, a graceful figure of authority who had lent his distinguished name to the chairmanship of the Pan-American Commission on Human Rights. Such was the stature of the Honorable Ambassador Don Ernesto de San Martín. I could see him discreetly called away from his diplomatic dinner for Angel Bello, wrinkling his aristocratic forehead as he listened to Alejandro's grave presentation of the urgency of the case of Justo Moreno Suárez.

Joan was finishing the tearful scene with her selfless benefactor when suddenly the screen went blank. Then it was filled with large block letters and two exclamation points: ¡AVISO ESPECIAL! Behind the words was the new state emblem, Angel's adaptation of the Soviet hammer and sickle—a hammer crossed with a machete. The mood of patriotic expectancy mounted with the rousing national anthem, "Angelitos Verdes." Now the confident, glowering face of Angelo Bello filled the screen, his deepset eyes more persecuted and accusing than ever.

"Loyal comrades of the Revolution—"

Marta appeared at the entrance from the bathroom, dripping wet, a toweled bathsheet draped around her.

"Your government is proud to announce that a cowardly and treacherous plot to overthrow your Revolution has been thwarted successfully. Implicated with the British imperialist agent *Mister* Claude Lewison are two members of the bourgeoisie who posed as revolutionary officials in order to stab the people in the back and help restore the corrupt reign of Victoriano Zamora. *I accuse* Justo Moreno Suárez, the former Provisional President, and Dr. Luis Levy, the former Secretary of the Interior whom some of you know as Garbo. If the defection of these two traitors leads our enemies to believe our government machinery has been disrupted, they delude themselves! We have been aware of their double-dealing for months and have held them under close surveillance. But it was not until we had all the evidence in our hands that our security cadre were ordered to move against them tonight. You will be relieved to know that two members of this unholy three are already in our hands. The third may think that he can evade our revolutionary justice. But we are ten million strong, united against the imperialists and the foreign interventionists who grow more desperate and more reckless each day that the First Socialist Revolution in the New World grows stronger and more successful! We brand the fugitive Justo Moreno Suárez nothing less than a common criminal who deserted his post in the face of the enemy and is guilty of the capital crime of conspiring with the enemy agents of the counterrevolution! If the fugitive Justo Moreno Suárez denies the charges brought against him, let him come forward like a man. Let him face the honest judgment of his fellow-citizens by coming here to defend himself publicly as would any brave man who has nothing to hide. Or let him forever brand himself the renegade tool of foreign intrigue and *yanqui* counter-revolution."

Angel's accusing index finger seemed to be pointing from the screen into Alejandro's guest room, as if he knew exactly where I was standing. "Justo Moreno Suárez, be forewarned that no hiding place will protect you from the righteous wrath of revolutionary justice. *Viva la Revolución!*"

A hoarse chorus of invisible Angelitos Verdes roared their predictable finale, *"VIVA* ANGEL! *VIVA* ANGEL! *VIVA* ANGEL ... !"

Over Angel's righteous face, now silent, reappeared the glorified hammer-and-machete seal of the Revolution. And once again the stirring march tempo of "Angelitos Verdes" filled the room, this time with the romantically revolutionary lyrics of our gifted poet Gregorio Solano. He had written the words to this new anthem in the first fever of joyous freedom, exulting in the overthrow of tyrants and the green wave of campesinos rolling down from the hills behind their incorruptible young leader. I had not seen my friend Goyo Solano for months. There were rumors that he had been carried off in the drive against intellectuals who had an emotional attachment to Angel but were becoming disenchanted with the tightening discipline. As I listened to his lyrical tribute to the new leader I wondered if I would ever see him again.

"My darling, what a fool I was ever to doubt you," the Spanish voice of Clark Gable resolved his idyll with Joan Crawford.

Marta strode to the television set and switched it off with a curse. "Excuse me, Clarita," she said. "But what a lying *pendejo!* Excuse me double, Clarita. He should be hung by the—"

"Marta!" I said, looking at Clarita. She was sitting hunched up in the window seat, hugging her knees. A frightened little girl ready to cry.

I went over and put my arm around her. "It is all talk. Just a lot of big talk."

Clarita nuzzled my arm for a moment and then seemed to remind herself that she was grown up. "I'm all right," she said and walked away.

"I'm sorry," Marta said. "But if he must have his Revolution why can't it be a truthful Revolution? Why does he have to make up a whole *cursi* plot about you and the Englishman and poor Garbo? Now the Holy Trinity is Marx and Angel and Juan del Campo. What a *quiniela!*"

"I wonder if they really caught Garbo?" I was thinking of those bright, watchful eyes behind their rimless glasses at our final press conference. "With his old underground connections, I would have expected him to slip back into hiding."

"Maybe he has," Marta said. "Your Angel is such a liar. Who can believe anything he says—in public or in private?"

"Popee—why did Angel keep calling you a common criminal?"

"It is very complicated, Clarita."

"I am not a child, Popee."

"Tell her, tell her," Marta said. "If she is going to be a political *asilada* she may as well have the answers." Marta limped formidably toward the bathroom. "I had better get dressed. Alejandro should be back any minute."

Clarita came and sat beside me on the edge of the great four-poster bed.

"Now what is it that is so complicated?" she said insistently.

"I will try to explain, Clarita. An embassy does not have to grant asylum to common criminals or deserters, as that would interfere with a country's right to run her own affairs without foreign interference. But an embassy does have the right to grant political asylum if the refugee is in danger because he does not agree with the people who are running his country."

"Then Angel is calling you a criminal and a deserter to scare the embassy into not letting us in!"

"True. It is just a chess game, Clarita, that Angel is playing with Alejandro's ambassador. But the Ambassador—I cannot imagine his turning down our application."

"So what you're saying is there really is no law that says they *have* to take us in."

"Of course there's a law. Havana—1928. Montevideo—1933. Caracas—1954. You learn those things in school." I heard my voice rising. "Of course there's a law!"

"But if it's up to what Angel says and what the Ambassador thinks—then it is up to the *men*," her voice rose with mine, "not the law!"

"Clarita, all laws are 'up to' men," I said. "Because men have to interpret laws."

"Then they aren't really laws," Clarita shouted.

"Clarita, if I tell you it's a law, it's a law!"

I had not meant to shout back at her but my nerves were too taut for me to argue reasonably the case for reason. Clarita flung herself on her belly on the big bed.

I put my hand on her shoulder, clumsily. "Clarita, don't cry. Everything will be all right."

She shook off my hand and sobbed louder.

"Clarita, darling, I know how you feel—"

"Beto was supposed to take me to the dance Friday evening. It took me three months to get him to invite me." She pushed her face into Alejandro's bedspread.

The door of the bathroom was thrown open and Marta came lumbering out. She had put her coarse surf-fishing clothes back on and the effect was startling. After a leisurely bath in this elegant suite one might have expected to see her in a long chiffon robe.

"Jesus, Mary and Joseph, what is going on out here!"

"I'm sorry," I said. "It was my fault."

Clara had pulled a pillow up to her face to mop the tears. As Marta went to her she scolded me without looking at me.

"Justo, idiot. She was trying hard."

Beyond the closed shutters I could hear the insistent rain. In the night storm I could imagine my pursuers in their ponderous raincoats trying to pick up the trail of their erstwhile President, now transformed by Angel's rhetoric into common criminal and deserter.

"All right, Clarita, enough! Stop crying!" Marta commanded.

I turned around to observe the small domestic miracle. Like a film actress whose histrionics are terminated by the director's curt command of "Cut," our daughter raised her head and stopped abruptly. Both of them stared at me, four eyes reflecting a single expression; it was like staring into a connected pattern of mirrors all throwing back at me from different angles the same image of inadequacy. Martyrs who die for a cause never seem to have wives or children, cousins or aunts. They stand and speak their piece and die and that is how they are remembered. I neither wished to be remembered that way nor could I follow Angel Bello's retreat from the human revolution he had promised us. Only the chronic inbetweeners, unable to dedicate themselves to a single absolute, ever know this feeling of guilt.

Marta was closer to the door when the knock came and as she pulled back the bar and unlocked it, Alejandro entered energetically.

"Good news," he said. "I have just seen the Ambassador. It was rather a delicate operation. Apparently Angel left the banquet in a terrible temper when he heard you had fled. I must say, not a moment too soon. Excellent timing!"

"It would be even better timing if we were already safe in the embassy," Marta said.

"Look—children—basically I bring you good news. The Ambassador says he will be delighted to receive you as his guests at the embassy."

"Thank God for men like Don Ernesto," said Marta, suddenly pious.

"It's not exactly a personal favor," I said, for Clarita. "It's his duty under the law. Just the same I am grateful to him."

"You will never find my Ambassador falling short of his diplomatic responsibilities," Alejandro said, with a curious smile. Then he added, with a tick of chagrin, "Before we can leave for the embassy, there is a detail that must be taken care of. The Ambassador will require ten thousand dollars."

Marta started to say something but put her hand to her mouth.

"My God, Alejandro," I said, "every embassy has an allotment of funds to take care of the refugees. And especially in our case, where we have held a position of impor—"

"Unfortunately, dear Justo, that is just the point. The public attack Angel has just made on you makes this a ticklish case for the Ambassador to handle. I am sure he will certify you as a political refugee, but to do so he has to prepare a careful legal answer in the face of Angel's protest. Our legal staff will be involved. There will be all sorts of emergency expenses."

"But ten thousand *dollars!*"

Alejandro looked pained but he had his orders.

"I will write you a check."

"Not on your National Bank, I hope."

I looked up, startled.

"My dear Justo, this entire subject distresses me, but you must realize that as of this moment you no longer have funds in the National Bank. The Ambassador would prefer cash—American dollars."

"But when I came back to join Angel I brought all my dollars with me and deposited them in pesos, to help build up the National Bank the Zamoristas had raided."

"He even gave his gold rings and watches to help the Revolution," Marta said.

"But most of us who came back did that. Alejandro, are you really telling me that Don Ernesto de San Martín, one of our leading spokesmen for human rights in Latin America, is—"

"Is a crook," Marta spoke up. "Yes, that is exactly what Alejandro is trying to tell you. Only of course he must live with the Ambassador. So let us all save time and grab the mop by the handle. Alejandro, I have five thousand good gringo dollars with me. Women seem to have more sense about these things. I will also write a check for five thousand more on my bank in Miami. Will that satisfy His Excellency?"

Alejandro rubbed the long curving nose that made him look like a Goya sketch of Spanish aristocracy. "I realize things like this should not be asked of you in these precarious moments," he said. "If I were the Ambassador—" he caught himself. "No, I will say no more."

"I understand," I said. "The Ambassador is performing a considerable humanitarian service by opening his doors to us when his resources are already strained."

"I am grateful to you, Justo, for being so understanding," Alejandro said.

"*Chinga* understanding," Marta said.

I was mortified. In front of Clarita. In front of Alejandro.

"Justo, I am sick of all this politeness. Being polite only takes more time. Let's get to the meat of it. How soon must the great humanitarian have his money?"

Alejandro looked pained again. Marta had hit the shark right on the nose, as we say. "As a matter of fact—"

Marta interrupted. "If I read that mournful map of yours correctly, Alejandro, your great humanitarian is waiting for his blood money this very moment."

"Marta," I said.

"I am sorry," Marta said. "In our circle it is not polite to call things by their right names. You want the money now, pronto, immediately."

Alejandro pressed his thin, sensitive lips together. Incomprehensibly I felt sorry for him. Marta was bullying him. I knew how it felt to be bullied by Marta. Even when she was right. Especially when she was right.

"Yes, love," Alejandro said. "It is all very distressing but if you could give me the cash and the check, I will rush it over to His Excellency."

Marta half-turned and fished her hand into the neck of her open corduroy shirt hanging loosely over her weathered beach slacks. She handed him a fistful of bills neatly rolled.

Alejandro fitted it nicely into his gold-tipped, soft black leather wallet and looked at us apologetically.

"And now the check," Marta said, digging into her big straw basket for her checkbook. She sat down at the long leather table.

"My pen," Alejandro said and gracefully produced from his pocket a slim gold one. He handed it to Marta with a bow. She took it without looking at him.

"How shall I make it out? To the embassy? To the Ambassador by name?"

"To cash," Alejandro said in a small, dead voice.

"Of course," said Marta and she wrote out the check.

"So you see, Popee, it's not really a law," Clarita spoke up from the corner. "If we have to pay to get in. A law is when—"

"Please, Clarita, this is not the time to go into all that again."

"These are complicated things even for grown-ups, little Clarita," Alejandro tried.

Clarita stared into her lap. Marta handed him the check. "I suppose he'll wait to call Miami in the morning and see if it will clear."

"We will get this settled tonight," Alejandro said. "So—very good, my doves, I will be back in thirty minutes. Everything will go well."

At the door I could not resist a final question. "Alejandro, it is hard to believe—did Don Ernesto actually refuse us admission until he had the money in hand?"

"Justo, try to understand. There have been cases when people promised, but once they were safely in the embassy— So, considering the extra expenses involved, the Ambassador has had to set a policy of—"

"Go," Marta said. "Go, Alejandro. Get this *mierda* over with."

"Lock the door from the inside," Alejandro reminded us. "And please do me the favor of not to worry. Tonight you will sleep safely in the embassy, I promise you."

"*Vete, Vete,* go—go!" Marta ordered. "We Latins and our flowery speeches. *Vete, Vete!*"

If anything significant was said in that hour of waiting, time has erased it. There was the sad, slurpy sound of incessant rain, the face of Marta, strong and indignant, and Clarita, incredibly but mercifully asleep on the wide bed, one hand tucked daintily under her flushed cheek. Marta's chain-smoking kindled my guilt for having dragged them into this predicament and for not being better prepared when it came. I felt guilty for having to depend on Marta's North American cash, for opposing the Revolution—and for not opposing it more effectively, for lacking the complacency that accepts political disenchantment with a shrug. I loved my wife and my daughter and my country and my democratic hopes and I was unable to serve them all.

In the silence of the long wait for Alejandro, I wondered how many countrymen could swallow Angel's charges. Lewison, Garbo and I would have been a far more likely triumvirate against Zamora. But I am being reasonable. That is one of my hobbies and one of my follies. Nothing could be more absurdly unreasonable than our waiting to pay for the rights to asylum that were granted us in half a dozen official Pan-American documents. Someday I would have to admit to Clarita that even though she had never written a treatise on the famous case of Haya de la Torre, her snap judgment was more profound than my authoritative study: political asylum was a law only on paper but not in fact if it had to be administered by mortals vulnerable and corruptible.

Finally there came a systematic knocking at our door and as I threw back the bar, Alejandro was in the room, the shoulders of his trench coat wet from the rain. "All right, loves, everything is ready. I will explain what we do, so listen carefully."

Clarita sat up and leaned against Marta. All three of us watched Alejandro's face like a team receiving locker-room instructions from our coach who was high-strung yet cool and knowledgeable.

"Marta, you and Justo are going to ride in the back trunk of the car. It will be a tight fit, but—"

"What about air?" Marta said. "We'll smother to death."

"Remember I have done this once or twice before. I have oxygen tanks for you. Have you ever used them at the beach?"

"Justo has," said Marta.

"Believe me, it is easier than swimming underwater. I will show you on the way out."

"And what about me? Where will I be?" Clarita asked.

"You will be sitting on the seat right alongside me, little one," Alejandro said. "Marta, give her some of your lipstick. If the militia stop us, I will tell them she is my date for a late party on the embassy grounds. Clarita, you will have a bottle of champagne in an ice bucket on the floor at your feet." His grin was reassuring. "I have been living my research."

"But look at me," Clarita said. "Who would ever believe I am your date wearing this old thing?"

"Wait, my beauty," Alejandro said. "I return in twelve seconds."

With her lipstick Marta transformed Clarita's pout into a deep red flower of seduction. Then she brushed her thick, auburn hair into an upsweep and topped it with a comb from her basket. Alejandro returned with a floor-length gold lamé evening gown.

"Here, princess," he said to Clarita, "take this into the dressing room. I think it will fit. Lamé is extremely"—he glanced at Clarita's chubby figure discreetly—"accommodating."

Delighted with all this attention, she took the gown from Alejandro and hurried off with it.

"I recognize that gown," Marta said. "It followed you home from a party while the husband was out of town on diplomatic business."

"Please," Alejandro said, "discretion, discretion. This gown insists on remaining anonymous."

When Clarita returned in the gold lamé with its daring neckline, it may not have shaped her into the golden goddess that Alejandro had lured home from his fancy diplomatic party. But as he had predicted, the metallic fabric was both stretching and clinging and our chubby fifteen-year-old appeared for the first time as a provocative young woman.

"Bravo!" said Alejandro, "Bravissimo! The lovely Señorita Clara will be the most dazzling princess at the ball." He opened a closet door and in a moment reappeared with a mink coat, not the conventional brown but a rare amber.

"Alejandro, you devil! I also recognize the coat!"

"No time to gossip. Time to move on."

With the grace of the born *galán,* he draped the magic mink on Clarita's shoulders. She drew it around her and seemed to grow up inside of it. This was her true coming-out party.

"Mon Dieu, quelle grande dame," Alejandro said with an elegant flourish of his hand. He bowed and offered her his arm. Marta and

I followed them down the elegant stairway and through the grand colonial hall to the large, high-ceilinged kitchen, where he produced the oxygen tanks and gave us instructions on how to use them. Then he fetched the champagne, prepared the silver ice bucket, and poured us each a glass of brandy.

"One for the road," he said. "May it be a short and happy one."

"May we all celebrate New Year's together," Marta said. "Where? —New York?—Paris?"

"Right here. With freedom," I said.

"Justo the dreamer," said Marta.

"I want a glass too," said *la duchesse*.

"Clarita—!" I was about to protest.

"Let her have it," Alejandro said. "If the militiamen should stop us it will be even more convincing if they get a whiff of spirits from her breath."

"All right," I said. "This is a special occasion."

"Popee—" the child voice of Clarita came startlingly from the damp red mouth and the amber mink. "You know those times I used to play with Sonia Alonso when her mother was out? We often locked ourselves in Sonia's room and drank and smoked."

I stared at her. While Tina was cuckolding her husband with Alejandro, her precocious Sonia was giving lessons to an innocent Clarita. On this sour note I was abandoning our comfortable bourgeois existence, in these final moments more aware of its sham and deceptions than of its virtues.

Through the softening rain we ran across the rear patio and through the garden to Alejandro's Mercedes. He told Clarita to jump into the front seat while he opened the rear trunk. I wondered how the two of us would fit into it. Marta was a big woman and I was both large-boned and overweight. We helped Marta in. In the spy films people always seem to be jackknifing nimbly into secret hiding places like this, but for us it was a clumsy maneuver, especially since Marta had trouble bending her arthritic knee. She lay on her left side, facing in toward the wall and Alejandro handed her the small oxygen tank. She took the mouthpiece between her teeth as he had demonstrated in the kitchen, and at that moment it struck me that Marta and I would not be able to talk to each other, that we would

be squeezed together in the dark metal container like twin embryos
held in the hard belly of the Mercedes. Alejandro had had the fore-
sight to remove the spare tire, otherwise I would surely not have
fitted in. He handed me a flashlight and a pistol, a .22 Bereta which
I took reluctantly because I always have had an antipathy to guns.
Then he helped me in, squeezed my shoulder and said, *"Merde,"*
with attempted gaiety, his way of saying "good luck." *"Listo?*—all
set?" I nodded and as I tucked my right shoulder in, he slammed the
top down.

I breathed deeply, slowly, in and out as instructed, but at the
same time I turned on the flashlight and in panic I made an odd discovery—that I was incapable of doing the two things at one time.
Somehow my fingering of the flashlight switch upset the coordination
of my breathing. I opened my mouth and the mouthpiece slipped
out. I switched off the flashlight and grabbed for the tube leading
from the small tank to the rubber mouthpiece. Of course there was
still air in the trunk compartment but my throat tightened with the
thought of *I am going to die* before I get that cursed tank working
again. *I am going to die* . . . I could hear Marta breathing rhythmi-
cally and I was glad but envious too. There was something undeniable and enduring about Marta that I could feel in the even breathing
of her body as I pressed against her. The manner in which she was
folded into me, pushing her spread of buttocks against my thighs,
was strangely similar to our lovemaking that last time in the
enormous bed at Papagayos. Our present position in the black confinement of the trunk compartment seemed an obscene caricature.

The Mercedes was moving now. We were adult fetuses breathing
through our umbilical cords to the life-giving oxygen tanks. In this
second fetal state, fear was my overriding instinct. As the wheels of
the Mercedes churned beneath us, the most obsessive fears moved
through my mind like a series of horror slides. If our car should be
stopped by Angel's omnipresent militia and Alejandro taken off for
questioning, we would lie there and gasp and expire like two fish
trapped in a waterless tank. Or if the most direct route to the embassy were blocked and Alejandro had to take an evasive course, our
precious half-hour's oxygen supply would exhaust itself. In frustration we would jerk the rubber gadget from our mouths and choke

and try to swallow the airlessness. We would press our mouths against the sealed crack of the locked luggage compartment door and die in agony like Jews in a sealed Nazi boxcar.

All this time over the muffled sound of the motor and the tires I could hear the regular inhale-exhale of Marta's breathing. That Marta, that rock, it would take more than the locked compartment of the rear end of an old Mercedes to do her in.

Then we were no longer moving. My hand was on Marta's shoulder. She reached up and squeezed it. In the darkness it was an act of reassurance and I loved her. If Angel's guards forced Alejandro to lift the lid or fire their automatic weapons through the metal skin, I would die with my hand in Marta's as if wedded again for the long sleep. I heard voices. Our measured breathing seemed too loud and I tried to use the breathing contraption more gently. I breathed in so cautiously that the canned air did not pass through the rubber tube into my lungs and I coughed. I choked. The ill-tasting, uncomfortable mouthpiece slipped from my teeth again and out through my dry lips and I was like a diver in panic: I would never be able to surface in time to reach the sweet fresh air. I was dying again and we were moving again. Moving where? By this time a security police guard could be at the wheel driving us to Angel's secret headquarters. Maybe it was better to choke out one's life than bleed it slowly away under police torture. Choke out my life, oh Christ, I wanted more, *more,* I wasn't ready, I wanted to prove—what? Something, to be better, yes, a chance to be better. Choking, I twisted, I groped —where was the *chingado* life-giver of a mouthpiece . . . ?

I heard the sound of a key in the latch of the compartment door that concealed us, the sound of the handle turning, the lid being lifted and my first thought was of air, precious air rushing in to save us. But who would be waiting when I looked up?

"Hop out, loves, we're here!"; the cultivated voice of our decadent archangel.

I gave Marta's shoulder a triumphant slap and then hands were helping me out. I was standing on my feet, swaying like a drunk while Alejandro and Clarita leaned in for Marta. My bearings came to me slowly. The Mercedes stood in the portmanteau by the side of the three-story embassy. We were safely inside the block-wide compound of the embassy grounds. I looked in the direction from which we had just entered. The dark of the night was penetrated by the rays of powerful street lights. Under the guise of diplomatic courtesy, Angel had installed modern neon overhead lights along this street so that the main entrance could be kept under twenty-four-hour surveillance. And behind the high iron grillework of the gate I could see through the rain the helmets and greatcoats of Angel's militiamen. There had been incidents when they had fired directly into the compound but almost always they used the excuse that they were aiming at criminals trying to escape justice by fleeing over the wall into embassy haven. Bullets actually spraying the extraterritorial grounds were explained as "accidental."

Alejandro must have had this in mind, for he said, "Pronto—follow me—side entrance—" He took Marta on one arm, Clarita on the other, and hurried forward. Marta in her old fishing clothes was lumbering, but rapidly, and Clarita in her amber mink was having trouble in her high heels. I was out of breath when I caught up to the reedlike Alejandro and his oddly assorted ladies. A key turned and the side door opened. A sleepy night security guard muttered, "Buenas noches." I was surprised at his attitude of boredom. A president and his family run a gantlet to achieve asylum and a security guard greets them as a sleepy portero would admit a familiar tenant to his comfortable apartment house. I hugged Marta and turned to kiss her but in our excitement our noses were in the way. We laughed and I turned to kiss the little-girl grown-up face of Clarita and for a moment we all held Alejandro in a close *abrazo*.

Then he pulled away and said, "Now to business!" He turned to the guard. "Manuel, who is on duty tonight? Call him so our guests can be registered properly."

As the guard left on his mission, Alejandro removed the astrakhan hat he had chosen for this adventure. Unexpectedly, he fanned himself with it like a comedian and grinned outlandishly. He was really an impossible man. Where would we have been without this impossible man?

A worn, disapproving embassy official appeared. He was a man in his middle thirties, of poor complexion and stale expression. He and Alejandro fell into a routine, meaningless *abrazo*. Then Alejandro introduced him formally, *"Licenciado* Huberto Alvarez, Assistant Secretary for Extraterritorial Personnel." The assistant secretary performed a disinterested bow and mumbled a routine "At your service" while Alejandro was introducing me with my full title, then "the Señora of Presidente Moreno Suárez, and their daughter Clara." Marta nodded as if to say *andale pues,* let us get on with it, Clarita curtsied from force of habit and Licenciado Alvarez mumbled, "Con mucho gusto," but with such lack of gusto as to underline the final absurdity of these ceremonial trappings.

"Señor Presidente," Licenciado Alvarez said in a voice that did not care, "I regret that our facilities for diplomatic refugees are now so overcrowded that we are unable to furnish you a private room as would befit your station. For the time being we will have to assign you to the male dormitory. As soon as you register in this book, I will escort you there. My assistant, Señora Lorona, will be here in a moment to escort your ladies to the women's dormitory. If there is anything you need that is in my power to supply, please do not hesitate to ask."

Everything Licenciado Alvarez said seemed to be contradicted by the manner of the man. I could see that he disliked me—no, rather that he regarded me and my family as an additional responsibility for an already overburdened official.

I turned to Alejandro and he opened his arms wide and we hugged each other in an *abrazo* of *compañeros,* as intensely as if this was a last time. He said not to worry, he would have special visiting privileges. He would bring a change of clothes for us and newspapers from the outside world and, he muttered, "I'll try to smuggle in a bottle of rum."

Then I took Marta in my arms. "I will see you in the morning."

"If the regulations permit it," Marta said.

"Ladies and gentlemen may come together for the midday meal in the courtyard," Licenciado Alvarez said with all the feeling of a railroad conductor.

"Don't worry, loves." Alejandro's voice was pitched even higher than usual. "I have the ear of the Ambassador. I can sweeten the life a little bit until your 'safe conduct' comes through."

"Ojalá," Marta said, in the sarcastic tone of "When we see it!"

"But thank you for everything, Alejandro. You are an *hombre* in a world of *pendejos.*"

It was a shrewd compliment and Alejandro seemed, almost physically, to stand a little taller with masculinity. Then I went to Clarita. "Popee!" she said and I felt limp with futility.

"Tomorrow, tomorrow, my little darling, I will see you tomorrow."

As I followed my indifferent host, guide, jailer, whatever Licenciado Alvarez was to me, Señora Lorona came waddling past us, an enormous woman, with the baby-face of a tart, framed in powdered folds of fat. "Oh you poor dears, you poor dears!" I could hear her saying to Marta and Clarita. It was faintly encouraging.

I followed Alvarez up a wide, red-carpeted marble stairway and then up a second stairway that was only half as wide, a narrow and rather nondescript ascension leading to a third floor so plain as not to seem to belong to the elegant floor plan below. From there we ascended a shorter stairway to the attic finished with regard for haste rather than taste. It was as if all of the money and all of the care had been lavished on the first two floors and the top floor was an afterthought. Licenciado Alvarez led me to a door at the end of a long dark hallway. He took a key from his pocket, opened the door and stood aside to let me pass through. It was dark inside and there was a smell that was both sweet and foul. I heard heavy breathing and sighs and troubled contrapuntal snoring. It was like peering into a tomb of mass burial where the corpses breathed. I hesitated. Then I stepped inside.

As my eyes grew accustomed to the darkness I began to see rows of cots, narrow ones set only a few feet away from each other in a long rectangular attic room. Bodies were curled and twisted and stretched in every conceivable position. Of the fifty or more, no two seemed to have chosen a similar posture for sleep. Even in this mass bedroom, amidst group unconsciousness, the underdog clung to his precious wisp of individuality.

I kept walking slowly down the dark aisle until I came to the empty cot. I sat down wearily and the springs protested but no one stirred. A great lump of a man was burrowed into the adjoining cot with the blanket pulled completely over his head. He stirred slightly and I heard the muffled sound of farting. The foul-sweet aroma drifted into my nostrils and now I recognized the odor I had sensed at the threshold. It was the funky compound of mass body excretions and communal wind-letting in a room lacking adequate ventilation.

On the cot to the left of me was a man sleeping on his back with the mouth in his gaunt face slightly open. It looked disturbingly like a death-head, but from the head rose the sound of gentle snoring punctuated by a muted whistle.

I removed my damp fishing pants and windbreaker and stretched out on my back. My legs were aching with fatigue but I could feel the nerves jumping. Calm yourself, Justo. In this tomb of bodies buried alive you must find ways to preserve sanity. Your job is to survive.

PART TWO

PART TWO

1

I have no idea how many hours I listened to the restless shifting of my multiple roommates squirming on their narrow cots. In fascination and in horror I heard the inadvertent sounds of slumber, the snoring, the moaning and the muttering. Occasionally a muffled voice would cry out, "No! No!" against some outrage in the private theater of his mind. After years of privacy, would I be able to endure among fifty bodies in a room that might adequately accommodate twenty-five?

Despite taut nerves I must have surrendered to exhaustion some-time before dawn because I remember the shock of that first awak-ening. My immediate impression was of shabby disorder, a scabrous room full of rumpled, spiritless bodies, scaly walls with abstract patterns of dirt, men who grunted and scratched their backsides and sat on their skimpy, soiled beds, or groped in meaningless wakeful-ness down the crowded aisle between the insidious rows of cots. They had been sleeping in their baggy trousers and undershirts, in their soiled underwear, in limp and ragged pajamas. A few were nude. A large group of men crowded together in undress is a sorry sight under the best of circumstances but the circumstances I awakened to that first morning of sanctuary were depressing beyond my most pessimistic expectations.

There were neither bureaus nor lockers for extra clothes or per-sonal effects, which added to the look of disorder and confusion. Here and there a shirt, a pair of trousers, some socks were hung on nails driven into the dirty stucco walls. A few of the more fortunate or farsighted had suitcases in the narrow space between cots to serve as bedstands for a book, an ashtray or cigarettes. Some had nailed empty cigar boxes on the wall to hold pencils, matches, small notebooks, toilet articles and medicine. Tacked above the beds were family snapshots of wives, children, sweethearts, a nondescript gallery of loneliness. Many had fixed crucifixes over their cots, and colored pictures of the Dark Virgin or of the Holy Family. Above one cot was a hammer and sickle and above another the hammer-machete emblem of the Bello Revolution but with this inscription crayon-scrawled above it: *Angelismo sin Angel!*—the kind of popular revolution I could still relate to, in principle, but now with the nagging doubt—can there be *Angelismo without Angel?* Or without a socialist *caudillo* by any other name who wields the power and jettisons promises once he grips the wheel of state? Doubts. Doubts. I despised them because they render a man paralyzed, no longer able to act and therefore an involuntary supporter of status quo. How to be profoundly, cynically honest with one's self and yet not sacrifice the gift of action—somehow I had to find the key to that conundrum if I were not to deteriorate into a meaningless cipher in sanctuary, at the mercy of both His Excellency the Ambassador and Angel Bello.

Near one cigar-box drawer was scribbled the inevitable "Yanqui Go Home," to which some wit had added a postscript, "And take me with you!" Between two cots an old-style chauvinist had written, "For Zamora, For God and For Country," which a critic had amended by drawing a line through the "For" and inserting the expressive imperative *"Chinga"* above it, and adding for good measure, *"Y chinga tu madre!"* This had been partly erased and scratched out, then rewritten once more, a graphic display of the ideological battles rampant among asylees whose opposition to Angel obviously was not sufficient to unite them.

The dissension on the walls, the nervous sense of vibration and countervibration were intensified by the verbal counterpoint of rival transistor radios—one blaring a jazzy cha-cha-cha, another bringing the official news from the capital, a third magically reproducing the Voice of America so that one could hear at the same moment that Angel's Revolution was an economic triumph and also that it was on the brink of disaster. Both sides argued with ample statistics while the sophisticated jungle music of Perez Prado provided the ideal musical background for propaganda warfare, "Cherry Red and Apple-Blossom White." There seemed to be a noisy truce, a policy of laissez-faire regarding the contending radio volumes as if each owner had become immune to the sound of the others.

Suddenly all the contending sounds were hammered into submission by a furious pounding on the door at the end of the aisle opposite the main entrance. I turned to see that it bore the letter C for *caballeros* and that the fellow pounding with hoarse oaths of eloquent profanity was a heavyset man with a ruddy complexion, soiled long underwear stretched below his waist by a paunch of impressive proportions. His nose was red and bulbous and decorated with broken blood vessels suggesting a life dedicated to serious drinking.

"*Cochino!* Come out, pig! Your time was up ten minutes ago! My bladder is exploding! I will piss in your face through the keyhole if you don't open the door!"

An imposing pillar of a man with a flattened nose and the Oriental, sunken eyes of an old prizefighter pushed his way toward the red-faced protester. As I turned to watch the confrontation I realized who he was. Búfalo de Sa had been our national heavyweight champion, a title that was always something of a joke because there were never more than two or three legitimate heavyweights in our country. Actually he had been a strong, free-swinging contender with a right hand that could shake up the best if only he managed to land it. During my exile in New York I had seen him in Madison Square Garden winning his first fight spectacularly and then being knocked out ignominiously in a rematch. There were rumors that he had bet his purse on the two-to-one underdog. There was the usual two-day boxing scandal and Búfalo came home in disgrace. Then he drifted into the business of making love to and blackmailing susceptible ladies of capital society.

Eventually this led him to prison where El Gordo Romano—in search of new talent—had him paroled as his special bodyguard-chauffeur. Búfalo had been at his side through the years of decadence and had gone into hiding after Zamora escaped to Miami as the Little Green Angels reached the suburbs of the city. I had known that El Gordo had been granted sanctuary in the embassy. As President, I had demanded his return to face justice for the common crimes of murder, armed robbery and extortion. So the Ambassador and I had been inadvertent partners: the harder I pressed for extradition, the higher must have been his price for sanctuary.

Since the cruelties and obscenities of Romano had drawn Angel and me together in common hatred of the man and his Tigers, it was more than psychological shock to find myself in a room with one of the most formidable of those enforcers. The shock of his presence caused a physical reaction. I could feel it on my skin. There was a release of adrenaline, a flow of juices spreading terror through my nervous system when I realized I was locked in with Búfalo de Sa. For now I knew whom he was guarding behind the bathroom door.

The man with the red, porcine face and the blue-vein nose was about to pound on the door again and deliver another obscenity when Búfalo shouted, *"Tu puta madre!"* and backhanded him viciously. His red face seemed to grow a shade redder and he put his hand to his mouth to feel the liquid that was blood. He stepped back and the fight was over. It was a curious fight because almost always a one-punch or one-slap encounter is an act of humiliation for the loser but this time the victim raised his head proudly and his puffy red lips split in an infectious grin.

My first impression was of a strong, lovable slob. There was such a variety of political opinions in the dormitory that I hoped his and mine would not be too far apart. While Búfalo assumed the position of sentry in front of the bathroom door with his legs spread menacingly and his thigh-like arms folded across his forty-six-inch chest, I introduced myself to his pudgy antagonist. Someone had handed him a dirty handkerchief with which he was, unconcernedly, mopping his mouth.

He spoke a guttural, earthy Spanish that would have had a Mexican lilt to it if there had been any song in his voice: "Moreno Suárez! *Sí, como no!* I recognize you!" He laughed through his swollen lips. The sound he made was unexpectedly cheerful in this drab dormitory-jail. "So the New Freedom finally caught up with you, eh?"

He nodded toward the babel of radios adding to the morning confusion. "We heard Angel on the radio last night. Calling you all the names."

In a good-humored, clownish gesture, he clapped his hands to his ears. "Most of the time I try not to listen. I plug up my ears. Angel's propaganda. The Voice of America propaganda. I hate all propaganda. I hate all politics. You know how I keep myself sane in here? Aside from drinking? I lie on my cot and I think about the best jai alai shot I ever made. I think about the most artistic señorita I ever took to bed. I think about the best paella Valenciana my wife ever made for me, full of tender chicken breasts and sweet little *camarones*. I think about the time when I was most gloriously *borracho.*" His soft, porpoise-body shook as he laughed. "I say fuck the mothers of all the dictadores. And fuck the mothers of all the políticos. A man has to live! All my life all I ever wanted to do was live!"

The way he shouted *vivir* sent a shiver through me. In front of the door, Búfalo scowled at him. I looked from one to the other uneasily. "Maybe you should put something on your lip, amigo?"

My new friend tapped his lip with his fingers disdainfully. *"No importa.* Every morning that *hijo* El Gordo-the-pig monopolizes the bathroom. Every morning his personal *pistolero* guards the door for him. Every morning I pound on the door and shout *cochino* and get a fist in the mouth for my troubles." He shrugged impressively. *"No importa.* If only I prevent El Gordo from enjoying a quiet shit it is worth a punch in the mouth. It is the small price I pay for my sweet little cup of freedom to speak."

He brushed his protruding bruised lip with the sleeve of his dirty long underwear. "By the way, allow me to introduce myself, here is Paco O'Higgins." (O-ee-geens is the way he pronounced it.)

O'Higgins. His name sounded familiar. "Of course. The old jai alai player." Now I remembered him, a back-court man, potbellied even then, a husky roly-poly who had a powerful return off the back wall and covered ground with amazing agility for one who carried that beer-drinker's bulge.

"The only Mexican who could stand up to the Basques," he said. Somehow his boast did not sound boastful.

"You were a real *tiburón!*" I was enjoying the memory. "I always used to bet on you. I had forgotten you were Mexican."

"Now I am a citizen here," Paco O'Higgins said. "I had to leave

Mexico when my brother Joselito got into trouble for denouncing our *cabrón* of a president, Calles."

Calles and his little clique had made millions at the expense of the peasants. The days of Porfirio Díaz all over again.

Paco grunted. "At the jail they tell me Joselito committed suicide. *Que bárbaro!* A typical Calles trick. I was so mad I got out my pistol and the next time old Plutarco appeared in public I took a shot at him."

"And the Callistas threw you in jail?"

"No, *hombre*, I was already a big name on the sports page—I was only deported. I went to Spain. But in every country there is some *cabrón* dictador who wants to tell you when to sneeze and when to fart. In Spain it was Primo de Rivera. I piss in the milk of his whore mother. I piss in the milk of all the whore mothers of all the dictadores. From Franco to Bello."

Then he reached over his belly and grabbed comically at his male organs. "My God, I should not use that word or I may have to do it here on the floor and turn this place into more of a pigsty than it is already!"

He rocked with coarse laughter and made a move forward as if to challenge the barricade of brawn set up by Búfalo, but at that moment the door opened and out walked El Gordo Romano in a cloud of pine-scented cologne. Among the unshaven, the slovenly, the unwashed, El Gordo struck an incongruous note. He not only looked like, but carried himself with the air of a hedonist who has just completed his toilette in the exquisitely appointed bathroom of a hundred-dollar-a-day luxury hotel suite. Dressed like a Buddhist monk, he was resplendent in a white silk monogrammed robe over matching silk pajamas and white velvet slippers with a gold embroidered crest across the toes. He had a large face which was now freshly shaved and powdered, a strong jawline and what is thought of as a heroic, Romanesque head.

El Gordo was followed out of the bathroom by a slight, birdlike subservient man who carried the master's toilet articles in a plastic bag. With a valet—I later learned his name was Jesusito—and a bodyguard, El Gordo had come to diplomatic asylum in style.

"Well, Mr. President," he addressed me with a mocking bow, "so you finally jumped off. Or were you shoved? Welcome to our club."

I did not reply to El Gordo's welcome. When he first took refuge here, I not only had signed his extradition papers but had supported the decision of the tribunal that found him guilty, in absentia, of mass murder and political extortion. As presiding officer of the Revolution that overthrew him, it was my role to make this clear to him: "I sentenced you to death. In my eyes you no longer exist."

It had become El Gordo's role to ignore Paco's rich vocabulary of obscenities and Búfalo's role to draw blood from Paco's lip as the price extracted for his morning exercise in free speech. I was beginning to learn the intimate rituals of hostile truce. One sensed in this room a tacit agreement of opposites, if not to respect, then at least to accept each other's differences. So El Gordo's welcome was not as sardonic as it may have sounded. We all had to live together in this crowded cage where human beasts of various political species sniff each other suspiciously and move stiffly on, lest the cage be plunged into a mortal free-for-all.

El Gordo Romano walked down the aisle like an imperious senator of conquering Rome, followed by the scowling Búfalo and the attentive little Jesus, and Paco O'Higgins bowed me grandly toward the bathroom door.

"After you, amigo. You may share my turn with me."

I hesitated. "What about the others?"

"This is my reward—for daring to challenge El Gordo's monopoly of the bathroom."

Paco followed me in and latched the door. It was a bathroom made of the cheapest materials that looked as if its ordinary size had been doubled under the pressure of events. There was a stall shower large enough for four, three small sinks, a urinal wide enough for three or four and the most unusual feature of the room, two toilets set side by side and inexplicably raised on a one-foot base so that they surveyed the room like a double throne. Paco immediately dropped his long underwear down over his fat red knees and lowered himself onto the toilet seat. Urine flowed as from a faucet opened wide. "Ay! Ay!" Paco cried out with uninhibited passion. "When you have to piss this bad it is a pleasure even sweeter than shooting it into women!" He reached down and cupped his testicles and pressed them slightly upward with tender care. "Ay, the poor things, they were not meant to suffer." Then, like a king who offers to share his throne with a royal cousin, he indicated the adjoining toilet seat. "Seat yourself, my friend."

Again I hesitated. Even in my student dormitory days there had been a large common room for showers, but the toilets had been private. I had sat on public facilities where the compartments had no doors and even that semiprivacy had been an embarrassment to me. There was nothing in the high-flown language of the conventions on diplomatic asylum that forewarned the asylee of the humiliation that awaited him in the form of double toilets exposed to view.

Paco gave a grunt of satisfaction. "Sit yourself, my friend, sit yourself," he said. "Do not be so timid. In this shithouse we do everything together."

I looked at the figure of Paco O'Higgins, hunched over his toilet seat like a friendly, giant, mottled, red toad.

"I must go and get my toilet articles," I said. "My toothbrush. My towel."

"Sit down, amigo," Paco insisted, "you do not have time to go back. We have a rule here, an unwritten law. After El Gordo, who enjoys special privileges because he has killed more people and stolen more money than all of us combined, the rest of us are allowed five minutes each—there is the fucking clock ticking away—" He bobbed his thumb toward a cheap alarm clock on a greasy wooden shelf above the toilet bowls.

"For everything?"

"*Todo, todo, todo,*" Paco grunted. "Five minutes to crap and brush our teeth and wash our beautiful faces. Most of us shower after breakfast or after our promenade or at night—that is not such a problem. Mostly it is the crapper that is the problem."

I moved to the sink to wash my face. Over the sink was a broken mirror. I had not shaved since the morning before, in my airy bathroom overlooking the beach. I was still wearing the dirty fishing shirt I had slept in. The cracked mirror reflected the image of what looked like a haggard bum. I thought to myself that I must keep up my appearance. I must shave every day and get Alejandro to fetch me clean clothes. I must try not to surrender to bearded slobbiness like my new friend Paco O'Higgins.

"You come into the crapper with me in the mornings," Paco was saying. "That way you will avoid plenty of fights. We have more fights about the crapper than we do about the big lovers who go sneaking into corners with other men's wives."

"Is there much of that in here?" I asked. "It seems too public."

"There's plenty of that in here," Paco said. "Even in a fish bowl there are rocks to hide under."

He rose and began to wipe himself. I looked away.

"I came well prepared," I said. "My wife is too old and my daughter is too young."

"Be careful, my friend," Paco said good-naturedly. "In this shit-house"—it was the only word I was ever to hear him use for our diplomatic sanctuary—"little by little everybody goes crazy. A cake of brown soap begins to look like a bar of solid gold. A sixty-year-old grandmother with breasts like empty paper bags begins to look like María Felix."

He pulled up his gray long-johns and moved to the sink to splash water over his ruddy face while I stood at the urinal. Then I joined him at the sinks, ran water over my hands and pulled the lever for a paper towel but the box was empty now. I wiped my hands along my sleeves and then brushed my sleeves across my face. Paco handed me a twisted tube of toothpaste and his dirty toothbrush. "Here. Don't be shy," he said generously. I accepted the tube. With my finger, I rubbed some of the paste over my teeth. As I left the bathroom, Paco was attacking his teeth with the dirty brush.

"Until later," I said.

"Good, good," he gargled with his mouth full of dental foam. "I will sit with you at breakfast. I am sick and tired of all the shitheads I am cooped up with in here. At least you are a new face."

"Thank you," I said.

"I do not say that to make an insult," Paco said. "What makes a man different from other animals is his love of variety. Otherwise he'd be content to fuck the same old lady all his life. Do I not speak in silver, my friend?"

As I stepped out into the dormitory, a line of about a dozen had formed at the bathroom door. An old man in a worn but once elegant robe called out irritably, "Come out, come out, your time is up."

"Tu madre!" I heard my gargle-voiced friend shout predictably through the door.

The old man muttered a semitoothless protest. "It is the same thing every morning. He is as bad as General Romano. We should all band together and take action against these dictators of the bathroom!"

I made my way down the aisle to my cot. The death-head in the adjoining cot was sitting up now, tall, bony-legged, narrow-chested, a living skeleton. It was pulling on its socks. I thought I would be cheerful with all but the known Zamoristas so I nodded and said, "Good morning!" but received no answer. The scarecrow simply stared at me balefully and drew on his other limp sock. "Since it seems we are to be bunk mates," I said somewhat louder, thinking he might be deaf, "permit me to introduce myself, Justo Moreno Suárez."

He stared at me with a disconcerting lack of expression. "Justo Moreno Suárez," he repeated in a flat tone of sarcasm. "As if you have to tell me. You should be ashamed of yourself, Mr. President."

"What have I done to you?"

"You lent respectability to the Communists. I hope they keep you here until you rot."

"You talk like a Zamorista," I said.

"Ask El Gordo if I am a Zamorista," the death-head challenged, nodding down the aisle toward El Gordo Romano, whose valet was helping him into his beige linen slacks. "Here is Rubén Silva."

He had been the publisher of a middle-of-the-road news-magazine, *Alegre,* that first had been cautiously anti-Zamora and then reservedly pro-Bello before it was confiscated for its slurs on a visiting Soviet trade delegation.

"I was loyal to the Green Revolution for the first nine months, before it began to show its true colors," said Rubén Silva. "That was the time for genuine democrats to make their position clear. Those of you who stayed on into the second year and the third have only my contempt."

"Silva, since we must be here together let us be honest," I said.

"If Angel had not gobbled up your private blackmail sheet you would be with him still. You are for anyone who allows you to make a profit."

"You are as much a Communist as Angel Bello!" he said.

I shook my head and turned back to the rumpled clothing on my cot.

When I drew on my trousers, the premonition of the asilado prompted me to reach my hand into my side pocket where I had folded my "tipping" money—about four hundred pesos. Before my fingers felt the emptiness I knew that my balance had been withdrawn. Then I grabbed for my windbreaker where I carried the lighter, the pocket flashlight, the silver cuff links, the pack of cigarettes I had brought at Marta's practical suggestion of small bribes for small favors. These pockets were empty too. I felt shaken by my loss, by the stupidity and disillusionment of my loss, and depressingly alone. All my adult life I had tried to believe not merely in brotherhood but in a system of brotherhood, a social order based on empathy and compassion and mutual sharing. To say it was discouraging is to understate my feeling of homelessness, statelessness, empty-pocketed self-disgust as I stood between those narrow cots and looked accusingly into the faces of fellow-asylees who either did not or pretended not to notice my loss.

Halfheartedly I made up my cot, as I saw others doing around me. At the end of the room there was still a line at the bathroom door. I wondered why we were not issued night-pots. It seemed to me a necessity, odorous but practical. I stretched out on my cot and stared at the ceiling. The stucco long ago had been painted a powder blue, but it had faded and gathered grime until it had become its own colorless color. It had cracked into a thousand veins and I tried to distract myself by tracing recognizable forms in the impromptu art of decay. There was a giant breast, with a perfectly formed nipple that inexplicably retained a penny-sized dot of the original color. There was a double line that seemed to form the trunk of a tree producing ornamental branches, fernlike leaves and bell-shaped flowers. Was I seeing a reproduction or merely dreaming of my favorite jacaranda tree spreading over the high wall of our house at Papagayos? I thought of the base of the tree with its airy blue carpet of fallen blossoms and the scent when I picked them up and held them to my face—like wild honey. I saw my jacaranda tree standing there, deserted. Then a stream of Papagayos impressions flooded in: who was giving milk to Dolores so she could nurse her kittens? Would my domesticated Mano go back to his foraging, jungle ways or be forever in a limbo of confusion waiting for the strange upright creature that came out of the house each morning to feed and converse with him?

My longing for all the familiar objects and living things at our lost house at the edge of the sea made me turn away from the half-uncanny, half-imagined reproductions on the ceiling. In a twitch of claustrophobia, I rose from the cot and went to the only window breaking the monotony of the long wall facing me. It was a dormer opening onto the rear patio placed between us and the opposite wing of the building. Looking directly across at me as if she had been waiting was the face in the tower window that had haunted my walks along the Playa de los Papagayos. Here again, the brooding, incomparable eyes of Adriana Ponce de Romano. Framed in the dormer window across the way, her face stared back at mine, motionless and yet full of imminent movement and promise.

I don't know how long I stood staring across the courtyard into the seemingly unseeing eyes of Adriana. It might have been a dream, like my vision of the violet jacaranda tree, except that I had seen the silken-covered El Gordo and the presence of that odious reality was proof unmistakable that I had reentered the orbit of the Romanos, and that the portrait in the dormer frame was the living model herself.

"Come, amigo." A meaty hand fell roughly on my shoulder. It was Paco O'Higgins, literally pulling me back into the mundane insistence of the sanctuary. "Time for breakfast. Shall we have *huevos rancheros?*"—I imagined a steaming plate of fresh fried eggs alive with red chili sauce and resting on a steaming tortilla—"or the garbage they usually serve?"

Paco pounded my shoulder, laughed hoarsely at his primitive joke and draped his arm around me as he led me in to breakfast.

2

In the dining room—or common room, for it was used for card games and checkers, reading and letter-writing after the morning service—was a table long enough to accommodate about thirty of us. Presiding over the table was a thin, frail, ancient waiter, a servant of the old school with a few precious hairs combed strategically across his bald head.

"My friend," Paco guided me into the crowded, chattery room, "here is our trusted servant 'Momentito.' Momentito was a kitchen boy in this shithouse of an embassy when Angel Bello was only a gleam in the eye of his father . . . when that old man was peeking under the skirts of the cook's fifteen-year-old daughter."

Then Paco turned to the old waiter, who was called "Momentito," I learned, because his invariable answer to every order was, *"Momentito, momentito,* in a little moment I am coming."

"Momentito, this is the President of our Republic, or at least he was until he decided to join us here a few hours ago. So we must all treat him with respect—even if he is a stupid son-of-a-bitch."

As Paco laughed loudly, Momentito bowed with a small, patient smile. Obviously he was accustomed to Paco's exuberance. *"A sus órdenes, Señor Presidente,"* he said. *"Café con leche?"*

"What else?" Paco said, taking a chair near the end of the table and indicating for me the chair at the head. "What else do we ever have but watered coffee and watered milk? Oh yes—stale *bolillos,* let us not forget the stone rolls left over from the Ambassador's dinner."

"I am sorry," Momentito said and the old waiter did seem personally embarrassed for the failure of the breakfast.

"Yes, of course you are sorry, Momentito," Paco said, holding out his cup for the servant to pour the coffee from a huge, battered tin pitcher. "And Apolonio the cook is sorry. And Don Ernesto the Ambassador is sorry. And, no doubt the Organization of American States is sorry. And meanwhile we go on drinking coffee that tastes like warmed-over piss—"

From the opposite end of the table came a growl of protest. There sat El Gordo Romano flanked by his Búfalo and his Jesusito.

"Quiet, you loudmouth!" El Gordo said. He seemed to be enjoying his coffee and breakfast roll. "Have you no sensibilities? Spare us your bathroom obscenities. Gentlemen are eating."

"Ha, will you please notice who is talking," Paco shouted. "He can force men who are dying of thirst to drink their own bloody piss but he's too delicate to hear the word mentioned at the breakfast table!"

A voice rose from the tentlike figure of the Bishop of San Cristóbal. "Please—gentlemen," he said in a sanctimonious voice. "May I remind you that we are breaking our fast. The morning meal has religious significance."

"Meal?" Paco literally snorted. "If God has anything to do with this pisswater coffee and indigestible stones, He should be ashamed of Himself!"

El Gordo glanced across the table to the Bishop as if to apologize for Paco's blasphemy. In fairness to the Bishop, I felt he recognized or at least sensed the difference between the frankly disrespectful disbeliever and the silky deference of a man who specialized in defiling fellow beings.

"My son, I understand your bitterness," the Bishop said to Paco with the genial smile he had perfected. "But remember that God's first duty is to cater to our souls. It is His secondary duty to cater to our stomachs."

"Your Holiness," Paco said, using the hard *bolillo* as a pointer, "it seems to me that sometimes He gets His first and His second duties confused. For instance, I see that He does very well indeed by *his* secondary duties"—he poked the roll in the direction of El Gordo—"and *your* secondary duties."

"Now, now," said the Bishop, "you must not judge too harshly. Life on earth is full of inequities—"

"You are new here," Paco said to me, "so you wouldn't know that of all the miserable monkeys in this cage, a precious few are able to have fresh *bolillos* and real coffee. I am not political—I am just a drunken ex-jai alai player, so it is not my place to point out that at this moment the only ones to enjoy these special arrangements are Zamora's secret police chief and the hand of the Pope."

The Bishop put down his fresh, edible roll and crossed himself discreetly. "I forgive you, my son. I understand the unhappy conditions that drive you to these outbursts."

Paco O'Higgins grunted. "Holiness," he said, "chew your roll and swig your coffee. For you are nothing but a man."

The Bishop shook his head and smiled a smile of human tolerance and chose to fall silent.

I tried to bite into my *bolillo*. It was as hard as Paco said. It took all my strength to break it in two. The inside was a little softer but not much. I dipped it into the *café con leche* which was little more than tepid, colored water. The Death-head, Rubén Silva, who apparently had forgotten he was not speaking to me because of my long-time allegiance to Angel, nodded sympathetically. "Now you see how they feed us. It is systematic starvation. I have lost thirty pounds in four months."

Others along both sides of the table spoke up. Breakfast was a scandal . . . The special fund to support the asylum obviously found its way into the pockets of the diplomatic thieves who conducted the sanctuary . . . There was a special government store for the diplomatic corps so they could have the best of everything, while the asylees were given only half a pound of meat a week and a quarter of a pound of coffee . . . Maybe they should all go on a hunger strike together to force the Ambassador to increase their rations . . .

As I listened to their grumbling while they chewed the stale rolls and sipped the pale coffee, I silently agreed that it was cruel punishment to serve this counterfeit brew to nationalists who considered our coffee the best in the world, and who liked it strong and thick with fresh hot milk to give it that rich, morning aroma. And our *bolillos* had to be just right, shaped like miniature gringo footballs, warm and crusty but soft and light on the inside. A fresh *bolillo* was a work of art and even our poorest workman would split the air with angry protest if his *bolillos* did not come from the bakery at exactly the right consistency. Some of us like to start our day by dipping into our women but all of us like to start by dipping a fresh *bolillo* into our rich coffee.

Across the table and down a few places from me sat a tall, sturdy man whose skin was the color of weathered bronze. This was El Indio Sandungo, who had rallied the barefoot campesinos of the southernmost province of Ocampo to the cause of Angel. He had been fighting his own guerrilla war against the big landowners when Angel was still playing right-wing forward for his *colegio* soccer team. The cry of "Here comes Sandungo!" was enough to panic a Zamora regiment and the price on his head had been as high as that on Angel's. In the days of their guerrilla alliance El Indio and Angel seemed to have no differences and for a time, in the euphoric early years, the black Indian guerrilla had been one of the saints of the Revolution.

I stared across at him. He was ragged now. Defeated. But still impressive. He must have recognized me from revolutionary rallies, for he nodded. But he did not speak or smile. He chewed at his hard roll and refused to join in the general, futile chatter of protest.

El Indio had believed truly in Land and Freedom. No one—especially his idol Angel Bello—had bothered to tell him that that phrase was merely a temporary slogan to bind the illiterate peasants to the Revolution.

My coffee was being removed from the table by Paco. Half-turning away to conceal his act, he slipped from his pocket a pint bottle, quickly poured a few ounces into my cup and handed it back to me.

"Here, my friend. If the coffee is weak, at least this will give it a little *zas*." I sipped it and the sweet-sharp bite of the rum was strong in my nostrils and burned encouragingly in my throat. Paco nodded and grinned, pleased with my introduction to his morning hospitality.

"*Le zumba el mango,* eh!" He said it in a hoarse chuckle. I felt a spurt of well-being, a sense of momentary luxury.

"Thank you. But how do you manage it? I thought liquor was not allowed."

"Nothing is allowed. I mean nothing enjoyable. Even on visiting days if anybody brings us packages, Angel's guards make sure to find the bottles."

"Then how do you—?"

Paco put his forefinger to his lips. "Shhh. A secret."

He drained his more-rum-than-watered coffee, poured himself another precious few ounces and then, with an elaborate gesture of deception that clearly did not deceive anyone, reached again for my cup.

"The best answer is—another drink. The only way to stay sane in this lunatic asylum—get drunk in the morning—stay drunk all day —fall into bed—I mean your lousy, hard, narrow cot—dead drunk at night. That way you may be able to live through the long wait for safe passage that never seems to come to anyone in this shithouse."

From the long table we wandered to a corner near the window with our illicit coffee cups. I asked how a Mexican jai alai player had come by the name of O'Higgins. I knew that Bolívar's chief aide had been the indefatigable Colonel O'Leary, but he had been a true Irish soldier of fortune. Who was his O'Higgins, or O-ee-geens, as Paco called him?

"Also, how you say, an Irish soldier of fortune," Paco said. "Only my grandpapa, Packy O'Higgins, was one crazy *hijo*. A professional prizefighter with his bare knuckles. He was a big boaster, he told my papa he even fought a famous champion by the name of Deaf Burke and almost won. Then he sailed to America and joined the gringo army invading Mexico. When he found he was fighting Catholics he switched sides and married my grandmother. So here you see a true Irish-Indian, with the worst traits of both races!"

He rose to his feet unsteadily. "Remember my advice, my friend, since sanctuary stinks, since it has nothing to do with the way it sounds in those fancy agreements, since words are always one thing and the facts another, there is only one thing for us to do in here— DRINK!"

He belched and laughed his drunken laugh again. "Now I go to take my shower."

I watched him stagger off, much as his two-fisted progenitor must have staggered, barrel-chested and whiskey-sotted, along the docks of New Orleans where the warship was about to transport him unwittingly to his new life as a Latin. And momentarily relieved from the pressures of enforced enclosure by Paco's spirited hospitality, I found myself thinking of all the *if-if-if*'s of the world that make a Paco O'Higgins.

If his grandfather Packy had not been a bare-knuckle fighter, *if* he had not lost to Deaf Burke and decided to try his fortunes in America, *if* he had not wandered down to New Orleans and fallen into the clutches of a deceptive recruiting sergeant who bought him enough drinks to sign him up for the Mexican War, *if* he had not inadvertently shot a fourteen-year-old cadet whose death-rattle clutch for his beads echoed profoundly in Packy's tortured Catholic heart, *if* he had not deserted and bedded with a Mexican *chica* who promptly presented him with a son, *if* he had not decided as a fugitive that he had no choice but to go native, go Mexican, all these unaccountable *if*'s, and these chosen at random from a hundred whimsical *if*'s, made Paco one in a billion, as each of us is one in a billion, victims and inheritors of the *if-if-if*'s that predestine us, shape us and face us, turn us this way and that way, spin us about until we are dizzy and then dare to challenge us—all right, man of soul, man of free will, man of independent spirit, go your own way, make your own life, we *if-if-if*'s who shadow you and haunt you, now dare you!

"Ay—*chinga!—imbécil!—no tengo nada!*" I heard the increasing tempo of the domino players. El Gordo and his Big One Búfalo and his Little One Jesusito were gone. So was the complacent Bishop. Sitting alone was El Indio Sandungo. He was there in the room but he was not watching the domino players or the card players. He was not reading a book or a magazine, as were some of the asilados. I tried to catch his eyes to exchange—what?—a smile, a thought, an expression of mutual sympathy? He looked directly at me, but his eyes were so strong in not seeing me that I turned away. I wanted to communicate with this man, this descendant of red Arawak and black Yoruba, but how? How does one approach a victim on the fifth level of the Inferno sentenced to sitting and waiting alone?

Could I remind him that I had agreed with his version of land reform, when communal lands had been set up as self-governing cooperatives? And that we both had objected when the co-ops were liquidated in favor of the larger collectives suggested by Russian experts? El Indio had denounced the state farms as he had the fifty-thousand-hectare fiefdoms of the Zamoristas. "We did not fight and die only to exchange one impersonal overseer for another," he told his followers. I had tried to dissuade Angel from sending our Little Green Angels to arrest his old comrade-in-arms, but one small vote was no match for Soviet money and Soviet advice. El Indio disappeared into the wild lands of the south, accused Angel of surrendering the original revolution and raised a new rebellion. When the Sandungo insurrection was put down, I had been relieved to hear that he had managed to escape and shoot his way into the embassy.

"El Indio. We were right. I still think if—"

For the first time El Indio acknowledged me. "What good is talk?" Then he withdrew into himself again.

The silence of El Indio and the sound of the magpie domino players drove me out of the room. Back in the dormitory most of the cots were empty, but here and there an inmate had gone back to his thin, narrow mattress. Some—I soon found out—were sick from hunger. Some were struck weak and dumb with melancholia. I would smile at them, either to be kind or because something in me still had to act the President, and they would look away as if to say, "Do not smile your eyes at me, Señor Newcomer. There is nothing here to smile about."

The single area of well-being belonged to El Gordo Romano who had two cots spliced together; on that makeshift double bed, he lay on his back in his silk monogrammed kimono with his white fleshy legs spread apart while Búfalo administered a strong-tender massage. His left hand was extended to the delicate Jesusito who was manicuring the master's fingernails with professional care. And on the ledge over his bed a Japanese AM-FM radio bathed him in Khatchaturian ballet music. He tried to smile at me as I had tried to smile at the sick and the lonely in their narrow cots. After all, the complete sybarite needs a circle of friends. He needs congenial people to be sybaritic with. But here in sanctuary, ostracized even by moderate Zamoristas, he had only Búfalo de Sa and Jesusito whom he paid well to love him, only this beast and this butterfly and the memory of his harem of fourteen- and fifteen-year-old girls trained in the art

of Oriental erotica—the feudal hacienda that was known as El Gordo's "Little Convent"—and of his torture chambers, where men's
testicles were removed slowly and handed to El Gordo as trophies of
his super-patriotism and determination to maintain Zamora law, Zamora order. Because he perspired easily and had a fetish for clean-
liness, he was known to change his fine silk shirts half a dozen times
a day. He was so fastidious that he had even air-conditioned those
torture chambers.

So now I avoided his smile, but I watched Búfalo's strong hands
working the muscles of the white hams that extended from the
master's knees to the master's groin. Partially exposed as his dressing gown parted for Búfalo's work, the testicles of the wholesale
castrator were large and low-slung like the fallen breasts of an
aging woman, and they were a strange shade of blue, a kind of
bluish red, suggesting the apparatus of some dirty business, like the
works that help drive the needle into the vein of the addict self-
seduced. I couldn't help looking. There seems to be an irresistible
curiosity, some atavistic challenge from Stone Age days, some
primeval competitiveness of the male. El Gordo noticed that I
noticed and drew his white robe together in a gesture so prim that
it would have made me smile if I could have erased from my mind
the shape and color of the horrors this sweet-scented syb had
authored and monitored.

"Mr. President. Would you like a cigar?"

It was Romano's talent to know every man's weakness and to
succor it quickly. Extended was the Corona Especial, the most expensive of all the fine ones. After the breakfast of weak coffee and
strong rum, there is nothing I would have enjoyed more. But he
was not going to bribe me into conversation.

I stretched out on my back and searched the ceiling again, but
this time I could not find my jacaranda tree. I was like an amateur
sky-gazer searching for fading astrological patterns in the sky. Under
my cot I had placed a few books—always the last possessions to be
stolen—and I reached down for a small volume I first had heard
aloud from my father, who read it with the reverence of a prayer
book, a text I could not quote from memory but every line of which
was affectionately familiar. It was *Ismaelillo* by Martí, *el apostól*

José Martí, the only figure I can think of worthy of double sanctity as the innovator of political independence and of a new purity in poetry. *"Ismaelillo* will live," Martí had written in the simple style he developed, shorn of the Spanish conceits and adornments that had cluttered the work of nearly all his predecessors and contemporaries. He was not at all a boastful man, only a clean and pure and sane one who could say, "My poetry will grow: in my grave/I will grow also."

I tried to close my ears to the Khatchaturian. Was it the source from which it poured, El Gordo's outlandish double cot, or had I always been critical of Khatchaturian? Melodic, yes, but so insistent on attention, like the public entertainer who needs to be loved by all the people all the time. I also tried not to hear a radio voice explaining, with Angel's style for repetition but without the emotion, how the Leader had *always* been a Marxist-Leninist. He had been a Marxist-Leninist when he led the Little Green Angels into the capital, a Marxist-Leninist the day he stood trial for attack on the Presidential Palace, a Marxist-Leninist when he delivered the graduation oration at his *colegio*—any moment I expected the fervent apologist to claim for Angel authority as a Marxist-Leninist in his kindergarten days . . . I turned toward the offending radio. It stood over the cot of a bony, jaundiced-looking little man who was snoring softly. Perhaps the sound of the propagandist who could not get at him was like music to him, as the Khatchaturian ballet suite was to El Gordo.

I tried not to listen. I could smell the fumes of the great cigar, but I tried not to smell. Unable to read, I shut my eyes so I did not have to see. The light still filtered through my lids, but I tried in the half darkness to see the image of my father reading *Ismaelillo* to me out loud on Sunday mornings. Papa was a schoolteacher, which meant we were raised with very little money. But the house was full of books and Papa was a compulsive teacher. Even on Sunday he could not resist putting the book down and delivering small, impromptu lectures on the style of Martí. Did I notice the inner illumination? Did I notice how the relationship of Martí's form and content was not master to slave but proud father to loving child? Thirty years later I still remembered that phrase.

How good it was to summon back the gentle memories of Father, to withdraw into a subjective glade of momentary personal peace.

"—Well, Justo old kid, long time no see!" I looked up to see someone lowering himself onto the cot next to mine, which meant his knees were pushing against me, an oval-faced fellow in his middle thirties with a small waxed moustache and toothpaste-ad smile. I had known him casually for a long time, although now I groped for his name. He handed it to me quickly like a professional card: "Johnie Valdez—now don't tell me you've forgotten your old palsy-walsy, Johnie?"

I had seen him at the Foreign Press Club dozens of times. He had spent a few years in the States and considered himself an expert on the gringo idiom even though his second-rate ear refused to inform him that he was ten years and sometimes twenty years out of date. "Johnie" Valdez—as he called himself, never Juanito—was always finding an empty stool near a defenseless guest at the Press Club bar and offering himself as a long-sought friend, "an old pal," I should say. He was an amiable hack who had conducted a daily gossip column. "What high-ranking member of the government would be surprised if he knew just how much his beloved *esposita* was enjoying her vacation!" There were Press Club rumors that Johnie enjoyed a secret salary as a blackmailer five times the size of his regular salary on the tabloid *Alegre*, the same one Rubén Silva had published before Angel and his little angels of censorship cut him down. Johnie Valdez a common blackmailer? I never believed it. It was a point of principle with me not to believe ninety-nine percent of the gossip I heard in the club. It was a snake pit, an amusing and informative snake pit if you could sift out that one percent of genuine revelation, a gathering place of sophisticated reptiles where nearly everyone liked to rattle his tail but few were ready to go for the vein.

It was a surprise to find Johnie here in this sour university. He seemed to be the kind of smiling cat who could squeeze through narrow cracks and, if pushed from a roof, fall neatly on his feet. Because he spoke perfect English and could take the soft-spoken, horny British correspondents to the right bordellos and because he quickly learned to write glowing columns about Angel and his friends, he had made himself useful to the new regime. How had he fallen off the train?

"Well, keed, it's no picnic in here, but it could be worse. That Angelito! How could we've been taken in by him? Oh, maybe I can understand it in myself, but you, a great political mind—" Valdez was always praising his companion at the bar—how well the chap looked! What a wise observation he had just made! What a *mango*-picker—a connoisseur of seduction—was the fellow on the nearest barstool who was buying the drinks. "Did you think when you saved his life that he was already a member of the Communist—?"

"Please, Johnie, no politics this morning."

Instantly, turning off one switch and flipping on the next, he obligingly flashed another color. "Forgive me, old pal. Of course you're sick of the subject. What'll we talk about?" It never occurs to a Johnie Valdez that boredom can be fought with silence as well as sound. "Women—what else? Show me the man who doesn't like to talk about the sweet fruit of this world, the mango, the papaya, half the time in this joint you think about getting out and the other half you think about pushing your sixth finger into the softest guayaba on the tree."

I glanced at the discarded *Ismaelillo*. This was worse than being trapped at the bar of the Press Club. At least there I could have ordered a daiquiri or greeted a correspondent just back from Colombia or Haiti, eager to bring me up on the latest political shenanigans. I could have found it necessary to make a phone call. Even a prison with separate cells began to seem preferable.

When Alejandro talked erotically, Marta and I had enjoyed it. At small dinner parties he might quote from Burton and the Kama Sutra and the unknown Chinese poets who were the John Donnes of erotic exploration and we would look at each other and appreciate his ability to seduce seemingly unassailable ladies and gentlemen. But Johnie Valdez seemed chained to his mangos and papayas.

"Boyohboy," he was saying, "wait'll you see the dogs we've got in the nunnery on the other side of this joint. You know how it goes, ladies who get into political trouble on their own are usually battle-axes, and if they come in as wives of the asilados, it's the girlfriends in the *casa chica* they had to leave behind who are the real mangos."

"Johnie, it's good to see you again, even under these circumstances, but I have a bad headache—so, if you will forgive me—"

"A headache! I'm the only guy in this klink who has a big supply of *aspirina*. A little peach who works in a drugstore comes to see me on visiting day. I return in one second."

Before I could stop him he was hurrying down the aisle. I should not have mentioned headache. But what could one mention? Whatever, Johnie Valdez would be at your elbow helping you cure your ailment, solve your problem, satisfy your whim. Too quickly he was back with a handful of *aspirinas* and an obliging glass of water. He watched me solicitously while I swallowed the pills.

"Hokay?" he said, as if they were expected to provide instant relief like the little dramas in the television commercials. Then he looked over his shoulder, toward El Gordo halfway across the room and lowered his voice discreetly, for, as Marta would say, he was a *pinche pendejo* all right but belonging to a particular category, *pinche pendejo discreto,* one of those who was always confiding in you and a score of others some precious bit of information about which he swore you to solemn secrecy, sharing with you an intimate personal secret that already had been whispered from one end of the capital to the other.

"Of course we have one *mango de bandera* in here," he whispered, "with the eyes of Dolores del Rio, the build of Sophia Loren, skoobie-doo!, and the secret garden of— But I cannot lie to you, my President, I have never set eyes on that treasure, El Gordo sees to that. In the courtyard at the general *comida* we all eat together, you will see him strutting like the Grand Vizar of Foqui-foqui. But Her Highness Adriana never comes down to eat with the common people. Romano is so jealous he puts a chastity belt on her chastity belt. So we all have to watch our step, pal. You remember the Maldonado affair—the dwarf, El Amante . . ."

"Look, Johnie, El Amante is dead. And no matter how many irresistible goddesses are combined in the inaccessible Señora, she holds no temptation for me."

"Holy smokes, I was only talking about our Mango Queen to

change the subject. You know me, keed, just making small talk to cheer you up."

When he put his hand on my shoulder, I was too weary or numb to move away from his familiarity. I lowered my head until my chin was resting on my chest.

"I know," he said. "I know."

If there is any phrase in this world that I despise it is "I know." Because nobody knows. There are those who admit it by their silence and those who expose it by saying, "I know." But I was too weak to argue, too low in spirit to fight off his insistent presence, like women who submit to men not out of passion but of depression, a resignation of the nervous system. In that state of physical indifference I accepted on my shoulder the obliging hand of Johnie Valdez.

There was a flurry of activity at the end of the room. "Here comes Bertie, our angel of mercy," Johnie said. He rose from the cot and, automatically, so did I. I noticed that some of those who had seemed too weak to move in their cots now struggled to sit up and a few of them even managed to rise unsteadily to their feet. A gregarious somnambulist, I followed Johnie and the others up the aisle toward our official receptionist of the night before, Licenciado Alvarez. "Bertie," as Johnie called him—most of the others accorded him full honors as "Licenciado"—had undergone an unexpected change overnight. Now he was refreshed and his perfunctory, official smile of the night before was replaced by a broad and bright-eyed smile of what seemed unlimited patience and affability. Under his arm he carried a thick bundle of manila folders which contained an up-

to-date record of the asylum cases he was handling. He was quickly
surrounded and pushed from all sides, but he never lost his aplomb,
his seemingly bottomless well of goodwill. Even when the irritable
old man who had been pounding on the bathroom door earlier
began to jostle the elbow of Licenciado Alvarez in his anxiety to
know if there was any progress on his case, our chargé d'affaires was
unruffled and courteous—in fact, encouragingly understanding.

"Yes, yes, just let me finish explaining this other case—one at a
time—I'm only one person, you know—but I will get to you in a
moment, Señor Gamboa. I think I may have a little bit of good news
for you." Then he added, "*Próximamente usted podrá salir.* You
will be able to leave very soon now." It was spoken with a genuine
smile of assurance that convinced me, on first observation, that my
original impression of Licenciado Bertie Alvarez had been a mis-
judgment born of our long night's ordeal, and that this was one of
those rare officials of goodwill who did not go through the bureaucratic motions but who really cared about the inmates in his charge.
When he came to the case of old man Gamboa he shuffled through
his folders and then explained to him with an encouraging smile
that he had had a satisfactory personal talk about the Gamboa case
with his opposite number in the Foreign Office who had seemed
willing to untangle the red tape. In this case the old man was claim-
ing that he was the *wrong* Enrique Gamboa, that an overzealous
member of the neighborhood Vigilante Committee had heard of an
Enrique Gamboa involved with the CIA and a Miami anti-Bello
action group, and simply had pointed his finger at the wrong Enrique Gamboa. "I am a poor, innocent druggist," the old man
insisted. "My only two sons, who were to take over my drugstore,
were killed for no reason in the last months of Zamora. And then I
am accused, also for no reason. To get money to hide I have to sell
my drugstore. I have nothing. I threaten nobody. My life is de-
stroyed. But I have a nephew who lives in Miami. He owns a liquor
store. He makes a good business. He will take me in. All I ask is a
little time to sit in the sun and to die in peace. Mariano Gamboa is
the name of my nephew. All they have to do is speak to him. He can
explain that you have the wrong Enrique Gamboa. The wrong Enrique Gamboa." He turned to me over his shoulder as if, somehow,

the more people he could enlighten as to this case of mistaken
identity, the more rapidly he would gain his release.

"Yes, yes, yes, yes," Licenciado Alvarez ran his *sí-sí*'s together
to assure the old man that he did understand. "There are left now
only a few small complications. The Internal Security Office has
acknowledged that there is another Enrique Gamboa involved in
this case. But their report must be officially approved by Major
del Campo. We are working on that. And our own consulate in
Miami is cooperating with the United States immigration authorities. Once you get your 'safe passage' from the Bello authorities, we
cannot arrange for your flight to the United States until the U.S.
officials are satisfied that you will be fully supported economically
by this nephew of yours. So there are only these two little things
that hold up your departure. But do not be discouraged. We are
working on it."

Licenciado Alvarez closed the thick file on the case of Señor
Enrique Gamboa—No. 5532792—I thought of the letters, affidavits,
memoranda, responsive memos, unresponsive memos, appeals to
the Internal Security Office, long-winded inconclusive answers as
the search for the real Enrique Gamboa dragged on, while off somewhere in Miami was the brand-new American citizen by the name
of Mariano Gamboa, who possibly could not be traced because his
place of business was called Marty's Package Store, and who had
dropped the last *a* from his name and maybe the *o* as well, so that
the old druggist Enrique Gamboa, who barely existed, was in quest
of a Mariano Gamboa who no longer existed, replaced by a scrappy
young citizen of the good old U.S.A., who rooted for his favorite
Miami football team and bought Cokes and hot dogs for his growing Cub Scout of a kid between the halves. But the smiling, refreshed chargé d'affaires patted folder No. 5532792 confidently as if
it truly contained the key to the mystery of exactly when the aging
ex-druggist, slowly withering away on this diplomatic vine, could
finally *salir*.

The old man turned away slowly, his hands trembling slightly, his
head moving a centimeter from side to side as if he were in an early
stage of palsy or Parkinson's disease. He was muttering, *"Gracias,
Licenciado, mil gracias,"* and to these thousand thank-you's the

agreeable go-between murmured his own liturgy, *"Próximamente usted podrá salir. Seguro, Señor, seguro!"*

Then it was my turn. There were others around us who insisted their cases should be taken up next as they had been waiting longer, but Licenciado Alvarez politely but graciously turned them aside. "Ah, our distinguished guest, Señor Moreno Suárez—" I noticed that he had dropped my former title, "Señor Presidente," and wondered if that had any significance. On such delicate and bending reeds do we lean in asylum. "How are you this morning? Were you able to get a good rest? I am sorry we cannot make things more comfortable for you, but you see how overburdened we are! But if there is anything I can do—anything in my power, that is—please do not hesitate to call on me. I am at your service."

He said it with more conviction this morning. Perhaps the night before we had interrupted a romantic assignation, or a sound night's sleep. When I asked him how my wife and my daughter were, he smiled gallantly, "What a fine, brave woman is your wife, and *que linda*, how lovely your little daughter! I made a special point to check with Señora Lorona, you remember, my assistant for the ladies' wing, and she said to tell you they are doing splendidly— very good 'sports,' both of them—whenever the private room becomes available I will assign it for them. At the moment it is being occupied by Señora Romano and her maid. You see, they came in very early when we were not so crowded," he said as he drew several official-looking papers from my folder. As long as I live, which may not be long, I shall never forget my number, 5556891—often I go to sleep or wake up chanting it like a treasured line of Martí's— *cinco cinco cinco seis ocho nueve uno* . . . Yes, my friends, there is even a poetry to the bureaucratic management of political persecution.

"Your government lost no time in delivering this official request to my Ambassador," Licenciado Alvarez explained to me, rather cheerfully under the circumstances. "It charges our embassy with"— and he half-read from his paper—"harboring a common criminal who has been indicted for major crimes against the state, and demands that we immediately deliver over to their jurisdiction the accused Justo Moreno Suárez so that sovereign justice may resume its normal course which has been suspended by the illegal entry of the aforesaid accused common criminal into the compound of this embassy."

I glanced over his shoulder at the long, detailed document, several pages of specific charges, drawn up in impeccable diplomatic language, putting the embassy on record that it was in violation of Article 1, Paragraph 1, and Article 11, Paragraph 2, of the Havana Convention, and going on to cite all the other violations under the more recent Caracas Convention, the same old diplomatic fencing match that Peru and Colombia fought year after year over the living corpus of Haya de la Torre. Except that I did not know how long and how hard the Ambassador Don Ernesto would fight for me. Still, he had our ten thousand dollars. If I were thrown back on the mercy of Angel's justice, I would have no reason to conceal the bribe. And Don Ernesto de San Martín might have to forfeit his place of honor on the Human Rights Commission.

"I am sure you understand how these things go," Licenciado Alvarez said. "The Ambassador has not yet had time to study this matter in detail, but he will answer that he has the case under personal investigation and that while we would never consider intervening in the territorial affairs of a friendly nation, under the provisions of the Rights of Man approved in Bogotá and reconfirmed again in Caracas he is unable to surrender you at this time."

"Of course, I understand how these things go," I said.

"Good, very good," Licenciado Alvarez smiled. "So many of the people in here are amateurs and I have to spend so much time repeating myself. But since you yourself have served as head of state—in fact I believe you signed an affidavit charging us with harboring a common criminal and requesting that we deliver him over to the jurisdiction of the state over which you presided so that *your* justice could resume its normal course—" He looked at me pointedly and smiled as if he had scored a neat forensic jab.

"But in that case, since obviously you are speaking of Carlos Romano, he *was* a common criminal, there were a hundred charges of grand theft, murder—read his dossier. Whereas my case is a matter of principle, profound political doubts—"

Licenciado Alvarez interrupted me with his smile. "My distinguished friend, we cannot take sides in these intramural quarrels. We are not a court. We are simply a diplomatic asylum living up to our obligations under the OAS."

Why was I letting myself be drawn into argument with this envoy of an envoy?

"There is something you have for me to sign?"

I had noticed the affidavit he had ready for my signature. It denied, point by point, the charges made against me by Juan del Campo. I now declared, in more elaborate form than I had done in registering the night before, that my sole reason for seeking asylum was not to escape justice, but because I was convinced that I could not expect justice from a territorial state from whose government my free conscience had driven me to defect—and that it was purely this defection, and no crime in the penal code of my country, that now placed me and my family in such immediate and mortal danger that I had no choice but to seek diplomatic asylum.

I nodded and complimented Licenciado Alvarez on a fine job— every curlicue as fine, I thought to myself, as he had composed for the super-criminal Romano. In fact it was the identical formal rebuttal with only certain words and phrases changed to meet the specific charges—in his case torture, extortion and murder, in mine, espionage, desertion and misappropriation of public funds. Romano was a monster and I still thought of myself as someone struggling against inhumanity in a world of dark imperfections. But in the filing cabinet of Licenciado Alvarez and in all those booklets spelling out the rules of diplomatic asylum at the various Inter-American Conventions, El Gordo and I enjoyed or suffered equal status under the law.

No, not quite, Licenciado Alvarez reminded me as he tucked back into his armful of bulging manila my personal folder, the still thin *cinco cinco cinco seis ocho nueve uno:* "I have one little warning. Until you are certified officially by His Excellency the Ambassador, you are still technically in provisional asylum. In other words your status has not been formally accepted by the territorial state from which you have fled. This is a kind of limbo where you enjoy physical asylum here but the state from which you defected still claims jurisdiction over you and may even try to assert their claim by *force majeure.*"

"You mean break in here and—"

"I do not mean to alarm you. We hardly expect anything that extreme. But we have had a few incidents where Bello militiamen have fired at provisional asylees—especially those against whom they bear a particular grudge. In every case, we file a protest, of course, but—"

"But the provisional asylee has already been executed inside the walls of the embassy," I said.

"Now, now," he said good-naturedly. "Let us not make too much of this. Let me simply suggest that when you go down to the compound for the mid-afternoon meal and the socializing and walking you are permitted until five o'clock, I would not stray too far from your fellows or venture too close to the gate. Not that we expect anything like that to happen. But why take an extra chance?"

Before I could respond, he added, "By the way, will you please raise your right hand and swear that what you have just put your name to is the truth, the whole truth and nothing but the truth, in the name of the Father, the Son and the Holy Ghost. It is just a formality, but I am also a public notary and I will stamp your document when I go back to my office."

Having served me, coped with me, lived up to the treaty obligations of his embassy for me, Licenciado Alvarez slightly turned from me and drew out another folder, another poetic number that reduced a human being to a sheaf of long-winded appeals and counter replies. Over my shoulder I could hear the supplications, "Please"—"What about me?"—"Have you heard?"—"Last week you said—" and could hear Licenciado Bertie Alvarez smiling, practiced, *"Próximamente usted podrá salir,"* and when the prisoner was asking for himself and his wife in the opposite wing, *"Próximamente ustedes podrán salir,"* and whether it was a firm promise or a diplomatic runaround, it floated through the long room like one of my favorite folk songs when it is sung by one of our husky-voiced back-country troubadors:

> Little little dove
> Little dove
> Where have you flown, my love?
> Have you found another nest?
> And brighter feathers you like best?

Or have you simply lost your way
And will fly back to me someday?
And so I wait   I wait   I wait . . .
For my love—
My little dove
Calling you home . . .

That is what I call typical of our songs, not as mournful as the
Mexicans, nor as merry as the Caribbean, sorrowful but always with
that little ocean-drop of hope that enlivened the ballad of Licenciado
Alvarez: *"Muy próximamente usted podrá salir."* As I walked down
the aisle to my cot I noticed that there were only three people who
did not swarm around Licenciado Alvarez and his manila folders
like bees around honey. El Indio Sandungo was sitting on his cot,
staring at what seemed to be nothing, staring into his dreams or his
mute Indian disenchantments. El Gordo Romano had finished his
ablutions and he was just as aloof and oblivious as the peasant
chieftain his Tigers had once hunted in southern jungles. Stretched
out in comfort on his double cot (I found out that evening that the
valet Jesusito slept on the floor beneath him on a straw mat), he
was reading a very thick book which turned out to be a Spanish
translation of *Gone with the Wind*. And from his extended shower
came Paco O'Higgins, back in his long-johns rolled down to his
waist—if one could so describe those rubber rolls of fat on old muscles that met in front of him to form that formidable belly.

"Paco," I called out. "Aren't you interested in finding out about
your safe passage?"

Paco performed one of those eloquent gestures of futility, shoulders pulled into neck and palms and head turned upward to the
heavens—the sort of thing that makes the gringo feel we are a
"colorful" people. "I will get out of this shithouse when I get out
and *chinga la madre* of little Bertie and his *próximamente usted
podrá salir.*" He went back to his cot, squatted down, reached into
his underpants and pulled out a pint bottle of rum that he had tied
around his waist with a heavy cord. He evidently carried his precious rum even into the shower for fear of having it filched. But
where the devil did he hoard that endless supply?

The departure of Licenciado Alvarez, our lifeline to the outside world, set off another congressional debate, with all of the senators on their feet delivering angry orations simultaneously. "What was the use of having a written agreement on diplomatic asylum if Angel thumbs his nose at the agreement?" "The Ambassador must be hand in glove with the Bello regime, otherwise he would protest! He would bring this scandal—this typical Communist violation of human rights—to the attention of the OAS!" "No!" shouted Rubén Silva, "he should call an emergency meeting of the OAS to expose Bello's cynical sabotage of the rights of sanctuary and safe passage to the entire American people!"

There were some who blamed the Ambassador for mendacity and timidity and there was a sharp, noisy, three-way division about Licenciado Bertie Alvarez. A party of the right thought he was doing everything that he claimed to do and that he was following up each case just as he promised. A disgusted middle group insisted that his smiles and promises were simply to cover up the miserable fact that it was all for show to keep the inmates submissive and manageable for another week, and that after each visit he stuffed our folders back in his filing cabinet and did not stir the papers that represented our existence until it was time to visit his zoo again. There was even an extremist group who believed that Bertie was secretly pro-Bello, and maliciously misrepresenting our cases so that he could punish us for our anti-revolutionary sins by forcing us to rot in this diplomatic halfway house between prison and freedom.

But the loudest of all drew me toward Johnie Valdez. He was standing in the aisle in the middle of the room. "My friends, my fellow-sufferers, let me remind you, it is not Bertie Alvarez, who has his job to do and who I think is hokey-doke. Do not get yourselves confused by the neutralists. We know who the real enemy is! If we did not, why in the name of Christ would we be here? The enemy is Angel!"

Our people adore speeches like that, and there were cries of "Petition! Petition! Let's all sign a petition!" Someone at the far end called "Hunger strike!" and there were some who called *"Como no?"*, *"Estoy listo!"*,—but—and this must be remembered and repeated both to our credit and discredit—someone else called out in a theatrically sexy voice, *"Yo también!"*, me too!, because *"Estoy listo"* means "I'm ready" and also has its double meaning for the boudoir. So the joke was made and the point was lost.

Momentito, the small, old-school servant from breakfast, appeared. "Gentlemen, good afternoon. In ten minutes we will be going outside for the afternoon meal. So if you wish to change or prepare yourself in any way—" As if by reflex he ended with a small bow. His manner was no different than if he had been addressing a formal gathering of the Ambassador's distinguished guests.

Change? I was still in my fishing pants and faded sports shirt. The same clothes in which I had left the beach house at the Playa de los Papagayos. In other words, I had arrived at this place with Marta the night before? No—it was as if the sun had fallen from its place of authority dividing night from day—and week from month. I had not seen my Marta in an eternity.

Ten minutes later I joined my fellow-asylees moving in single file up the aisle toward the corridor. A stairway would lead us to the outdoor compound where we would all have our *comida* together, where Marta and Clarita would be waiting.

From the second floor of the embassy, Momentito led us through a door marked Emergency Exit. I found myself following Paco and the old druggist Gamboa, and walking alongside Johnie Valdez. Johnie was chattering to me, but I wasn't really listening to his *charla.* We had stepped out to a metal landing that descended to the patio below. The storm of the night before had passed over us. The sunshine—it was a tropical November day—had an immediate effect on our motley parade. I saw the old man Gamboa, his hand still trembling, lift his face to the sun as he held on to the rail and

walked down the long steps a few rows ahead of me. I would not
go so far as to say that a live wire of animation sent its charge
through the long line of nondescript asylees descending the fire
escape. But there was a noticeable lifting of spirits—the sunshine,
the fresh air, the promise of something to fill the empty belly, the
prospect of a change of scene from that dormitory to out-of-doors
and, best of all, the anticipation of women. I had never been in
prison, which in these days of systematic injustice is something of a
confession, but in one day I had come to realize what suffering there
is in the physical absence of women. It was not even a sexual problem, or let us say not entirely a sexual consideration. When one is
cramped, dislocated, caged, committed to an atmosphere of oppressive confinement, reduced to a string of numbers in a bureaucratic
file, sex is not the first of the hungers. But there is something about
men, males, a regiment or a prisonful or a crowded dormitory of
them bedded together in narrow proximity that produces a depres-
sive state of apathy. It is like a color spectrum that omits the stripe
of life we call red.

As we made our way down the metal stairway, moving slowly
because some of the older ones like Gamboa had to cling to the
railing and take one step at a time, I had a chance to look over
the high walls that surrounded the embassy grounds. I could see the
ring of Bello militiamen, sharply uniformed boys with gleaming
automatic weapons. Their precision was frightening. I wondered
how deeply it penetrated the wearers of the handsomely fitted uniforms who executed their turns so smartly and handled their weapons
without the old, familiar, dangerous but rather heart-warming
carelessness? I remembered when we flew back from Mexico to
celebrate Angel's triumphant entry into the capital and to accept the
provisional presidency how the excited rebel kids would swarm into
the Hilton lobby playfully swinging their automatics like noisy little
boys with toy guns that go "Ta-ta-ta-ta-ta-ta-ta—you're dead!" In
the crowded elevator of the Hilton on my way up to meet Angel in
the penthouse suite from which he was directing the newborn Revolution, a ragged kid in improvised camouflage showed his high spirits
by swinging his automatic around by its strap. "*Joven*, you must be
a little more careful—that thing could go off," I said. "Oh, comrade,

forgive me," the green boy said (we were all comrades in those delirious early days), "I did not mean to scare you—I was just feeling so happy—no more fighting—no more killing—Viva Angel!" And as a sign of good faith, of good feeling, he handed me the automatic—as an overjoyed child hands you his favorite toy on the day of the Three Kings. Now my peach-faced sixteen-year-old rebel might be a member of that crack militia besieging our sanctuary and staring up over the wall at us. I stared back at them, my young comrades of the early days when all of us except the terrified Zamoristas were drawn together in a daily and seemingly endless celebration of hope. "As soon as we have consolidated our Revolution," Angel Bello had shouted to a million people jammed into the Zocalo between the Presidential Palace and the cathedral, "as soon as we have tried and shot the Zamora *gusanos* who are still hiding among us, we will not even need an army. I tell you, we will have Boy Scouts directing traffic, and we will use the military funds that Zamora squandered to build schools and hospitals for our poor little farmers who have never even set eyes on such institutions!"

And now these Boy Scouts wore black boots manufactured in Germany and glared at us with attitudes prefabricated for export to the Soviet satellites. I could see them outside the gate too—there was a rear gate as well as the front gate through which Alejandro had driven us the night before. Two of them were within a meter of that rear gate. "Look at them," Gamboa grumbled. "They would just as soon shoot us as—"

"You think it has not happened?" the death-head Silva asked. "Just before I came in those butchers fired right through the gates."

"How can the Ambassador allow such an outrage?" someone behind me said.

"The Ambassador is a *puta*." The coarse voice of Paco could be heard further down the metal stairway. Then the same drunken voice, this time directed at Angel's militiamen tensely watching us descend, bellowed as through a megaphone, "*Hola,* you little green worms, go back to your big *melón* of a boss and tell him that one of these days he is going to open his mouth so wide he will choke on his own *cojones.*"

There was laughter, some of it nervous. "Hombre, for the sake of God, are we not in enough trouble already?"

"—in the eyes of their mothers," Paco called back.

"Paco, old kid, take it easy," Johnie called down the stairway. "We all feel the same way, but let's try to live a little longer, hokey-dokey?"

"Hokey-dokey up your much-abused ass," Paco roared.

Johnie shook his head and chuckled as if Paco had paid him a gallant compliment. "That Paco—what a pistol!" he said to me. "Any time you want to get drunk just stand in front of him and let him breathe on you."

By this time we had reached the first-floor landing and could no longer see over the brick and stucco wall. I stepped off the bottom rung of the fire escape onto the sandy dirt floor of the courtyard. What we had entered was not the entire al fresco grounds of the embassy, but only a rear area which had been fenced off from the rest. The sun baked into the dried-out patio and the late autumn air was warm but fresh. Now it seemed that I had only partially sensed how stale and fetid was the air of our overcrowded dormitory. But my next impression was that the promenade and common eating-area were bare, unimaginative and uncared for. There were only a few trees, a silvery green olive tree and a date palm, and both of them looked as if they were struggling for life in the sandy soil. Beneath the olive tree was a primitive shrine, with a crude white cross rising from a small Gothic arch in which a homemade dark Virgin had been placed. In curved niches to either side of her stood smaller images of two saints intended to serve as her guardians. On the ledge in front of the Virgin some small flowers had been offered, some small white blossoms that had gone limp in the sun and a spray of pale orange bougainvillea from a vine that was making a feeble effort to spread itself up over the rear wall. There was a long table, at one end of which Momentito presided, assisted by a very young and very homely maid who was helping him set up the large terra-cotta pots from which they would soon be serving the main meal of the day on chipped pottery dishes. Meanwhile the line was already forming, a colorless line of men in washed-out, wrinkled clothing.

"What do we have for lunch?" I asked Johnie Valdez.

"Are you keeding?" he said in English. "One day we have black beans and rice and the next day we have rice and black beans.

Thanks to that *melón* who sold our Revolution down the river—"

It occurred to me that the inadequacies of our menu were more to be blamed on the embassy obligated to protect and sustain us than on the Bello regime. But Johnie seemed to blame every circumstance of our ordeal on the inspired egomaniac whom we had trusted so eagerly with our Revolution.

"And the ladies?" I said. "I thought they were joining us."

Johnie gestured toward the fire escape. "Here come the old girls now."

Following closely behind the billowy Señora Lorona were Marta and Clarita. Clarita still wore the gold lamé evening gown which had worked so well in the masquerade of the night before. And I was surprised to see that she had not removed her makeup and that her coiffure was still the chic upsweep that had helped to pass her through the Bello cordon.

"*Chihuahua!*" Johnie said. "There's a juicy-looking little perch. I better get to her first before every *macho* in the yard takes a bite out of her."

"That is my daughter Clara," I said.

"Justo old pal, a thousand pardons. Of course I had no intention —such a charming young girl, so genteel—one can see at a glance she is a well-brought-up young lady, not one of these *gallinas* that—"

But by this time I had left Johnie and his apologies and was hurrying forward to embrace Marta and Clarita.

"Marta! Marta! Clarita! My darlings! How are you? What's been happening? Already it seems like years."

"The longest day of our life," said Marta.

"Popee, you and Mama want to talk," Clarita said. "I will take a little stroll, it feels so good to be out."

"All right, *querida*," I said. "But do not stray too far away. There are many strangers here."

"Popee," Clarita said reproachfully. "I am not five years old."

I nodded and smiled at Marta who had changed out of her old fishing outfit into a faded print dress that fitted her oddly, loose around her shoulders and breasts and tight around the hips.

"Julia loaned me this," she said. "The very latest in what lady asylees will be wearing this season."

"At least you can still joke."

"I'm not really joking," Marta said.

"Do I know Julia?"

"Doctora Julia Bécquer," Marta said. "She sends you her love. She stayed upstairs to help an old lady who's very sick."

"Oh—la Doctora!"

Julia Bécquer had served as our Secretary of Health and Social Welfare for the first year of the Green Revolution. In the days when the underground was helping the Bello rebels by sabotaging the Zamora regime in the cities, Julia had been one of Garbo's most effective lieutenants. She had helped him turn the largest hospital in the capital into an elaborate network of anti-Zamora activity. It was there that Angel's rebels were hidden when Romano's Tigers were trying to hunt them down.

"I thought Julia had escaped to Mexico," I said.

"She's been here ever since she defected," Marta said. "Well, she didn't really defect. It's like our story—she kept waiting and waiting, hoping she could still have some influence on Angel because she had done so much for him. And then one night Garbo told her a special detachment was coming for her and he couldn't do anything to help—he was already under suspicion as a non-Communist. She's been here for seven months."

"*Próximamente usted podrá salir,*" I said.

"So they say that in your wing too? Señora Lorona's exact words."

"She and Licenciado Alvarez must take '*Próximamente-usted-podrá-salir*' lessons together," I said.

"You are also able to joke."

"Joke? The conditions here, when I see what a mess it is—this whole farce of 'immediate safe passage'—what we should have done—"

"That is what I came downstairs for," Marta said. "Not to hear how much you miss me, or to enjoy the delicious black beans and rice which I understand is the specialty of the house, but to have you tell me what we *should* have done. *Mierda!*"

Even though it was galling that Marta should stab so quickly at one of my most vulnerable shortcomings, this expenditure of spendthrift energies on the might-have-beens, still it was warming to have her at my side spicing her language with the coarseness that was as much a part of her as her handsome face, her blunt honesty and her hearty enjoyments.

"Marta," I said. "From the way things look now we are going to be in this shithouse—"

"Justo—that does not sound like you!"

"I know. It sounds like my friend Paco O'Higgins. But it is a shit-house where we're treated worse than the poor burro of the most heartless *guajiro* and—and—I've forgotten my point—"

"Justo, you seem a little drunk to me. Have you been drinking?"

"No, of course not. Well, maybe a little. O'Higgins is a good friend. Oh—now I remember what I was trying to say—we may be in here a long time. It will be a hard life. The mattresses are very narrow and very hard. When the fellow in the next cot farts—"

"Justo—what is happening to you? I'm the old bird who is supposed to lay the blue eggs in this family."

It's true. I was not in the habit of using vulgarities. But try to sleep eighteen inches away from the next man in a dank room full of strangers, or men who would be strangers if the net of ill fortune had not swept you all up into the live-bait tank of sanctuary, and something in you will need to say fart and need to say fuck and need to say shit. It is the universal language of the wretched and the damned, of the *hijos de la chingada*, that growing international association, the first and probably the last international, where the powerless *chingadas* squirm and fume, hunger, curse and beat help-lessly against the great wall of the fortress controlled by the one power audacious enough to usurp the place of God.

"Justo—" Her strong, self-confident voice cut through the heat of the equatorial sun. The sun was beating into my head and making the rum boil up in my brain. I felt fuzzy, dizzy, but pleasantly so. I felt apart from the other *hijos*. Out of focus in the background I saw them forming a long, listless *cola* for their daily rations of black beans and rice. "Justo—are you listening to me?" I saw several shapeless women and an old man genuflect and then go to their knees in prayer at the base of the shrine. "Listen to me, Justo. We have things to talk about. The time is passing too quickly."

Through the sunlight baking into the sandy floor of the courtyard,

I saw the unfamiliar figure of a young lady, pleasingly buxom, in a gold evening dress and golden slippers with extremely high heels. In fact, they were so high and so narrow and she had such difficulty walking on them that she seemed—to me—touching and outlandish. But to the men she was not outlandish. To the men she was exactly what Johnie Valdez had called her in his first, spontaneous moment of desire, "the tastiest little perch in the lake." I saw them on the lunch line watching her, their eyes on the two halves of her large buttocks moving under the clinging, concealing-revealing golden fabric that glistened in the afternoon light like human skin oiled to enrich its tawny surface in the shine of the tropical sun. I saw the nudging and sensed the wicked *picardías* that rippled along the line. Clarita walked along that line without once looking at the men, yet encouraging them to taste her body with their eyes. The same Clarita whom we had thought of as backward, who, even when she had confessed a liking for a young schoolmate, Beto Morales, had been too shy to know how to go about prompting him to invite her to the *Quinceañera*. Marta had had to plot secretly with Beto's mother to bring the miracle about. "Poor Clarita, she seems so lost, such a permanent child," Marta had said. "At her age I was madly in love —with a different *machito* every week. I knew how to handle them."

"At Clarita's age you would have been a little whore if only someone had told you there was money in it," I had said to Marta. We had laughed together and reassured each other—every young tree had its own time to blossom. That had been only a few months ago.

"Marta, there must be someone who can loan her a dress. And the lipstick—the rouge—her hair. How could you let her go out like that? She looks like a ten-peso *sancha* swinging her ass along the Avenida Miranda. You complain about my rum but what were you doing? You should have stopped her."

"I tried. I told her. She refused to listen."

"Refused to listen to her mother!"

"I am telling you, Justo—not only refused—when I tried to wipe it off with a towel she ducked away from me and ran out to the fire escape. There was no way I could stop her."

Placed around the patio were crude tables with benches attached, as in public parks, and at one of them, waiting for Jesuscito to bring them their special *comida,* sat El Gordo Romano and Búfalo de Sa. Búfalo winked at his master and made a suggestive Latin gesture. Inside his freshly laundered Yucateca shirt, El Gordo shook with laughter. I could feel his eyes undressing Clarita even though I could not see them behind his dark glasses.

"That *cochino*," I said.

"My God—Romano," Marta said. "How is it someone hasn't strangled him in his sleep?"

"It may happen yet."

Marta looked at me. She knew I was a peaceful man. Then I saw Búfalo rise and approach Clarita. I couldn't hear what he was saying, but he was being very gallant, very Latin, the experienced assistant *gallo* who had delivered a thousand ripe little hens into the claws of the king *macho* of the aviary. I saw Clarita look up and smile and toss her head and half-ignore his advances, temptingly, as if she had just graduated with honors from a finishing school for coquettes. I jumped up and ran to her side. I grabbed her arm and pulled her away. I was so close to the large, heavy-bearded face of Búfalo de Sa that it seemed as if I had run into the terrain of an onrushing bull. Clarita spun her arm free of my grip. "Papa—leave me alone! Never do that again! Never!"

There was a change in her voice. I felt a rage of frustration at losing control of her, and especially with those Calibans enjoying the small drama they had created. I dragged her along with me. She tried to twist away and I slapped her. Marta had slapped her occasionally, but for me it was the first time.

Marta came between us. Clarita was crying. I was crying. "Justo! Stop hitting her! And with everybody watching!"

I glared at her. My nerves were trembling. "Whatever you do, everybody is watching! Where is there any privacy in this—"

"Justo—enough!—No bad language," Marta commanded, as if she had not disturbed me with the frankness of her conversation in front of Clarita all her life.

A child again, Clarita allowed herself to be embraced in Marta's strong, protective arms.

"Clarita," I said. "I am sorry—I—forgive me. But those two men—are very bad. You mustn't go near them or encourage them."

Clarita turned away and pressed her face against Marta's shoulder. During the years of our struggle against Zamora she had been too young to understand. When we all flew home from our last exile in Mexico we had told her that Zamora was a bad man and that now we were going to have a better life under the system we called democracy. Marta and I both thought we should spare her the lurid accounts of the excesses of the Tigers of Romano. But now I wondered if we had overprotected her. It was like trying to tell the young Germans of the postwar generation of the genocidal insanity of their fathers. In fact, I remembered a Sunday breakfast a few years earlier when I had mentioned the name of Himmler, and Clarita said she had never heard of him. And then I asked her if she knew the names of Goering and Goebbels and she said no. And then I became fascinated. I thought of all my shibboleths of the nineteen thirties and forties. Did she know Mussolini? Laval? The fascist wars in Ethiopia and Spain? Did she know the names Churchill and FDR? No—no—no. It didn't seem possible. How could the names and causes that had obsessed one generation be totally unknown to its children? I went on with the catechism—had she ever heard of Joe Louis, Judy Garland, Manolete. . . . To her, "No, no, no's," I said to Marta, "I can't believe it—that wide a gulf between us and Clarita's generation—imagine not knowing—" Then suddenly Clarita had run out of the room, sobbing, and I realized that what I had intended as innocent intellectual curiosity had pushed Clarita into a corner that was thoughtless and cruel.

But now I wished that we had informed her of her own home-reared Francos and Himmlers because in her ignorance or innocence it seemed merely as if I were scolding her for flirting with older men, better dressed, more self-confident, and in this *chingada* atmosphere, rather more attractive men than the motley collection meekly waiting on line for their daily plate of beans.

"Clarita," I repeated, wanting to sound firm but unable to keep my voice from shaking, "I want you to promise you will never go near those two men again."

"You are not going to order me around like that," she said. "You are not the president of this place."

"I am still your father."

"I will talk to anyone I please."

"Marta, tell her who they are," I said. "And make her wipe off that obscene lipstick. Wash her face."

"All right, all right—why don't you go and stand in the food line. Bring us three plates."

"I'll bring two. I have no appetite."

"Bring three," Marta said. "Julia tells me the evening meal is a pea soup as anemic as the morning coffee. No matter how upset you are you need food to keep going—even their *cursi* beans and rice."

So I stood on line—only a short one now—with the other grumblers. Everybody was grumbling. How rotten the food was. How hot the sun. No comfortable places to sit. No shade. No consideration . . . Momentito dipped the beans and rice onto our cracked clay plates with practiced humility as if we were at a diplomatic affair. But obviously he and the homely little waif Reencarnación were under orders to serve subnormal portions. One scoop of rice and one scoop of beans. Now I could understand why some of the old hands did not dawdle in the sunlight when they reached the patio but took their positions in front of the line, even before Momentito and Reencarnación carried out the brown clay pots. That way, if the single scoopful per diner had not exhausted the supply by the end of the line, there might be meager second helpings for the persistent.

I carried back the three plates and the three tin spoons I had picked out as the cleanest of the fly-specked utensils on the weathered wooden table.

"You mean they actually give us spoons?" Marta said. "I thought we were supposed to eat with our fingers."

A frail-looking woman with gray hair in an old rag of a dress nodded from the other end of the table. There was always someone agreeing or disagreeing or at least monitoring your conversation in sanctuary. "Like animals they treat us. Worse than animals."

I nodded. The complaints, the grumbling, the frustration, the nagging, gnawing, niggling nothingness of sanctuary. Of course they had a right to complain, for they were legitimate political refugees, most of them, and there was nothing in the official literature of asylum that even faintly suggested that they were to be treated like political prisoners. The rub was that we were being treated just as Angel Bello wished us to be treated, not as the sovereign republics of America had agreed we should be treated.

We tasted the beans and looked at each other in dismay. Black beans and rice sounds pedestrian, but I have eaten our national dish in expensive restaurants and in poor sugarcane villages and hundreds of times in our own home when Marta had kept a knowledgeable eye on the cooking of María Magdalena, when each bean had had its own identity, had been flavored with chunks of salt pork, green peppers, bay leaves, ground black pepper and simmered in pure olive oil. They had been cradled in a round white bed of rice cooked *al dente*—Marta knew a hundred ways of preparing rice, all minor but not necessarily unimportant works of genius. The rice had to be of the finest quality, poured slowly into the pot of boiling water. Marta and María Magdalena worked with the precision of alchemists. At exactly the right moment the flame was lowered, a cover was put on the pot, the rice allowed to simmer, and all the Virgins protect us from the wrath of Marta and María Magdalena if anyone should lift the lid before the work of art was completed. Then a great slab of fresh butter was encouraged to seep through the steaming, separate white kernels. The thick, rich gravy of the beans alive with spices would make love to the rice and the final touch was the addition of the crisp green onions fresh from our garden that María Magdalena chopped quickly and expertly like a living and loving machine for Marta to sprinkle generously over her chef d'oeuvre. That was black beans and rice in its glory, and my mouth or maybe just my mind salivates with longing when I call it back to memory.

But my mouth dries and tightens in bitterness at the travesty of the national dish that Momentito had scooped up with his ancien régime, apologetic smile. The beans had been overcooked until they had lost all identity in a flavorless paste. The rice, a victim of cruel neglect, too long abandoned in too much water, had become a tasteless mush. The gravy was a sickly cousin of the morning coffee, pale-colored water. I tried to swallow but literally gagged on it.

"I think the cook must be a secret agent of Angel Bello," I said.

"The cook!" Marta said. "The cook is a little nothing. Not even a *pendejo*. He has nothing to *pendejo* with. This was cooked by a culinary eunuch. Maybe the real secret agent of Angel is your friend the Ambassador, and this specialty of the house—this Garbage à la

Embassy—is the secret weapon with which he plans to poison us so he won't have to bother with all the legal complications."

I looked around at the various tables in the courtyard where nearly a hundred asylees were partaking of this gray picnic. Most of them had emptied their plates. Some were now arguing with the helpless Momentito that the kitchen should produce another large bowlful. "But look at all these people," I said. "Somehow they manage to survive."

"I suppose you build up an immunity," Marta conceded. "As with any poison. The human body is God's masterpiece of endurance."

"God? That sounds strange coming from you. I can't remember when I've heard you mention God except as a curse word."

"When I was Clarita's age I think I believed in God."

We rarely discussed religion. Marta had been a casual agnostic, too much occupied with the trivia and the realities of life to work either toward a serious atheism or a revitalizing of the traditional faith of her family.

"And now?"

"Now?" She laughed. "I've got my own religion."

"What do you believe now, Marta?"

"I believe there is a Mad Scientist in the sky who keeps inventing new creatures and testing their ability to suffer—to see how far He can go before they reach their breaking point where they deny Him, blow up His laboratory and finally destroy Him."

"In other words, make a revolution. Isn't that what Angel is trying to do?"

"No—I mean another kind of revolution—where you blow up the Mad Scientist in the sky without replacing Him with a Mad Scientist down here testing our ability to suffer. What kind of revolution would you call that?"

"That will be the revolution to end revolutions," I said. "When the leader no longer uses the slogan 'Death to Tyrants' to pull down the old tyrant and leap into the power seat himself. Ready to commit murder in the name of mercy."

"In other words, never."

"Well, at least not until we understand our own humanity. Until we no longer enjoy torturing each other."

"You know what I think," Marta said. "I don't think we should wait for that revolution. Everybody's always waiting. For two thousand years they've waited for the Second Coming. Sometimes I think the whole human race are *pendejos*, just hanging there upside down like bats in a cave, waiting. I don't want to wait. I don't have the slightest interest in saving humanity. I just want to save you and me and Clarita and get our *nalgas* out of this hellhole and start to live again. No more theories. No more politics. Revolutions—dreams—always turning into nightmares . . ."

"Because man is still not ready—" I began.

"Maybe man is not ready," Marta said, "but Justo dear, woman is ready—at least this old pigeon is ready—to move to Miami or Rio or Mexico City and have champagne and marvelous jelly omelets for breakfast and make love after the four o'clock siesta. I want to have witty friends to dinner and help Clarita make a brilliant and happy marriage—there you have my own little personal revolution and to hell with Rousseau and Marx and Angel Bello and Sartre and all the public prophets—maybe that includes you—who help to make such a public mess of what could be a beautiful, private world."

All this time Clarita was sitting as far away from us as possible, at the extreme end of the long bench and facing away from us.

I felt something moving against my leg and looked down to see a small, bony, tiger-striped cat, not yet fully grown but already with a belly beginning to swell with embryo alley cats. It looked forsaken with its lusterless fur and its skinny legs, which were all white to the knees as if it were wearing high white stockings beneath a dusty, worn, shrunken tiger skin. Although it rubbed against my legs, it drew away in fear when I tried to stroke its head.

"Don't touch it," Marta said. "It looks so ratty. It could be carrying some disease."

"*Pobrecita*," I said. "Poor little thing. You would think a cat in an embassy—"

"It probably sneaked through the gates just like us," Marta said. "Why should they treat a cat any better than they treat a president, or a madonna of the hospitals like Doctora Bécquer? Hmm?"

There was no answer. I stared at the lumpy food that unexpect-

edly had provoked our philosophical debate. The mangy cat returned and caressed itself against the back of my legs. I thought it
was begging for food and started to lower my plate when I heard,
"Here, kitty, kitty, here little mother cat." I looked up to see
Clarita calling the stray to the plate she had set on the ground in
front of her. The misshapen little cat—in the quick way of knowing
that is the great talent of their kind—looked up, studied Clarita
carefully and then went toward this new benefactor on her cautious,
skinny white legs. She sniffed at the hem of Clarita's glittering gown
and then at the plate near her feet. She did not grab at it as I
thought a hungry cat would. She slowly moved her nose and white
whiskers around the entire plate. Then she took a few tentative licks.
But apparently soggy rice and mushy beans were no more to the
liking of a half-starved cat than they were to humans accustomed
to gourmet cooking. She drew her mouth away and looked up at
Clarita with bright yellow-green eyes. Clarita reached down, picked
her up and cradled her. "Good little girl," she said. "Good little
mother cat."

I was feeling badly about Clarita and this seemed a good excuse
to approach her. Marta was right. She was only a child, thrown
without warning into an adult world—no, not merely an adult world
but a malformed corner of that world.

"Look how she lets you pick her up," I said. "You always had a
way with animals. Even when you were a baby."

Clarita half-turned away from me and hugged the little cat.

"She's so friendly," I said. "She ought to have a name."

"She already has a name," Clarita said, still not looking at me.
"Dolores."

"But we have a cat called Dolores."

Clarita shook her head. "We do not. The only one we have is this
Dolores."

"The mother cat—at home."

"We don't have a home any more," Clarita said. "So nothing in
that house belongs to us any more. So there is no cat that belongs to
us by the name of Dolores except this sweet little one." She held the
new Dolores above her head and looked into its blinking face.
"Your name is Dolores." The cat made a small meow of protest and
Clarita lowered her to a more comfortable position.

"Dolores and I are going to take a walk together, all around the courtyard, aren't we, Dolores?"

As she turned and walked away, lowering her face to nuzzle the dirty little stray, the gold lamé of her gown caught the sunlight and came alive like a net of shimmering little fish. A glimmering, confused half-woman of fifteen and a shabby eight-month-old kitten unprepared for motherhood . . . And at home—but Clarita was maddeningly logical like her tough-minded mother—our home was now only the memory of a home. If ever we were to escape this prison-asylum, it seemed unlikely or at least unreal that we would return home to the beach at Papagayos. And even if we should return on the wave of still another revolution, that "clean revolution" I was forever seeking like the Holy Grail, even then it would never again be the home we left behind, of which the original Dolores and her fecund supply of kittens, and María Magdalena and Don Pepe, our toothless butler, and all the other familiar faces of our human, bird and animal world were such an integral part. No, once more, Clarita, no matter how deep her present confusion, spoke the hard truth and I was the dreamer. If we did not have a home at the Playa de los Papagayos then of course we no longer had a cat there by the name of Dolores. Clarita spoke the existentialist truth: the only cat by the name of Dolores that she possessed was the one she held this moment in her arms.

I took a step in the direction of my daughter and was about to call after her that I didn't want her to wander around this courtyard unescorted, but Marta had read my intent. "Let her go," she said. "It is difficult, but we cannot be at her side every moment. If you nag her, you'll only drive her further away."

I nodded. I watched her go. The part of her from the waist up that was tenderly holding the pregnant stray was the plump, overweight, little-girl Clarita who had joined us at Marta's studio shack on the beach. The part from the waist down that was moving in a way calculated to catch the eyes of men hungry for more than food was the new Clarita to whom I had not yet been introduced, the loving daughter of yesterday now a hostile stranger.

"Come, we will walk around the yard too," Marta said. "The time passes so quickly. Soon we will be back in that stuffy jail. We need the exercise."

So we walked, arm in arm, slowly because Marta was favoring her bad knee.

"Maybe Doctora Julia can help you while we're here," I said.

"A pregnant woman, an old lady who's dying, a mother with two small children who keep getting the colic from the terrible food—Julia has enough on her hands," Marta said. "I'm strong—I'll live. The knee doesn't bother me too much physically. It's the psychological part that hurts. It keeps saying, 'Marta, old girl, you're not as young as you think you look. I'm putting this stiffness in you so you will act your age and not make a fool of yourself.' "

"Nonsense," I said. "Look at the way those men are enjoying you as we go by their tables. I'll have to watch you as carefully as Clarita."

This was not entirely in jest. Marta carried herself with her old flirtatious self-confidence. And despite the extra flesh over the old ballet muscles, she still had the sachet of sexuality that made men look up as she passed, as if they were saying, "There goes an old one—an old one but a good one!"

Marta laughed, pleased. "Thank you. I confess I've had quite a few temptations in my time. Some of your friends—it would surprise you what they've tried to do behind your back. But I don't plan to put horns on you with any of these *pendejos*. Why should I when I have the only handsome man in this whole fiesta?"

My hand was between her upper arm and the side of her breast. I moved it surreptitiously. "I wish there were somewhere we could go. Right now."

"Señora Lorona explained everything to me, very discreetly," Marta said. "Friday is the Day of Matrimony. Married couples are given the use of private rooms on the second floor. Actually I think they belong to Señora Lorona and Licenciado Alvarez. But for one hour—"

"How romantic! What does Señora Lorona do—knock on the door when our time is up?"

"We will learn about it on Friday," Marta said. "Señora Lorona, who is full of fascinating information, also informed me that we are allowed visitors once a month on Sunday afternoons. And there is also a special luncheon—a quarter of a pound of meat, chopped beef or one pork chop—"

"Cooked by the same assassin who tries to poison us with the rice and beans?"

Marta suddenly stopped and embraced me. "Oh God, Justo, are we ever going to get out of here?"

It always unnerved me when Marta showed fear.

"Of course we are," I said automatically. "The Ambassador isn't going to hand me over to Angel. He knows I would tell what really goes on if he let them put me on trial. He has our ten thousand dollars."

"But what if he turns you over but keeps us here? Then he might assume you'd keep silent to protect us."

Marta's logic was painful. Of course I was the only one the Bello regime was charging with common crimes, the basis for demanding my return to its jurisdiction. Marta and Clarita would continue being diplomatic guests of the embassy. But if I were to reveal the brisk trade in human misery conducted by the eminent Ambassador, who knew what would happen to them?

"We should walk a little more," I said. "The sun is dropping over the wall."

We were approaching half a dozen stone steps that led down to a laundry room in the basement. Leaning against the wall enjoying one of his master's big cigars was Búfalo de Sa. The door was open and we could see a row of washtubs—it seemed like a large bare cellar room that led to other subterranean chambers. As we passed, a small, plump woman with artificially yellow hair appeared. She looked around anxiously, paused a moment to adjust her hair and although she obviously saw Marta, pretended not to and hurried off.

"That is a lady by the name of Señora Gamboa—she asked me to call her 'Cookie.' Her husband is a druggist. She has been telling me how—"

"Yes, yes, I know the story," I said. "The wrong Enrique Gamboa."

"They've been here almost ten months. She says she is going out of her mind."

Coming up the laundry room steps was El Gordo Romano. His white Yucateca shirt was not as immaculate as when I had seen him earlier. It was wrinkled now and the arms had become smudged from leaning against the basement laundry walls. He paused on the top step, took a deep breath, called Búfalo's attention with an imperious *ssst,* and they strolled off in the opposite direction from Señora Gamboa. Across the yard near the wall the old druggist was dozing in the fading sun.

"Señora Gamboa may be going out of her mind, but she is finding a bit of diversion on her way to the madhouse," I said.

Marta smiled. "At breakfast this morning she was boring me with how worried she is about her husband. He has a weak heart, he already has had two attacks and Cookie is afraid if they don't let him out of here soon—"

"She'll have a *criatura* by El Gordo and there will be one more little monster in this world."

Marta laughed. "This place is a mess!" But she did not say it with the sense of outrage at the casual courtyard cuckolding of old man Gamboa that I might have expressed. I'm afraid Marta was a true daughter of Rabelais. As we were about to pass the gate I remembered Licenciado Alvarez' warning. I could see the young militiamen patrolling half a dozen meters away. I was still in limbo, a fair target. I paused. "Shall we go back the other way?"

"It's prettier on this side," Marta said. "There's still a little sun along the wall."

"No," I said. "The sight of those simple country boys in those tight Soviet uniforms depresses me."

"Whatever you wish, Señor Presidente," Marta said lightly. Apparently Señora Lorona had informed her of the matrimonial conveniences but not of the inconveniences of venturing too close to the open-grilled gates. "Anyway," Marta went on, "there is Clarita. You see, once she has the kitten in her arms she's perfectly content. She is simply looking for something warm to hold on to—apart from us."

"As long as she doesn't hold on to El Gordo and Búfalo."

"If you nag her with those names," Marta said, "it will have exactly the opposite effect."

"I will strangle them. If they touch her I'll strangle them."

"No—Búfalo will strangle you, he's a professional. That is the way he makes his living. And El Gordo will look on with great pleasure."

Probably true. I had heard that Búfalo and Jesusito stayed awake in four-hour watches throughout the night—with Jesusito under orders to awaken Búfalo the moment anyone approached or made a threatening move toward El Gordo.

By this time we had reached Clarita. A young man I had not noticed before, frail in stature, slightly stooped and sickly pale, was stroking the head of Dolores II.

"Listen, Mama. She is purring," Clarita said. "Momentito told me he would find a little liver in the kitchen for her. We are going to make you a nice, fat, happy cat, aren't we, little mother?"

She kissed the cat on its small, dry nose. It was a case of genuine love or the need for love and at the same time of course she was showing off for the young man. He was standing shyly with his head lowered to his chest, as if he were embarrassed to look us in the face. "Oh, this is Miguel Flores," Clarita said, "My mama, Señora Bravo de Moreno"—then she seemed to include me with reluctance—"and my father, Señor Moreno Suárez."

The young man bowed slightly and mumbled his *"A sus órdenes',"* and *"Con mucho gusto's"* and *"Muy amable's."* The hand he extended was limp and damp. "Flores," I said. "You are not by any chance related to Professor Flores? Alfonso?"

"My father," he said.

"So you are the brother of—"

"Tacho." He nodded. The same Tacho whom Alejandro had inadvertently lost to the Little Green Angels who broke into his house before Alejandro could smuggle him into the embassy grounds.

"I met him once at the University," I said. "He came up to speak to me after a lecture I gave."

"I remember," Miguel Flores said quietly. "It was in the first months after we won. I should say, 'thought' we had won. I was with Tacho when he came up to the podium."

"Of course," I said. "Forgive me. Of course I remember."

But I did not. Miguel Flores was one of those pale, shadowy brothers that so many dynamic older brothers seem to have. Tacho had been lean and wound tight like a spring. I could see him vividly —his dark hair falling forward over his forehead because he spoke so vigorously, his manner of emphasizing his speech first with a gesture of his right hand and then his left. But this younger brother Miguelito, shy and retiring, had faded into the background.

"And now if you will excuse me," young Flores said, and he

politely mentioned each one of us by name, including Dolores II to whom he bowed as nicely as he had to the rest of us.

"What a nice young man!" Marta said.

Clarita said nothing. She looked at me and moved several steps away, the cat still cradled in her arms.

"You see," Marta went on, "you make yourself and Clarita so upset over a few moments of small talk with that gorilla of Romano's and the next time you look around she's having a pleasant conversation with a well-bred boy from a very fine family."

"My God, Marta," I said, "you make it sound like a romantic promenade around the plaza on a Sunday evening. This is a zoo where all the animals roam together—little fawns exposed to lions and tigers."

Instead of answering, Marta took my hand and pressed it in our old signal of love in a way that spoke to me clearly: Yes, it is hard, hard, but hold on to yourself.

Señora Lorona waddled up to us. "Ladies," she said, including others at nearby tables or strolling past, as if she were a kindergarten teacher in a schoolyard herding her brood together, "it's time to go inside again. Will you kindly assemble at the bottom of the stairs." She went from group to group, expertly shepherding them toward the fire escape.

Marta and I embraced briefly. I turned to Clarita, but Marta said, "Not yet. I will tell you when."

My vision was blurred by tears. I wanted to take my daughter in my arms. I wanted to say, "Sleep well." Or, "I'm sorry." Something. Instead I stood helplessly and watched them join a cluster of other women moving slowly, reluctantly toward the fire escape behind their formidable leader, Señora Lorona.

Clarita turned from the straggly line for a moment and handed the new Dolores to Momentito. He accepted the small cat sympathetically. But as he carried her away, the neglected Dolores, obviously unused to so much attention, scratched his hand and jumped out of his arms. Momentito looked at me apologetically. *"Pobrecita,"* he said. "I will try to find her later and feed her the liver as the charming Señorita requests."

I thanked him. Humble and powerless, a mere menial in a great embassy, he seemed to represent a tiny grain of humanity on a vast beach of unfeeling, empty shells. I moved toward the steps and watched the ladies ascend. Around me was the small talk, lewd comments on legs, backsides, the revealing of upper thighs as they raised their legs to the next step, the comparative sizes of their bosoms, some of them moving with a life of their own, coarse observations about the youngest, most succulent addition to the mango tree that I was not supposed to overhear.

I turned away. It was understood that the men had an additional ten minutes while the ladies were led back to their quarters. Marta was right once again. I must hold on to myself. I must trust her to protect and handle Clarita. I must think positively of a future that held the promise of freedom in some distant land where the family could be reunited and knit closely again. I thought of Clarita, a little too large and heavy to be sitting on my knee, but still begging, as she had only a week or so ago, "Please, Popee. Read me *The Little Prince.*"

Tears. I was ashamed of my tears. I didn't brush them but pulled them out of my eyes with the tips of my fingers. The president, even the provisional president of a revolutionary "republic" should not cry. For the true twentieth-century revolutionary, there was too much killing to permit tears. In the name of an abstract humanity, he must kill multitudes of people, traitors, counterrevolutionaries, enemies of the people. In the name of People he must kill people. The true revolutionist eludes the secret police until he is in power and can install his own secret police. It was said of Stalin that he never cried. Instead of tears, he sentenced his fellow-comrades to Lubianka so that they could cry for him. And although Khrushchev was softer and Mao was Oriental and Angel Bello was an erratic Latin whose moods and mind could change like our tropical weather (where sun and heat and rain and storm and sun again often occur in the course of a single hour), they all had in common the consolidation of the Revolution in the form of personal power. From the French Revolution of the eighteenth century to our own Revolution, it is no haphazard coincidence that these revolutions devour their children. It is not even according to some fatal flaw of the individual but to some inexorable law of social upheaval that has bedeviled mankind and that must be exorcised if ever we are to free ourselves from that deification of ourselves that encourages us to take the lives of our fellowmen with the rational apology that we must send them to the wall to protect our Paradise on Earth.

My reverie, or day-mare, was interrupted by Momentito.

"Señor Moreno," he said. "Here is a package and a note for you."

I quickly tore open the envelope. It was from Alejandro. His name was not printed but engraved on fine Japanese parchment.

My dears: Forgive me for not coming to visit you this afternoon. I have been unavoidably detained. Nothing serious. Meanwhile I send a change of clothes for the three of you. More, much more, tomorrow. *Ciao.* I embrace you. A.C.

I frowned. For Alejandro, the playboy, the Pagliaccio, who liked to show a suave and charming face to the world, the note hinted of demons at which I could only guess. Was he being harassed by the police? Or by an irate husband? Or a discarded male lover? With Alejandro it could be such a variety. He was involved in so many virtues and so many vices.

I don't know if I raised my eyes inadvertently or whether I subconsciously searched for that third-story dormer window. I don't know if I believe one's eyes can be drawn by the eyes of another. But once again I found myself looking up into the face of Adriana Ponce de Romano as she looked down at me. Three stories above the level of the courtyard is a considerable distance, but the force of her beauty reached through and brought her closer. I could see the majestic upsweep of her dark gold hair and the cheekbones molding her opaline skin, and the large nose that accentuated her beauty. I couldn't be sure from the distance but I thought she parted her lips and smiled as she raised her hand in gesture to me. Then I could see that she was holding something. A folded newspaper? A fan? She might simply have been fanning herself against the heat of her private attic room.

"Hi there, Justo old palsy-walsy," I heard a voice behind me. Even if he had not been speaking what he considered gringo talk I would have recognized Johnie Valdez. "Yom yom. I don't blame you. The sweetest mango is always the one you can't reach."

With the faintest twinge of guilt I turned my eyes away from the face of Adriana.

"You have excellent taste, my friend," Johnie went on. "But remember my warning. El Gordo never permits her to leave that room,
and Búfalo—if he even catches you looking at her that way—will
swat you against the wall like a mosquito."

"Johnie, your best stories were always the scandals you invented
yourself. The mark of a true columnist."

He slapped me on the back and laughed. "Hokay, keed. You
know what they say—never try to keed a keeder."

Momentito was approaching. Inmates were beginning to move in
reluctant clusters toward the fire escape.

"But I wish you luck," Johnie said as he turned to join the others.
"Maybe a *mango de Manila* is worth the risk of falling from the top
of the tree."

At that moment I hoped fervently that he would be the first asylee
in the compound to receive his safe passage. Then, alone again, I
raised my eyes to her window. She was still looking down at me.
This time I felt certain of it. It was only when I turned away and
glanced back over my shoulder that I saw Adriana also turning
away. But again it might have been only coincidence. In sanctuary,
every moment, every imperceptible speck of experience, becomes
magnified a thousandfold like an amoeba in the eye of a microscope.

5

Back into the dormitory the men came grumbling, abusing the
anemic lunch with such violence that the protest was transformed
into a kind of perverse satisfaction. Perhaps that is why verbal exhaust plays such an important part in the system of prison or army
life. From what I have read it was lacking only in the German
extermination camps. Those victims were too far gone, too close to

the gas chambers and the trenches of mass burial to grumble about starvation diets and the disciplined cruelty of the guards. To grumble is to affirm that one continues to exist: the disgruntled trumpeting of identity.

Most of the returned asylees listened to each other's charges against the embassy handout as if they had never heard them before —and then leaped in to score their own points as though convinced their arguments would result in a positive program of dietary improvement that could be put into effect.

On every other issue from politics to women there was dissension, but on the subject of beans and rice, enthusiastic harmony. My fellow-inmates seemed to enjoy the verbal competition for the most vividly foul description of their daily sustenance. The metaphors of obscenity mounted in imagination and intensity.

While I unwrapped the package from Alejandro I half-listened to the inevitable denouncement: "Petition!—we should draw up a petition!" And the inevitable counter-suggestions: "We should all sign it and send it to the cook!" "Alvarez—he'll promise anything to keep us quiet and throw our petition in the *basura*. Send it to the Ambassador!" "A waste of time—he'll simply send it to the cook and the cook will wipe his *nalgas* with it!" "Maybe we should add it to our other petition—the one for safe passage!" "Yes!—put in everything!" "No!—the other one is an official protest, it should go directly to the OAS calling for an emergency meeting!" "Why not send both petitions to the OAS?" "Hey, pals, wait a sec, listen to me!" shouted Johnie Valdez. "Since the real scorpion is Angel, send that *chinche* the petitions—with copies to the Ambassador!"

There were speeches and counter-speeches, oaths and counter-oaths and as I removed the contents of my package quietly—the change of clothes Alejandro had managed to get through to us—I realized that what the dormitory represented was a microcosm of our country in those rare periods when there was no *caudillo,* no *gran chingón,* and instead so many individual voices that no one thing was ever accomplished. Haiti solved the problem with a voodoo—tyrannical "Papa Doc." In Brazil it was the army—regardless of whom they called "President." In Mexico the politicians and the businessmen had wrested power from the generals and ran their country with a benevolence lined with greed through their one-party system, which was at least an improvement on a one-man party. In our tiny country called Sanctuary, there was neither an oppressive centralism nor an effective majority. We were simply a crowded dormitory full of disgruntled apostates, speaking in tongues for a score of rival apostasies. As I unfolded the new slacks and shirts, thoughtfully wash-and-dry, and similarly practical dresses for Marta and Clarita, I thought half in amusement, half in rue, there will be no petition, only a score of conflicting suggestions for petitions. There will be no agreement, neither regarding safe passage nor beans and rice. Even if they carry this debate on into the dawn, they still will not have decided whether to address it to the Secretary General of the United Nations or to the perspiring cook in the stained apron in the embassy kitchen. There are simply too many individualists in this country. That is why it's a political miracle when they join together to rise up and overthrow a Zamora. And then they break up again into hundreds of pieces of conflicting opinions that can only be held together through block committee spies and holy (or Central Committee) terror.

As I listened, while shedding my gamey fishing clothes for the clean gray slacks and fresh sport shirt, I was struck by the odd contradiction: the more irreconcilable individualists we had here, the easier it was for the new power group to bring the masses to heel and impose on them its "voluntary" authority.

Almost everyone was involved in this informal dormitory assembly meeting except El Gordo and his retinue, El Indio Sandungo, Paco O'Higgins and young Miguelito Flores. El Gordo had allowed Jesusito to help him into his silk robe; Jesusito then had folded a large, clean beach towel over his arm as he and Búfalo followed El Gordo up the aisle to the shower. For a man crawling with filth on the inside, Romano was the unchallenged possessor of the most immaculate exterior in our sanctuary. This was at least the second or third of the half-dozen showers he took every day. I had never—thank my democratic saints—been summoned to his central headquarters in his days of power, but after the fall of Zamora, the picture magazine *Alegre,* published by my critical cot-neighbor Rubén Silva, had run a lurid exposé on Romano's headquarters,

showing the barrels of skulls and bones that had been removed from
a torture chamber, and also the private sauna where El Gordo
sweated off some of his self-indulgence each afternoon. The large
modern shower adjacent had cleansed him from a dozen shower
heads and his electronically controlled dressing room revealed forty
silk monogrammed shirts waiting to replace the one he had damp-
ened with perspiration in the previous hour. After the murder of
Duncan, Lady Macbeth merely went through the motions of washing
her hands. El Gordo was a twentieth-century power machine and
could call on the latest developments in electronic plumbing to wash
himself clean of the stain that all but he could see.

As El Gordo and his faithful attendants disappeared into the
bathroom, I followed them down the aisle and glanced into the common room. There the endless domino game was in progress. They
played it with a sense of desperate monotony. There were cries of
triumph and groans of frustration, but somehow it was all a frieze,
an action *en suspenso,* a circle of hell where the damned were playing out their roles of eternal torment.

When I returned, Paco was snoring in sprawled and drunken
splendor on the slender cot straining under his weight. Miguelito
was lying back against the wall reading the thumbed copy of Neruda.
I was tempted to go over and talk to him. Already I had begun to
miss serious talk, but the pale young man only nodded shyly, as if
wishing to keep to himself and his Chilean poet. Johnie Valdez
called out to me heartily and I nodded but kept walking toward my
cot.

I lay there with my eyes closed, letting the idle talk swirl around
me. Now it had moved inexorably from food to women. The inter-
mingling of the sexes had stirred and in some cases satisfied the
glands and there was the external boasting, which was like the oaths
of the domino players. They laughed about Cookie Gamboa—the
old druggist was out of earshot in the common room with the domino
players—and how Gamboa dozed blissfully in the sun while El
Gordo hung another set of horns on the old man.

"His head has so many antlers he looks like the national forest!"
The busy voice of Johnie Valdez.

"You should talk—El Gordo's not the only one. You helped put
them there!"

Johnie sounded pleased. "If someone leaves a pie on the window-sill, can you blame the thief for poking his finger into it?"

"His *little* finger," a growl rose from the supposedly drunken slumber of Paco O'Higgins. "I bet Cookie thought you were using a matchstick."

Again the congratulatory accusations: "You should talk, *bor-rachito!* That little water pistol of yours has hit that target once or twice."

"*Silencio!*" Paco shouted. "Can a man never get any sleep here?"

There were rude suggestions as to how best Paco might put him-self to sleep.

"He doesn't need a woman—he's married to his rum bottle."

This was too much for Paco's manhood. His Latin breeding overwhelmed his Irish blood. The Irish boast with their fists. The Latin boast with their—Paco spoke from his prone position with his eyes shut. "Ask the maid Reencarnación how she liked the candy bar I slipped her after lunch today."

"You mean that skinny, walleyed trout?" Johnie said. "I wouldn't go near that with a ten-foot pole."

"You don't have a ten-foot pole," Paco said, still with his eyes closed.

"Ha, ha," Johnie said. "You know what Cookie says about yours? It's so full of rum it flops around like a drunken sailor who can't find his way up the gangplank . . . and falls asleep on the dock!"

"*Silencio!*" Paco shouted again. "Can a man never get any sleep in this shithouse!"

I pressed my face into the pillow so I would still seem to be sleeping while the idle talk moved on from the bony, pathetically-in-demand Reencarnación.

"How do you like the new little perch they threw in our tank today?"

"Did you see the way El Gordo went after the bait?"

"I give her two weeks before he plants a flower in her belly."

"If Paco doesn't climb through the rear window ahead of him."

They were Dante's personification of the carnal who have sacri-ficed their reason to their appetites. Suddenly I wanted to throw a bomb that would wipe out our hideous circle of sanctuary.

"Shhh—" It was Johnie Valdez, thoughtfully reminding them that the proud father of the fat little perch, the latest target for their long knives, was lying within earshot. And so the talk, the *charla,* the prattle, turned from Clarita to other familiar forms of dormitory gossip. Like a prurient game they obviously had played day after day, they speculated as to what El Gordo and Búfalo and Jesusito did when they locked themselves into the showers for so long a time. I could picture the unwholesome human sandwich they described, with the sensual fat of El Gordo pressed on one side by the giant instrument of Búfalo while his own overindulged and punitive organ was being labiated by the obedient and tender Jesuscito. I wiped my arm across my eyes to erase the scene. Sex in sanctuary was no longer *sensualis santis.* It was the obscene adagio of El Gordo Romano. It was the barnyard accessibility of Cookie Gamboa. Most frightening of all, it was the wholesale acceptance of our Clarita not as a troubled child to be protected, but as just another ripening mango ready for the plucking.

Sleep, forget, escape, I tried self-hypnosis to blot out the filth, the sound, the images. I drew on Marta's pragmatism to remind myself, dwell only on what you can effect and don't waste energy on might-have-beens or should-have-dones. Bless Clarita, protect her, help her, save her from the haphazard fornication of the El Gordos and the Búfalo de Sas and, yes, even my rum-soaked compañero Paco O'Higgins. I loathed myself for exposing her to the bestiary glorified as sanctuary. For waiting, waiting for the ax to fall instead of escaping in good time while I was still a president who enjoyed the confidence or at least the tolerance of Angel Bello. Why do we sentence ourselves to walk the treadmill of disenchantment?

Dis-en-chant . . . despite the exterior and interior distractions I must have dozed, for I was awakened by a sense of movement in the room and of the familiar voice of Momentito calling us to the evening meal. This was served from an enormous earthen bowl and was supposedly pea soup. It is possible that a green pea or two had been drowned long ago at the bottom of the pot but basically it was pale hot water, colored sickly green.

Some of the older and bonier asylees were lifting the chipped bowls to their mouths and pouring it down greedily. I wondered how I would survive on a diet calculated to starve all but the most healthy

or resourceful. I took a deep breath and then swallowed some of the
hot green water. Across from me El Indio was finishing his. I said,
to the room at large, that the soup was a scandal. El Indio shrugged
and rose and brought his bowl back to Momentito. *"Un poco más,"*
he said. There was another bowlful for him which he accepted with
a dignified "Thank you" and went back to his seat.

If ever I were to write *The Making of the Dictator,* the black
peasant who first raised the banner of Land and Liberty would make
a key witness. Was he not the landless peasant seduced and abandoned as had been each generation of peasants since the Conquest?
By the Church, by the Creoles, by the liberals, by the old revolutionists, by the new revolutionists . . . ? I must find some way to
reach this silent black Indian who drank down a second bowl of
watered soup in self-contained determination to survive.

Two hours before midnight Momentito had retreated with the
emptied soup tureen and the table had been cleared for the domino
players who rattled their game on into night. As I went back into
the dormitory, I saw that Paco was still deep in noisy nasal slumber,
sprawled on top of his cot in his dirty long underwear. El Gordo had
returned and was spread comfortably on his double cot reading
Gone with the Wind. Each time I passed I tried not to look at him,
but this time I was distracted by a glistening that a second glance
convinced me were tears forming in his eyes. He was deep in the
book and perhaps he had reached one of those soggy parts, when
Scarlett returns and finds the old plantation in ruins. The book had
become a standard tearjerker in Spanish and I wondered if the
mournful scene evoked tears from the hard eyes of El Gordo because it is a classic saga of disestablishment, of the fall of castles
high. El Gordo had had his turreted mansion at the Papagayos and
his three-story house in the city and his secret police headquarters
and his air-conditioned torture chambers—swept away now, gone
with the wind. No wonder it brought tears to his eyes. In the next cot
Búfalo leafed through an old copy of *El y Ella,* our imitation of a
Yankee scandal sheet that combined features on boxers and wrestlers
with full-page displays of starlets in bikinis or less. Jesuscito was already dozing on the *petate* that separated him from the floor under
his master's double cot.

I undressed carefully to keep as fresh as possible the new clothes

Alejandro had sent. I hung them on a hanger I had borrowed from
Paco and climbed into bed. There was no reading light—I was told
I could rig one up if I could get one: another item to add to the
growing list for Alejandro. So I listened to the voices talking to fill
the void and the rousing cha-cha music, interrupted by another triumphant newscast describing the capture and forthcoming conspiracy trial of turncoat President Justo Moreno Suárez, Claude Lewison
and Dr. Luis (Garbo) Levy. The Voice of America, from the
adjacent bed of the Death-head interrupted a Louis Armstrong medley for a counterannouncement: Dr. Luis Levy, the phantom Garbo
who had haunted the life of the capital in the days of Zamora, was
up to his old tricks. The Bello propaganda machine was trying to
convince the people that Garbo had been apprehended and was being held incommunicado in the old fortress that used to protect the
maritime approaches to the harbor and the capital city that sprawled
behind it. But from somewhere in the capital the elusive Garbo had
broadcast a shortwave message of defiance to the Bello Revolution
for which he had risked his life so many times.

I tried to imagine Garbo, broadcasting from the soundproof basement of an imposing townhouse or a rickety corrugated metal shack
on the outskirts of the city. So he had gone back to the old life of
fly-by-night and hide-by-day, the ingenious Garbo, whom I remembered as cold, aloof and inhuman, risking torture and the rough trip
to the *paredón* as if it were the most routine of white-collar jobs. I
wondered which was the more true, the Voice of the People, as the
local radio central hailed itself, or the Voice of America, as the rival
propaganda mill advertised itself. They were equally unreliable,
since truth was not their first concern.

I thought of Marta in the other wing, gossiping with new friends
or sizing up potential enemies, of Clarita with her red mouth and
her newly discovered powers. There was a radio musical debate now,
a Shostakovich symphony fighting a rock'n'roll group, fighting and
losing as a furious group that called itself *Los Cocos Locos* was doing a loud Latin imitation of a North American juvenile imitation
of the Beatles. I beat them off with remembered lines from favorite
poets.

Góngora, Sor Juana, Martí, Darío, Lorca, come to my rescue, let me soar through this putrid, flaking faded blue ceiling to—the moon, *la luna asoma,* the moon appearing to me in my private sky, the enclosed cyclorama of my inner eye, where the moon rises as the sea covers the earth, and the heart—the eternal *corazón* of our eternal Spanish songs—feels itself an island in infinity—and *green,* how much I want you green, green wind, green boughs, green hair, green eyes—no, with eyes of cold silver, the silver of El Gordo Romano, the silver-green eyes of Adriana, the green hair of Adriana, the green flesh of Adriana, silver-green, silver-green because everything that belonged to El Gordo Romano was touched with the silver of Romano. But her eyes were not silver, they were dark green and glistening, moist as with gathering passion, and she was as beautiful as the moon, Lorca's bashful moon, only closer and warmer and in a trance I saw her, the remote Adriana slowly moving toward me through the dormer window and across the open space between the attic floors of the two wings fifty feet apart, and floating through the dormer from which I had first seen her here in sanctuary, floating toward me waiting in my narrow cot and opening her arms toward me, the silver-green arms of the remote lady of the tower remote no longer as she came to my bedside and reached out to touch me with desirous fingers that begged me to respond and weaken and harden and weaken and draw me into her, fingers touching and probing and awakening and—it was only then that I realized that it was much, much later and that I had been sleeping and that the hand actually reaching out to me, poking my shoulder with quiet but not so gentle insistence belonged to Paco O'Higgins who was on his knees between my cot and that of the sleeping Death-head Rubén Silva.

As I opened my eyes I was relieved to inhale the strong breath of rum and to realize it was the simple Paco and not the complications of Adriana at my bedside. In the darkness he was so close to me that I could half-see, half-feel him putting his finger to his lips. I rose on one elbow and stared at him. He beckoned me to follow. To the bathroom for a midnight swig of rum? I shook my head. But he beckoned more strenuously. The heavy musk of rum grew stronger as he leaned over me and aimed his hoarse whisper into my ear, "Follow me. Important."

I threw off the single worn blanket and followed him down the aisle, straining my eyes to see the grotesque silhouette a few feet in front of me performing a kind of hippopotamus tiptoe. He managed to be remarkably silent. I was more clumsy. I drifted six inches off course and bumped into the end of a cot. There was a groan. I had disturbed none other than Búfalo de Sa. But he didn't awaken. Neither did El Gordo, who lay on his back in relative, double-cot comfort and snored authoritatively.

It was Jesusito's turn to take the watch, for he was crouched between El Gordo's cot and Búfalo's with his narrow back against the wall, his thin knees drawn up. He was an imperfect sentinel; although he didn't snore like his overseers, his head was resting on his chest and he didn't raise it as we tiptoed past his sentry post. Like an educated thief, Paco opened the door to the hallway. I followed, in somnambulistic obedience, wondering if he was heading for the women's wing. I had heard that the partition was locked during the night. But Paco was sly. Perhaps he had fashioned a primitive open sesame. Perhaps he was on the prowl for Cookie Gamboa or some other cooperative asilada. I would feel like a damned fool bursting into the women's dormitory and could imagine the tangy reception that Marta would have ready for me.

But instead, Paco turned toward the staircase leading to the second floor. "Paco, *adónde?*" I whispered, but he turned and put his finger to his lips again and continued his way down the steps. I was burly, neither as roly-poly as Paco nor as agile on a creaking staircase. Even on tiptoe my tread produced sounds that made Paco caution me again. We came to the door at the bottom of the stairs. Paco reached down into the opening of his long-johns at the crotch —his secret vault—and drew out instead of the expected rum, a key tied to a string. With this he quietly unlocked the door which led to the precious second floor strictly off limits to asylees. I followed him down a dark, narrow hall where he opened another door and we were in a room I could not immediately discern, with a cold tile shelf along one side and a large table that felt metallic running down the middle. "Where are we?" I whispered. This time Paco startled me by speaking, not loudly though it came at me like a shout because the human voice was no longer expected. "The kitchen!"

Paco had an air for the dramatic as well as the comedic and his exclamation mark to the sentence was to swing open the door to an enormous North American General Electric refrigerator. A light inside went on automatically and there before us stood an unforgettable sight—four wide shelves stocked with food—a huge platter of chicken and rice, a bowl full of marinated shrimp, a large plate of raw *filetes*. And fruit, papaya and grapes and plums and guava. I pulled out a bottom drawer filled with fresh vegetables, lettuce, tomatoes, squash and green chilies. One of the trays in the door of this gleaming, overstocked miracle was laden with cheese, Port du Salud, Camembert, imported Swiss, Gruyère and the best of the local ones. Another deep tray must have held five dozen eggs and still another was stocked with bacon, Italian salami and spiced beef. It was an awesome treasure of culinary supplies that lay open to our hungers.

"Eat, eat," Paco grunted. "Help yourself. Take all you want."

"But I don't understand—how are you able to—?"

Already Paco was munching on a stuffed hard-boiled egg obviously left over from a diplomatic cocktail party in the marble foyer at the bottom of the winding staircase. "The cook is my old friend," he explained. "Apolonio. He was cooking here when I was still playing jai alai." Paco's mouth was full of soft, mashed, delicious egg yolk that dribbled down his chin. "Always a gambler, a very big gambler. His whole month's salary he would bet it on a single game. I met him in the jai alai bar one night after a thirty-point game he'd lost on the Blue, thirty to twenty-nine. I was the back-court Blue who had missed the final point. You see, I was betting heavily on the Red. I told him next time he should catch my eye when the game was getting close to thirty. If I rubbed my belly, he should bet me with all the pesos he had left. If I rubbed my *nalgas*, as if I had a muscle ache there, he should bet the other team. Yes, Apolonio was a little fellow, but he was a very big aficionado of the jai alai. And, with a little help from me, a little instruction on the fine points of the game, he won enough money to buy a nice little house and a nice little *casa chica* for his girlfriend, and to get his oldest daughter, the ugly one, a good husband who sold television sets to the campesinos at a low price; when they fell behind he would simply take back the sets and sell them to some other stupid campesinos. Ah, is it not wonderful the ways of the gringo from whom we learn so much!"

I was eating the shrimps, cold, sweet, crisp *camarones*. Quickly I ate half a dozen and went on picking them out of the bowl, chewing too fast, swallowing too fast. I'd forgotten how hungry I was.

Paco reached into the rear of the refrigerator and drew out a quart bottle of amber Carta Oro rum. Now I knew the secret of his endless supply. He wiped the egg yolk from his mouth with his flannel underwear sleeve, twisted the top of the bottle and swigged great gulpfuls. Then I drank from the bottle as he chuckled at his own story.

"Apolonio never forgets his old friend in the back court. When he hears I am in this shithouse, he sends me a key to the second floor with a little note saying he will leave the kitchen door open for me, and a bottle of Carta Oro to wash it down with. So fuck El Gordo and his money belt. I have Apolonio."

He reached for a breast of chicken nesting in a generous bowl of

paella. As we sat there on the floor in front of this embarrassment
of gourmet riches, I was reminded of adolescent forays . . . nights
at the Marine Academy when I was fifteen or sixteen years old,
when together with the incorrigible captain of the soccer team, I
would sneak out of the darkened dormitory into the commissary to
raid the icebox, less motivated by hunger than by the adventure of
our illicit marauding.

It made us feel daredevil brave, those midnight adventures after
"lights out," and now when I was no longer sixteen but almost fifty,
I felt some of the same bravado elation as Paco and I squatted in
front of the refrigerator and gorged ourselves on shrimp and chicken
and yellow peppers and fresh twisted bread and tangy rope cheese,
and for dessert mango mousse which was one of the specialties of
Paco's Saint of the *Cocina*, Apolonio. I reached for the golden rum
and drank to the absent cook and to the idle corruption that had
brought Paco and Apolonio into this illicit partnership, a toast to
benevolent conspiracy. Yes, Paco was a scoundrel, but now he was
my scoundrel, and facing the great god refrigerator from a position
not unlike that of the Buddhist priest addressing himself to Lord
Buddha himself, I stuffed more and more food into my mouth as if I
had never eaten before and would never eat again. Paco belched
heroically, opening his mouth to give vent to the full sound and
pleasure of too much food. "To eating and drinking and fucking," he
said, lifting the rum bottle in formal toast, "and death to the politicians who fuck up the fucking."

He drank deep and handed me the bottle and I drank, holding my
own with the guzzler and ready to affirm yes, yes in this shithouse
of a world where every fight for freedom became, once won, a fight
to murder freedom, what else was there indeed but eating and
drinking and fucking and stealing the good quick moments from the
long, nothing days?

We drank to Apolonio's long-suffering wife and to his sanctified
children and we drank to Apolonio's nineteen-year-old sweetheart
and his illegitimate brood, which were many drinks, and by this
time I was talking like Paco because it was difficult not to talk like
Paco O'Higgins when you made yourself into a glutton and a drunk-
ard and a thief in the night like Paco O'Higgins, and I said, "Paco,

my friend to the death, my compañero, I do not believe in God, or maybe since I lost my faith in this Revolution, in anything any more. But some kind fate which is almost as good as God must have brought you to me because I do not see how I could have survived in this shithouse without you."

And I belched almost as profoundly as Paco.

Paco trumped my belch. "Ay! You will survive. With me or without me. With my rum or without it. If I leave before you, you will find something else to hold on to. Maybe the Señora with the face of a green-eyed angel of fucking."

"You mean Señora Cookie?"

"No, hombre! It is too late in the night to play the innocent with me. Cookie Gamboa is a peroxide blond pincushion. While the old *cabrón* dozes in the sun, every *macho* in the yard sticks his needle into her. No, no, no, hombre, you know very well who I mean."

I did. But I remained silent.

"The madonna at the window! Look, my friend, you think I do not see you standing there trying to catch her in your *cesta*. For those of us who get tired of making insults and playing dominoes, what else do we have to do except watch each other watch each other?"

"Of course I was aware of her."

"Aware of her!" Paco mocked me. "Hombre, speak to me in silver. Already you've said to yourself, 'If I could only put my hot knife into that juicy mango pie, if I could only put horns on that *hijo* of an *asesino,* El Gordo, I could learn to live happily in this diplomatic shithouse forever!' "

"Speak for yourself, Paco, you horny old bachelor. At least your wife's far away, but mine is right across the patio. And even if she's no longer as beautiful as El Gordo's prize, Marta and I are still like *this*." I clenched my fist tight.

"Drink, faithful husband, noble liar, drink," Paco said. "You can drink to fidelity and I will drink to infidelity and my rum will piss out of me as purely as it went in because it passes through a more truthful bladder."

I'd never known a man who could drink as much as Paco O'Higgins without losing control of his senses. At the afternoon *comida* in the yard he had seemed a trifle woozy and incoherent.

But his siesta had revived him and although his tongue was a little thick, his tone somewhat hoarser, his eloquence was expanding.

We both had stuffed ourselves to the point where it had become an effort to reach into the refrigerator. Paco slammed the great door shut and, in the darkness again, we rose to our feet like the two overweight, overfed *borrachos* we were.

"Paco, a thousand thanks," I said. "That was a banquet."

I wished I could have filched some for Marta and Clarita. For a moment I thought of hiding cheese and fruit in my crotch, O'Higgins style, but I saw no practical way to preserve them through the night and the morning shower and all the time intervening between this raid and the mingling of the two wings next afternoon.

As I was following Paco to the door, I noticed a telephone on the wall. Whim, rum, the heady sense of foray from the old Academy days prompted me to pick up the receiver, dial for an outside line and then call a number I could pick out in what was now semi-darkness.

"Hey, *cabrón*, what are you doing?" Paco turned back, for the first time alarmed.

"A joke," I said, and then into the mouthpiece, "Bueno?—Alejandro? Here is Justo."

"Justo! Mon Dieu! Where are you?"

I'd thought Alejandro would be amused, that this would be his kind of *quixotismo*, but his voice sounded unnatural and taut.

"In the embassy, of course. I have just—"

There was a click and the phone went dead. Benefactor Alejandro Castillo who courted danger like his current seduction had hung up. It sobered me. I tiptoed up the stairs behind the barrel-shaped, surprisingly graceful Paco. From the few words Alejandro had spoken he sounded frightened. Or perhaps he was startled. It was a foolish, childish, show-off whim I had indulged. Alejandro—frightened. It unnerved me to think of the effete, lion-hearted Alejandro surrendering his poise and giving in to fear, even for a moment.

Like those adolescents in the innocent days of boarding school, we sneaked back into our dormitory. The sweet-foul atmosphere of sleeping male bodies was familiar to me now. Even many of the different forms in the cots were becoming familiar. Young Miguelito was sleeping with his knees drawn up like an embryo and the blanket pulled over his head. He was so young, so frail to be so deeply in trouble. A pure young Socialist. I felt sorry for him, because there is no country in the world that can tolerate pure young Socialism. I had been a pure young Socialist once and now I knew better, and worse. The people were not ready. Being people, being susceptible to the infections of their humanity, they may never be ready for the dream: *From each according to his ability to each according to his needs.* It's like the Ten Commandments and "Do unto others"— altogether ideal and therefore still beyond the reach of man. I felt a sudden, irrational urge to pause at Miguelito's bedside, to tuck the thin, insufficient blanket closer around him and even to kiss the back of his thin, barely sufficient neck as I had kissed the child Clarita's. Miguelito coughed in his sleep—he coughed frequently, to himself, shy, introspective coughs—but I fought back my impulsive, paternal need to comfort him and went on down the aisle, that creaky wooden valley between the snoring and heavy breathing and turning and tossing and farting and dreaming, dreaming. Even El Gordo lying on his back with one heavy leg on one cot, the other speared through the sheet and blanket that should have belonged to Jesusito, even El Gordo seemed to be dreaming. He whimpered, faintly, an unexpectedly tender sound from the imperious face of the husband of Adriana, and I wondered, what was he dreaming, of what were the dreams of an El Gordo made? Had sleep carried him all the way back to muling infancy and was he whimpering for the warm nipple of his mother? Or was his incongruous whimper a schizoid transference? Could he reach back in sleep to change places with one of his thousand departed victims? Were the needles piercing the tender flesh that hid beneath the nail? Was the electric prod delivering foul messages of torture to those fleshy blue testicles? Good night, unsweet El Gordo, I wish you bad dreams, I wish you nightmares multiplied to the square root of your victims.

He sighed with a deep intake of breath that seemed almost like an answer. Sigh, you *chingón.*

Paco patted my shoulder in a silent *buenas*, turned off at his cot and fell upon it like an exhausted sea lion. I padded down to mine. In the adjoining cot, an arm's length away, the Death-head was mut-

tering to himself, incommunicably. Again the muffled protest "No!
No!" rose from a tangled, troubled mattress, answered by a nasal
groan from the far side of the long, cluttered room. My stomach
growled. I tossed and worried, thought of Marta, Clarita, the Ambassador, what extra steps and pressures I might bring to bear
through Alejandro to extricate ourselves from the web of this
enormous diplomatic spider. I tried to quiet the nerves dancing
their St. Vitus under my skin. Becalm myself. Think of the sea, my
beach of pink sand curling to its protective arm of coral rock. Think
of pelicans in formation against the vermilion sunset sky. Think of
jacaranda trees in airy purple bloom and a lone black cormorant
skimming over the surface of the darkening bay. Think peace.
Think, there is nothing I can do right now but sleep in peace and
drift on, slowly floating on the still waters of a protected cove until
sleep becomes the bay of peace and peace is sleep asleep asleep . . .

And so at last I managed to snap off the switch of consciousness
but not the more inaccessible switch of inner tension. Faces re-
volved and exploded in my head like blazing pinwheels and fireworks triggered in the middle of screaming, scattering crowds at
village fiestas. The faces would zoom in at me, larger larger
LARGER until they filled the screen of nightmare in which I was
both actor and spectator. I saw Angel Bello hurling his revolutionary
jingo invective into my frightened face and I saw Chino the one-
eyed fisherman and the old taxi driver whose teeth were being slowly
extracted one by one and the Caliban dwarf El Amante leering at
my exposed testicles, the ravaged Captain Maldonado's testicles. In
my sleep I felt I was falling falling and fainting and there was the
green-eyed Adriana gazing at me, only her dormer window was in
this room at my bedside and she had slipped her dress down from
her shoulders to her waist and her breasts were like the great moons
of the Kama Sutra standing high and spiraling to pink, round
nipples passionately erect. Oh, and she raised both of her hands and
placed them around her left breast and made a forward movement
as if to offer it to me. Closer and closer to my mouth it moved until
I saw no face, no hands, only the great, warm breast of Adriana,
sculpted of ivory turned to flesh, and I could not, could not receive
it for fear of consequences, and I turned, twisted my head away,
felt an earthquake, growling movement somewhere in the land or in

my body and then too late realized it was in my throat, trying to force its way through my mouth, the vomit. Vomit wrenched me from my nightmare dream, jolted me to sour consciousness, just in time to catch and swallow down most of it, though the first aborted mouthful poured over my chin, onto the bedclothes and down the shirt-neck of the fresh cotton pajamas that Alejandro had sent me.

I felt myself to be a sick, green, miserable slob who had over-eaten, over-rummed in stupid animal greed. My stomach was taut, burning, twisting. There was a hard, hot knot at the point where my rib cage divided. I climbed out of the cot and hurried up the aisle to the bathroom, lowering my head over the bowl just in time to let it all explode, shrimp, egg, cheese, guava, rum in one putrid outpouring. I'd forgotten to bring one of the clean towels Alejandro had thoughtfully included. I wiped my face with coarse toilet paper. Then I cupped water to my hands and washed out my mouth and gargled, and let more water trickle slowly down my wretched, scummy throat. Better. A little better. But I must ask Alejandro for pills. I had never really joined the great neurasthenic twentieth-century club of pill-consumers, but now I wished for seda-tives, painkillers, sleeping pills, happiness pills, and some for re-newed energy after the total debilitation I was feeling. My legs resisted me, my nerves were beating out of rhythm, my head throbbed and ached at the temples. I put my forehead against the bathroom door and pressed hard as if to keep my brains from erupt-ing like my belly. I leaned against the door until I felt some control. Then I went back down the dormitory aisle to my cot. I removed my pajama shirt, but the faint odor of vomit still clung to me. Once more I tried the mental sedative of beach and sea and birds and evening sky to help me over the ledge into a deathlike sleep that would spare me the tossing and distraction of troubled dreams. The muffled "No, no," the coughing of Miguelito, the jumble-talk of the Death-head: each cot gave forth its own peculiar sound, its own foul bouquet. But finally my brain was too tired to hear or smell or think and I drifted into black hours of exhausted sleep.

7

"Cochino!" The battle cry was like a hand grenade hurled through the window of my unconscious, exploding in fragmented echoes. It took me a few moments to realize that I was awake and that this was morning reveille: O'Higgins Time. I grabbed my toilet articles and the last of Alejandro's clean towels and hurried down the aisle just in time to see Paco receive his daily blow on the mouth from Búfalo. My friend's bloody lip, and El Gordo's disdainful glance as he finally emerged from his Número Uno position in the toilet, had become part of the daily order and logic of sanctuary. Paco bowed me in ahead of him and this time I was able to overcome my original inhibitions and squat down alongside him on the elevated seat. At least I was able to perform the act despite my inhibitions. The remainder of the morning ablutions were hurried, as I could feel the pressure of other asilados at the door. Paco was more immune. He would mutter a *tu madre* and keep on brushing his mouthful of unbeautiful yellow teeth or wiping with a dirty towel his ruddy, stubbled, agreeable, porcine face.

After the predictable breakfast, amidst the constant clacking of the dominoes, I glanced at the official Party paper that had replaced all the others. This time there was no mention of the great espionage case. All three of us, Lewison, Garbo and myself, had been dropped from the front page as abruptly as we had been projected there. That was one of the conveniences of a state-controlled press. One was not bothered with inquisitive reporters digging for follow-up stories. When Angel wanted his front-page story, when the infamous trio was useful again, he would push the propaganda button and the Party hacks would go flailing away with their typewriters and their scare headlines.

I felt the hours stretching like worn-out but still durable ropes. As eager and restless as a child waiting for the coming of the Three Kings, I looked forward to the mid-afternoon *comida* in the yard, the fresh air, the sight of Marta and Clarita. Then I was in the middle of the pack moving down the metal fire escape. This time the ladies were already in the yard. Apparently we alternated as to which group was led down first. Sanctuary seemed to be run with scrupulous equality between the sexes.

Marta and I embraced. She looked fresher in the new print dress Alejandro had sent in for her. Clarita had put aside the gold lamé for a simple blouse and skirt, but her lipstick and make-up were as provocative as on the day before. In her mind she was still wearing lamé.

"So, Justo, another day. Did you sleep well?" Marta asked.

"*Así-así*, I had some bad dreams."

"You look pale. As if you've lost weight."

"It was a long night." I wanted to spare her the unpleasant details. "I hope yours was better."

"It's hard to sleep in a room full of old bags. They snore louder than the *cabrones* on your side of the stable."

"Never mind, Marta. Soon. Soon we'll be sleeping together again."

"Clarita whimpered all night. Once she woke up and came into my bed—even though it's too narrow for her mama. Those cots are made for skinny English ladies, not for magnificent Pan American backsides like ours." Then she added quickly, glancing in the direction of Clarita who was wandering off from us again, "I'm worried."

"I know. Her comfort and security pulled away so suddenly. She has to punish us. And her only weapon is defiance."

"Excellent, Dr. Freud," Marta said. "But that doesn't solve anything. What should we do?" And then she added, characteristically, "We should get her out of here."

"Of course," I said. "Like that. With a snap of our fingers. Or did you pack our magic lamp?"

"You're as cheerful as a hungry dog in an empty cage."

"You describe me well. How do you expect me to feel when I come out into the fresh air with nothing to look forward to but watching my daughter turn into a *sanchita?*"

"Justo! I've heard enough of your *cursi* complaints. And if any of those *pinches pendejos* come near her, I will grab it and break it off!"

"Bravo," I said. "But first you have to catch him. As Paco says, 'This place may be a great big fish bowl, but there are always rocks to hide under.' "

"Your friend Paco better keep his *chiquito* away from her too."

"Marta, your language gets more interesting every day."

"In a barnyard, Justo, my noises are like the other animals'."

Men and women were queuing for the big earthen bowls of mush and Clarita had gone ahead to queen it along the line as she had done the day before. But then she saw the lean stray cat Dolores II and reached down to pick it up and nuzzle it. It had been wary the day before, its small, mangy body defensive, but now it knew Clarita.

"Alejandro!" Clarita saw him first and hurried to greet him, Dolores II still cradled against her shoulder. He brought a flash of color and life to the enclosure and a great smile, the smile that made his elongated, jagged, homely face handsome and engaging. He was dressed as if for a sunny winter's day picnic on our old beach, in mustard-colored slacks and fine blue Yucateca *guayabera*. Around his long neck was tied a silk maroon ascot. His crepe-soled beach shoes were almost the same color as his slacks. In each hand he carried a large picnic basket smartly covered by oblong napkins, imprinted with ruby grapes and bottles of wine.

"*Ciao*, my loves," Alejandro's high voice piped squeaky, welcome music, "see what I have brought you—a feast worthy of the President and his lady and the lovely Señorita!" He set the bulging baskets down and managed to embrace all of us at once. Then he scanned the enclosure with his special brand of effete practicality. "Now let us see—where shall we have our little picnic?—as far away as possible from eavesdroppers and intruders and envious eyes." He nodded toward the fencing that divided the asylum compound from the embassy grounds proper. He unfolded a white embroidered tablecloth and then from the baskets proceeded to set his feast, a large, firm Genoa salami, a precooked ham, a fresh round loaf of rich, dark bread, a tin of ripe Camembert and a crock of brandied Cheddar. There was a fresh pineapple and blue grapes, a jar of green chilies *Jalapeño*, which can make your eyes water with joy, and an Oaxaca string cheese imported from Mexico. For Clarita, there were Swiss chocolate bars and sugar wafers, for Marta, a carton of those North American cigarettes which were one of her vices, and for me, a box of Corona Especiales. Alejandro had saluted the occasion with a resplendent half-gallon jug of Valpolicella.

Instead of paper cups he had brought real glasses, fine-stemmed, into which he poured the red Italian wine with the style of a black-tie banquet.

"A toast," Alejandro raised his glass. "To the same picnic a year from today—in Positano."

"Positano!" Marta said. "Alejandro, you have the most delicious ideas! Next year in Positano!"

"Next year in Positano," I murmured. The taste of the wine and the ritualistic sounding of the small Italian coastal town had a euphoric effect on us.

"You may wonder, my cherubs, why I say Positano and not Porto-fino or Ischia or Capri. Well, this very morning I had a letter from my old friend the Countess Guarini, you remember my speaking of my adorable Lily Guarini. Lily is the unofficial mayor of Positano, I should say mayoress. She must be seventy-five and she still has lovers fighting over her. Dear Lily always falls in love with sculptors —exclusively sculptors. And my loves, her house! It is built on a great rock over the ocean with a huge window facing the sea and a bedroom in an alcove above it that can only be reached by climbing a steep seagoing gangway. The little kitchen is fitted out like a ship's galley. In fact the Countess Lily's house even has a prow on it and when the waves pour in and strike the rocks and the spray flies up, you begin to feel you are rocking and moving over the sea."

"Especially if you are up in that alcove with her," Marta said.

We all laughed uncontrollably. We all wanted to laugh.

"Yes," Alejandro said, finishing his wine, "that is true. But it is not only in the sailor's hammock that she rocks the boat. When she makes her entrance into her salon, with her vivacious old-young face made up outrageously as if she were playing *The Madwoman of Chaillot*, it is like a bolt of lightning in the room. She flirts, she is full of daring ideas, she has read every new book and all the old ones, she gossips shamefully one minute and talks wisely and even profoundly the next—you will absolutely adore her!"

Alejandro put me into such a good mood that I forgot my queasy stomach and dug into the ham and string cheese and even the irresistible green chilies *Jalapeño*, cooling the fire with a swig of the Valpolicella.

He was at his gay best as he distracted us with tales of the Countess Lily. As he talked, we could picture the house built on the monumental rock over the sea with half a dozen guest houses built on adjoining boulders connected by catwalks. Guests who could afford it paid for the guest houses they visited. It was a kind of informal hotel not on a European or American plan but on the Countess Lily's own haphazard Marxist plan, from those most able to produce the necessary lire to those most in need. The Countess had the knack and the originality of living graciously and richly without money. We could see her through Alejandro's stream of loving words, surrounded by her young, artistic lovers and her doting friends and guests—"with a heart so large that there is room for all of her lovers in it"—Alejandro was saying, "and they all become friends in an odd fraternity of the spirit and the bed."

"I might as well tell you my secret," Alejandro went on, refilling our glasses. "As soon as I see you safely out of this mess, I am going to have myself transferred to Italy. To be a cultural attaché here is becoming stifling. A pox on all the Bellos and Stroessners and Francos. We will drive together to Lily's. From Naples we will take that crazy mountain road to Sorrento—the one that curves and curves and curves, up and up and up and then down and down and down through the mountain, dodging oncoming cars and buses on the wrong side of the road and donkey carts, so that it's only by some happy miracle that we are suddenly looking down on Positano, on the little terra-cotta houses that cling stubbornly, beautifully to the steep hillside and refuse to go tumbling on into the bay. We will all stay for a month or a year and Lily will introduce you to everybody who comes to Positano, the white-faced dancers from Paris, the muscular Germans, the bucktoothed Oxford poets, the durable antiques of Positano who seem to have lived there since the days of the Saracens, and the wicked children with innocent and beautiful faces who wind themselves into the most outrageous orgies." The words poured from Alejandro like wine and were more intoxicating. "To Positano and the white cupolas that the Moors brought with them, to the Buca del Bacco and the little beach where we will hold moonlight picnics—next year in Positano at the villa of the Countess Lily Guarini!"

Over Camembert and the Valpolicella, Alejandro reached into another bag and like an elegant emissary of the Three Kings produced movie magazines for Clarita, copies of *Paris-Match, Vogue* and *Réalités* for Marta, and for me *The New York Times* and the London *Observer.* Also for Marta, the latest Sagan trifle and to show how keenly he remembered details, the final volume of Durrell's Alexandria Quartet which she had not read. Marta was delighted. She had rather fancied herself as Justine. To round out the literary bouquet there was Baldwin, the gifted black North American's *Another Country.*

"Here you have black faggots and white faggots and lesbians and a lot of highly charged American writing and even a message," Alejandro said. He often referred to faggots unselfconsciously and it made me wonder if he did so to throw us off the scent. At the same time he was disarmingly frank about the catholicity of his sexual interests. When he smiled his mischievous handsome-ugly smile I realized that his description of the Baldwin extravaganza was deft mimicry of Marta who enjoyed shocking wellborn ladies with talk of queen faggots and bull dykes.

For me there was an old favorite, Silone's *Bread and Wine,* but in a new revision by the incorruptible Italian political novelist. I had followed Silone since the anti-fascist middle thirties when I first read his warm, defiant novel, *Fontamara.*

"Thank you, Alejandro," I said. "I don't see how he could improve it, but he probably has."

"Every few days I will bring you more, my loves. I promise you, you will never want for food, or books, or any creature comfort I am able to carry in."

"Alejandro, I adore you," Marta said.

"Yes—you make us feel that everything is possible," I added.

"Next year in Positano!" Alejandro sang. We were all feeling a little giddy with the wine and the promises in the warming light of the winter sun. "I will write the Countess Lily that we're coming. I will write her that new lovers and old lovers are on their way to frolic with her in her triple-sized bed."

Clarita had slipped off and was standing under the pale olive tree. She had scooped up Dolores II again. And Miguelito, whose skin was almost the color of the sickly pale leaves of the tree, was at her side.

"I must be tramping on now," Alejandro said, gathering his empty baskets. "Tramping" was one of those special words he had picked up from the speed-set in London when he was racing motor-cars. "Please, no more phone calls, Justo. Now be of good cheer, my loves. I promise I will have you out of here—"

"If it takes you the next twenty years," Marta interrupted.

"Marta, you have a wicked tongue," Alejandro scolded. "As surely as I got you in here, I will get you out. *Ciao, amori!*"

We watched as his slender, nervously athletic figure moved away from us. He walked rapidly with style to his gait, softened by a faint touch of grace. At the entrance to the embassy grounds, off limits to us asylees, he turned and blew us an airy kiss that became a reassuring wave.

"Who cares how many Tina Alonsos or beautiful beach boys he has, he is an angel," Marta said.

"Our private winged messenger to the outside world."

"Ah, Justo, next year in Lily's triple-sized bed!" Marta said. "Even if she has to be there between us, I will be too overjoyed to be jealous."

"You hand me those seventy-five-year-old Loreleis with your usual generosity."

"The Countess has a twenty-five-year-old body with that seventy-five-year-old mind."

"Alejandro is a dreamer. A romanticist in the guise of cynic and libertine. Undoubtedly she is just the opposite—an arrested adolescent in a seventy-five-year-old skin."

"Just as long as we find her—in Positano—I won't care if she is one hundred and seventy-five and has the brain of a retarded chimpanzee."

Momentito and Reencarnación were carrying out the large earthen bowls now emptied of their unappetizing contents. The Bishop was fingering his beads in front of the simple shrine in the middle of the courtyard and grouped around him were half a dozen women. Except for funerals, baptisms and a few high holidays, Catholicism was left to the ladies.

I could see the dolefully jaunty Bertie Alvarez, our shepherd, come to summon his flock. The courtyard had the look of a joyless Brueghel. There was old man Gamboa snoring in the sun, El Indio Sandungo staring at the wall, Clarita and Miguelito flirting with the mangy cat between them, Paco draining his flask, Búfalo at the steps to the laundry standing guard over El Gordo's perpetual fornication . . . senseless, loveless, compulsive. To this level of hell were the captives of sanctuary reduced. I could imagine El Gordo and Cookie grinding away together throughout eternity.

Again the women were the first to go up the fire escape. I brushed Marta's cheek in a brief, hasty embrace. "Tomorrow is the hour of the married ones." In her blunt way it sounded almost like a threat.

"An hour," I said, "in a strange room. A long way from Positano."

"I'd rather have a taco tomorrow than wait a year for paella Valenciana."

"Marta, you are a terrible woman. But when you put it so delicately, I must agree. Now go. *Vete*. And keep a sharp eye on our poor little plum."

Clarita did not offer me so much as a *hasta mañana* before turning away, her right hand in Miguelito's and her left arm cradling the scrawny cat. I thought of our walks together along the beach and the evenings she had leaned against me like an overgrown kitten while I read to her from Saint Exupéry, Hudson or Cervantes. I could feel a heaviness in my chest at her cutting off from me so abruptly. If I had thought only of her safety, I would have slipped the country while Angel was still riding me with a loose rein. But there was principle at stake in hanging on. Much more was involved than the idle procrastination that my indecision had seemed to Clarita and even to Marta. When should the left-wing democrat or the liberal Communist jump the revolutionary ship as it swings further and further toward hard left rudder? Ask Masaryk. Ask Camus.

Hearing the rapid clicking of high heels on the stone steps behind me, I turned to see the blondine head of Cookie Gamboa emerging from her makeshift boudoir in the laundry room. She broke into a funny, roly-poly run to catch up with the female pack that the hulking sea lioness Señora Lorona was leading up the fire escape.

8

Back on my cot I unfolded the newspapers Alejandro had brought. It was strange to lean back and browse through *The New York Times*. Now forbidden in our country, it came to us through Alejandro's diplomatic pouch. It had been a pleasure to read it at the beach house, a fat, gray journal, full of facts and reasonably unbiased. It always seemed less a Yankee than a British paper, thorough, conscientious and rather bloodless. Still, as we say, if someone gives you a burro, do not complain of its age. *The New York Times*, safe to read behind sanctuary walls, was a joy: there was the struggle for Negro rights and the seesaw battle between the northern Democrats and the axis of Republicans and southern Democrats. There was the Yankee obsession with containing Communists, not only at home where they had the might if not the right, but in Asia, where they seemed to be drifting ineptly into a great land war for control of a continent they would never conquer. It was not Panama or Nicaragua or the Dominican Republic. The geopolitics were different. Only the military policies were the same. I turned page after page and suddenly I was looking at a picture of myself. It was their daily profile on the man in the news and that man was me. I must confess I read the two columns with relish, even though I did not quite recognize myself. It was too glowing. I was the legendary

Latin democratic leader perennially in search of the ideal society. It reminded readers that as a very young man I had organized a brigade of young students to go to Spain to fight against Franco and for the legitimate government (though a government eventually and tragically infiltrated by the Communist apparatus). It described my efforts to fight corruption in my country in the days of Zamora. It recalled my crucial vote that had saved Angel from execution, my escape, my years in exile and my return on the wings of the victorious revolution to serve as Provisional President of a country that I had hoped to lead along the unfamiliar road to social democracy. It speculated on my growing disenchantment as the Green Revolution turned ever more Red. And it made me out a kind of democratic saint, more pure than Juan Bosch and less tainted with Yankeeism than Muñoz Marín. It gave me an odd feeling to read it here with my head against the dirty stucco wall of the embassy catch-all for Angel Bello's political freaks. In one way, it was all true. And in another, all lie. I had been a mere soldier in the ranks in the fight against Zamora until driven to an act of conscience at the trial. And again, I had had no significant influence on Angel's regime. My hope to change it gradually in my direction had been an exercise in futility, crowned by having to run for my life at the warning of Suzi Cisneros. In two carefully chosen and well-written columns of *The New York Times* I sounded like all the paragons of democratic virtue rolled into one courageous ball of resistance. But how could they know all the doubts, the fears, the hesitations, the failures of the spirit and the flesh that resulted in the procrastinations of Justo Moreno Suárez when life seemed to be calling on him for acts of faith?

Johnie saw me reading and hurried to my side in that over-friendly manner of his. In fairness I should remember that he was raised in the world's largest orphanage, where five thousand children who had come into the world haphazardly all bore the name Valdez. Johnie had been born to dormitory life with five thousand ready-made, alas too readily made, brothers and sisters. There were probably only two ways to survive in a family of five thousand. Either you advance, to the point of becoming a glad-hander, an obnoxious extrovert, or you retreat into yourself and hide in the shadows of the inner mind. I could understand Johnie Valdez, the insufferably cheerful advance man for Johnie Valdez. But long-run understanding is not always the antidote to short-run irritation. I turned away and went on reading.

He cheerfully ignored the slight.

"Howdy doody, Bigshot!" By this time he was leaning over my shoulder and reading my "notices." "*Chihuahua!* How does it feel to be El Señor Bigshot in New York?"

"It would feel much better if I were in New York."

"I am proud of you," Johnie said. "Proud to have you for my friend. If you ever get to the good old U.S.A., you are the logical leader of the next anti-Bello Revolution. And if that *cabrón* ever lets me out I offer my services—I will be your press officer."

"If I ever get to New York, I am finished with politics. I have already been the President of one 'Democratic Revolution.' If the General doesn't become President, the President becomes a General. I am like the other Garbo. All I ask now is to go into exile and be left alone."

Johnie winked at me. "Hokey dokey, if you want to kid a kidder, I get the point."

"Thank you, Johnie," I said as the quickest way to send him back to his corner of the room. "Thank you for understanding."

He gave me a pat on the shoulder, a conspiratorial pat. "Here is Johnie Valdez at your service, at your service until the death."

I stretched out on my back and relished *The New York Times*. After the violent colors of our one True Voice of the Revolution, *Verdad*, it was like enjoying a pastel canvas by a careful pointillist. It was imperfect and it was slanted in its own way, but at least it was a journal of little opinion and much news, while all that was left to us was a paper that was all opinion with a party-controlled trickle of information.

After I had read it from cover to cover I looked around to see if anybody was watching and then tucked it into my pillowcase to save for Marta. I strolled across the aisle and stared down into the courtyard, hot and dusty in the sun. The only object moving was Dolores II sniffing without conviction at the high wicker rubbish basket where the paper plates used for *comida* had been tossed. Suddenly

I was worrying about Dolores I. Had the soldiers driven her away? I hoped someone would recognize her unique qualities and take her in. Meanwhile there was Dolores II, scrawny forager of meager refugee leftovers, the perfect pet for us scabrous asylees.

A vicious-looking black and white tomcat jumped up on the wall, its head full of scars like an old fighter's. It leaped down with a yowl of aggression and Dolores II ran. Around the corner of the building, out of sight, I heard the jungle scream of cat fight, then a terrible moan of victory.

I decided to take a shower. This would be an off hour when I might find the luxury of a solitary shower. I might even be able to sit and think quietly to myself. I had never realized what it was to be deprived of privacy. All day and all night to be aware of human movement and sound. They were not sticking long needles under my fingernails or applying electrodes to my testicles or pulling out my teeth without anesthetics as they did in Belsen and Lubianka and Romano's and Juan del Campo's secret police chambers. Nobody was sealing me into a crowded cattle car or shoving me into a gas chamber. By those twentieth-century standards I was living in comfort. Yet the need to close a door behind me that would shut people out and leave me silently alone was a thirst as real as the dry-mouthed lack of water. Even Paco, my crony and fellow-thief in the night, could wear me down with the knowledge that I could not get rid of him, that we were chained together like lunatics in a medieval asylum.

As I passed the cot of Miguelito, the young man put his book down and called, "Señor Moreno, may I have the honor to speak to you?"

My reluctance was reflected in his earnest face.

"It will only be for a little moment," Miguelito continued. "I have written a declaration of my feelings for Señorita Clara. But I did not think it was right to present it to her until I had your permission."

Miguelito was a well-brought-up young socialist.

I nodded. "Read to me, *joven*, read to me."

He read the poem somewhat tentatively at first but gaining in volume and confidence as he went along. All poets like to recite their own work but in our country poetry reading is almost as popular as our bongos and maracas. Often I have been amazed at the way a noisy, hard-drinking nightclub crowd would become hushed and listen with rapt attention to a master of ceremonies who suddenly launched into a passage from Lorca or Jiménez or Alfonso Reyes. So it was not quite as mad as it may sound for Miguelito Flores to intercept me with his recitation on my way to the bathroom.

It was not a bad poem although it hid behind a conceit that I found psychologically revealing. Miguelito had died and was looking down at Clarita and wishing that he had not been too timid to declare his love while he was mortal and able to sweep her into his arms and claim her as his one true love. It was written in an elegiac style, imitative of Lorca's rhythms but rather effective in its own right. The lad had talent. It ran in the Flores family. In a different world, under "normal conditions," a state consistently foreign to ours, Miguelito might have made an interesting suitor for Clarita. But here in our diplomatic prison I felt I had to tell the intense young man:

"Miguel, I like the poem. As a literary exercise. But as a personal statement, it seems to me you are rushing things. You have only known my daughter a few days."

"It is all I need," Miguel said. "I love her with all my soul. I dream about her—"

"Yes, yes, I am sure you do. But remember, Miguel, these are abnormal circumstances. All of us cooped up here together. A man we would hardly talk to on the outside becomes our inseparable friend. A woman we might not look at twice when we are at liberty becomes a passionate obsession. I think, if we are to preserve our sanity in this place, we must guard against these obsessions."

"Señor Presidente," Miguel insisted, "I swear on the head of my father and my mother and my martyred brother, Tacho—I will always be in love with your daughter."

"My young friend, always is a long time," I said, "and meanwhile none of us knows what is going to happen tomorrow. I would advise you to continue your friendship with Clarita, enjoy your talks and your walks with her in the yard and let it go like that until we know our fates a little more clearly."

"Yes, I thought that is what you would say. So you think I should not say my poem to her."

"Oh, say the poem, as long as you think of it as a poem and not a solemn pronouncement. Or a lifelong commitment."

"Thank you, Don Justo," the young man said gravely.

I went on down the aisle to the bathroom. The door was not locked, but it should have been. When I stepped inside it was into another world of humid steam and hot rushing water. Sitting on the toilet seat but using it as a chair, with the lid down, was El Indio Sandungo. He was naked and with the sweat glistening on his tall black body and the steam from the shower shrouding him he looked like a black jungle god, St. Lazarus having become St. Babalu. I had traveled into his primitive jungle village, lying along the mysterious Río de los Muertos, when the rain came pouring down over a land so hot that the rain itself felt warm and clouds of steam drifted through the mangrove and the wild orchids. If he noticed me he did not acknowledge me. Swaying backward and forward and slapping the rounded edge of the toilet seat as if it were a bongo, El Indio was reciting a prayer in his native language full of Oriental glottal stops like all the other Indian tongues. He stood up and bowed once in each direction, to the four winds, then turned east again and delivered another prayer with his great black arms extended. I could not tell if he was crying or if the tears were sweat beading and rolling down his face.

When he stepped into the hot shower, letting the water strike hard against his broad, hairless chest, it was like watching a wild African horse in the city zoo and wishing you could free him and return him to his forest haunts. El Indio was not a man of politics to be caught up in the technicalities of ideological dissent and diplomatic asylum. And yet he represented a greater danger to the Bello regime than any of his more sophisticated fellow-internees. For Angel had to justify suppression as being for the benefit of the peasants, and here was Sandungo whose name was synonymous with the old rebel cry, "Land to the peasants." A Justo Moreno allowed to go unmolested no longer had a power base and was hardly a threat to the Bello regime. But an El Indio Sandungo free to return to his native province could arouse the tribal passions of the bottom-dog

peasants who wanted land and even cooperatives but not the state
farms that had replaced reactionary masters with commissars. El
Indio could heckle, embarrass and harass, and hold up a revolutionary alternative to the landless who wanted a country of their own
that would not salute the flags of Washington, Moscow or Peking.

At first oblivious to my presence as he washed his body in the
steaming spray, now he turned directly toward me and solemnly
beckoned. I stared at him. He beckoned. I took a step backward.
He beckoned again, inviting me into his jungle world of wild water
and heavy air. I backed away until I felt the door behind me, quickly
opened it and escaped into the aisle of the outer room.

"Wasn't that Alejandro Castillo you were having your picnic
with today?"

It seemed as if Johnie had been waiting for me.

"Yes, it was. Why do you ask?"

"I just heard it on the radio. He's being expelled."

"No me digas! For what?"

"For helping to sneak you into this embassy—"

"He has a right . . . diplomatic immunity."

"—and for being in with you and Garbo and that guy from the
London *Observer*—the espionage ring working with British Intelligence and the CIA."

"But—there is no espionage ring!"

"Garbo is broadcasting from underground."

"How do we know that? He could be in jail with poor Lewison.
The whole thing sounds like one of Angel's dreams of paranoia—
with subtitles supplied by Juan del Campo."

"Wait a minute, pal. Rein in your *burrito*. Angel doesn't fool me
any more than he does you. I only tell you what I hear, not what I
think."

Asylum without Alejandro! I had not yet absorbed it. I felt like a
deep-sea diver on the bottom with his air-line severed. Well, not
quite. I suppose I would not die in sanctuary. But without Alejandro to pull the right rope would I ever surface and breathe free air
again?

From a nearby cot a radio was blaring Perez Prado's "In a Little
Spanish Town." The announcer was winding up an hour of popular

music with a passionate commercial for *Verdad*—"keep up with the Revolution. Only *Verdad* tells you the truth—The day-to-day miracle of the only republic in the New World to break the chains of Yankee domination."

Only *Verdad*, indeed, I thought. Only *Verdad*, period, since there is no other paper.

"And now *Verdad* brings you '1700'—the late news of early evening."

"You can hear it for yourself," Johnie said. "I am sure it will be on again, in more detail."

I followed Johnie toward his cot. On the wall behind him were two photos, one an autographed picture of him with Yvonne de Carlo, another one in which he had managed to place himself between Lyndon Johnson and some South American presidents at an OAS conference. On a shelf over the cot was a Viscount AM-FM radio. He offered me his cot as a good host would indicate the most comfortable chair in a living room. I sat and listened to the usual bulletins about cigar workers who had volunteered a day's work each week without wages as their contribution to the Revolution, the encouraging statistics on rice production, Angel Bello kicking in the soccer ball to open the national championships. The daily diet of progress and propaganda. Finally the announcer's voice became very grave. "Comrades and friends of the Revolution, the espionage plot involving the turncoat President, Garbo of the CIA and a British agent posing as a journalist, took on additional Pan American complications when it was revealed after careful investigation by the Internal Security Office that one of the best-known figures in local diplomatic circles, the cultural attaché Alejandro Castillo, has been using his diplomatic immunity to spy on the People's Republic. The First Colonel of the Revolution, also serving as Foreign Minister, has protested to Castillo's ambassador, Ernesto de San Martín in the strongest terms and is demanding his immediate departure. Failure of the accused cultural attaché to leave within the time stipulated by the People's Republic will result in a warrant for his arrest to stand trial with the rest of his conspirators who face revolutionary justice at the hands of the People's Tribunal."

It all sounded so convincing. I thought of Lewison, brooding somewhere in an isolated cell, of Garbo, who seemed fated to live his entire life underground like a mole, a brilliant rodent with a bald head and myopic eyes always faintly contemptuous even of the comrades who risked their lives with his, of Alejandro, born to the life of international playboy, but flawed with the propensity for involving himself in the plight of his friends. Next year in Positano. There had been a military coup in his country. How would the army dictators greet him when he returned to the capital? Already the attaché job had been a polite form of exile. Perhaps they would use this espionage story as an excuse to get rid of an aristocratic maverick, a sexually and politically unreliable troublemaker. I hoped he could make it safely to Europe. I could see him living out his days in decadent frolic on the coast of Italy. Ordinarily I believed that people had a responsibility to involve themselves in the political and social problems that plague our society. But for Alejandro Castillo I was prepared to make an exception. Let him live where he wished to live as he wished to live, the total hedonist. He, at least, had a special gift for it.

Ever since I had taken sanctuary I had counted on Alejandro. He would bring us food and books and periodicals and, most of all, hope of receiving safe passage. Axes did not fall on Alejandro Castillo. Like an expert boxer he would slip the blow and turn around to laugh at the clumsy ax. That was my image of him: slipping through the best-laid traps, always having the last laugh. An Alejandro caught, humiliated, ordered to turn in his credentials, depart the country in so many hours and perhaps even forced to face the disciplinary music of the military at home, this was not my Alejandro Castillo. It unnerved me. If we could lose Alejandro at the snap of a dictator's fingers, anything could happen, we could rot here in sanctuary or even be turned back to face the new "justice."

I sat for—I have no idea how long. I heard someone ask if I wanted to come to supper, but I shook my head. It was Johnie. He patted my shoulder. "Amigo, are you all right?"

I nodded.

"There is nothing I can do?"

I shook my head.

"I know how it is, keed," Johnie said. "The first big letdown. We all get it in this lousy place. First you are in a daze . . . then you meet people, make friends, get a little hopeful. Then whammo, it hits you, here you are, stuck—for God knows how long. It hits you like a ton of bricks—the big letdown. But you'll get over it. Just like we all get over it."

He put his hand familiarly on my knee and squeezed it. I resented it although I was almost too numb with despair to care about indignity.

"It's that broadcast," he said. "You're worried about the espionage charges. You're afraid that *sinvergüenza* Angelito will—"

"No," I said, barely audible. "It is not that. It is something—personal."

"Cheer up, my friend." I couldn't bear to look up at his ingratiating smile. "Look on the happy side. Tomorrow is the Day of Matrimony. You lucky family man! Tomorrow you will be united with your lovely *esposita*."

I was not thinking about "my lovely *esposita*" (and who else but Valdez could attach that *cursi* phrase to my sturdy wife). I was thinking of Alejandro and his earnest assurance of only a few hours ago, "I promise you, you will never want for food or books or the creature comforts." It had given us a sense of security. Now it made me feel bereft and bitter. Man should never promise anything. The word "promise" is a lie. It should be stricken from our dictionaries. Man is too frail to promise anything.

The Day of Matrimony brought a welcome variety to the routine. Rolls were just as stale and coffee just as pale, but there was a lively sense of anticipation that brought zest and humor to the morning gathering. When old man Gamboa dipped his *bolillo* into his cup, Paco said, "Don't be afraid, old man, push it all the way to the bottom—good practice for the second breakfast you're going to have today." And Johnie, our other self-appointed Matrimonial Day master of ceremonies: "Here, Gamboa, have another roll, you are going to need all your strength."

Those who were not enjoying the special privileges of the Day of Matrimony seemed to take a vicarious pleasure in sharing in the sensuous anticipation. It passed from place to place around the table like potent wine that made everyone giddy. Almost every word in Spanish has a double meaning and this morning whatever I mentioned—if I asked Momentito for a saucer I would be told that I would have one to my liking soon enough. If I asked for a knife to cut the hard *bolillo* I would be told that if I did not have a knife of my own the matrimonial visit would be a total loss. I laughed and accepted the *picardías* as part of the Day of Matrimony. In captivity one goes to extremes. There seems no answer, no release, no escape. And when monotony is broken it is like a village fiesta, when the agonies of daily existence are put aside, when the overworked peasant puts on a mask and a gay cloak and loses himself in the carnival. Even El Gordo was not immune. He limped to the table and one of the Zamoristas who would talk to him asked what the trouble was and he said he had a slight attack of the gout and the Zamorista said, *"Ni modo*—the job you have to do today is not done with the foot." And El Gordo managed a self-satisfied smile.

The ablutions were no less ceremonial. It was the accepted custom of our dormitory that each *matrimonio*—or *Don Juan Cuerdas* as we were more rudely called—was permitted twenty minutes of uninterrupted preparation in the bathroom. Señor Gamboa emerged from his private toilette reeking of sweet lavender lotion and with his few hairs combed lovingly in a circle to simulate a full head of hair. Then he put on the clean shirt he had been saving and the one shiny dark suit he had managed to preserve. He even wore high-laced shoes for the occasion.

Paco came down the aisle to study him ostentatiously, for the benefit of his audience. *"Pues, hombre,"* he said, "are you sure you are going to an *aventura amorosa?* You look more as if you're going to church."

"It's the same thing, Pacocito," Johnie chimed in, like the second half of a vaudeville team, "since the door of the church is always open on Sunday."

"That particular door is open every day," someone muttered at the far end of the long room and laughter crackled down the aisle like a lighted fuse.

I felt sorry for old Gamboa, but he was busy preening for his weekly encounter with Señora Cookie. And since he was hard of hearing, the wit of his comrades was lost on him. Or, did he hear more than we thought, I wondered, remembering my own reaction when they had spoken of Clarita.

"Take a good look at him, boys," Johnie said. "Is he not a regular peacock!" Then he addressed himself to the ancient druggist with exaggerated solicitude. "Wait a little moment, amigo, I will fix the back of your collar." As he did so, he held up two fingers behind the unsuspecting Gamboa's head. "There, my good friend, now you are the envy of every *pendejo* in this grand hotel." And he turned to the rest of us, still hoisting the two shameful fingers above the old man's head. "Am I speaking anything less than the truth, boys? Don't you all envy druggist Gamboa his beautiful *esposita*? And is not imitation the sincerest form of flattery? You bet your life—every one of you would like to be in his shoes!" And then he added, inaudibly to the grinning Gamboa, "And most of you have!" Then he shouted in his ear, "Good luck, you proud peacock! Enter the fray! Show her who's boss in your family!"

It was wicked what Johnie Valdez was doing to Enrique Gamboa, but the laughter of cruelty comes even more readily in confinement.

Entering into the spirit of the occasion was Alvarez, dapper with a carnation in his buttonhole and an air of professional gaiety. As soon as he saw Licenciado Alvarez, Señor Gamboa began to protest that the authorities had made a mistake and that they were accusing the wrong Gamboa. But Bertie waved this aside with a practiced smile. "Señor, this is not the day to discuss your file. It is the Day of Matrimony! So enjoy yourself, Señor. Next week we will be discussing your case and perhaps we will have some good news, yes? Now come with me. Your private room is ready."

As Bertie led the ancient bridegroom to his rendezvous, he paused at my cot and said in a confidential tone, "I will be back for

you in half an hour. Each *marido* is permitted one hour, but with
Señor Gamboa"—he shrugged expressively—"after five minutes
they begin to argue."

I did not respond. I shied from these public displays of intimate
matters. Memory called back a night when Marta was visiting her
sister in Mexico City; after many *Gonzalones* at the Press Club I
went on with some of my drinking companions to a nearby bordello where I drank for another half hour in the crowded after-hours
bar of Tía Felisa's Casa de Amor with a large-eyed Indian girl who
told me her troubles with a sad-merry smile. It was the same old
tale of girls in a slum *vecindad* who find themselves impregnated
by their uncles or their cousins or even their brothers when they are
thirteen or fourteen and who drift into prostitution as naturally as
little celluloid boats floating in a bathtub drift into the whirlpool
under the drain. With our drinks still in hand we went up the stairway to the bedrooms on the second floor. But there we found half
a dozen other couples waiting their turn. All the rooms were occupied. Tía Felisa was doing a rushing business. Abruptly the impulse
to make love to this pretty little celluloid boat was gone. I felt
obscene, depraved, a vulgar public spectacle to be waiting in line as
men queue up for a crowded latrine at the boxing matches. I
pressed some bills into the small hand of the child, muttering something senseless like, *"Lo siento,* I am sorry, *chica,"* and hurried
down the stairs, past more couples on their way up, into the cool
night air of the street.

This time we were in another kind of bordello where Marta and
I also had to pay our way, but from which we could not flee simply
by hurrying down the stairs and out the door. I watched Alvarez as
he paused at El Gordo's section. Apparently the General and I
would go to our legal assignations in tandem. I was eager to see
Marta. At the same time I was surprised at the depth of resentment
I felt toward El Gordo for his tryst with Adriana.

He was in the bathroom more than the custom-established limit
of twenty minutes, with Búfalo and Jesusito accompanying him,
and when he finally emerged he was a model of tropical masculine
well-being. The musky scent of expensive cologne preceded him
down the aisle. A few of the Zamoristas who had never lost the

habit of complimenting the masters of the fallen regime volunteered to inform him what a splendid spectacle of manhood he was.

But dependable Paco O'Higgins, rum bottle in hand, was more than a match for the sycophants.

"*Halo*, Gordo!" he said. "Are you going to take Búfalo along to help you do the job?"

Búfalo made a move as if to reprise the ritual at the bathroom door in the morning, but El Gordo restrained him with a gesture. He was a fastidious man and he probably feared bloodying his immaculate white suit at such a delicate moment.

When Bertie returned with Señor Gamboa, catcalls and double entendres greeted his reappearance. The old *marido* fell prone on his bed, to the accompaniment of dormitory laughter, and then began to remove his old-fashioned celluloid collar.

"Well, *viejo*," Johnie Valdez called out. "What took you so long? Was the rabbit unable to find her little carrot?"

"*Sinvergüenzas*—shameless ones," the old man said. "There was a time when matrimony was a sacred institution. Is there nothing sacred any more?"

I admired the injured dignity of Señor Gamboa. The Revolution had driven him here by bureaucratic accident. His was undoubtedly a case of mistaken identity. The state was doing it to him and the embassy was doing it to him and his peroxide kewpie of a wife was doing it to him and his fellow-asilados were doing it to him. He was the eternal husband, the eternal fool and yet, somewhere in the depth of his humiliation, he found the strength to rebuke his tormentors.

Now it was our turn, mine and El Gordo's. Carefully ignoring each other, we followed Licenciado Alvarez down the stairs to the door to the second floor, the same one Paco and I had passed through on our nocturnal raid of the refrigerator. From an impressive cluster of keys, our keeper selected the one that admitted us to the gold-carpeted hallway where he told me to wait while he led El Gordo to his room. I watched the resplendent, white silk figure pass through the door the chargé d'affaires opened for him and then Alvarez returned, amiable but businesslike, and gestured for me to follow him in the opposite direction. We paused at an ornately carved door and my protector or jailer produced another key.

"I am sure you will find everything very comfortable, Your Excellency. I will return in one hour. Here is Licenciado Alvarez, at your service."

I managed a thank you. I was anxious to get this obsequious official out of my sight. But he hesitated and added, "I am sorry it is necessary to lock the door—from the outside. It is nothing personal, you understand. A man of your stature we trust completely."

"All right, all right, I understand," I said.

Injured by the impatient tone of my voice, he quickly unlocked the door and stepped back for me to enter.

He had not told me that Marta would be there ahead of me. She was sitting on a small sofa across the room, in front of the double windows.

"Marta," I said. "How long have you been here?"

"I don't know. Some *puta* in our cell-block stole my wristwatch. The only safe place to hide it is inside your *raya* and even there I wouldn't trust those *brujas* I have to live with."

She made me laugh. How good it was to hear that mouth again.

"I miss you," I said. "After a quarter of a century it's not so easy to sleep without you."

"A habit!" she said. *"Que romántico!"*

"A sweet habit," I said. "You know what I mean."

"I was only teasing." She came to me and her limp seemed more extreme.

"Your knee?"

"Enough with my knee. So I may not be able to run the high hurdles in the next Olympics. My knee is the least of our worries."

Our temporary love nest was a spacious bedroom furnished in Spanish décor, not in aristocratic colonial taste like Alejandro's villa but neither in the synthetic modern that had begun to contaminate our indigenous style. There was a large double bed that seemed to be waiting for us obscenely, like the bed that was the only piece of furniture in the rooms of Tía Felisa's. Actually the room was not like that at all, but I could not shake off the sense of indignity.

I led my tough old bird of a wife to the bed but not for the reason planned by the establishment. Despite her offhandedness, her knee was getting worse. To anyone of her encrusted independence, physical defect was anathema. It foreshadowed old age and the final humiliation of material deterioration awaiting all of us who are not lucky enough to die in our sleep or unlucky enough to be awakened from sleep and dragged to the *paredón*. She sat on the edge of the bed and rubbed the offending kneecap while I paced.

"I suppose you heard the news," I said. "Alejandro?"

"From all sides. That *cursi* whore who thinks she is a countess, Señora Romano, was the first to hear it. She has a radio that can pick up a crystal set in China. She could hardly wait to spread the good news."

"I heard she was a recluse, that no one ever sees her."

"Recluse!" Marta said. "She sits in her room like a queen, combing her hair and summoning the peasants from our *cárcel* to hold an audience with her. I haven't had the honor yet, so I have only heard about her special suite. It must be like the bridal suite of the Hilton. Well, not quite, but after the pigsty we are living in— Don Ernesto should be ashamed of himself. In the States money talks, but here it is a deafening scream. I wonder how much that *pendejo* pays for his lady's chamber. I'll bet he's squeezing the *cojones* of El Gordo like a nutcracker, our eminent Ambassador."

"I wonder why they aren't living together."

"Well, she's in the women's wing. And even though Don Ernesto could make one of his 'special exceptions' he's smarter than that. This way he gets it from both ends. She pays to have the private room and he pays because he doesn't—which makes him even more anxious to get his safe passage. But they say he'll never get out until he tells Angel where his millions are hidden, and Don Ernesto won't arrange the Romanos' visa unless El Gordo splits with him."

"*Pobrecito*," I said. "My heart bleeds for him. But what about us —without Alejandro? And what happens to our Alejandro when he flies home and those damned generals are waiting for him?"

"Alejandro is a cat," Marta said. "He will land on his feet—or better yet, on his back in that enormous bed by the sea. But we will still be rotting here on this manure pile unless we take steps."

"Maybe I should send a personal note to Don Ernesto."

"With Alejandro gone, maybe's are too expensive," Marta said. She had stretched her legs out straight on the bed now, with her back against the headboard. "As soon as Doctora Julia told me the news, I asked Señora Lorona to deliver a note for us, asking the Ambassador for a private interview at his earliest convenience."

"Good. There must be a way out of here."

"I was counting on Alejandro. But now, even if we send her off alone, we have to get Clarita out of here." She looked at me. "Immediately. She can stay with my sister in Mexico City. Surely Don Ernesto could arrange that one little favor with Angel."

"Good God," I said. "Are you saying that Clarita—has she—"

"Who can tell? But she's acting strangely. It almost seems as if we left the real Clarita behind and some strange spirit has taken her place."

"You talk like an Indian! Have you asked her directly?"

"Of course. You should know me by now. I put it to her not mother to child but woman to woman, just as I would to Tina Alonso. 'Tell me, Tinita, who is fucking you this week,' I used to ask her."

"Marta, I don't want to hear about your obscene conversations with that slut. I want to hear about Clarita! What did Clarita say?"

"Clarita said, 'It is none of your business, Mama,' and she walked away. And when I speak to her in her cot, she pretends she's asleep."

"I can't believe it," I said. "No, I won't believe it. Not with the old pigs we have on my side of the fence. Maybe with young Miguelito. At least he is her age, and gentle, intelligent—"

"I have a surprise for you," Marta said. "That is not the type we girls pick to do it with."

"Marta, damn you! You almost sound blasé about it. If this has happened, it's a tragedy!"

"Of course it is, stupid idiot. I know it as well as you do. But going around groaning 'tragedy'— All we can do now is think practically. Not waste time on emotions. Get her out of here and to Mexico City as soon as possible."

"This slime of a fish bowl. If that sadistic pig and his Neanderthal man have done it to her, I'm going to kill them—even if I go with them."

"Be quiet," Marta said. "That would be a big help. Stop sounding like a *macho* father. They are always going around pinching everybody's *nalgas* and then ready to shoot the *machos* who pinch their wives and daughters. It's a national disease."

"I am not pinching anybody's *nalgas*."

"Not yet," Marta said.

"Marta, in the name of the devil, what are you talking about? You're a wonderful woman, but there are days when an hour with you and I am ready for the *manicomio*."

"You are already in the *manicomio*," Marta said. "I want to help us get out of the *manicomio*."

"All right," I said. "It is agreed we will try to see Don Ernesto and we will ask him to help both of you to get your safe passage."

"I want to wait here with you. My sister will take good care of Clarita."

"If you can go, I say go. Why suffer this filthy life any longer?"

"If you can bear it, so can I."

"Let us see what happens. Let us see how you feel after we've talked with Don Ernesto."

"Justo?"

"What?"

"Do you still love me?"

"Oh my God, Marta, what a stupid time to ask such a stupid question."

"Is there ever a better time to ask it?"

"Do middle-aged people have to keep reassuring each other with 'I love you'?"

"Maybe especially middle-aged people."

"All right, then. I love you. I love you, Marta."

"You used to purr it in my ear. You used to say it in a way that made everything in me open up to you like a flower."

I stepped close to the bed and looked down at her. "Marta, dearest, I do love you. But I feel wrong here in a strange room with a jailer in a business suit holding a time-clock on us. It may have to wait until we are free again and know that Clarita is free again before I can say 'I love you' and what is more important, do something about it."

"I'm as concerned about Clarita as you," Marta said. "But at this moment there is nothing we can do for her. At this moment all we can do is something for ourselves." She reached out from the bed and lay her hand on my leg above the knee. Then the tips of her fingers marched lightly up my thigh until they came to rest. They paused a moment and then pressed gently.

I was wondering if Bertie Alvarez was watching from a peephole. Or maybe the fat Señora Lorona. Or the entire embassy intelligence staff might be listening. It was a fish bowl all right and maybe my friend Paco was wrong and those who thought they were hiding under rocks were only fooling themselves.

In spite of my anxieties, Marta could draw on all the good years to know how to excite me. I felt a swelling and a pressure against the binding of my clothes. I was a caged male pigeon, helplessly mated and induced to passion.

"I don't think we have time to undress," I said.

"So we will not undress," Marta said. Slowly and carefully she undid the zipper. Then she cupped her hand under me and brought her face close. I leaned into her and closed my eyes and weaved back and forth.

"Ay," she said, after a moment. "I love to feel them in my hand, getting hot and hard."

"Marta, I want you."

"I will turn on my other side," she said, "and you can—"

"Yes, yes."

I began to climb onto the bed. The springs were very old and they protested.

"Come to me, come to me," Marta said.

I lifted my other leg onto the bed. I felt clumsy with my clothes still on. I was suspended between desire and self-consciousness. Marta had raised her skirt up over her hips, and worked her underpants down to her knees. What I saw was large, plump, erotic, and not exactly beautiful.

"Come to me, come to me, Justo darling," she murmured into the pillow and tried to fit her bare *nalgas* against me.

I thought I heard a movement, a brushing at the door. I drew back. Then I heard human voices. Then a light, discreet knock on the door.

I jumped up. I zipped my fly. A bit of my shorts caught in the mechanism and for a dread moment I thought I might be apprehended that way.

"Señor Moreno?"

It was the voice of our jailer.

"Yes, yes, of course."

Again I felt not at all the martyred President but like a guilty schoolboy caught in the act. I tried to make my voice sound matter-of-fact and businesslike. Marta and her appetites. Something had strongly told me that this was not our time or place.

The voice of Licenciado Alvarez came dripping through the door. "We trust we are not disturbing you but—the hour has passed."

"Oh, of course. Quite all right. We were just talking." For some fool reason I felt I had to appease, to reassure Bertie Alvarez. Marta was already sitting on the edge of the bed and had arranged herself as I went to the door. I unlocked our side and then Alvarez unlocked his. Our hour had run out so quickly. I wished I could turn the sand-clock upside down. One of the lessons to be learned in sanctuary was not to misuse the rare private moments doled out to us.

Señora Lorona was also at the door to waddle Marta back to the ladies' wing.

"Well, did you have a pleasant visit?" Bertie Alvarez asked, smiling his most ingratiating smile.

Sensing the frustrated Marta winding up for one of her truck-driver expletives, I put a restraining hand on her arm.

"Embrace Clarita for me," I said. "And Marta—"

"Yes, my love. Viva the Day of Matrimony."

I watched as she walked away, limping badly and looking straight ahead so as not to have to engage in conversation with the simpering lady shepherd. Yes, Marta, I love you. Now I could have told her without the prompting. I don't know why but it was usually when she was walking away from me that I felt an impulse to shout out to her my true time-tested feeling.

10

A color, one single spot of color can change the entire mood, the entire ambience of a room. I felt it even before I saw it as I crossed the threshold into our dormitory. The color was green. It was the green hair of Goyo Solano. Goyo was the bohemian original who believed it his artistic duty to obey his impulses. Inspired by the Green Revolution, with a theatrical gift for dramatizing his political passions, he had startled the literati by appearing in public with his hair dyed to demonstrate his loyalty to the original conception of the agrarian revolution.

I hurried down the aisle to him. Obviously he had just arrived. Momentito and another embassy *mozo* were setting up a narrow military folding cot for him between mine and the Death-head's. The canvas cots were hardly a foot apart instead of a foot and a half.

"Goyo! What a surprise!"

"How goes it, dear one? I have wondered how you were."

We fell into a deep abrazo. Marta had always complained because Goyo flirted outrageously with the young men at our parties. But I could accept his affectations and eccentricities because I believed they were spontaneous and inwardly generated. When he wore his hair sunflower yellow it was because he was going through a period when he felt like a sunflower. When he exchanged his bed for a coffin it was because he felt more than a sense of mourning for the young men put to death by Zamora and Romano. He felt his life was a living death while the youth of our country were being murdered. There were no conveniences in the coffin. No pillow, no mattress to soften the hard wooden cubicle. Of course it was masochistic. Of course Goyo Solano was wildly neurotic, to the point of insanity by conventional standards. And like all sensitive men in our culture he was fascinated with death. In the winding staircase of his home, built in the shape of a giant S, there were human skulls set artistically in niches, illuminated by soft blue lights. And in his private theater, which was built like an elegant jewel box, carpeted and draped in red velvet, he liked to produce the little verse plays he had written about death. All the characters were skeletons and the plays were performed on a black stage with the white bones of the performers standing out in incandescent paint.

I remembered Goyo Solano at one of his "evenings" on the stage in an elegant purple tuxedo trimmed in maroon, with his hair deep bougainvillea pink to suit the occasion, welcoming his illustrious guests—the intelligentsia of the country. Painters, writers and musicians vied for invitations to Goyo's entertainments—to his "little cycle of playlets on our old friend, Death."

And again, it was not morbidity for its own sake that inspired Goyo Solano. It seemed that all good Latin poets were in love with death. "Although I know the roads, I shall never reach Córdoba," is the sad song of Lorca. "Oh, Death is waiting for me on the road to Córdoba." Death is always waiting for our poets on the road to somewhere. And for us it is not merely a figure of speech. A black bull from Guisando was waiting for Lorca's friend Ignacio Sánchez Mejías at five o'clock in the afternoon. A Franco firing squad was waiting for Lorca on the road to Córdoba. And for his friend César Vallejo, the eternal dice were thrown and the hollow eyes of death turned up, as that displaced Peruvian puts it, like two funereal aces of mud. No, Gregorio Solano was in the great tradition of Latin poets who cannot wait for death to embrace them but instead go forward to court her, seduce her, ravage her if necessary. For the Latin poet the couch of love is nearly always a coffin and it was only the theatricality of Goyo Solano, or the courage of his conviction, that inspired him to sleep in a black coffin and to dress his actors as cadavers.

I remembered Goyo under the purple spotlight of his elegant theater reminding us that we must dwell upon death in order to save ourselves from the momentary presumptuousness of life. Man is a tiny button on the great cloak of death, he had recited from the stage. The tiny button drops off and the cloak does not even notice it is gone. Only the tiny button is aware of its falling. Help, help,

help me! it cries out in its tiny voice. But the cloak never hears this. He is too busy sewing on new little buttons.

"But if you say life is meaningless, why do you protest the excesses of Zamora by sleeping in a coffin?" Goyo had been challenged one evening. It was the kind of question he enjoyed. "I do not say life is meaningless. I only say it is foolish to give it too much importance. Still the emphasis should be up to the individual. What I resent is Zamora's presumption in deciding for them when they should die. Our life is our only real possession. To steal it from us is the most brutal kind of theft. Death should be a private affair. I demand the right to commit suicide. And for my lovers to commit suicide. I would die before I let anyone write my poetry for me. When Zamora lets Romano torture our young men to death because they do not agree with him he is writing their poetry for them, he is depriving them of their sacred right to die when and how they choose."

Zamora and Romano had tolerated such utterances from Goyo, shrugging him off as a pervert-eccentric until he was featured on the cover of Rubén Silva's *Alegre,* stretched out in his coffin. It was captioned "Gregorio Solano, *El Poeta de los Muertos,*" Poet Laureate of the Dead. Ostensibly, in the sensationalist style of *Alegre,* it was a prurient exposé of the bohemian excesses of a mad poet, his dyed hair, his Black Masses, his transvestite costumes, his love affairs with other celebrated *maricones.* But superimposed on a collage of photographs of beautiful young men was a poem of Goyo's called *"Volveremos,"* "We Will Return," which said, in lines reminiscent of Lorca, "You may kill one of us, you may kill two of us, you may kill five of us, twenty of us, a thousand of us, or twenty thousand. *No importa!* For we will return—for every one, five, for every thousand, ten thousand. Yes, we will return, the tortured, the mutilated, the men-children whose captial crime was youth. From our shallow graves our skeleton teeth sing a merry song, like castanets they sing with spirited assurance, *y Volveremos, y Volveremos,* over and over again, We Will Return."

The Tigers of Romano who came to Goyo's home after the sensational spread in *Alegre* would not admit that the arrest had anything to do with an offensive poem. They pretended that the Solano compound was being raided on moral grounds. And it was not a case that had to be invented. On the half acre of his unique estate on the outskirts of the city, Goyo maintained a rare museum of pornography. There was a large room devoted to the wood carvings of his brother Baltasar, an exhibit that was overwhelming. Every sexual position was represented, man to woman, man to man, woman to woman, all worked exquisitely in our native mahogany. It was explicit, realistic, but Baltasar Solano never let you forget that it was an artist who had shaped the dark mahogany to warm human flesh and form and molded the lovers together.

It was a thrilling and for some viewers devastating experience to walk through the room of the Hundred-and-One Positions, as Goyo called it. He was a devilish man, Goyo Solano, saturnine, attractive, with the face of an eager and self-satisfied cat and the body of a torero. Full of energy and excitement, he would dance from sculpture to sculpture, pointing out his favorites, laughing, making witty and irreverent comments. One of his favorite games was to introduce well-bred North American girls to the Baltasar exhibit. They were from Vassar or Radcliffe and they had read his poetry and they came impressed. Casually he would ask them if they would like to see "the sculpture of my crazy brother." And then he would relish their discomfort or titillation. Beyond the exhibit was the Room of Venus. Here was a small indoor swimming pool, sprinkled with gardenia petals, large enough for a dozen nymphs, and beyond that, raised by half a dozen marble steps, an enormous circular bed in a room lit like a stage in subtle pastels. There were always beautiful young men around, the models of Baltasar, the lovers of Gregorio, and it would delight the feline host to arrange for the seduction of the "respectable" *gringas*. There were peepholes through which Goyo and his other guests could watch the sport. And sometimes if he felt the moment was appropriate he would join the enchanted *gringas* in the magnificently canopied bed and make love to his young man who in turn entertained a young lady who thought she had come to commune with aesthetic gods. "You see," he would explain, calling them deeper and deeper into the forest like Pan, "it is not anything to get so complicated and involved and emotional and guilty about like you North Americanos. It is to laugh, it is to enjoy, it is to feel, it is to raise the most beautiful hell for one little moment between the hard birth and the hard death. We are all skeletons making love, all dead people reaching out for our one little moment to be alive. That is why I cannot be faithful to one person. I must have a hundred, or a thousand if I am lucky. I can only be faithful to Gregorio Solano the poet. I am one rotten son-of-a-beetch, yes?" And he would fill the room with outrageous laughter.

But the Tigers of Romano, suddenly transformed into soldiers of morality, swooped down on "La Casa de S" and carried off the singular exhibit and with it the inspired madman who presided there. They threw Gregorio into a large prison tank along with pickpockets, dope addicts and common thieves. Rubén Silva, my death-head cot-neighbor who played all sides, ran a follow-up spread in *Alegre* with photographs of the lurid sculpture and the Pool of Diana and some of the voyeur photography purchased from a captain of the Tigers. It was typical of Silva to have it both ways, to use Goyo's poetry against the Zamora-Romano regime and then to make a public display of Goyo's extravagant vices that played into the hands of repressive officials who protested that the poet was being arrested not for his political resistance but for his scandalous behavior.

In the common tank Goyo had refused to eat. He was known for his conviction that eating was an art, like sexual expression. The slops offered him by filthy guards disgusted him. He wrote poetry on the walls in chalk, blasphemous poetry against the Tigers of Romano, some of it obscene but quite wonderful. (Later it was published in *Libertad,* the anti-Zamora organ in New York, as "Poems from the Wall of My Prison.") Meanwhile Goyo insisted that he would not have to starve very long because the artists of the world and his fellow-poets of Pan America would come to his rescue. He was right. The International P.E.N. Committee on the Political Persecution of Writers released to the press a strong cable to President Zamora. Pablo Neruda protested from Chile, and Alfonso Reyes, Octavio Paz and Carlos Fuentes from Mexico, the pious Molinari from the Argentine. Zamora had enough trouble without taking on the intellectuals of Latin America. He had Goyo removed from the common pen to the prison hospital and from there to the airport. Goyo Solano lived through the last year of the Zamora regime in Greenwich Village. It was there that he wrote some of his most exquisite poems, expressing his longing to go home again to the land of the royal palm trees taller, more beautiful than skyscrapers. In his exile in New York City, like José Martí half a century before him, Gregorio Solano dreamed of a creative revolution and a new era of contentment for his country. Bello was his new Martí and as *"Volveremos"* became the marching song of the young student and campesino guerrillas, Goyo became the poet laureate of the coming Green Revolution that would regenerate the life of our country. It was during that year in Greenwich Village that he began to wear his hair green to symbolize his fealty to the Little Green Angels.

Now, again driven out of the territorial state imposed on his beloved country, he was still wearing his hair green—but for another reason. Before it had been to remind the Zamora regime that the Angelistas were coming. Now it was to remind the Angelistas of the fresh green promises they had broken. He had been a hero in the early months of the victory of the Revolution. And his revised song, *"Volveremos—Los Angelitos Verdes"* had been adopted as the national anthem of the new Republic. Angel had even invited him to share the podium with us so that he could read his poem to the hundreds of thousands gathered in the Plaza of Independence. Angel had given Goyo a warm abrazo and so had the other comrades, Juan del Campo and Elena Concepción and Garbo and myself, all bathed that day in the same rosy light of revolutionary dawn.

Goyo had written new verses dedicated to the triumph of the Green Revolution. The skeletons of the martyred young had promised to return. Now the militant campesinos and their student allies were pouring down from the hills and out of the jungles to free their little brown brothers from the rich ruling families, from the tyrants who did their dirty work and from the American sugar and coffee monopolists. It sounded like a radical poem. It was easy to confuse Goyo with the Marxists and the Communists. It was easy for Goyo to confuse himself. But in truth he was no Pablo Neruda crossbreeding his genuine art with Communist doctrine. He was simply carried away, like so many of our romantic nationalists, with a profound longing to be free. And since the longest shadow was cast by the North Americans, Goyo seemed to be echoing the extreme Left in identifying intervention and oppression with Wall Street capitalism protected by gringo militarism.

In fact, in those free and easy days of the Green illusion, Goyo had been invited to come to the United States to read his poetry in several of the eastern universities, but the passport division of the American embassy, with their usual political subtlety, refused him a visa on the grounds that he was considered a dangerous Communist.

A nonpolitical mystic and dreamer contemptuous of the United States because he saw it as a symbol of mechanized mass-man, Goyo Solano had begun to sense the phalanxism in Angel's Revolution. Despising organized fanaticism, he had defied the Revolution by writing a poem entitled "An Open Letter to My Young Friend Yevtushenko" that had shaken and divided the intelligentsia:

> My comrades are those
> who will not say Comrade . . .

It may not have been a great poem, but like some of Yevtushenko's own work, it had become a rallying point for our intellectuals who had welcomed the overthrow of Zamora and were now torn between their personal loyalty to Angel and their dread of being Sovietized.

Goyo had not been arrested immediately by Angel's security police. As in my case, he simply had been ignored by the government press, was no longer seen in public and, with guards posted outside his home "for his own protection," found himself under unofficial but unnerving house arrest.

Now we were sitting together on my cot. He was wearing an odd costume, an old-fashioned golfing suit of green corduroy knickers and jacket with a yellow lining. He glanced around at the long, monotonous row of cots. "What a disgusting place. I was very angry with the Ambassador for not providing me with a private room. I should think he would for you as well. After all, we are hardly ordinary asilados."

I smiled. "Every one of our 'cell-mates' is extraordinary—in his own eyes and in the eyes of Angel. Otherwise he would not be here."

"Justo, you are an unregenerate democrat."

"And you?"

"Still a disciple of Ortega y Gasset. The cult of individual excellence. Poets and mystics. That is why I adored Angel. I thought at last we would have a sweet prince of creativity in the Presidential

Palace. How frightening it is to discover that Christ and Judas can turn out to be the same man!"

He looked at me with his yellow-brown Mongolian eyes that seemed to take on some of the pigmentation of his green hair, which was cut in bangs that fell halfway down his high forehead. Other asylees were staring at him, but he seemed totally unselfconscious. He was accustomed to being stared at, laughed at by the Philistines. He flaunted his green bangs, the single earring he affected, his whimsical clothing and his *mariconismo*. "Mind you, dear one," he had said to me with princely condescension, "I have nothing against men going to bed with women. I simply think it is boringly pedestrian and vulgar. Believe me, I have tried it. I have tried everything. I even tried making love to a duck once while a young friend held it for me. But I did not like the way it quacked. And the feathers made me sneeze." Then he laughed uninhibitedly, delighted to have shocked me.

"Tell me, Goyo, how did you manage to escape the guards—and to make it into sanctuary?"

"My heart is broken," Goyo said, not really listening. "The love of my life has been taken away from me. My poor baby. My poor Marcelito."

From the sleeve of his green corduroy jacket he took a small lace handkerchief and dabbed his eyes.

Goyo had discovered Marcelo Luna on a trip far into the mountains of the Santa Marías, where the primitive Mocaño tribe still lived as they had two thousand years ago. Cultivating hallucinatory mushrooms for their religious services, they were a singularly beautiful people with dark bronze skin, eyes like fawns, with richly formed, sensuous lips and high-bridged "Roman" noses. Goyo immediately fell in love with the twelve-year-old Marcelo whose dark lashes were so long as to look artificial and whose dark eyes had myriad colors behind them like the fire opal. For a few hundred pesos Marcelo's family was happy to sell him to the wealthy outsider. There were ten other ragged children living in a one-room thatched hut blackened by the charcoal brazier over which the worn-out mother cooked the daily meal of corn and beans.

Marcelo brought his homemade flute with him, showed an aptitude for music, and at fifteen gave his first violin recital in Goyo's private theater. There was no doubt that Goyo had made an unusual discovery. The dark, grave Marcelo Luna was not only a joy to look at but to listen to. Goyo, a strange cross between a proud father and a proud lover with a gifted young mistress, had hopes of bringing him all the way to New York and Carnegie Hall. His "Ode to Marcelo" was a poem recited in all the Latin capitals.

Now Goyo was desolate. Although he was under house arrest, Marcelo had been allowed to pass through the guards to give a concert at the University. When Marcelo was hours overdue, Goyo's brother Baltasar came to inform him that Marcelo had been arrested. The pretext had been that Marcelo had engaged in a political argument with some pro-Angel students and had made remarks about the Revolution that clearly stamped him as a dangerous counter-revolutionary. Goyo's first impulse had been to storm down to the police station and demand his protégé's release. But Baltasar was convinced that they were not after the innocent Marcelo at all. They were hoping that Goyo would come down and provoke a scene, an *escándalo,* that would "force" the police to take him into custody.

"All that night, I do not sleep a single minute," Goyo was saying. "I pace. I cry. I drink cognac. I have attacks of my cursed migraine headaches. I have nightmares without sleeping about what they are doing to my beautiful baby. His face must be so frightened. Ever since he came down from his village he has known only luxury and love. You know I am a son-of-a-beetch. I have a very poor character for being trusted. But always with Marcelito I was loving and kind. When we made love it was like in the Bible, when the big animals lie down with the small, the gentle and defenseless ones."

Goyo's interpretation of the Bible may have seemed unconventional. But there was no denying the depth of his feeling for the innocent manchild, lured from the security of his Mocaño tribe, caught in the web of conflicting ideologies he would never understand.

"In the morning when I looked out, I saw guards who moved like mechanical men taking orders from a computer. It made my heart sick."

He crossed his legs and ran his long fingers along his green bangs, a characteristic gesture. "Escape is not really that difficult," he said. "I called in my cook Anabela and asked her to loan me one of her dresses. Fortunately she was not the least bit suspicious. That is the advantage of being a little bit crazy. I often wore dresses . . . you remember the marvelous orange sequin I wore in my production of *Carmen Meets Marquis de Sade* . . . Well, I slipped a pillow under the dress, put on a black braided wig from my theater, tied a scarf over my head, got a big laundry basket in which I hid these clothes and a few precious books, and sallied forth. It was such a good performance that the guards even said 'Buenos días' and passed a few jokes."

"And on this side?"

"The same thing. I said I had some laundry for Señor Alvarez. I said it like this—" Goyo demonstrated a passable falsetto—"and waltzed right through."

"And then?"

"Licenciado Alvarez received me. He was not pleased." Goyo looked up with mischievous eyes. "I had managed to get in without paying any *mordida*. I have heard the Ambassador asks as much as ten thousand. Alvarez grumbled that there was no room left, that he had no idea where they could squeeze me in and that he was not sure the Ambassador would validate my case, since I was a poet and not really a political personality. I said, 'Nonsense, every time we have a new regime here I write a poem that gets me into trouble, so I must be more political than I realize!' And—here I am!"

He gazed around the long room of cracked walls and faded paint. At that moment El Gordo entered from the common room with his attentive Búfalo and Jesusito. Búfalo nudged his general and pointed at Goyo Solano. El Gordo, unmindful of the gout that obviously had been causing him pain, nodded and laughed, a hearty, dirty horselaugh. Even the sad face of Jesusito tried to smile to accommodate the master.

"The thought of having to sleep in the same room with that beast," Goyo said. "I shall die. I am simply unable to bear it. Look at him! He looks like the father of all toads, decked out in his white silk. Like an ogre from *Alice in Wonderland*." He pointed at him theatrically and then drew his hand back to cover his eyes. "It makes me feel physically sick to my stomach to look at him."

At this moment El Gordo turned and challenged Goyo directly. *"Que tal?* How goes it, little poet? You sad excuse for a man. So, you were so anxious for your Angelito to return, eh? *Volveremos!* Writing marching songs for him, eh? You thought you'd wind up in the Presidential Palace with him, sucking his—"

Búfalo let out a roar and the giant toad fell back on his double cot, pleased with his repartee.

Goyo brushed nervously at his green bangs and turned away. "He makes my skin cold and wet," he said. "I think I would die, literally die, if I had to stay in here very long. Thank goodness the P.E.N. already knows about this. And the Association of Pan American Writers. I managed to get word to them before I slipped through the guards. You will see. It will be like last time. They will make too great an *escándalo* for Angel to keep me here long."

"Yes, Maestro," I felt I should reassure him, "with the P.E.N. and the Pan American Writers and the great poets of the world on your side, it should be only a matter of days."

"The first thing I will do—I will arrange the release of Marcelito —my poor baby. I cannot bear the thought of his sleeping in that horrible tank with those filthy men— Oh God, if they touch him, if they dare to put their filthy cigars against his clean brown skin, Justo *cariño,* I will die, I will physically die."

"Hold on to yourself, Goyo. If he was only being held as a decoy to lure you into their parlor, I doubt if they will keep Marcelo very long. They know he is no threat to the security. They may be heartless, but they are not idiots. Marcelo is probably home this very minute, practicing his violin."

"I do not think I can live without him. He is my whole life."

"Goyo, in here the only thing you must concern yourself with is surviving. Think of it as a battle against the Philistines. Against El Gordo. Against the old death-head over there trying to hear what we are saying."

"Sounds very noble. Are you surviving?"

It was a question I had begun to ask myself. "I'm trying. At least I make notes for a book I hope to write, about the making of a dictator. Not the man—but the anti-democratic flies always spoiling the beautiful broth. I hope to devote each chapter to a different leader who dreamed or talked of democracy and wound up with a dictatorship."

"My dear Justo, that would mean a thousand chapters," Goyo interrupted. "Good Lord, in our own time every country is crawling with them."

At least I had distracted him from dwelling on the fate of Marcelo, and for a few moments had pushed to the back of my mind my fears for Clarita.

"True, Goyo. Almost everywhere you look the generals with the blessings of the gringo State Department know the art of frightening or buying off the politicians. Even a politician like De la Torre, the old radical—after spending years in a sanctuary like this, when he's finally allowed to return to Peru, he turns around and makes deals with the same dinosaurs who had driven him into exile."

"Yes, we keep trying to fly," Goyo said, "but our wings are always getting stuck on the flypaper of broken promises. It is all so depressing! And what of our own brilliant examples? When Zamora was leading his 'Revolution of the Corporals' remember what he was promising us? Freedom! And look at our darling Angel, raising the *grito* against Zamora for failing to keep his promises. Oh, Justo dear, all those lovely things Angel was going to bring us, freedom of conscience, intellectual freedom! And now—the president of the Writers' Union gets a long-winded bouquet in the official press for his dreary orthodox poetry. While the independent, experimental writers have to publish their works abroad—if they're lucky! Depressing, Justo. Maybe our generation has eaten its last supper. And since we no longer believe in resurrection, it is the *niños* still in secondary schools who will free us from this cycle of fraud we are caught in."

"Maybe. Maybe. With my own ears I heard Angel in court defending his attack on the Presidential Palace. I not only heard him, I believed him. Obviously this is not word for word, but I remember him saying, 'My answer to Zamora is the Democratic Revolution. To respect all ideas. The ideal revolution satisfies man's material needs and also his hunger for freedom. So I say to Zamora, since you allow us no other means, we have the right to overthrow you by

force. But once our Revolution comes to power, it will be farewell
to censorship, to political harassment, to persecution and oppression . . .'

"Ah yes, I remember. The promises, the hopes, the dreams. I
used his words in the new anthem. But how long was he in power
before he was announcing, 'I am now a Marxist-Leninist'? He had to
become a dictator because, for all his fine words, he was too big
an ego for popular government."

"It goes deeper," I said. "Not just ego but no real faith in popular
government. The real tragedy is that the people have never known
a popular government. So all they have to believe in is Angel. And
the sense of pride he has given them for standing up to the new
conquistadores whose flag is the dollar sign. Good, if only they
were not conditioned to being led around by the nose, to waiting
for Angel to solve their problems for them—or to tell them to go
back to the fields and work harder. I don't want to turn the clock
back to the time of Zamora. But if only we could turn it forward—
to the new world Angel described so eloquently at his trial and when
he first came to power. I don't know what I am any more, Goyo, too
liberal for the Communists, too Communistic for the liberals . . ."

"I have no politics," Goyo said. "Except that people should love
each other. Man has talked about that from the beginning. We'll
probably still be talking about it when the world is blown to bits."

"I hope you will be here only a few days, Goyo," I said. "But
even if it is a matter of hours, write poetry. Think of all the great
poets who fought the darkness of captivity. Close your eyes and
compose. Lie on your back and compose. Give us another 'My
comrades are those who will not say Comrade . . .' "

"I will try, Justo dearest," Goyo said. "I will try."

"It is not easy here. It is not a prison, but your soul begins to cry
for privacy. There is never any real silence except late at night when
all the lights are out. Our only chance is to concentrate on our work
and make our own inner privacy."

Goyo Solano nodded. His long, slender fingers played thoughtfully along the fringe of green hair on his forehead. *"Claro, cariño,
claro.* Sor Juana said that the silence is peopled with voices. But the
reverse is also true. In a hall full of voices you can insulate yourself
within your own silence."

"The only way to save your sanity," I said. "Not that I have been doing it so successfully."

Goyo patted me on the shoulder, tenderly. "Then we must try to help each other, Justo dear. For me it is very fortunate to find you here. I do not see you often, but every time I do, I feel close to you."

His long, delicate fingers continued to rest on my shoulder. I did not resent it as I had the insistent touch of Johnie Valdez. This was not resentment but a faint sense of unease.

I made a move to stand up and Goyo's hand removed itself like a gentle bird, a turtledove.

"Come, Goyo, I will give you a tour of the palace."

"Ay, I will see it soon enough," Goyo said. "But there is one thing I am curious about. Alvarez says we must all share a common bathroom? That is something I have an abhorrence of. Have you ever watched a cat? They cannot bear to be looked at when they are squatting in their box. I am simply a bigger cat. I would constipate myself until I became a heavy stone before I would let anyone see me attend to that."

I led Goyo down the aisle past the blaring radios to our communal bathroom. It was locked. Señor Gamboa and one of the sick asylees in a bathrobe who spent most of his time in bed were waiting at the door. Gamboa rapped irritably. "Come out of there, you two. Your time is up. *Vamos, vamos!* A little consideration, *hombre!*"

Goyo looked at me in horror.

"Two go in together! Always?"

I nodded. "In the morning, anyhow. There are two seats, side by side. A regular double throne. Like Ferdinand and Isabella."

"Obscene," Goyo said turning away. "I do not even wish to see it. The Ambassador is getting rich on this business. He could afford to give us a little privacy. After all, we are not criminals. We should be treated like honored guests."

I glanced at the handsome Swiss watch Alejandro had taken off his own wrist at our last picnic.

"Almost time for *cena*. You must taste the nourishing soup spooned out to the honored guests."

"How long have you been here, Justo dear?" he asked gravely.

How long? I hesitated. I should have kept track of the days in the traditional ЦЦ's on the cell walls of prisoners who fight against

the loss of their identity in a vacuum of timelessness. I shook my
head helplessly. Five days? A week? It seemed much longer than a
week. Two weeks? Three? It did not seem measurable in the units
of time we had used in the outside world. It was more like crawling
through a long dark tunnel wearing a watch the face of which is not
illuminated. You know only that it continues to tick and the fact that
you can hear it proves you are still alive.

That night in our cots so close together we could hear each other
breathe, Goyo and I amused ourselves in a memory duel of poetry.
I recited some of my favorite lines from Martí discreetly under my
breath, but Goyo was a performer, a little theatrical in his emphasis
perhaps, but with a real love for the rolling sound and cadence of
our language.

. . . *Díme, díme, Señor: Porque a nosotros nos elegiste para tu batalla?*
(Tell me, tell me, Oh Lord, why did you choose us for your battle?)

There was an angry shout from down the aisle, "*Silencio!* You
Communist fairy poet!"

I recognized the voice of the critic, El Gordo.

But Goyo was never to be stopped in the middle of a quatrain.
Over El Gordo's interruptions, he persisted.

Y después, con la muerte, que ganamos?
La eterna paz o la eterna borrasca?
(And afterward, in death, what do we gain?
Eternal peace or eternal storms?)

Again El Gordo's rude voice in the dark: "Listen you *charros con
sarten,* you cowboys with cunts, enough of that butterfly poetry, we
men are trying to sleep."

"You listen, you fat skinful of pig droppings," Goyo said. "You
could not censor me when you were Chief of Police and you certainly cannot censor me here. You left your power on the other side
of the river. And the bridge burned long ago." In the dark there
were some "*Olé's*" and some hisses. A large figure loomed up. It
was Búfalo, staring down at us from the ends of our cots.

"*Basta, basta.*" I could feel the gravel sound rising out of his
thick neck. "One more sound out of you two and—*zap!*"

Like an overbearing governess, he waited another moment. I was
afraid Goyo would talk back, with that wild, effeminate courage

of his. But there was a heavy silence in the room. And coughing that came from Miguelito. The hulking shadow of Búfalo returned to its post. Silence. Coughing. A fart. A groan. Contrapuntal snoring.

I had no idea how much later it was that night when I felt I was slowly rising up out of a deep dream as a deep-sea diver is drawn slowly upward from the bottom of the sea. I felt anxious to pull myself up out of my sleep, to break the surface of consciousness, into the fresh air. I felt something soft and warm and wet on my finger. Then my eyes were open and I could see where my finger was —in the mouth of the sleeping Goyo Solano. He was sliding his mouth along my forefinger and caressing it slowly with his tongue, moaning softly, "Marcelito, ah my sweet Marcelito . . ." I withdrew my finger slowly so as not to awaken him and embarrass us. But now I could not sleep. His face was too close to me. There was moonlight in the dormer window and faintly but unmistakably I could see his bangs, his slant eyes, his catlike face evil or perhaps merely mischievous in repose. I could hear Miguelito coughing again. I went to his cot and leaned over him. "Miguelito, all right? You need a little water?"

Looking pale and fragile, he shifted his small body and murmured, "Papa?"

I turned away. Everyone in the dormitory seemed to be somewhere else. In sleep they had all slipped home again.

I was half asleep when I felt a hand on my shoulder. My first thought was *Goyo*. It was good to have someone I could talk with, share ideas with, but it was going to be hell if he mistook me for his lost Marcelo. Then I felt the hand more firmly, not caressing me but

rather impatiently shaking me. I peered up through the semidarkness
to see Licenciado Alvarez.

"I am sorry to disturb you," he whispered. "But the Ambassador
is able to see you now."

"What—what time is it?"

"It lacks five minutes to one."

I sat up quickly. Safe passage! Why else would the Ambassador
send for me at such an hour?

As I dressed hurriedly in the dark, my mind was running out the
corridor and into the office of the Ambassador. And then on to the
waiting car, the airport, the jet flight to Miami . . . poor Goyo, poor
Miguelito, poor Paco, poor old Gamboa and all the rest of them, I
felt guilty to be leaving them behind. But once I was a free man I
could use my influence to gain safe passage for the others.

I followed the silent Licenciado Alvarez through the magic door
to the carpeted second floor, down the great marble stairway to the
main floor. There was the sleepy night-guard Manolo, who had
admitted us. After confinement in the dormitory-common room, with
only our daily visit to the aslyee courtyard to vary the monotony,
this was as heady an adventure as stealing down into the kitchen
after hours. Manolo led us down a corridor to a door which he unlocked with a number of keys. At the far end of the next passageway
a soldier admitted us. We were in the Ambassador's mansion now.
There was a royal red cord looped through heavy golden rings leading us to the second floor which had the elegance and unlived-in
feeling of a French seventeenth-century museum. At the end of the
circular mezzanine corridor, lit by a large crystal chandelier, was an
ornate door with rococo paneling outlined in gold leaf. Alvarez
knocked, was admitted by a neatly moustached aide and presto! I
was in the presence of His Excellency the Ambassador. Don Ernesto
de San Martín was standing near his walnut desk with its finely
veneered surface. The high forehead, the trimmed Vandyke, the old,
intelligent eyes, sophisticated, amused, watchful, presented a model
of Spanish American nobility. He was wearing a beautifully fitted
silk tuxedo with a maroon dress tie and a matching miniature carnation. I became conscious of my wrinkled shirt and my lightweight
slacks, the clothes Alejandro had sent me, now long in need of

pressing. Clothing is superficial, of course, but the poor peon in his dirty white working pajamas is made to feel humble by the soft suede boots, the fine-fitting trousers and the double-breasted black jacket with silver buttons of the *hacendados*. I knew it was foolish, I knew that it needed only an uncontrollable turn of the wheels to reverse our positions. But I knew it only in my head. My body felt damp and squirmy with subservience. In the animal world that lived just beneath the skin of the civilized world, I was in his power.

"Don Justo," he said with an elegant bow, "forgive me for inviting you here so late. I have just come from a dinner party we gave for Angel. What a world of intrigue we must live in here. Just a few minutes ago this hand that just took yours in friendly greeting was grasping the hand of Angel Bello."

He moved from his desk and ushered me to a large black leather chair. "May I get you something, a cognac?" He nodded to Bertie Alvarez who had come awake full of ready smiles as soon as he saw his Ambassador. "Your lady will be here in a few minutes," Don Ernesto said as Bertie handed us the brandy. "I am sorry to disturb her at such an hour, but I thought the matter was too important to put off for another day, and tomorrow I am going out into the country to inspect some new rural schools that Angel is opening. I must admit he is doing a good job on the illiteracy problem—a good deal better than some of our so-called Latin democracies."

I breathed in the expensive fumes of the brandy. I was not quite prepared for comfortable, civilized discussions. It took time to fit this handsome den into the shabby jigsaw of sanctuary life.

"We could educate the illiterates without forced labor camps and island prisons for dissenters," I said.

"Indeed!" my host hastened to agree. "I am hardly suggesting that this regime has turned me into an Angelista. But as you know, I am a consistent advocate of compromise. In our world the sides tend to crystallize and harden too quickly. So the dialogue is always being spoken from the mouths of cannons. At the dinner tonight, for instance, in the form of a toast, I released a trial balloon of a compromise. I suggested, ever so gently, that Angel call off his guerrillas trying to ferment Marxist revolutions in our Pan American republics. And in return, I would recommend that my country use

its prestige to open the door for Angel to rejoin the American
family of nations."

Ordinarily this was the kind of thing that would fix my attention.
Could Angel be induced to follow the Moscow line of "Socialism
in one country"? Would he grow more conservative or at least self-
protective like the Russians, if his internal economy developed and
his national security was no longer threatened? But, alas, the life of
the asilado is not ennobling—one does not become more selfless in
exile and confinement. I found it difficult to make conversation
about Don Ernesto's high-level diplomacy. I was impatient to break
in, to say, "Your Excellency, I am no longer President, even in
name. I no longer have the slightest influence on Angel. I am the fly
he brushes from his shoulder. All I can think of is getting out of
here, out of the crowded dormitory, out of the sun-dried enclosure.
I want to get out. Help me to get out of here!"

There was a knock on the door and Señora Lorona plodded in
with Marta. I was shocked to see that Marta was wearing slacks. No
self-respecting lady wore slacks in our country unless she was climbing a pyramid or vacationing at one of our smart watering places.
Certainly not when calling on the Ambassador.

Don Ernesto pretended not to notice. He moved forward like the
black silk he was wearing and neatly kissed her hand. "Señora, en-
chanté."

"Sorry about the pants," Marta spoke up. "I was dressing in the
dark. It was the fastest thing I could find."

"Of course. I understand," Don Ernesto said. "These are such
difficult times. I feel badly that we are not able to provide more
comfortable quarters—"

"Not as badly as we feel," Marta said.

"Naturally," replied Don Ernesto, unruffled. "I try to empathize,
in my mind I try to put myself in your place, but—"

"But you do not have to eat the atrocious beans and rice," Marta
said.

He looked pained. "I must apologize for the cuisine. Our budget
for embassy asylum was based on the expectation of helping a handful. To feed and house a hundred or more extends our resources.

You have no idea how many letters I have sent back to the Foreign Minister asking a larger appropriation."

On the panels dividing his leather-bound books were plaques and diplomas attesting to Don Ernesto's distinguished record as a humanitarian. The framed documents, if not our daily prison rations, said, "I care."

"Don Ernesto, I am sure you have written many letters," Marta said, evenly but in a voice I recognized as dangerous. "And since you are one of the most accomplished writers in Latin America, I am sure they were beautiful letters. You can put them in a book sometime, so that no one will ever doubt how concerned you were during our time of hardship."

The Ambassador smiled his practiced, diplomatic smile. "Look, my friends, we are three civilized and, I think, practical people. My job is not to keep you in political asylum. It is obviously to get you out, to influence Angel to grant safe passage for as many as possible. As quickly as possible." He cradled the bowl of the brandy snifter in his hands and inhaled the fumes. In another age I could see him in a white ruffled collar, painted by Goya as a highbrowed, decadent aristocrat. "And tonight in my friendly talk with Angel I feel I won the domino game."

"You mean that *ladrón* will give us safe passage?" Marta said.

"Not all three of you," Don Ernesto replied. "At least not all at the same time. But he did agree to let you fly out, Señora, and your daughter."

"And Justo?"

"Unfortunately his case is more complicated. I had to warn Angel not to raise his voice at me for refusing to turn you over to what he calls 'the People's Justice,' Don Justo. He is demanding your extradition. He insists he will carry this so-called conspiracy case against you all the way to The Hague. Which is all right with me. I am ready to advise my government to defend your asylum before the World Court if necessary."

"I thank you for that," I said, edgily.

"Not at all. It is my duty—"

"—as a celebrated humanitarian," said Marta.

"As a representative of a great freedom-loving nation," replied Don Ernesto.

I thought of his freedom-loving country, a handful of have's and fifteen million have-not's locked in feudal violence.

"Of course, to be perfectly candid, I must walk a very careful line until conditions in my own troubled country find their own level again. The generals who have just overthrown our civilian government have no particular love for me. After all, I am a liberal like yourself. But I am also a career diplomat the generals will probably want to rely on—our diplomatic corps has weathered many such storms. I am sure, Don Justo, as a recent head of state, you understand the delicate balance."

"*Pobrecito,*" Marta said. "We are very sorry you must suffer this delicate balance. Meanwhile, you want us to decide if Clara and I should leave Justo behind."

Don Ernesto nodded. "I will need your decision immediately. Angel's mind is like quicksilver. Tonight he is convinced it is good for him to appear merciful to the ladies. Tomorrow a headline, a setback or even some unexpected whim can change his mind. I would strike while—"

"—his limp thing is still *pendejo,*" Marta suggested.

Don Ernesto, descended from the great line of San Martín, stared at her. I thought he was going to choke on his cognac or bite the lip of his glass. In our country, only *putas* talked like that.

He looked at me with compassion. His manners were still oriented toward Old Spain.

"If you would rather discuss your decision alone . . ." Don Ernesto made a move as if to withdraw.

"I see nothing to discuss," I said. "If my wife and daughter are free to leave, I would like you to arrange the first flight possible."

"I assumed that would be your choice," he said. "Licenciado Alvarez has the necessary papers."

The chargé d'affaires produced them with a flourish. "This is the formal application for safe passage."

Marta spoke up. "Just a moment. I am not ready. I am not signing anything this evening. When I married my husband I signed a contract. It may sound old-fashioned but I came here to be with my husband."

"Bravo," Don Ernesto said. "I deplore the passing of those old-fashioned values. I salute you, Señora. But these documents we are offering you are becoming very rare. Including a visa to our country, for instance, with permission to move on to the capital of your choice. Ordinarily this requires many, many months. But we have ways of cutting through the red tape."

I had heard of this red tape. First you bought your way in and then you bought your way out.

"How much will it be this time?" Marta asked.

The Ambassador stiffened. He liked to put things differently.

"It is not an actual charge, my dear lady. It is simply the need for reimbursement for legal services. Our Immigration Department needs a deposit to prove that you will not become a ward of the state on the other side. Of course in your case this is merely a formality."

"What is the price of the formality?"

Don Ernesto looked at Alvarez. "Our chargé d'affaires handles those details."

"How much, Señor Chargé d'Affaires?" Marta asked again.

There was a pause. "Five thousand dollars, Señora."

"Five thousand dollars," she said. "You are in the misery business, Señores. In the humanitarianism business by day and the misery business by night."

"Madame, I beg you to understand," Don Ernesto said. "This sum is not my personal consideration. It goes to my government, as reimbursement for our legal and emergency expenses."

"Yes, of course. Whatever you say." Marta smiled. "And now, shall we get on with it?"

Don Ernesto glanced at me, as an ally. "I choose to take no offense," he said. "The lady is understandably overwrought. I apologize for the unfortunate circumstances. Even though I am sure you appreciate the fact that I have no control over them. If I had my way you would all be free."

I believed the Ambassador. He had written forcefully about the need for constitutional democracy and deeper regard for human rights in Latin America. But the misery market has always been an attractive field of endeavor. The web had not been of his making. He merely found himself in a favorable position to catch or release the flies.

"It is up to you," Don Ernesto said. "When you decide, Licenciado Alvarez will do everything he can to expedite your departure.

If all goes smoothly, you could be on your way within forty-eight hours." He rose and kissed Marta's hand. "Don Justo, I hope you will join me sometime soon again. I know that you are a student of Martí, one of my favorites also. And I have read your study of the Haya de la Torre case. Most illuminating. We must have a good long talk about it one day."

"Thank you, Your Excellency," I bowed. It was easy to fall into his style. We were like two professional colleagues meeting politely on the University campus. There was not the faintest suggestion that the latest Haya de la Torre case was me.

"Haya lived on the top floor of the Colombian embassy for seven years," Marta said.

"A most regrettable affair," replied Don Ernesto. "Some of the world's greatest jurists were divided on the issue." He sighed. "Even though I have had a long day and the hour is late, I called you together because I wanted to be helpful to you."

"How kind," Marta said. "If we decide to accept your proposal, we will be helpful to each other."

Don Ernesto glanced at the brass clock on the wall. "Now if you will excuse me. I know you would like a few minutes to yourselves. Licenciado Alvarez will wait for you in the corridor." He bowed, murmured his *Buenas noches* and retreated through the rear door behind his desk that led into his private quarters. At the same moment Licenciado Alvarez vanished obediently.

"Tu madre," Marta said to the door through which Don Ernesto had left us.

She moved to me and threw her arms around me, using anger as a tourniquet to squeeze off the flow of tears.

"Oh *mierda*," she said. *"Mierda, mierda, mierda, mierda!* The trouble is, I love you, Justo. I pretend and I joke a lot, but the truth is I'd feel cut in two living in Miami or Mexico City without you."

"Marta, dearest Marta," I said, stroking her hair. "Selfishly, I do not want you to go. But for you, personally, and for Clarita, the time has come. To have to worry whether she is pregnant or not pregnant—you must take her out of here."

"I say 'yes.' Then I think about you and I say 'no.' Let me talk to Doctora Julia. Let me think about it overnight."

"No. Don Ernesto is right. Angel can change from hour to hour.

Tonight he may open the door a few inches. Tomorrow he may slam it in your face. I say go. Go while you can."

"Justo, I love you. I am as sick of that *cursi* phrase as you are, but—"

"But if Angel refuses to let me through, it makes no sense for the three of us to rot in here, no matter how much we love each other. I say pay the miserable five thousand and—"

"We have a life together too, Justo. At least I hope we have. Let me think. One more day."

"You always accuse me of being the sentimentalist of the family. Thinking of old promises. Putting off decisions. It isn't like you, Marta. You're slipping into sentimentality."

There was a knock on the door. Automatically we drew away from each other. The door opened and Alvarez presented himself.

"Forgive the intrusion but now it is nearly two o'clock. And I have a number of cases to process in the morning. Including yours, if you should decide—"

"Vámanos, Licenciado," Marta said. "We must not delay the wheels of justice."

"Thank you, Señora."

"Por nada," Marta said.

The bored chargé d'affaires, no longer having to perform for his ambassador, led us quickly into the corridor where Señora Lorona was waiting, sleeping on her heavy feet like a tired horse. Behind these two we trudged out through the trellised passageway, into the embassy reception hall, up the great marble steps to the second floor and on up the narrow steps to the cell-block. I held Marta's arm. She was limping badly.

At the passageway separating our two quarters, we paused and I clasped her hand tightly with both of mine.

"Sleep well. And tell Clarita I send her my love."

"I'll try," Marta said. "I feel sorry for her. But I could choke her just the same."

"Pobrecita. The innocent victims of history."

"Chinga history—"

Señora Lorona had opened the door to the ladies' wing. I watched Marta limp resolutely through. I watched until the door closed behind her. And then Alvarez, my impatient keeper, ushered me into the familiar night-odor.

I could feel my way to my own cot with my eyes closed now and as I lowered myself to it to pull off my clothes, I felt a human body.

"Goyo!"

"Oh—oh—forgive me, dear. I must have fallen asleep in the wrong bed. They are so close together."

Goyo moved to the adjoining cot and I got into mine. The pillow smelled sweet with the perfumed lotion from his green hair.

"Sweet dreams, dear Justo," he said softly. Then he sighed. "Oh, my Marcelito, my poor baby, poor baby . . ."

And so at last we fell asleep, I with jumbled dreams of Clarita and Marta and the bony, pregnant cat, Goyo with visions of his lost Indian child-lover. Each vulnerable internee was finding solace or the shadow shapes of fear in his private journey through the stench of communal night.

12

The morning began with its ritualistic violence at the bathroom door, only with this difference: to the amazement of everyone, Goyo ran forward and retaliated for the punch to Paco's mouth by slapping Búfalo sharply in the face.

The audacity of the act from this unexpected source electrified the dormitory. And it had a surprising effect on Búfalo. For a moment he stood there paralyzed, staring at the man with green hair as if he were some sort of a Martian.

By the time he had gathered his senses and was ready to lumber up to Goyo, a crowd had gathered in a protecting semicircle around the poet.

One might have thought that the effete Goyo would have been terrified of a muscle box like Búfalo de Sa. But then, it is also true that it takes madness, or courage which is a form of madness, to be an eccentric who dyes his hair to suit his mood and sleeps in an open coffin. Goyo had the unstable courage of the great Gypsy bullfighters who one moment performed the most incredible acts of bravery and the next moment lost their faith and vaulted the *barrera* in panic.

"I must warn you," Goyo said, "I cannot bear commotion around the lavatory. The morning wash should be a spiritual ceremony."

Those who might have laughed remained silent out of respect for Goyo's bravado, and because of the novelty of the situation. The ogre of this place was monotony. Everyone was familiar with the look of everybody else, his posture, his daily habits. Paco, who had seemed so exhilarating during the first days, had become tedious, overbearing, even disgusting. No, men do not come to love each other by sharing adversity, especially the monotony of enforced confinement. The group around Goyo, who might have made easy laughter about his green hair and his green corduroy suit and his pastel behavior, were grateful to him for creating this morning diversion. It would sustain them through the day.

At the moment Búfalo had regained his primitive poise and was ready to respond to Goyo in the only way he knew, El Gordo emerged from the bathroom in his white *guayabera* shirt, his neatly pressed slacks and his white suede shoes. Behind him Jesuscito peered uncertainly over his shoulder. The crowd fell back a little, like water pushed aside by the great bow of a ship. El Gordo sized up the situation quickly with his small, black, busy eyes.

"Búfalo, leave him alone!"

With the instant obedience of a trained animal, the bodyguard made a way for his master and shadow-manservant through the group of us blocking the corridor to the bathroom.

"Fascinating!" Goyo said. "Why would that beast Romano come to my protection?"

"Because, while all of us acknowledge that he has enough power to enjoy certain privileges, he acknowledges that we have enough power to prevent him from going too far. Even with Búfalo as a shield, he's lucky not to be torn to pieces in here. So we sniff each other like a pack of dogs who bare their teeth but know the fight will kill them all."

"But I am not a dog," Goyo said. "I shall die here if my fellow-artists fail to get me out within the week. I shall physically die!" He gave a deep, exaggerated sigh and rolled his soft, hazel eyes.

Paco was already squatting on one of the toilet seats with his baggy trousers pulled down over his purple-red knees. Through the door which he hadn't bothered to close he grunted, "Ask Greenie if he wants to come in, too. Otherwise he'll be at the end of the line. A man could piss in his pants while waiting for all the rest of these *chingadas* to drop their loads in the morning." And he gestured brusquely to Goyo through the doorway, "Come in, hombre, come in. Nobody else in this house of shit has ever slapped Búfalo. Did you see the expression on that big ass of a face?" He laughed hoarsely and the movement led to a noisy release of his bowels. "Ay! That feels better!" he announced, at the same time cheerfully waving Goyo to come in.

Goyo drew back. His eyebrows arched. His nostrils flared. He looked like a great, indignant cat. "—I—I cannot—I cannot bear—I insist on privacy—" He escaped down the aisle. Johnie Valdez fell in behind him and mimicked the mincing gait for a couple of strides. A few were now ready to laugh. Búfalo thought it was very funny. But if Goyo Solano noticed them he pretended not to.

I went into the bathroom, closed the door, and lowered myself to the throne adjoining Paco's. I still had not overcome my squeamishness, but now I was resigned to it.

"Compañero!" Paco suddenly shouted out. I think he actually preferred it this way. It appealed to his full-bodied gregariousness. He was the kind of a man who would like to do everything together.

This was the morning known affectionately as *"El Día de Que Próximamente Usted Podrá Salir"*—Bertie Alvarez' famous "You-Will-Leave-Very-Soon-Day." He arrived with his customary pre-fabricated smile, the worn manila folders under his arm. And, as usual, the impatient ones swarmed in while the cynical ones circled the swirling periphery or kept to their cots.

"I put the Señora's papers in motion an hour ago," he shouted to me over the shoulders of his "cases." "I will personally walk them

through for endorsements this afternoon. Hopefully we will have
the final approval from *Inmigración* by five o'clock in the afternoon." I nodded. Our keeper seemed to think he was passing on to
me festive news. I dreaded the separation. Suspended in sanctuary,
helpless to move forward or backward, I felt myself the poorest of
paupers, bereft of choice. Marta was suddenly rich in decision. She
could leave or she could endure with her husband. How long? To
think in terms of time was a conceit. Peru's Haya de la Torre and
his seven years. Mindszenty. There were skin and bones around me
fading in captivity. *At five o'clock in the afternoon. Death laid eggs
in the wound at five o'clock in the afternoon.*

Oh damn your morbid Latin souls. Lorca in search of death on
the road to Córdoba. Bolívar on the dusty road to Santa María
walking slowly toward his death. Martí rowing through a storm to
join Maceo the Centaur, the frail poet and the machete-wielding
giant both on their way to deaths they had willed and already described, Martí wishing only that his chest could be fuller so the blow
could strike deeper. And Antonio Maceo whose body was already
riddled with a dozen wounds that never had time to heal offering
that great target of muscle and bone and battle-toughened flesh to
the Spaniards he despised. We Latins worshiped death and found
it sweet like skeleton candy. Only a Latin mind could write, "There
is no woman so beautiful as death . . ." In love with, and hypnotized
by it, we transform our morbidity into a flamenco of castanet merri-
ment, and the more the castanets sound like the burial bones in a
rocking coffin, the louder the laughter.

"One case at a time!—please, gentlemen, let me follow my list!
In a moment, a moment, give me time, give me room!" Alvarez
pushed and bustled his way down the aisle. And as if from a man-
sized talking doll, "Soon—very soon you will be able to leave!"

I watched him work his way down to the cot of Paco O'Higgins.
It was the only cot on which the sheets and blankets were a tangled
mess. Paco was sprawled out in his dirty long underwear grinning
at the harassment of Licenciado Alvarez as if it were a show put on
for his amusement. Our chargé d'affaires pushed aside the most
insistent of the asilados and went over to Paco. He leaned down and
whispered something in the old jai alai player's ear. Paco jumped
up and hugged Alvarez and kissed him on both cheeks. Then, to the

delight of the audience he was attracting, he held the startled official in a rough embrace and kissed him fully on the mouth. Onlookers clapped and whistled. When Alvarez finally broke away,
Paco's guttural laughter was infectious. Only El Gordo and Búfalo
and a few other Zamoristas whose loathing for him was a passion
resisted the epidemic of laughter that spread through the dormitory.

Paco stepped onto his cot and stood up to make an announcement. "Gentlemen—and ladies. For Paco O'Higgins the waiting is
over! My good friend Alvarez has just told me—in strictest confidence which I would like to share with all of you impotent goats—I
am leaving! Tonight I will be in Miami, eating my good wife's *chiles
relleños* which she knows how to make better than anybody in the
world . . . I will go to the jai alai and bet on my little nephews . . .
and look at the *muchachas* who come there in tight slacks for the
benefit of mankind . . . and what do you bet I will catch one under
the stands? Sí, Señor! *Adiós,* you poor bastards."

Alvarez looked pained. It was asylum protocol for the fortunate
inmate not to inform his fellows of his departure. The quiet slipping
away of an asylee did not inflame the frustrations and restlessness
of those left behind. Anyone tapped for safe passage was advised to
guard his good news as a diplomatic secret.

But this unwritten rule would not restrain my friend Paco. To the
silent exasperation of Bertie, Paco had almost the entire personnel of
the dormitory gathered around him as he threw himself into the
spirit of the occasion.

"Hear me, you cuckolds and tutti-fruttis," he shouted hoarsely.
"I solemnly declare this the Day of Paco O'Higgins." From his
crotch he pulled up the pint bottle of rum that hung from the wrap-
ping cord tied around the folds of his waist. "To health, wealth and
love," he offered our favorite toast, "and time to enjoy them." He
tipped the bottle to his lips and let the dark rum pour into his
mouth. Then he handed the bottle to me and told me to drink and
pass it around while he fished another one from a cache in his mattress. He climbed up and stood on his cot again.

"And now for the things I will not be needing—I might as well
give them to you as let the embassy guards and Angel's thieves of
the customhouse steal them off me on my way to the plane."

There was appreciative laughter from the audience, among whom the rum bottle was passing. Asylees did their best to hold onto a wristwatch, a transistor radio, an expensive ring on their way through safe passage. But the story was always the same. It was the price one was expected to pay for personal freedom. You entered the new country of your choice shorn of your worldly goods.

"My first gift is to my good friend, El Presidente," Paco said, nodding down at me with a mischievous grin. "It is my right to pound on the bathroom door when El Gordo is dropping his morning enchiladas."

There was laughter, loud, raucous, even slightly hysterical. It had been a long time since they had had any excuse to laugh together. They laughed as if they had forgotten there were any controls to laughter, full volume and only a beat away from sobbing.

"What about the punch in the mouth?" somebody shouted. "Do you also make him the gift of the punch in the mouth?"

Everybody turned to look at Búfalo. His bull head lowered to a thumbed copy of his favorite sports-girlie magazine, *El y Ella,* he pretended not to hear.

I was not so sure about the honor of the punch in the mouth, not at all sure I could accept it with the stoicism and aplomb of O'Higgins. But I had to speak up. "I accept the gift—including the consequences." There were cheers. Paco was unquestionably the favorite figure in sanctuary and some of his popularity was passing to me vicariously. They could hardly wait to see me receive the ritualistic morning punch in the mouth.

Paco balanced on the cot and took another swig from his bottle.

"Now what else, my friends—my transistor radio—I give it to old man Gamboa—he can take it outside with him to the afternoon meal. It can keep him company if his little wife happens to be busy."

There was more laughter. But old Gamboa did not seem to get the joke. He reached a bony hand out to Paco and accepted the radio gratefully.

"And now my wristwatch. It is eighteen-karat gold and tells the days of the month and the months of the year. I give it to young Miguelito Flores—not because he likes luxuries. I know all about his crazy socialist ideas. I give it to him because he is poor and idealistic and doesn't have money or anything else he can use for *mordida* to get himself out of this shithouse."

Miguelito rose from his bed, put his hand to his mouth, gently, to protect others from his cough, and accepted his gift with a pale smile.

"What else?" Paco said. "On my finger I have this big sapphire ring. The Jai Alai Association gave it to me after my biggest season. It would break my heart to see it on the grabby finger of some customs' official. So I give it to—"

He looked around. In the back of the room was the towering, silent Sandungo. "*Hola*, my big black friend," Paco shouted, slurring his words hoarsely, "since you keep so silent, since you never complain like these other donkeys, I give you my ring. Maybe you can sell it to buy your freedom."

Paco held it out to him, but El Indio did not move. "I want nothing." His voice came from low in his chest, rumbling through the room like black thunder. "No money. No big stone on my finger." He spoke with an inflection that suggested Jamaica, calypso, the Caribbean, different from any other speech in our country. "I want only our land. That is all I want—our land!"

Paco frowned. An exaggerated rum-potted frown. El Indio's deep voice and simple slogan had interrupted the festivities.

"I am sorry," Paco shouted from his perch on the cot. "I cannot give you back your land. All I can give you are these little presents I hold in my hand. Don't ask me for land and liberty. Ask for my ring or my radio. Or some friendly telephone numbers if you ever get out of here."

El Indio was silent again. He leaned against the far wall with his long, muscular arms folded across his chest.

"So—what will I do with this damned thing?" Paco said. "Here—here—take it—whoever catches it!" He tossed the ring up in the air, down the aisle. Lawyers, professors, journalists, businessmen scrambled for it like eager children. It would make a handsome bribe.

"Look, look—it fits me perfectly!" a voice cried out of the pack. "Scubie-doobie-doo!"

"I'll see you in Miami," Paco laughed. He drained the last drops from the rum bottle in his hand and held the empty up for everyone to see.

"Now who shall I give this empty bottle to?" he looked around.

"I know—to Búfalo. He can hold it for his master to piss into. And then he can drink it. The next best thing to kissing El Gordo's ass!"

Waves of laughter swirled around Paco. He tossed the empty bottle up the aisle to the floor where it shattered. "Leave it there," he shouted happily. "Maybe El Gordo will forget his slippers next time."

The laughter mounted until it again verged on hysteria. All of us watching Paco balance and sway on his cot were feeling full of love and an overflowing sentimentality. What would I have done in this gray asylum without him? He provided the laughter, the rum, the food, the color, the life. With his fleshy nose crisscrossed with drinking veins and his old, hard, self-indulged jai alai back-court player's belly, he was an appealing figure. At this moment I loved Paco O'Higgins. At this moment everybody in the dormitory except the most virulent of the Zamoristas was actively adoring Paco O'Higgins. Stepping down from his cot, he reached into his mattress and, as if from a bottomless well, produced still another bottle of the precious rum. He unscrewed the top and offered me another swig. "I am saving my best gift of all—for the last." His whisper was a rum-scented rasp. "My little key to the kitchen. But do not tell the others. Apolonio could lose his job. I hope you will not have to be here too long after I go, but meanwhile you will eat and drink the best, eh, *compañero?*"

He embraced me vigorously, pounding me on the back while I patted his strong, fat shoulder in gratitude.

"Thank you, Pacocito, you have been a great shipmate."

"Until Miami," Paco said, "or Mexico City, wherever the luck takes us. We will go to the Frontón together and the prizefights. I will take you to one of my *casas chicas*. We will drink too much and stagger to the bedrooms with our little *chiquitas* and we will do a lot of laughing together."

"Que te vaya bien," I said. "You deserve a happy life, Paco."

"Deserve, deserve, who deserves anything? But I am going to enjoy myself—even if it kills me."

He laughed as if this was the greatest joke of all and climbed back up onto the cot to continue his giveaway party.

"Now let me see—what else do I have—ah, is anyone interested in a pair of dirty, long underwear? When I get to Miami, I am going to buy everything new—I don't want a single shoelace to remind me of my seven months in this ambassadorial pisshouse."

I felt a tug at my sleeve. It was Momentito.

"Señor, I have a message for you. Urgent. Follow me. Your Señora is waiting."

I followed the jockey-sized house-servant through the sanctuary exit to the corridor leading to the ladies' wing. There was Marta waiting with Señora Lorona. Momentito and the plump matron moved discreetly away.

"Justo," Marta said. "It's decided. Clarita and I are leaving. As soon as we can. Tonight if possible."

"It happened?"

"Yes, I'm afraid it happened."

"You're sure?"

"Almost. She missed her period. More than three days now. Of course she only turned woman six months ago. She is not yet regular. I talked to Doctora Julia about it."

"And?"

"She says it would take at least another week to be positive. But—there are symptoms—"

"Oh, that son-of-a-whore. Whoever did it. I will have to kill him."

"Who needs a hero? What we need is to get to Miami—a good doctor—while it is still simple to do."

"Little Clarita. I still think of her—"

"Justo, there is no time for that. I have sent a note to the Ambassador urging him to get us out. As soon as I hear from him I will give Señora Lorona the message for you."

She put her arms around me briefly. "I am sorry about that promise. Never to leave you. I meant it. It teaches me a lesson. A promise is like signing a check with no date on it and not knowing if you will still have money in the bank when it comes due."

"I know, Marta. I know."

"Life stinks," Marta said. "I will talk to you later."

She turned away, motioned Señora Lorona and hobbled off on her increasingly lame knee that she had to favor but refused to indulge.

I went seething back into the dormitory. Paco was still standing on his cot giving the last of his sanctuary treasures away. But there was too much blood rushing into my head for me to be able to see or hear anything clearly. All I could think was Clarita, Clarita dishonored, Clarita deflowered, Clarita split open like a tender peach, Clarita nailed like a defenseless kitten pounced on by the first tom to trap her in the alley, Clarita's girlish bloomers pulled savagely to her knees by a greedy lecher's hand, Clarita implanted with the alien seed, Clarita's virginity sacrificed to the hard thrust of momentary pleasure. I saw sperm and blood as a foul elixir poisoning my baby Clarita, beating in my head and clouding my vision.

"One of you *putos* has done it to my daughter!" I shouted. "One of you degenerate swine has left his poisonous eggs in my child! Well, I know who you are, you syphilitic goat, you cradle-snatching whoremaster—and I'm going to kill you for it! Maybe you think I am an easygoing pacifist reasonable intellectual—well, I am also a man. I also believe in honor—vengeance! I'm going to tear it off and stick it in your mouth so it does no more harm to innocent children!"

Paco stepped down from his cot. He still had the rum bottle in one hand but the party was over. I could feel everybody watching me, guardedly waiting as if I were the rattlesnake coiled and they were unprotected flesh shrinking back from the venom.

I was trembling, screaming, too numb to hear myself over the din of my own shouting.

"With my bare hands! I'll tear it off and stuff it down your throat, you scum-bag of a sex maniac!"

I stared around at the room of frightened faces, singled out El Gordo and walked slowly toward him. Búfalo braced himself, ready for his role. I should have been afraid, but the blood and the adrenaline were flowing. Blood and sperm produced a poison called rage. "Búfalo, out of my way, *hijo!*" I was actually looking forward to the judo chop of his enormous fist. I was crouched ready to leap forward, ready to kill El Gordo or enjoy trying. It was exhilarating. How long had it been since I had released righteous, violent anger.

"Wait! Wait!" someone was saying. Someone was grabbing my

arm and pulling me back from Búfalo and El Gordo. "Justo, wait—
wait, *hombre!*" In the confusion I recognized Paco.

"Justo, it was me!"

I looked around, more dazed than if Búfalo had struck me between the eyes. I reeled backward or fell backward, and hands
caught me. I was balanced on the edge of a cot. I felt sick and dizzy,
struggling in the coils of a nightmare.

"No," I was saying, something meaningless like that, "no, I refuse to believe it, no, *no me digas*, don't tell me that!"

"Listen, my friend, Paco is a son-of-a-bitch. But he is no coward,
and no liar. It happened like this: El Gordo is one big bastard—king
of all the bastards. He gets your child in the laundry room. I am
standing close enough to hear what is going on. She is crying for
help and calling, 'Popee, Popee.' You are at the other end of the
yard with your wife. So I butt Búfalo in the face and run in. I pull
the bastard off her. I have muscles under this fat and I send him
flying. She falls in my arms to thank me. Her dress is still pulled
up where El Gordo was trying and—and—these things happen, my
friend. Like the way I used to leap up and take the *pelotas* high
off the back wall. The crowd was surprised I could move so fast
with all this belly, eh? Well I outjumped El Gordo for this one too.
I feel shame to tell you this. My head wanted to save her but—I
must tell you the truth. I can't let Búfalo smash you to a pulp for
nothing. It was me."

Sperm and blood spinning in my head. This was what it was to
go crazy. "No," I said. "I cannot believe you. My best friend here.
The only one who looked after me. I do not believe it."

"Look, hombre," Paco said, "I am your friend, you are my friend,
but here it is every man for himself. We are all starving to death, so
if a tasty morsel is served up to us, we eat first and apologize later."

"Pig," I said, "you are nothing but a pig. A filthy pig. I thought
you were a slob. But a slob of a human being. You are a slob of a
pig." In our language the word *cochino* is much stronger, a real
epithet of an insult. When one says *cochino* in my country, one is
prepared to fight.

"I am not the only one," Paco said. "I am just the only honest
one."

"No—no!" I said. "Your brain is swimming in rum."

"Ask them!" Paco shouted. "Look around and ask them."

I looked at the wall of sanctuary faces watching me. "Well?" I said. "Well? Tell me! Tell me, you sons of *putas madres*."

No one answered. Were they all guilty? Enough were guilty to make them all feel guilty. So everyone was doing it to Clarita. A pigpen full of pigs. Doing it to a younger version of Cookie Gamboa. In every fish bowl there are rocks to hide under. Nothing about this in the noble conventions of political asylum. Fuck conventions. Fuck principles. Fuck fucking. I made a fist, punched it into Paco's face and was pleased to see that it drew blood from his nose.

"Please, no violence," I could hear Goyo Solano saying. "I cannot bear violence. I abhor violence. I sympathize. He is a pig. Most men are pigs. But please, Justo dearest, no more violence."

I tightened my fist and struck it into Paco again. He did not duck and he did not strike back. "Good. Good, amigo," he said. "Hit me. You have every right to hit me. Hit me harder. I am sorry for you. I feel for you, amigo. But I do not feel guilty. It is human nature. I would do it again. So you deserve to hit me again."

"You are a son-of-a-bitch," I said. "Go to Miami. Go to hell."

I could not hit Paco any more. I was tired, finished with the energy of rage.

"I wish you only good," Paco said. "But you are in for much trouble. You have too many ideals. Illusions. I am more fortunate. I have none. I am going to enjoy my life."

How could I have liked this man, I wondered, or even at odd moments thought that I loved him? This animal no better than El Gordo or Búfalo.

"Come, Señor O'Higgins," a voice said. Bertie Alvarez. Had he been there all the time? My brain was too blooded to keep track of goings and comings. Staggering down the aisle, vaguely aware of Goyo and Johnie's trying to help me, I fell on my cot, buried my face in my pillow and lay there a long time without sleeping.

I wasn't listening to the familiar babel of the room—I was throbbing with shock and hatred and disgust. I tried to soothe myself with seascapes from our windows at Papagayos, but the visions of that lost place only deepened my depression. I saw Clarita with her baby cat calling, "Popee, Popee, look at me, watch me, Popee" as she went down the slide backward, or "Wait for me, I'm coming, Popee" as she ran down the beach to join me in a walk to the coral rocks at the far end of the pink crescent. I groaned and worked my face deeper into the pillow. The frustration of having life run so completely counter to what I desired ached inside of me. "I can't bear this life can't bear this life can't bear this filthy life . . ." I was writhing and slobbering into the pillow.

"Justo my dear—" A warm, gentle hand was caressing the back of my head. "Justo my dearest." I turned to see Goyo sitting on the cot next to mine. His saturnine face was softened in sorrow. "Don't cry," he said, "or I will have to cry too. Maybe I can cry for you and that will save you the trouble."

"Goyo, Goyo, you have never been a father."

"You are so conventional," Goyo said. "When I think of some filthy prison guard forcing himself on my beautiful Marcelo, is it not somewhat similar?"

"No, it's—oh, I don't know—Goyo, I'm sick—I feel cold and green all over—I want to die."

"Live, live," Goyo said. "For today it is sad, but your little dumpling will recover. She will meet a young doctor or a lawyer or a prosperous businessman in Miami and your wife will think it is a splendid match and the bridegroom will never know what happened in the courtyard. Young ladies are masters at covering up their tracks. They are much much better at duplicity than their *macho* mates. Your daughter will be all right. Just like your wife. A very sturdy lady. Built to survive."

I was almost beyond reach of solace and yet some faint spark in me responded to his twisted common sense. It was not quite the "fate worse than death" that the sentimental gringos used to call it. I could see Clarita surviving it in Marta's hardheaded way. Still I could resent Goyo for suggesting it. For he was as wrong as he was right. A Clarita would survive it, perhaps, but a new Clarita, a different Clarita, and I had a right to push my head into my pillow and mourn the death of my first one.

"Diplomatic asylum," said Goyo
"is a Garden of Eden

where the snakes have taken over.
It is the snakes who sunk their fangs
into the apple.
Snakes who do not bother to remove their skins.
It is the snakes
Twisting through the leaves
Who strike at tender fruit like Eve's."

He took my hand, which was hanging over the edge of the cot, pressed it gently and then held it with a tender firmness.

"Justo, I love you. I am not being unfaithful to Marcelo when I say that. I love you in a different way."

I withdrew my hand.

"Goyo, go away. Go away."

13

That evening, having passed up the supper of watered soup, I was standing at the dormer window looking out at the opposite wing of the building. The sound of a racking cough interrupted my thoughts. Miguelito was lying in bed with the thin blanket up to his neck, his eyes staring at the ceiling.

"Miguelito?"

He said nothing.

"Maybe I can bring you a little hot soup?"

He shook his head.

"The soup is not much, but at least it will warm you."

He shook his head faintly, his dark eyes still fixed on the ceiling or rather at some distant horizon of his own beyond the dull reality of the cracked and faded blue ceiling.

He coughed again and I patted him on the shoulder, but he didn't seem to care. I stared at him a moment, helplessly, and went back to the window. Adriana was there. In the dusk she was all the

Renaissance portraits, rich, classic, stately, brooding. She smiled and across the fifteen meters of evening light separating our windows, I could feel the erotic energy of that smile. No wonder El Gordo had to tie a golden cord to her leg like a prize falcon.

Then she was speaking to me and I strained to read her lips, but I could not understand. Moments later I wasn't sure if the encounter was real or the product of a lonely imagination. Did Adriana Ponce de Romano only exist in my mind like one of those erotic projections of Genet's?

As I stood musing, I felt a tug at my shoulder and Momentito was there again. He handed me a letter. To my surprise it was from the Bishop of San Cristóbal. I had not seen the Bishop for many days. Under the peculiar expansion and concentration of time in sanctuary I had lost sight of, and therefore forgotten, him. He wrote on his crested stationery:

DEAR MORENO SUÁREZ:

I understand, through our excellent asylum telegraph system, that tonight may be the last under this roof for your Señora. I would like to offer you both my personal quarters so that you can have a farewell visit in privacy. Meanwhile, I will use your cot in the dormitory. Like all of us I am hopeful of receiving safe passage in the near future. But before I leave I would wish we could have a nice visit together. Until that moment, I remain, attentively . . .

I followed Momentito to a large room on the second floor. It was more elegant than our matrimonial room, in classic Spanish, dark leather, carved wood and red-and-gold-leaf. Over the wide bed with its intricate headboard was a large silver and ebony crucifix that looked like one of the prized possessions the Bishop had brought with him from his rectory.

Marta was standing by a large window that opened onto the inner patio. I went to her quickly and we held each other as Momentito closed the door behind us.

"Lock it," Marta said.

As I did so, I wondered where our host the Bishop was. I had not passed him on the way. Would he find instant Christianity by resting on a narrow cot and sharing the dormitory for one token visit with fifty less fortunate asylees?

When I returned to Marta I could see that she had been crying.

I took her face between my hands and kissed her eyes and then her mouth.

"I hate tears," she said. "I wish I could be stronger."

"If you were any stronger, you would pull these walls down around you like a Lady Samson."

"If only it were as simple as walls. It's that slimy diplomatic red tape that keeps slipping through our fingers."

"Once you get her out of here you'll feel better," I said. "To have something to do, settle down somewhere, put Clarita in school, get her back to normal relationships."

"After the abortion," Marta said. "First things first. We don't want to bring a little El Gordo into this world."

"A little rum-pot jai alai player," I said. "A little Paco."

"Paco? What makes you—?"

"He told me."

"That was nice of him."

"He wanted to save me from Búfalo. Because I was about to attack El Gordo."

"That *was* nice. If he had kept his pants buttoned it would have been even nicer."

"Of all the people in here I had to pick that pig for my compañero."

Marta shrugged. "Why punish yourself? Outside this place you would never spend ten minutes with a Paco O'Higgins. You would put him aside as a *cursi* clown you might like to get a tip from at the Frontón matches. But in here—I see the same thing on my side of the fence—he becomes fascinating, an inseparable companion you are wondering how you ever lived without."

"Yes, damn him, you're right," I said. "We all go a little insane in here. Only we don't notice it because everybody else is suffering from the same symptoms."

"I'm going to get you out," Marta said. "This is one thing the entire anti-Bello refugee colony should unite on. And I will promise Don Ernesto an additional *mordida* if he can talk Angel into letting you out. That humanitarian will do anything for his fellowman— especially if there is money in it. In three months we will be together."

"Next year in Positano."

"Who knows? Every day life gets a little crazier. Meanwhile, don't worry about Clarita. An abortion is not the end of the world. I had one when I was not quite seventeen."

"I thought you were a virgin."

"I know you did. I told you I cracked it from riding horseback so young."

"Who——?"

"What does it matter now? A hundred years ago."

"I'm not jealous. Just curious."

"That isn't true. I can feel you getting jealous about it. Men are impossible."

"Was it—someone I know?"

"Just before we met. A young stable boy at my grandfather's ranch. So you see," Marta laughed, "at least I wasn't lying. It did come from riding horses."

I slapped her sharply on her spreading rump. "Marta, you're incorrigible."

"I'm frank, that's all."

In an age of liars and hypocrites, her faults, her bad manners, stood out like stars—like virtues.

"Marta, I am going to miss you. Already I begin to miss you."

"I will work hard to get you out of this peso-pinching madhouse."

"I know and I will try to get on with my *Making of the Dictator*. I think about it. Only without a quiet office to work in— But I will try. It will give me something to hold on to. Maybe we will celebrate its birth with champagne in Naples, en route to Positano."

"A tamale in Mexico will be all right too," Marta said. "Or a tamaleburger in Miami."

"For you that is unexpectedly *cursi*."

"Getting safe passage and sleeping in a real bed tomorrow night and arranging for our daughter's first abortion and leaving you behind, it is all so *cursi* that I am allowed to say *cursi* things."

We were sitting on the Bishop's soft bed together.

"I wonder if the Bishop masturbates," Marta said.

"Marta, Marta," I said, half shocked, half pleased. "Is nothing sacred to you?"

"Surely not the Bishop's cock."

I shook my head and laughed. "Life is going to seem very stale. You've always added the salt and pepper."

"Salt and pepper," Marta said. "I want to be the whole enchilada."

"The whole enchilada." For years that had been a favorite Marta phrase. In the emotional vacuum she was going to leave behind I knew I would keep hearing those Marta-isms . . . her whole salty, outrageous, opinionated vocabulary.

There was a light scraping of knuckles at the door. I went to it and found Momentito bowing. "The Licenciado wishes to know if you would like your supper served in the room?"

"You mean that watery pea soup that looks as if it dropped from the bladder of an anemic eighty-year-old Spanish grandee?" Marta asked.

Momentito blinked. Years of embassy service under many regimes enabled him to maintain his equilibrium. "Señora, this will not be the usual *cena*. This will be the same dinner we serve to the Ambassador."

"Well, we're paying for it," Marta said. "We may as well see what His Excellency is getting for our money."

As seasoned a diplomat as Don Ernesto, Momentito bowed with the grace of the Ambassador, mumbled his dutiful "at your service" and withdrew.

For the next half-hour or so, time clung to us uneasily. It was as if we had said all we had to say for the moment and yet were locked together. At our home on the beach at Los Papagayos I would have made myself a tall rum drink, offered one to Marta, wandered out to the portico facing the water, watched the pelicans fly in formation against the darkening sky. This was not a concentration camp with barbed wire, brutal guards, police dogs, gas chambers. But there was the quieter torture of monotony. They say that baboons will suddenly tear at each other in boredom. Natives like El Indio Sandungo may be more fortunate than the highstrung primates. Somehow they have taught themselves to conquer boredom. I have seen Indians in my country sit for five or six hours or all day if necessary on the side of a dusty road waiting for an uncertain third-class bus to carry them to visit their *parientes* in the next village some thirty or forty kilometers away. Some call it stolidness. To others it may seem an Oriental virtue, simplicity. Whatever it was, a sublime inner eye or simple lack of imagination, Marta and I did not possess it. We sat uneasily on the large bed together and talked of the past, the future, repeating ourselves, reassuring each other and boring each other with our repetitions. In romantic novels people rise to the occasion. But I was inhibited by the pressures of the occasion and Marta's tough, breezy small talk was inadequate in a different way.

It was a relief when the meal arrived on the practiced hand of Momentito. With my ex-compadre Paco, I had gobbled my share of cold food from Apolonio's refrigerator but I had forgotten the taste of an elegant, hot, cooked dinner. There was osso bucco, wild rice, small native squash, *calabazitas* baked with a topping of yellow cheese and chilies, and on the side a generous helping of fresh diced pineapple flavored with native rum—an Italian meal with local flourishes. "His Excellency the Ambassador sends his felicitations and wishes you to enjoy this with your dinner," said Momentito and from beneath an embroidered napkin produced a bottle of Chilean wine. There hung over the occasion the ambivalent atmosphere of a second honeymoon feast and the forced festivity of that last meal for the fatally condemned.

"Suddenly everybody is being kind," I said. "The Bishop. The Ambassador. Apolonio the chef."

Marta shrugged. "I think the osso bucco is a little overcooked. And the *calabazitas con queso*, I like mine better."

"Shall we send it back? Let me call the waiter."

Marta laughed. "You never send anything back. You are too kind. It's a funny thing. You look like a powerful hulk of a man, and I know you have strong convictions. But you do not like to hurt people's feelings. Maybe that is why we have been so well married for such a long time. I love to hurt people's feelings."

True. It was a trait that ran deep in Marta. She would embarrass me sometimes by going out of her way to be rude to inefficient waiters. But she was no snob. She rode her friends just as crustily. I admired the honesty while often deploring the cruelty.

"I drink to my favorite monster," I said.

"Until next time."

We drained our glasses. The wine was comforting. It felt good to let it trickle slowly down the throat. I was living in a world now where each new sensation was to be tasted and treasured. As I reached to pour another glass, Marta put her hand on mine.

"Let's save a little for afterward?"

She rose from the small table that had been set for us and moved toward the bed. I felt challenged in a way that made me uncomfortable. I loved Marta and still could take her with pleasure, even while I yearned for the lean and slender body of the ballerina that lay buried beneath the layers of thickening flesh. Sometimes I would close my eyes and indulge in a kind of chronological infidelity by calling back the image of the lithe eighteen-year-old Marta Bravo y Del Rio I had lusted for. But now, now, this afternoon in a borrowed room, on time borrowed from state bureaucracy, with lifelines being pulled apart where they had been braided together, I felt it would be forced and false. I realized why captive animals resisted cohabitation. It was like being watched, told when to eat, defecate, copulate.

Marta sat on the bed and began to undress. A tough lady, Marta: the blood of two grand families flowed in those sturdy veins, the Bravos and the Del Rios, but there was almost no trace of the aristocrat in her. She was a freak, a sport, a maverick, and seemed to toughen and grow coarser as she grew older. The street language had been piquant and original when she wore a size eight. Now that she was a fourteen she not only talked like a truck driver but had the burly figure and rough swagger. With it all, her femaleness was undeniable. It filled the room with the earthy, musky perfume of her body. I was reminded of the Mexican Pre-Columbian earth goddess Coatlicue with her skirt of intertwined serpents, an overpowering figure that you could both fear and love.

"Marta—I love you—you know that. But—here on the Bishop's bed with Momentito coming back for the dishes any minute and Bertie Alvarez or that lady hippo knocking on the door to tell us our time is up . . . Like on that damned Day of Matrimony, I am no longer a lion with a perpetual erection, any time, any place."

"Justo, don't make such a speech about it." Marta was still

waiting for me on the bed. "I know I am too blunt for my own good. I know I should let you coax me and want me first. But I have always been the practical one in the family and our time is short."

She was lying back, half dressed, with her brassiere loosened over her large breasts. What perfect, breathing flames of nature they once had been. On our honeymoon in Mexico, Diego Rivera had insisted on painting them into one of his gaudy revolutionary murals. I had stayed in the studio because I knew Diego's reputation with models and I was a jealous young husband and did not trust either of them.

"I know," Marta said again. "I understand. But just hold me a little while, Justo. Come close to me. Because I do not want to leave you behind. I am afraid for what is going to happen to us. I have a loud mouth and a nasty disposition and a dirty mind and I hate all the *mierda* of sentimentalism. But I love you, Justo. As much as the most sentimental of weepy wives. So lie with me for a little while. Let us think about the good days when we had all the time in the world and all the right places to do it in."

I climbed on the wide bed and lay beside her with my hand on her large, soft breast and it was warm and comforting.

"You remember the first time?" Marta said.

"Yes. Yes. I was thinking of it too."

An old-fashioned ball at the mansion of Marta's parents: it was the summer the rebellious Spanish generals with their Moors and their Nazi and Italian Falangist "volunteers" had gone for the jugular of the young Spanish Republic. I was feeling resentful of the ruling class that dominated our capital and I had just refused to drink some old fool's toast to a Franco victory while the brigade I had thought to join was dying on the Ebro. Marta had led me away from political argument by offering to show me the rear garden, bordered with roses and beguiled by the scent of jasmine. At the end of the path was a latticed summer house. I remembered kissing Marta's bare shoulder. I remembered the small hooks that undid themselves for me down the back of her lace evening gown. In the cool shadows of the summer house I remembered Marta, lying under me, saying, "I had no idea you were such a good dancer!" and swatting me lustily on my backside as a signal to get off.

"What a mango from Manila you were," I said with my hand still on her breast.

"Were . . . I will thank you not to put me in the past tense. You didn't seem to mind it so much our last time at Papagayos, when the sun was staring in from the ocean."

Her hand caressed me. "Ah, my beauty," she said. "Ah, ah, I wish I could take this with me."

"So do I. It's not much use to me here."

She reached through the buttons until her hand was inside, and then it was outside, standing straight, an unexpected icon on the Bishop's bed. She raised herself to a sitting position and ran her cheek along the length of it. And then she paused and held the tip of it between her lips and I forgot about the Bishop and Licenciado Alvarez and His Excellency the Ambassador and Article V of the Caracas Convention on Diplomatic Asylum. I bent to kiss that second mouth and then, timelessly we floated in a pleasure void until Marta lay back and guided me into her. We cradled and rocked and groaned and breathed hard in unison together, shuddered together, cursed and gasped a final cry together. And then we rested in silence. Silence.

I was back in sanctuary.

"One of our best," Marta said. She was always grading them like a schoolteacher of erotica. "Even with our clothes on. After all these years we still make perfect *caldo zopilote* together."

"Marta, you know I loathe that expression."

She laughed. "Why do you think I use it?"

I drew her to me again and held her closely.

"Oh Justo—Justo dearest. I'll spend all of my time, I'll spend money, I'll throw tens of thousands of pesos to the políticos in Mexico, I'll use public opinion and private *zipizape* to get you out of this cage."

"I believe you," I said.

"After all, that *pendejo* Angel can't keep you locked up in here forever."

"Not if he's read Article V. But you know him, he's probably mislaid his copy."

"Justo, please. Try not to be bitter. I am the one who is supposed to be bitter. You are—"

"Sweetness and reason. Señor Job. Well, my good friend Angel and my good friend the Ambassador and my good friend Paco

O'Higgins are gradually changing me from a *pan dulce* to a tooth-cracking *bolillo.*"

There was a knock on the door. *"Señores. Con permiso."*

Marta and I moved quickly, fumbling at buttons, straightening clothes.

"In a moment," I called out. Then, "Never enough time. We still have so much talking to do."

"We will always have talking to do."

"Yes, yes, but I mean plans, last-minute things. And I must see Clarita."

"Later," Marta said. "When you come back to us in Mexico."

"No, Marta, I refuse to let her leave without a word between us."

There was a louder knock on the door. *"Señores, por favor!"*

"Coming, coming," I said to the impatient invisibility of Licenciado Alvarez. "A little, little moment."

"You sound like 'Momentito,' " Marta laughed.

"I am the sum total of all the traits in sanctuary. But—about Clarita. I expected to see her at lunch today, but when she didn't come—"

"I say wait," Marta said. "Right now she blames you for everything. For being here, for what happened, for your friend Paco, everything. Give her time to grow up to herself. Then she may begin to understand what has happened. She may even become proud of you."

"I don't care if she is proud of me. I don't feel like a hero. I feel more like—"

Alvarez knocked more insistently.

"—like an egg that misses the pan and falls on the floor— For God's sake, Alvarez," I shouted, "give us two more minutes!— If only Clarita would—"

"I know, Justo dear, and she will. Give her time. She is so mixed up. On top of adolescent confusion she has this asylum confusion. Along with the Paco thing, she thinks she is in love with young Miguelito. And she even feels guilty for that because when she left the Papagayos, she thought she was in love with little Beto."

Beto Morales. Her schoolboy escort was a faint flicker from a planet burnt out and fallen from the galaxy.

"Love," I said. *"Amor amor amor* . . . a tired old song. A worn-out medieval notion. I am sick of hearing about love."

"You and I?" Marta said. "Isn't that love?"

"That is different," I said. "That is *us*. A life together. It needs another name, *cariño*."

This time when Alvarez knocked with his fist shaking the door Marta hobbled hurriedly to open it and our impatient keeper bustled in.

"I am sorry to interrupt but I bring good news! Good news, Señora! The safe passage has come through. And with a Number One priority. We have been on the phone to Mexico City. Everything is in order on the other end. I will be driving you to the airport myself in exactly one hour. Now you must hurry. Inspection of your private articles. Papers to sign. You must follow me and hurry, Señora."

Practical, always practical, Marta was ready for our farewell abrazo. But I was not. In sudden, paternal panic I said, "Marta, wait, no matter what you say, I can't let Clarita go like this. In silence. It will eat into my mind. And no matter what she may feel now, when she looks back she'll think we failed each other."

"All right, I'll talk to her," Marta promised. "I will do my best to convince her."

Our turnkey glanced at his watch.

"Alvarez, I insist. I have a right to see my daughter."

The face of the chargé d'affaires wore its uniform: studied neutrality. Marta answered for him.

"I will try to send her back with Señora Lorona. But if she is not here in ten minutes—"

"I'll wait. I'll wait. Do you hear that, Alvarez? Stop looking at your watch. While my wife attends to the packing, I want a few minutes alone with my daughter." And then, answering the question in Marta's eyes, "I promise I won't lecture her. I simply want to— In the event that—"

We looked at each other and finished the sentence together, in silence. Would it be weeks, months, years, a lifetime? We kissed hurriedly, not at all like those prolonged farewell kisses in our melodramas, though we did mutter last-minute promises—write—soon—love—forever—

Joining Señora Lorona in the corridor, Marta moved forward with her familiar stride that almost succeeded in hiding the limp. I watched intently, knowing her well enough not to expect to see her face again. It would have been *cursi* to look back for a farewell glance.

I was pacing in the Bishop's room, imagining Clarita's defiance when the door opened, then closed again quickly and we were alone together for the first time since our talk in Alejandro's halfway house.

"Mother said I had to say good-bye."

I went toward her, hoping to embrace her, but she made no move to accept me. She was no longer wearing lipstick, nor the rest of the disguise that had made her look like a secondary-school actress trying to play the role of Cookie Gamboa.

"I hoped you would want to come, not be ordered to."

"Why should I want to come, to be called a bad name? You called me a very bad name."

"Clarita, I love you. That is what I want you to remember."

I saw the baby fat of her cheeks soften a little.

"And, whatever happened, I'm with you. No matter what I said, it's this place that I blame. These animals. I blame myself for exposing you to them. And—I hope you will forgive me, Clarita. If not right now, then when you are safe and have time to think about it."

She was silent, listening soberly, as in the days when I used to read to her. I reached out and this time she did not resist me. A moment later we were together, weeping together.

"Popee . . . Popee . . ."

"Papa loves you, Clarita. Every night when you go to sleep remember that. Papa loved you. Papa loves you."

There was a soft knock on the door and the soft voice of Señora Lorona behind it. "Señorita, I am sorry but—"

"Five more minutes!" I called out.

"I'm glad she isn't my mother."

"So am I. Now— Well, I suppose it's time to go back and help Mama pack. And—try not to be frightened."

"Popee—how—how do you try not to be frightened?"

She was beginning to sound more like the half-grown Alice-in-Wonderland I thought we had lost at the Papagayos.

"Mama will show you. She is very good at not being frightened. And—she has been through it herself, when she was not much older than you. So—"

"Yes. I know. She already told me, Popee. She says it is not much harder than—brushing your teeth."

Marta. Marta. I could hear her voice saying that. Could feel her and smell her and taste her. The salt and pepper, all the seasonings of my life were in her.

"Popee, don't cry. We will be fine. You must take care of yourself, Popee."

"So—what was I trying to say—you can see from Mama that it is not the end of the world."

"Popee, I want you to take care of Dolores. In a few weeks she will have her babies. I asked Señora Lorona if I could take her with us. All she says is No! No! No! Everything is against the rules. Because she is fat and smiles a lot, people don't see how mean she is. She doesn't like cats. She told me."

"I will ask Momentito to look after her and I will remind him about the liver. And in the yard I will pick her up and tell her the story of *The Little Prince*."

When Clarita laughed I heard again the sound of little bells in that life we had left behind.

Through the door came the sweet-fat voice of Señora Lorona. "Señor Moreno. I am sorry to say this but it is our job. Time is up. I must take our young lady back now."

Clarita stuck out her tongue at the invisible intruder. I was hugging her, kissing her, talking—"I love you. Take care. And take care of Mama. Sometimes she talks a little tougher than she really is."

"I know Mama," Clarita said. And I felt that she did, better than ever before.

In the hallway my eyes were wet but hers were dry. "Write to me, Popee. And Miguelito, tell Miguelito that I love him. I am not sure that I do but maybe it will make him happier. Ask him to write me a poem every day. It will give him something to do."

Then she was on her way, making it clear by attitude and distance that she was not walking with Señora Lorona. I waited, but somehow I knew from the way she was growing into Marta that she would not look back either.

As I entered the dormitory I noticed a tight, tense group crowding around the bathroom door.

"Stand back—back—don't crowd—get back, you *hijos*—"

With Paco gone, Johnie Valdez seemed to be in charge. I pushed my way closer. "What happened? What's wrong?"

Johnie nodded over his shoulder. "The kid."

From the bathroom four asylees were struggling to carry a limp body through the doorway. Because Miguelito had looked so ashen in the final days of his life, he hardly looked more dead than he had before. Except that he was not coughing any more.

"What happened? What happened?"

"I found him hanging from the shower pipe. By his belt. He left this note for you."

I studied the handwriting a moment. It was so graceful and sensitive that it looked unreal—like those overly elaborate scripts inserted in motion pictures. Addressed "To My Estimable Father-in-Law-Never-to-Be," it apologized for his abrupt exit. It said that from the moment of Paco's confession he knew there was no other honorable end.

I leave nothing of value except possibly my poetry. You will find it in a sheaf under my pillow. If you are ever in a position to publish it, I dedicate it to Clara, whom I consider a fellow-victim of tyranny. If the book should enjoy any financial royalties, I bequeath them to the Movement of Revolutionary Students, in honor of my martyred brother Tacho. Mother and Father forgive me. Long Live *Free* Socialism. And remember

MIGUEL FLORES Y PENA.

I stared at the letter. It covered only one side of a page but it contained a lifetime of yearnings and confusions, on every level, from personal desire to national politics. And at every turn, young Miguelito was sentenced to frustration. Poor little socialist sheep who had lost his way. Was that the meaning of the death of nineteen-year-old Miguel Flores? Did he die, as he thought, from disillusioned love? Or was it physical deterioration? Or Sanctuary V? I felt like shouting it at my fellow-prisoners. Look it up. Read it. It doesn't give them the right to keep us here until we rot or kill ourselves. It says, keep us here only long enough to arrange safe passage. Where in hell are our Pan American governments? Where is the UN? Where are the so-called civilized people of the world who are supposed to be looking out for us? As usual, napping, yawning or looking the other way.

Was I thinking this, reading Miguelito's letter and thinking this? It seemed so, but as guards from the lobby of the embassy materialized with a stretcher and were carrying out the wasted form of Miguelito with a blanket over his face, I realized I was on my feet shouting:

"Read it! Read it! Miguelito didn't kill himself. He was crucified. That shower pipe is a crucifix. The same hypocrites who murdered Jesus murdered Miguelito. In the name of diplomatic asylum! Read your blessed Articles. From Havana to Caracas! I studied them! I wrote a treatise on them. I tell you, *hijos*, they killed young Miguelito when they strangled Article V!"

"Justo, ol' pal, ol' pal!" Johnie was easing me back to the cot. "Gotta get hold of yourself. You were screaming like—Angel winding up for one of his talkathons. I know it's tough, real lousy, but you mustn't let it get you, keed. Listen to your Uncle Johnie. Am I right? Or am I—right?"

I looked around at him slowly.

"Okay," I said. "Okay—Johnie. Was I really screaming? I didn't know. I think I must be going mad."

"Try to relax," Johnie said. "Try to get a little shut-eye. And if there's anything you need, just remember your old pal—always at your service."

This time I was grateful. If I was conscious of resenting his manner, at least that was a reminder of sanity.

In the middle of the night I was either awakened from a dream or, tossing restlessly on my insomniac sea, I was dreaming that Goyo Solano was standing naked in the middle of the aisle with a candle in his hand proclaiming a nonbeliever's mass for the passing of Miguelito Flores.

"Ladies and gentlemen," Goyo was saying, as if he were on the stage of his private theater about to announce one of his own black comedies. "I wish to speak a few final lines of poetry to Miguel

Flores. A man of nineteen should not die by his own hand in an ugly bathroom far from home among strangers, enemies and Philistines."

A gravel voice in the darkness behind me called out, *"Basta, hombre!* Blow out the candle. I was right in the middle of a juicy dream. Let me catch her before she gets away."

It sounded like Búfalo. There was a shrill cackle from a cot beyond.

"Pigs," Goyo Solano said, looking like a soft devil behind his candle. "Is that not the fate of all poets? To live among pigs and to die among pigs."

"Señora, for the sake of God, go back to bed with your *nalgas* in the air so your neighbor can bugger you up to your belly button. And may you stick together like dogs in heat."

Goyo said in naked dignity, "Miguel Flores will be laid to his eternal rest with some words of poetry if I have to scream them over your boorish voices."

There was silence. Then a grunt of resignation from Búfalo.

Goyo began, in that tone of familiar affectation that was nevertheless touching and sincere.

> *Adiosito, Miguelito mío*
> *Hasta las mananitas.*
>
> What is so special about dying?
> People do it every day.
> Anybody and everybody can do it.
> The bullfighter beckons it with his cape on Sunday afternoons.
> The soldier dies and dies and dies . . .
> The old man goes in his sleep without a whimper.
> A child is run over in the street.
> People die by overeating.
> Or by killing each other.
> In Mexico they eat skeleton candy
> Drink too much and dance on the graves
> On the Day of the Dead.
>
> No, there is nothing special about dying.
> We do it every day.
> In pain and in conflict
> In sickness and in health
> In profound disgust and serene satisfaction.
> No, death itself is as ordinary as dirt.

Only the man who returns to that dirt
Is extraordinary.

So think:
There will never be another Miguelito Flores.
In the unfolding generations there will be men who look like
Miguelito Flores.
Who sound like Miguelito Flores.
Who think like Miguelito Flores.
And who may even die like Miguelito Flores.
But
There will never be another Miguelito Flores
Never before and never again *this* Miguelito Flores.
The exact reproduction of
Miguelito Flores.

No, there is nothing special about dying.
There is only something special about Miguelito Flores.
So, Miguelito Flores, I bid you good night.
Miguelito Flores, I wave you farewell.
To wherever you are going, farewell, farewell.

Now you are one of the million million
Corpses
Rotting and forgotten.
No, there is nothing special about dying.
Only about living
For one brief moment
As Miguelito Flores *el único*.
And now that candle flickers
Out.

Goyo blew out the candle. There was a loud fart. Búfalo was snoring. I heard groans of fatigue. Rubén Silva padded to the bathroom in the service of his weak bladder. He was followed by old man Gamboa. I knew the sound of every cot as if it had its own voice. Even the silences. The silence of El Indio Sandungo was deeper and stronger than the silence of lesser forms huddled under the thin blankets.

Naked, Goyo returned to his cot next to mine.

"That was well done," I said. "It was right that someone did something."

"We need our ceremonies to separate us from the animals," Goyo said. "Otherwise we would simply be carried out of this world like sides of beef."

"It was a good poem. One of your new ones?"

"Very new," Goyo said. "I made it up as I went along. I couldn't bear the thought of that child leaving here with a shrug of indifference."

I could see the outline of his triangular eyebrows and his Oriental satyric eyes in the darkness. He leaned toward me, only a few inches, discreetly, like a seducer who does not want to frighten off his prey.

"Justo *cariño,* I am so lonely. I am so full of love I do not know what to do. I believe that you love me a little bit, Justo."

"Goyo, I admire you. I feel tender toward you. I respect your talent and your heart. If you want to call that love."

"Yes, yes," Goyo said. "I call that love. You are afraid to call it by its right name because you are conditioned by our Philistine culture to think only of women. You are more subtle, but you must prove that you are *muy macho* like the rest of them. But under the *machismo* I feel the true sensuality, the true sensitivity of the Greeks."

"Goyo, go to sleep," I said. "Sleep. I wish you good dreams."

"All right," Goyo said. "I will close my eyes and think of Indian boys as smooth and delicate as rainbow trout in a freshwater pool."

During the night I awoke with a pounding in my head. In sleep I had seen terrible things: The blood of Miguelito pouring from the shower faucet. Paco O'Higgins as a giant frog trying to swallow a little tadpole that was crying out "Popee . . . Popee" as they disappeared behind a rock in the fish bowl. Then I was making farewell love to my wife. But when I withdrew it was not from Marta but Adriana. What a pig I must have rooting in my brain to think *Adriana* when my right mind was grieving for Marta. Marta, forgive me. Clarita, forgive me. Marta . . .

Somehow, slipping off to sleep again, Adriana had replaced Marta on that inner screen. Again she was standing at the foot of the bed and I was reaching out to draw her into the deep soft of the four-poster featherbed in Alejandro's guest room where conscience or consciousness drove her away. And again I was left with the reality of the hard, narrow cot.

14

When the first light slanted through the dormer window next morning, the changed atmosphere of my existence in the dormitory came
to me on two levels. Marta and Clarita were gone. Already there
were thousands of miles between us. The evening before, the final,
abortive embrace seemed not so much long ago as unreal. In sanctuary, whatever was unrelated to the immediate present did not
exist. Now my immediate belly-deep concern was not—would I ever
get out of here, would I ever embrace my wife again?—but what
would I do in the face of Búfalo de Sa standing guard at the door of
the bathroom without my stout defender Paco O'Higgins in front of
me to absorb that daily, ceremonial punch in the mouth? That
lovable, loathsome betrayer had handed me on a silver plate the
right he had earned with his bloody mouth. Our dormitory might
have seemed to an outsider a gathering of motleys disordered and
chaotic, but there was method and structure in the mess. The law
of the sanctuary was strange, unwritten and yet clear for all to see.

I would lose my position, my face, my place at the head of the
line if I did not emulate O'Higgins. But I could not pound the door
and shout obscenities like that departed hero-boor. It was not my
style. Still, the eyes of my fellow-inmates were waiting. I had to do
something. Make up my own kind of *escándalo*. I instructed Goyo
to follow me up the aisle. As soon as El Gordo had his prescribed
time, I would make my move. I was frightened of what Búfalo
would do to me. I had boxed and played tennis in younger days, but
I was badly out of shape now. And as in all prisons, from the most
genteel to the coconut camps where Indians were bullied by *mestizo*

guards, there was a pecking order. My fellow-asylees were waiting
for the erstwhile Presidente to prove he had a beak.

In pajamas and robe I went uncertainly toward the bathroom
door. At my shoulder marched Goyo, wearing a silk black Oriental
robe trimmed in Chinese red. I waited until El Gordo had had his
allotted time. A dozen asylees had gathered behind us to watch the
game. Búfalo watched me with the expressionless look of the bodyguard. He did not move except that his enormous chest rose several
centimeters. He stood still like a predatory animal ready to spring.
I looked around, wishing there was some way out of this. But the
eyes were waiting. El Indio was waiting. Johnie Valdez was waiting.
The familiar faces of the caged were waiting.

"All right, El Gordo," I said, but not loudly enough. It was difficult for me ever to raise my voice unless I had many drinks or was
under emotional stress. But this time my voice was even fainter than
usual. It seemed to get stuck somewhere in the lower part of my
throat and emerged as a kind of unfamiliar whisper. There was
laughter behind me. I cleared my throat, took a deep breath and like
a neophyte trumpet player trying to produce a sound through the
formidable brass apparatus, I forced the tone through my lips. "All
right, El Gordo, time is up. Even if Paco is gone we are not going
to let you spend all morning in there."

"Atta boy, my President! You tell 'em, keed!" Johnie half-
mocked, half-encouraged me.

Búfalo's heavy features creased slightly, especially around the
slit, scar-tissue eyes, in what was meant to be a smile. To draw an
aggressive response from Búfalo, the challenge would have to be
stronger. I felt like a gnat trying to bite a rhino. I tried to remember
how Paco had done it, and what Marta might say. Heavy-legged with
fear, I let out another notch in my aggression belt. *"Asesino!"* I
shouted to El Gordo through Búfalo's wall of a chest. *"Asesino!*
Come out! Your time is up, you *pinche pendejo* of a murderer!"

This time I was rewarded. Búfalo did not strike out or punch me
as he was accustomed to doing with Paco. But he did accommodate
me with a sharp backhand slap across the mouth. It stung and I fell
back. I put my hand to my lips. Yes, there were a few flecks of blood
on my fingers. I turned around to my audience. There was an audible

murmur of approval. Everybody seemed satisfied, even Búfalo de Sa. We had struck a new balance. That is how the wolves and the sea lions work out their arrangements. A moment or two passed before El Gordo emerged, sleekly bathed, resplendent in white silk and smelling of his fine French cologne. Nothing had changed except the degree of gout. Now he was walking with the aid of Jesuscito, whom he used as a small human cane.

Inside the bathroom Goyo stared at the double toilets and hesitated. I immediately aimed the accumulated water of the night into the toilet bowl. Goyo looked away.

"Justo, my dear friend, as I told you, I am very sensitive about these things. Ever since I was a child. No one—not even my closest ones—has ever seen me in the bathroom. Would you be a dear and wait outside the door a few moments?"

"Goyo, you must understand the arrangement here. Once I step outside I lose my turn, and someone will come in to replace me. Those are the rules of the bathroom. I succeeded Paco, and with the privilege of the slap on the mouth I am permitted to bring you in with me. Otherwise, since you were the last to arrive, unless you make some special fight for it, you will be the last to relieve yourself."

Goyo looked as if he might cry. "I cannot bear it," he said. "I shall die."

"I doubt it," I said. "You will suffer. You will feel humiliated. But in the end you will get used to it like the rest of us."

"Never." Goyo shook his green hair emphatically. "If you offend my aesthetics you plunge a knife into my soul."

"Look, Goyo, how will this be? I will take my shower, hot and steamy. It will be like a curtain between us. But you will have to try and be quick about it. In less than five minutes the next customers will be pounding at the door."

"Que bárbaro!"

"That is true. But if you want to survive in here, you will have to toughen up, Goyo."

"I am not going to toughen up or soften up or shrivel up. I am going to live and die as myself, as Gregorio Solano."

"Everyone changes," I said. "Everyone shifts their sails to the wind. Or tries to steer with the current. That is only human."

Goyo raised his eyebrows. "Who ever said I was human?"

"Goyo, sit down like the rest of us, before they begin breaking the door in."

I stepped into the shower. Through the splashing of the hot water on my shoulders I could hear other sounds. Yes, poets may talk more grandly, but they are as prone to nervous stomach as the rest of us.

Goyo did not go into breakfast. In silence I dipped the stale *bolillo* into the pale coffee. The Bishop was present, ready to discuss his liberal Catholicism and his bleeding ulcers, but I would not encourage him. When I returned to the dormitory I found Goyo lying on his cot with his Chinese robe opened at the neck. He had lost, for the moment, his chipper poetic stance. He thought of himself as our Dylan Thomas, our Yevtushenko, but a running of the bowels is a grim leveler. Standing over him I could see for the first time the gray roots of his green hair.

"Goyo—are you all right?"

He gave an expressive, soft shrug. "I cannot bear the color of that ceiling."

"It's faded. It could be worse."

"Not really. It reminds me of the color of—"

"Look at the designs," I interrupted. "After a while you will get to know it as a Mayan astronomer knew the skies over Yucatán."

"Thank you, I do not wish to know it so well. I am still counting on the Association of Pan American Writers to get me out of here before I go mad."

"Goyo, how can you go any madder in here than you were out there?"

Goyo's face exploded into laughter. He loved the idea of being crazy, of shocking respectabilities.

"Yes, I am crazy! I am an angel with green hair and yellow wings, flying upside down. But this place will drive me seriously mad."

He patted the cot. "Sit down, Justo. Close to me. Hold my hand. I feel lonely. Do not be afraid. I am not going to attack you in public. Your poet laureate has better manners. He does not make love in broad daylight in the middle of the barnyard like a pig."

I sat down, on my own cot, across from him and tried to be careful without being unkind.

"I know how you feel, Goyo," I said. "Lonely. With Marta and Clarita gone—already it feels, not a day, or a week, a different century or a different planet."

Goyo sighed. "You are a poet, like me. I think you would have made a good President, Justo, if they had let you be more than a figurehead."

"Not really. I would have been out of my depth. Not enough of a politician."

Goyo was lying with his arms folded behind his head. He looked as he had in happier days when lying in his hammock in his eccentric country home on the outskirts of the city.

"Politicians are for countries that are going concerns," he said. "Like the United States. They need not merely a politician but an engineer, a businessman, a man of the practical moment. But for our poor country, which has not yet found itself, which is undeveloped, undernourished, unrealized, here we need a poet who can see around corners, not just of buildings but of time—who can imagine the future."

"Swords into plowshares and politicians into poets."

"I am serious, my dear Justo," Goyo said. "Sometimes I say things I do not mean to stir people up—I am my own court jester. But now I speak my heart. Listen to our radios. The news. All bad. On every continent riot and hatred and hunger and war. Any fool can see where we are heading. By the year two thousand I will be a very old man and I would like to live out my days on a grassy island in the Caribbean with a small boat anchored in a green lagoon. I will try not to think of all the billions of people following their little flags and singing their silly anthems. I will try not to think about what the politicians and their engineers and generals and computers have done to the world."

In that characteristic gesture, Goyo ran his fingers down the green fringe of hair overhanging his forehead. "Maybe only poets who have the intuitive wisdom to see into the world of the unborn can save us from destruction. That was the power of Jesucristo. He was a child in a world of generals and governors and practical men. He was a poet. He not only knew how rotten was the present and the past, he could see that there was a sweetness in man yet to be released. But we know what happened, my dear Justo. The poet was

crucified. The poet dies. The one true church is taken over—infiltrated—by the generals and politicians and power-grabbers who
become the popes and the bishops and the cardinals. Exactly the
opposite of the ideas of Jesús the poet becomes what is known as
Catholicism. Only every once in a while a poet comes along to remind the powerhouse of what it was in its beginning, what it might
have been."

"True, Goyo, but not every poet can be trusted. Look at Angel.
In his student days he was a poet-revolutionist. In jail and in exile he
was still a poet. That was how he swept us along—with his imagination. But once he came to power it was a different soup."

"Yes," said Goyo, "our country thought it needed Angel, but you
know who it really needs?" With a long, graceful finger he pointed
to himself. "Gregorio Solano, the poet, the dreamer, the lover. You
know I was raised a Catholic—weren't we all?— But the medieval
emperors, in the name of selflessness and the golden rule, you know
what they did to heretics—put them to the rack and the torch and
poured molten metal down their throats! The emperors used and
abused the poet Jesucristo. Just as their modern counterparts
torment a true son of Jesús like Gregorio Solano. But there is a part
of me that still remains Catholic, Justo dear. And that part of me is
in defiance against the power structure of the Church. Think for a
minute of the Grand Inquisitor of Dostoevski. Think of the implica-
tions, Justo. I read it as an epilogue to the New Testament. It should
be included in a modern version of the Bible."

Then Goyo the Poet-President reverted to Goyo the Wicked with
whom I was more familiar. He rose on his elbows, raised his butterfly eyebrows and said, "The part I love most is where the Grand
Inquisitor and the Savior kiss when the story ends. I see Jesús and
the Grand Inquisitor putting their tongues into each other's mouths.
A coming together of rival philosophies that is not of the mind."

He laughed his arch, evil laugh.

"Poet-President," I said, "you may be able to see around the
corners of the present into the vacuum world of the future. But you
are still a venomous witch."

Goyo laughed, delighted. "But of course. I am terrible. I am the
most terrible person in this room. Including El Gordo."

There was a flurry of activity at the entrance. It was Bertie Al-

varez with the manila files under his arm. "Wait—wait—don't push
—one case at a time!" And the eternal chant, *"Próximamente usted
podrá salir."*

I hung back. I knew from the Ambassador and from the pressure
Angel was keeping on him that I was going nowhere. At least not
soon. At least not next. But Goyo rose from his cot and pressed in
like an eager puppy. "Señor, Señor, you must have some word for
Gregorio Solano. There must be some word for me. I am no ordinary peon to be pushed around. I am a poet!"

"Please, please," Alvarez was smiling. "Give us time. Of course I
recognize your importance. But each case we process is reviewed by
the territorial state. We can only request safe passage. We cannot demand it. But soon, soon. You will not live here forever, I assure
you."

Goyo came back to his cot grumbling, "I cannot understand it.
The Pan American Writers? One of the three most famous poets in
Latin America. The author of the marching song of the Revolution.
This is ridiculous."

"Goyo," I said. "I am sick of all the complaining. We live in a
complaint factory. On a revolving belt of complaining. You can take
your bitching and your boasting and—"

Goyo tossed his head in a wild laugh. "Thank you. I accept!"

"Goyo Solano, get away from me!" I said. "You are depraved.
A priest of depravity!"

"Flatterer," Goyo said archly.

I moved away. I left the poet laureate camping on his cot. I was
glad he was here. Not glad for him but selfishly for me. Especially
now that Marta was gone, he helped to fill the void. At least he was
someone I could talk to—as long as I could keep our friendship on
the level of the mind.

Wondering how I would survive now without the steadying afternoons with Marta, I drifted to the window. I stared out at the courtyard, sun-paled and dusty and more forlorn than ever without the
promise of Marta. Marta. I closed my eyes and tried to imagine
where she was *this second*. I could see her hobbling, tough, going
about her business with Clarita. Yes, and I could see her still flirting at cocktail parties and encouraging tall young men with dark

lashes and a predilection for attractive older women. Damn her. Jealousy. The most debilitating of all the emotions.

When I opened my eyes I was looking into the window across the patio and instead of Marta, there was Adriana. Adriana the untouchable. What was she like? What went on behind that come-hither-but-keep-your-distance *misterio* of a face? Marta might have been able to tell me. Sooner or later she would have cut to the heart of the secret. Again I wondered if Adriana had come to the window especially to find me. It might have been chance. She paced her room as I roamed our dormitory and a window is for looking through and for escaping four walls. And yet, I felt some sense of power in the appearance of Adriana at the window. She was not wearing a dress but a silken, rose-colored kimono. I could see her fine ivory neck rising from her shoulders and the fullness of her breasts that rose and fell and breathed and were alive. She knew that she had only to move, ever so slightly, to make a statement in silence that was overpowering.

She was not flirting, she was using her body for me, a frustrating fifteen meters away. Just as the powerful yellows of Van Gogh strike yellow notes as well as images, I felt her so strongly that I glanced around to make sure I was not being noticed by El Gordo or by Búfalo de Sa. But all was *muy tranquilo*. El Gordo was lying back on his double cot nearing the end of his Spanish translation of *Gone with the Wind* while Jesusito fanned him with a folded newspaper and Búfalo sprawled on his sagging cot, his thick bull's back resting against the wall as he ogled the ample backsides of the ladies featured in his old sports magazine.

We continued to gaze at each other until I turned away. Back on my cot I concentrated on Marta until I could almost hear the boldness of her laughter.

At lunch time, following the others into the mid-afternoon sunshine of the courtyard, I took a walk inside its perimeter. Goyo wanted to accompany me, but I was able to discourage him with only slight injury to his feelings. A walk alone around the circumscribed sun-bleached area is not exactly privacy but it is the nearest thing in asylum. I wanted to walk alone. I wanted to look up at the pale tropical sky alone. I would pass other asylees and pretend not to see

them. Johnie hovered nearby, but I kept my eyes on the sandy earth
trod flat by the feet of too many people penned together. I managed
to avoid his "What-can-I-do-you-for?" For several full circles of the
enclosure I hid within myself. Dolores II crossed my path. Her body
was growing more distorted each day, a ludicrously disproportioned
figure of a cat, with a great pregnant belly hanging down between
long, skinny legs. I could count the ribs like miniature railroad ties
under the thin fur of malnutrition. She looked at me and tried to
meow, but no sound came forth. The sand was too hot, the air too
still and energy long spent. I thought of Clarita and how she had
cradled the cat as she promenaded her defiance down the yard. I
picked up Dolores II and scratched her head. A flea jumped onto
my forearm, then several others. Dolores II was crawling with them
—what Marta would call a "flea trolley." It seemed cruel to put her
down, but there would be tiny red, itching bites along my arm. I
stroked the mangy head, matted with flea scabs, and gently set her
on the ground again. Why, I wondered, had she chosen asylum along
with the rest of us? What moral decision, what political rejection
had led her to our dung heap?

My thoughts were interrupted by a shrill screech. I turned to see
Dolores II rolling over and Búfalo laughing his gravel basso as he
withdrew his heavy foot. Dolores II found her feet again but was
limping. Her hip was bruised or dislocated. I was trembling for the
senseless pain Búfalo had put into that life-bitten cat. It gave me the
courage to scream at him. "Sadist! When you did your torturing for
El Gordo at least you were under orders!"

Búfalo stared at me, his small eyes dark and uncomprehending.
I think he let me go on because he was not a listener. He heard
sounds. And then, like a trained animal, he did what he was told.

"But this," I went on, excited with hatred, "—you are a *cochino!*
I will not say I piss in the milk of your whore mother because I do
not think you have a mother. I think you were put together out of
pig shit!"

He stared down at me in the hot sun. I was ready for his big
fist in my mouth. Frightened. But resigned and ready. He curled his
right hand into a club and drew his arm back to aim it at my head.

"Amiguito," he said. "Little friend, you are afraid, eh?"

"Yes, physically I am afraid," I said. "But not psychologically. Psychologically I am not afraid."

I did not expect to say that. And I did not expect him to react as he did. He laughed. Whether or not he understood the word "psychologically" I do not know. Maybe it was merely the sound of it that struck him funny. But he laughed his cement-mixer laugh. "*Vete,* beat it, little friend, beat it!"

I moved on. Everything in sanctuary is test and challenge. I felt I had won this one, so far. Paco had had his style and I had mine, but I was standing up, winning some skirmishes at least. I walked on. I looked for Dolores II. She was on a table, trying to lick the place where Búfalo had kicked her. I approached her and moved as if to pet her, but she rose and limped away. I am not trusting any more two-legs today. You two-legs are not consistent like cats. I wished I could prove myself to Dolores II. I wished I could carry her to some haven of regular meals and soft pillows where she could give birth in comfort and dignity. I felt inconsolably sad for Dolores II, who was of course Clarita and Marta who were myself. Inconsolably helpless because Dolores II would now confuse me with Búfalo. In the jungle every movement of the leaf was your enemy.

Once again I felt myself caught up in a will that was stronger than mine and there she was at her dormer window. It was open to the sunlight in which she was drying her hair. Fluffing it to let the rays of the sun caress and warm it, she was like a tawny lioness stretching and performing for its mate. Or was this performance an instinctive searching for a mate? It was a heady thought. Ever since the Maldonado affair she might have denied herself to El Gordo. She had not been his prisoner in that tower room but a self-willed exile from his attentions. Perhaps his elaborate toilette for the Day of Matrimony was an enormous bluff. The poetic justice of his plight was so compelling that I tried to believe it was true. Beckoning with the comb that she moved slowly through her burnished gold hair, she was advertising herself in the window.

Now she was gazing down at me. I was sure of it. She was drying her hair for me and for no one else in the courtyard. I could feel her opening, slowly, slowly, like a morning glory in the first light. Then, suddenly, her expression changed and she disappeared.

A rough hand on my shoulder spun me around. "Hey, *estúpido*, what the fuck you think you are doing?"

"A cat can look at a queen."

"Maybe yes, maybe no," Búfalo growled. "A cat can also be swung against a wall and squashed like an overripe melon. *Cuidado*, Señor. Remember Lieutenant Maldonado."

"But you have no El Amante here to do that for you."

Búfalo laughed and anyone would have thought he was responding good-naturedly to some harmless joke.

"Ha, ha, we have other ways. The General has the gout. He gets into a very black jealousy when he has the gout and cannot go to the Señora."

"The Señora cannot go anywhere either. Even if she wanted to. She is a prisoner in that room." I wondered if it was gout or her denial that made him insanely jealous. Maybe the Day of Matrimony was a torture for the torturer, her revenge for the gift he had made of Maldonado's prize. No wonder the humiliated *gallo* was the compulsive rooster who crowed over Cookie Gamboa in the laundry room.

"Move away, *mano*," Búfalo was saying, "or I squash you like a cat."

At the trash basket, Dolores II was poking her foot through the diamond-shaped wire spaces at the brown spots on a broken plate, the stain of beans rather than the substance, but a starved cat paws at the faintest of possibilities. Her foot caught in the wire side and she let out a cry for help. I moved forward to release her but Búfalo was ahead of me. He grabbed her and yanked her free. One of the claws or even part of the paw must have been torn off, for she let out an ear-piercing yowl. He squeezed her hard in his big hand and she screamed—growled—cried and wriggled to scratch at him. His hold on her slipped to her tail. Over his head he swung her around— while she snarled and cried for her life. Then he let her go, with an obscene flourish, like a hammer thrower. I shut my eyes but I heard the scream, the crunch, the squash, the sacrificial collision of Dolores II and the sun-baked stucco wall. A crash of bones and blood and sinews holding together the desire to live. I looked and the horror was the crawling, accusing mangle of a former cat still able to flop in a last, ludicrous effort to walk. Blood was dripping from her mouth and her ears. She was flopping and falling and bleeding and trying in all her blood and futility to hang on to her life and the lives of her unborn.

Búfalo was laughing. "See what I mean, my little friend? I will pick you up by your legs and swing you against the wall and your brains will go squash like a ripe papaya."

"Kill it," I said. "For God's sake, kill it. How can you laugh at it like a hyena?"

Búfalo laughed his kind of laughter.

"You kill it, my little friend. If you give so much of a soft fuck about it, you put an end to it."

I had seen bulls die like that—writhing, thrashing, vomiting blood —after the fourth or fifth sword. But even a misplaced cowardly sword into the lung was cleaner than what was happening to her.

But I did not have the toughness to end the agony. Búfalo knew this. He was laughing at me. I looked around for help. There was El Indio. Without expression he came forward, bent over the bloody mess and gave it a violent chop with the side of his long black hand. The thing lay dead at last. I looked away. El Indio went to the trash basket, found a piece of discarded newspaper, wrapped up the remains of Dolores II and put them in the trash. Rest in your grave of garbage and refuse, Dolores, a true child of your age.

I did not thank El Indio. He walked away from the trash basket without looking at me. The peasant plants his corn with a pointed stick as had his ancestors a thousand years before. He was not afflicted with the curse of tongues. El Indio had talked to the people when he wanted them to follow him into the Revolution. I had heard of these speeches, short and simple. "They have land and do not work it. We have no land but we have hands to work. Now the time has come to take back the land of our fathers. Bring your machetes and follow me."

I stared at the bloody dust where Dolores II had thrashed her final minutes away, remembering the mangy cat in Clarita's arms. I covered over the stains with my foot and cursed Búfalo through my futile tears. Then it was time to follow Momentito up the metal fire escape to our attic lockup again.

15

By now I could identify each snore in the night, each groan, each letting of wind, but that did not make them more agreeable. Once again I tried to focus my mind on constructive preoccupation. In sanctuary, time was the only coin and I was squandering it. Where was *The Making of the Dictator?* Even with Johnie Valdez talking and the Death-head muttering and El Gordo snoring, there must be a way back to it. Think Bolívar. Think Martí. Think Madero and Zapata—and the pendulum swing to repression that cuts them down. Let the book overcome the insistent stagnation and the verbal and nonverbal obscenities of sanctuary. Think. Think. Book. Book. Fuck the sanctuary.

You see. *Chinga.* I would not have used such language at home. Sanctuary was vulgarizing. Sharing the toilet. Sharing the stink. Think book—think . . . Marta. My mind roamed down from her face, from her mouth. That first time. In the garden house. Lie here, Martita. Let me undo the hooks in the back. Oh, she complies. How charmingly, turning her head away. My fingers are excited. From behind I reach my hands through her long hair and under her arms to cup her breasts. The brassiere resists me. I hurry to remove it. My fingers fumble. She smiles and helps me. I turn her to me, bury my face between her breasts. They are unfamiliar, firmer, bolder and I look up to see that Marta has been replaced. Adriana. How many years I had wondered and fantasized about those nipples. Were they small and pink or large and amber? I could feel them tightening hardening rising to the touch of my tongue. From nipple to nipple teasing one against the other while hand roamed smooth flesh of warm belly until fingers touched the hidden hair. I kept my mind pressing into her. Think *boca*. Think *chocha*. Think moving into the soft mango deep of the most beautiful woman in the country. Have you ever tried to make love silently in the dark? To put all of yourself into the explosive act of love without making a sound? It can be done, but it takes art, concentration and stealthful care. My mind drove me on, exploring, feeling the soft inner layer of her, teasing her, making her rise to it and draw it deeper in, to the bottom, touching the bottom of her, so full of my own pleasure I could hardly hear her gasping, "Oh Justo, my God how big ay ay you are going to split me in two—no don't stop don't stop more more more push it into me harder ay! ay! I want to die don't stop harder harder faster faster we are going to kill each other love of my life hard love of my life I can feel your balls buried in my cunt and the tip of it all the way into me until it is coming out of my throat coming coming coming ay! ay oh . . ." I raised the sheet to my forehead and wiped away the sweat. Lord, what kind of old fool was I? At my age. I looked around quietly. The Death-head was snoring. Goyo mercifully was turned away. The dormitory was asleep. Justo Moreno Suárez, Naval Cadet and First President of the People's Republic had made love to Adriana under the very eyes of El Gordo and his watchdog Búfalo. I fell asleep in her arms, the grateful arms of Adriana.

Once again I heard bells chiming in the distance. The cathedral that had been tolling off the hours for four hundred years. What a procession of peoples and periods and politics and petty and majestic lives and deaths had listened to that awful clanging that tourists considered beautiful. The colonial clanging half-awakened me and I peered up into the semidarkness of pre-dawn and wondered if someone was staring down at me.

"Goyo . . . is that you?"

"Shh." The face of Goyo Solano was an irregular cloud hovering over me. "Don't be nervous. I was just memorizing your face." His whisper was a snake hissing at me. "Do not feel disturbed. I am going to write a poem about you. You have a beautiful face. A cross between an Old Testament prophet and an arena *poncheador*."

"For God's sake, Goyo, let me sleep."

"Shh. I am ready to go back to my cot now. I will write a poem in my mind describing your face."

He patted me tenderly on the shoulder, then worked his body back into his own cot, so close to mine that our shoulders were almost touching. I moved as far away as I could. Within seconds my mind was flooded again with visions and fantasies of Adriana. In the next cot Goyo was whispering to himself. We both fell asleep entwined in our wish dreams.

In the morning the door-pounding ceremony was more intensified by the senseless murder of Dolores II and the erection for Adriana that had awakened me and the coquettish *Buenos* look from Goyo. Thinking of the writhing pulp of Dolores, and of those boarlike blue-veined balls of El Gordo touching my Adriana, and of having to share the bathroom with my friend and pursuer, I shouted and banged on the door more in the manner of Paco O'Higgins than of the former Presidente. And Búfalo responded, mechanically, more the way he had toward Paco: he hit me much harder on the mouth than he had before. And now I saw or felt why Paco had no need to fight back. There was a strange satisfaction in creating a disturbance that forced Búfalo to strike at me. It may be difficult for bourgeois, comfortable people to understand this. I had been bourgeois once, yes, and even a personage, but here in the dormitory I was a have-not. I had my few clothes and my few books and a laundry bag and that was all. Except for my dreams. They could not deprive me of my dreams, my fantasies, my secrets. My private pleasure of Adriana. Hit hard enough in the mouth to draw blood, I could not *understand* in my mind but *feel* on my wet thick lips the idea in the minds of student rioters who taunt their police and their national guards. You insult them, you call them terrible names and the doing of it makes you for that moment a free man, and then if they thud you with the butt of a gun or poke you with a bayonet or blind you with tear gas, what more can they do for you than kill you? So you stand up to it, enjoy it, make them punch you in the mouth, make them make you bleed. When Búfalo gave me his morning gift of the taste of my own blood, not only could I understand those riots, I was the riot, I became the revolt, and Búfalo was the mercenary stalking the university or guerrilla hideouts for rebels to squash like cats.

At breakfast there was the usual clatter, the backbiting and the bickering, but it was as if I were wearing a hearing aid and had turned the volume low. In my pocket of near-silence I let my mind leap to the window of Adriana. The live bird stirring against my thigh would never let me rest now. There had to be a way. When Paco had spoken of rocks to hide under, he had meant in the courtyard, the laundry room, or against the wall beneath the fire escape. But Adriana never left her room. Until the Romanos received their safe passage, El Gordo had sentenced her—or had she sentenced herself?—to solitary confinement. There must be a way. That persistent swine of a seducer O'Higgins would have found a way. What if he had? I felt all the emotions of a jealous lover. The thought of that fat fish swimming into Adriana's pool titillated and tortured me. It was hard enough to think of El Gordo offering his swollen testes to my lady. No, no, it was sheer masochism and I drove Paco from the door of my mind. Behind that door I had Adriana to myself. There had to be a way.

Back in the dormitory Goyo was lying in wait. He had not gone into breakfast with the rest of us. His face always had been drawn tight against its bones, giving him that look of a devil fawn. But now he was much paler than when he had first come and the wickedness that was always in his eyes was not smiling as in sweeter days. And—how long had he been here? I was never able to separate the days, weeks, months that ran together in sanctuary. There was a quarter of an inch of gray at the roots of his hair. For the first time in the fifteen years I had known him, he had begun to look old. I never had thought of him as a man with gray hair. It would destroy the image of the ageless dancing leering satyr. I was surprised that a man as vain as Goyo would not have thought to bring green rinse along to keep his hair from betraying him. But then, he had not expected to stay more than the first few days. His fellow-poets would pressure Angel into safe passage before the infection of gray roots had time to spread upward and ravage the glorious green he had worn with such élan.

"Justo dearest, I have been waiting for you to finish that elegant breakfast so I could read you your poem."

Like most self-assured poets, he did not wait for an answer but began, in his well-known rhetorical style. It was a poem about my face all right, about the "gladiator nose" and the "sturdy ram's head" and the "vibrations set off between the twin tuning forks of physical toughness and an almost feminine sensitivity." It was a sonnet and it reminded me of the scholarly arguments about Shakespeare and the sonnets he seemed to have directed to men—was the Bard as aberrant as a three-guinea note or was he merely praising his benefactors in the extravagant style of his time?

"A—nice piece of work, Goyo. I can see it in a future collection."

"Thank you for assuring me a future," Goyo said with a trace of evil glee.

"But if it is meant as an overture it simply makes me uncomfortable."

"Justo my dear," Goyo talked to me as an affectionate teacher to a schoolboy, "I recognize that you are a heterosexual. Or to cut closer to the bone, you think you are. I am not one of those doctrinaire Baudelaires who sneer at conventional love. Conventional love is a necessary—I will not say evil like some of my friends— simply that it is necessary. We may turn away from the conventional but we cannot cut ourselves loose from humanity. Women must breed. There must be men to plant the seed. Who am I to play God and say an end to reproduction? In the world of physical love I have declared myself. Egalitarian. All intense feeling, all love of man for woman, man for man is part of the life force. The love force. If it exists, it is part of life, even the Sadisms of the Marquis. You think I am crazy? He was so crazy he was coming out the other end and becoming sane."

I smiled and edged away, trying to avoid him without offending. His were deep feelings, rare sensibilities, and although the end result of those sensitivities ran counter to my own, I felt bound to respect his right to his ways.

"No, Justo my dear," Goyo went on, warming to his subject, "I have never said, 'Down with man entering woman.' I am only saying man is the only animal to rise above the basic, to beautify, to heighten. You know your Roman and your Greek poets, the French Impressionists and the Shelleys and the Swinburnes. You know your Gide. Could anyone say it more beautifully? There is no love more aesthetic than man for man. Two beings locked in an embrace of pure passion. Hart Crane said it so well. And those puritanical boys from the southern United States. Tennessee Williams and Truman Capote. Don't you adore them! They say it well! Yes, the Anglo-Saxons—they have a gift for it. What a lovely time I had when I gave a reading at Oxford. They are beautiful boys, the English. Those children of Bloomsbury. So many beautiful boys. I remember one night in Rome I walked alone into the Colosseum. A young boy came up to me, shyly. Curly-haired. Like a Renaissance angel. He was a child, but the urchins of Rome know the gift of all the centuries of love. I remember throwing my head back in a final gasp of delight and—"

"*Basta,* Goyo, you must stop this. I have told you—we have different ideas of expressing affection. Now let us remain friends."

Goyo Solano made his mouth into a pout. Dramatically he clasped his knees and lowered his greenish white head to them like an aging Pierrot.

"Friends, friends," Goyo said. "All of the old heteros want to be *friends*. But you will see. Time will bring you to me. You belong to me. Justo, my dearest. I have something of the witch in me, you know. I have never been wrong about this." And he began to recite:

> "A brilliant body that hears
> and a glorious body that speaks
> in the meadow where nothing speaks."

I stood up. "Screw you, Goyo! You rotten Donna Quixote. You are not going to seduce me with Gabriela. I know your poetic lecherous tricks."

Goyo laughed, pleased. "Sooner or later you will come into my parlor. You will see. You will see."

"Never."

I went to the window, but she was not there.

16

Like a top that blurs its individual images into a whirl of impressions, time was spinning on. The backhand slaps in the mouth from Búfalo, the ingratiating small talk of Johnie Valdez, the chronic complaints of old man Gamboa, the snide restlessness of Rubén Silva, the occasional visits in the courtyard with the Bishop still trying to smile through the pain of his ulcers, the secret cover of night . . .

The lights and the lines and the hungers spun on: Bertie Alvarez was there. Safe passage? "I am sorry, Señor Solano, of course we are working on it. But—" Goyo shaking his head in disbelief, a head now two centimeters gray at the roots.

"Hey, kiddos, look at the poet," Johnie Valdez had called out one day to break the monotony, "now if he could add a layer of red to his hair he'd look like our national flag."

Goyo pretended not to hear. The vain Goyo Solano. It was not easy to look at him. Each hour as his hair grew out he was looking older, more seedy, and, for the first time since I had known him, dilapidated, depleted, bereft of style. With his friends and admirers he had always been on stage and now it all had been taken away from him, his stage and his dressing room and his make-up kit.

Still he pursued me, from the depths of his despair and his loneliness. Sometimes he would follow me to the window when I went there to commune with Adriana. We had grown bolder as if the fantasy of her presence in my cot every night was driving us to neglect our earlier caution. It was more than eyes. Now there were imperceptible gestures, the secret language of assignation.

"Beware, my romantic friend," Goyo had said, suddenly coming up behind me one late afternoon. "If El Gordo or his Beast should catch you at this game, you will never get out of here *intact*."

He had raised his eyebrows in an arch look and had sounded his sardonic laugh, a hollow echo of his mocking laughter in happier times.

"It is only a look, an idle glance to pass the time."

"Ah, but the glance of the morning is the passion of the evening. An idle thought today is a carnival of lust tomorrow."

I was annoyed, as if he were poking his fingers into my most intimate night games.

"Goyo, I am sick and tired of your cleverness. I will thank you to *chinga* yourself with your cleverness."

"What else?" Goyo had said, sad-clown-faced under his motley hair. "I should say, *who* else? It is much nicer with a friend than by yourself. But since I seem to have no other friend here but myself, I will try to do as you so kindly suggest."

Then Goyo had walked away, to sulk on his cot with his face lowered sadly over his worn copy of Mistral. I felt guilty for treading on this already injured Pan. I wanted to like him and for him to like me. But in our cursed sanctuary was there room for like?

That night I waited, an impatient lover, and what a warm basket of delights she brought into my cot. My bird rose to the feast as she beckoned me on, moving slowly back and forth in the tradition of sensuality up and down but each time closer to her mouth to the parted lips of her mouth while her eyes gleamed in the dark like the courtesan insatiable. Then it had crawled like a tense snake all muscle in a straight line driving surely on beyond breasts up the column of her neck and finally she received it in the soft warm womb of her mouth while her tongue played Eastern music double, triple tonguing the instrument until it seemed it must overflow its thick liquid music and at that moment my luxurious duchess paused and moved herself up along my body until we were *cuerpo a cuerpo* again and then everything she had done to pleasure me was only a foretaste of the prolonged ecstasy of pleasure pleasuring . . . ah, Adriana my passion, I lay there spent and secretly satisfied deep in the dream of sleeping inside of her.

There was snoring all around me and body fumes were heavy in the dark air. A carnal yogi, I stopped up my ears and nose with the concentration of my fantasies. The bodies huddled in rows became unreal or nonexistent and the only reality was the need to do it again better deeper always with new variations of the ancient art. This time Adriana performed like an erotic contortionist arching her back and bending downward from our cot to the floor, only to rise to engulf me not to conquer me but to join me couple with me for the final crescendo.

In the frenzy of this accomplishment, I lost my last thread of caution. There in the hollow of my blanket, poled over my knee, in my tent in the inciting folds of my imagination Adriana crouched eagerly obedient to pleasure. I lay back on my pillow and moaned as my body shivered in the darkness.

"*Cariño,* what a waste of a lovely wand," Goyo said.

He had not come to me in a prescient night dream as had Adriana. He was there on his knees, leaning over my cot. I could smell the perfume on his hair and sense the unicorn outline of his head.

"Here," he whispered, "let me do it for you. No one will see us. All the apes in this monkey house are fast asleep. Lie back, Justo, I will please you."

"No Goyo. No! Go to sleep now." I pulled the cover tighter around me.

"Please, Justo, only this once. Lie back and close your eyes. I will put the blanket over my head. No one will see us."

I rose on my elbow. "No, damn you. Keep away from me."

My harsh whisper might rouse the Death-head and my other neighbors, but I had to keep his hands and his mouth from silently raping me in the dark.

"Justo, shh, we must be careful not to wake them. Now be sweet . . ."

His hand insisted under the blanket. I sat up, put my two hands on his chest and pushed him as hard as I could. He fell back against his cot toward the death-head's.

There was a snort of broken snoring and then I heard Rubén Silva sputtering, "What the devil! What is going on here? *Por Dios!*" Now he was crankily awake. "If you two want to play go in the bathroom and leave us to our sleep."

"Goyo," I said without whispering now, "get back to your own cot. I warn you, if you come near me again I will have to hurt you."

"Beast." He was climbing back into his bed. "Brutal *macho* beast. I hate you. I despise all of you. You belong in this pigsty because you are pigs, every one of you."

By now the others in the dormitory was stirring. Voices rose in irritation. "For God's sake, hombres, silencio!" "Shut up, down there!" "Save it for breakfast!" And one shrill, pseudo-feminine voice that I recognized as Johnie Valdez: "Here I am, sweetheart!" There was loud laughter and an ugly joke. I lay there feeling spent and depressed. My own solitary lust had invited Goyo's advances. I felt guilty of having entrapped him, like the notorious vice police in plainclothes who solicit young men in the parks and then arrest them for male prostitution. Now I could hear Goyo on his cot sniffling and trying to choke the sound of his weeping as one fights off an embarrassing sneeze. The vain, self-styled peacock Goyo Solano, crying to himself in the dark like a chastised schoolboy.

Next morning I rose from my cot on the side away from him, took my towel from under the pillow and made my way up the aisle to the bathroom without looking back. At the door my imitation of Paco was halfhearted. I accepted my backhand slap in the mouth, waited for El Gordo to limp out in scented, silken obesity and then realized from the ring of waiting faces that I was expected to choose a new partner for the privilege of the bathroom.

By what strange code had I come into this position of authority? Now no one questioned my ascension to the throne. Some may even have forgotten how I had come to my high rank at the head of the line. But we are creatures of habit and order, and my preeminence was part of some vital, silent arrangement.

I looked around and hesitated. I saw Johnie giving me his big orphan-columnist eyes. And old man Gamboa pleading. Even Rubén Silva forgot his political antagonism and managed to smile at me. Johnie moved forward like a spurred bantam rooster.

"Here's your new stuffed chili partner, pal."

Gamboa who had never made a single move to offend anyone stepped between Johnie and me. "No," he said. "You are a young *listo*. You must have done something to get in here. I have done nothing. I have no politics. My only bad luck is that my name is

Gamboa. They accused the wrong Gamboa. So at least I should now be favored with second place to the bathroom." He appealed to me, "Honorable President, take pity on an old man forced here for no reason."

Johnie pushed the old man's sunken chest. "I am sick of your cry-baby complaints. 'I am innocent—the wrong Gamboa—no politics.' Well, I have politics. I despise Angel as a traitor to our original Revolution. I say give the bathroom privilege to a real revolutionary, not a dried-up *cabrón* of a druggist."

"Do not call me that!"

I should have acted instantly, but I waited. Gamboa went at Johnie with the strength of a man who no longer cared. I tried to separate them. Gamboa's rage was out of control. "*Cabrón! Cabrón!* . . . Everyone calls me *cabrón!* You think I am deaf. You think I am too old. Yesterday when I was sitting in the courtyard I said to myself the next man who calls me *cabrón*, I will push my fingers into his eyes."

As he screamed he was demonstrating his threats on the startled Johnie. They clutched and swayed together and fell awkwardly to the floor. Others tried to pry them apart. I looked around helplessly. I was angry at myself for waiting too long again. Now one group held the thrashing Gamboa. Another restrained Valdez. Johnie had fallen and cut his forehead over his right eye. The indignity of the blood had carried him into a fury. "Let me go! Let me put that old *cabrón* out of misery so his whore of a wife doesn't have to cuckold him any more!"

"*Tu madre, tu madre,*" the old man was screaming. "Your mother was a whore in the dark. If the customer could see her he would throw up in her face."

It would be all screaming now. I hesitated at the doorway. El Indio stepped forward. He had been standing at the rear of the onlookers as usual, coolly observing the scene. Now he spoke.

"You and I will go together."

It was just. Maybe not outside justice but sanctuary justice. After the commotion I could favor neither Johnie nor Gamboa. El Indio chose himself at the right moment and the asilados felt the rightness of it and it became part of the unwritten law.

I was pleased. At least El Indio would spare me the byplay conversation that Paco used to enjoy. And he was not a sexual threat like poor Goyo. We avoided each other in the bathroom, he self-contained within his Black Indian world, and it became the nearest thing in sanctuary to the luxury of being alone. The black giant did not need me to be his friend. He did not need to smile at me and receive a reassuring smile in return.

For the rest of the day I was able to avoid Goyo. I did not see him at the *comida* and promenade in the yard. When I came back to the dormitory late in the afternoon I caught a glimpse of him, lying on his cot reading. He looked up for a moment but I walked away. I managed to get through the evening, undress and slip into my cot on the opposite side from Goyo without seeing him. Then I lay with my back turned to him so our eyes would not meet. I concentrated on Adriana.

I had read my share of romances in which men become obsessed with love and in the early years of my life with Marta I had wanted her with an intensity almost as strong as this that seized me now. Of course I still loved her, but I had to force myself to think of her just as I had to force myself not to dwell on Adriana. I would try all the old tricks of distracting one's mind from a single obsessive idea. I would try to lull myself to peace with favorite scenes of contentment, the pink sand and the coral rocks and the aquamarine shimmer of the sea at our lost Playa. I would close my eyes on the cot, on the toilet, on a bench in the courtyard, on the metal fire escape, or leaning against the high stucco wall with the broken glass cemented along its ridge, close my eyes and try to think *beach green water* blending out to stripes of *blue-green* and finally *deep water blue* think *beach* think *bay* think old friend *Mano the parrot* think *red hibiscus* and the powder-bluebell *jacaranda*. I could place myself on the old, lost beach but then my mind would wander to the tower where Adriana looked down at me. I saw her everywhere in time past, time present, not only with my eyes open but with them closed.

I wandered in a daze of uncontrollable desire like a man dying of thirst who tries to satisfy the need with a few drops of his own dry saliva. Once I sat under the latticed shade of the fire escape and was

on the verge of abandoning myself to the image of my lust when
Johnie happened to come around the corner. "Hey there, old pal,
howdy doody? Been looking all over for you. How about a walk
around the yard? These other *pinches* are beginning to bore me."

In payment for my guilt I had to endure the small talk, gossip
and *chistes* of Johnie Valdez two full turns around the yard. As we
were joining the rest of the group on our return trip up the fire
escape, Johnie asked in his favorite gringoese, "How gives it with
your friend of the green hair? I know there are not too many *vita-
minas* in these lousy beans and rice they hand us. But has our poet
laureate given up eating for the duration?"

I had been avoiding Goyo so studiously that I had lost track of
his movements in our enclosure. Each time we went out to *comida*
and our daily exposure to fresh air, Goyo had remained in his bed.
When we returned he was still lying in his bed. Of course I had seen
him, but my guilt, or my subconscious or even that part of me that
was attracted to him while the rest of me was repelled had blocked
him from my sight.

This time, when I came into the dormitory, I went down the aisle
and sat close on the cot next to his, facing in his direction. Now
that I came so near to him, I was glad that I had. He didn't deserve
to be abandoned. He didn't deserve to lie there forlorn, with his
hair nearly an inch gray at the roots, his ruddy pink cheeks fading,
his risqué eyebrows drooping.

"Goyo?"

He looked up in pleased surprise.

"Well, my President, I thought you had forgotten my name."

"You are not eating anything?"

His eyebrows arched and something of the old, gay, outrageous
Goyo Solano returned.

"Ah ha, so you noticed! Excellent powers of observation. No
wonder you were the first and last President of our Free Republic."

"How long have you gone without eating?"

He shrugged with the exaggerated gesture of a ham actor. "Who
knows? All I can say is— Not as long as I have gone without love."

"But Goyo—you must eat."

"Why, Justo old boy? Why must I eat?"

When he turned his head to me—the gray and faded green bangs fringing his high forehead like a striped awning left out over the winter—I thought how difficult it is for an eccentric to maintain his eccentricities in captivity. It is what must have driven the mad de Sade even madder.

"You must eat to survive this house of swine and wretches," I said. "You are our greatest poet. The world is full of bankers and generals and politicians. And the new Republic will be full of bureaucrats and self-important majors and proletarian politicians. But how many poets, how many free poets?"

"How many wild birds when the whole world becomes a cage?" Goyo asked.

"Exactly," I said. "Exactly. You must live."

"I am on a hunger strike," Goyo announced joyously.

"I know. Give it up, Goyo. If it is—because of what happened with me—that is not important—"

"Maybe not to you," Goyo said. "To me it is love—life—offered—rejected."

"But Goyo, I do love you. I want you to live."

"I will live, my warmhearted and hopelessly conventional friend," Goyo said. "I will live, yes, and I will escape this *manicomio*. Only I will do it my way. Not by starving to death—obscene!—but by threatening to starve to death—so Licenciado Alvarez will hear—and the Ambassador will hear—and the poets of Pan America will hear. And then the land will tremble with the shouting, "Freedom for Gregorio Solano!—Freedom for Gregorio Solano!—until even the ears of Angel will burn with the shame of it and the voice of Culture and Love and Liberty will be too strong for those Thermidor guerrilla ears and he will tell his Communist jailer-in-chief Juanito del Campo, 'Go. Tell Solano he may go. To any damned country he chooses. Let him write his silly verses. Give him safe passage. So that—when I am ready to guerrilla-ize all Latin America—I do not have that cursed butterfly of a poet on my revolutionary conscience.' "

Goyo was positively in love with his hunger strike. Not only was he sure it would work, but it gave him the martyr's privilege of talking about himself in the most heroic terms. A man bent on his own destruction and resurrection is entitled to fits of egomania.

17

During the night Adriana came to my cot again. But something was always interrupting us. This time it was the strange laughter of Goyo, merry in a mournful way, ripping through the silence like lightning in a midnight sky.

"Goyo? Are you all right?"

"What? Oh? Come in, old friend. Marcelo and I were just taking a bath together. That's why you see me in this samurai robe. Marcelo says I look exactly like the samurai warriors in those Japanese prints. The forty-seven Ronins. All I need is my samurai sword! Only I abhor swords. I am always afraid one is going to swing and cut off my proudest possession."

He laughed again, uncontrollably.

"Are you all right, Goyo?"

"All right?" Goyo had to check his laughing to get the words out. "I feel absolutely marvelous. I feel so light I could fly to—not to Heaven, Heaven must be frightfully dull, all those good people sitting around with wings on their shoulders, playing dreary hymns on their harps. Can you imagine what that would sound like? God must have a tin ear. No wonder he's deaf to most of the prayers of the poor trusting Christians. Where shall I fly to—to Olympus? At least the Greek gods knew how to have fun."

"*Silencio,*" the disgusted voice of the death-head Rubén Silva called out.

Goyo laughed again. "Some of us are too happy for *silencio.*" He broke into song, in Italian:

> "*Volare—*
> *oh, oh!*

Cantare
Oh o o o!"

The song was punctuated by grouchy commands—"Shut up!" "Quiet, you fairy!" "Men are trying to sleep, you buggered Yucatecan!"

Goyo laughed with malicious joy.

"Nel blu dipinto di blu
Felice di stare lassù . . ."

The catcalls increased. The entire dormitory had come to life. Goyo sounded delighted with himself.

Then a deep voice sounded, from a mouth that almost never spoke.

"Silence! Let him sing. He sings it well." It was the voice of El Indio Sandungo.

There was a moment of quiet, then a few rude refutations of El Indio's unexpected defense of the poet:

"He sings like a soprano!"

"No wonder he sings about flying. He has no balls to hold him on the ground!"

"You shut up too, you stupid black Indian."

I could recognize the speakers in the dark.

"Who calls me *estúpido?*" El Indio said in his voice of quiet thunder.

Silence.

"Who is the white-face coward who calls El Indio *estúpido?*"

Silence.

"Coward," El Indio spoke into the silence, "to hide in the dark."

Only once before, when El Indio had talked to me about land and liberty, had he spoken so many words.

The dormitory remained silent. The asylees had little or nothing to do with El Indio. As a group we were more afraid of him than we were of Búfalo de Sa. Búfalo bullied us. But El Indio challenged our very existence by ignoring us. With El Gordo it was his money and his hired muscle. With El Indio the power of his pride and his scorn for us spoke louder than Búfalo's fists.

In the silence Goyo resumed his happy song, his voice cracking expressively:

"E volavo, volavo felice più in alto
   Del sol ed ancora più su
   Mentre il mondo pian piano
   Spariva lontano laggiù
   Una musica dolce suonava soltanto per me . . ."

What a strange song, not like a song at all but a hallucinatory poem, painting your hands and your face blue and flying into the infinite sky, a human blue missile soaring soaring and listening to sweet music sounding only for you. Some mad Italian had written it but it might have been composed by Goyo Solano himself on one of his own drug-induced expeditions into inner space.

"Volare o o
   Cantare o o o o . . . ."

Goyo's voice fell to a dramatic whisper. I felt as El Indio had. I was enjoying it as a welcome release from monotony, even though it was a reflection of Goyo's hunger strike, intense melancholy turned to celebration.

I was flying myself, through a curtain of twinkling copper celestial needles, Adriana with me. She looked more beautiful than ever with the wind pleating through her loose, flowing hair and molding her silken nightgown to her ivory flesh. Silence at last. Goyo was either fantasizing or sleeping.

There was a loud fart from somewhere down the aisle.

"Please gentlemen, no more singing this evening, I have a very busy day tomorrow."

He was a clown, that Johnie. I would think that Angel Bello would grant him safe passage. Surely Johnie was no threat to any society, left, right or center.

A sweet stench hung over the room like a barnyard sunset.

I heard chuckling and "Ay, *chihuahua,* it is so funny . . ." the voice of Goyo laughing in his sleep. I went on flying with Adriana through my own copper-shining sky.

In the morning Goyo was lying on his back, with his eyes half closed, smiling.

"So, Goyo, how do you feel this morning?"

"Lovely. Like a feather in the sky. Starvation is good for the soul."

"You must eat something today. We cannot afford to lose you."

"Of course the world cannot afford to lose Gregorio Solano. Which is exactly why I am on this hunger strike."

"But what if—nothing happens? How long do you think you can hold out?"

"Indefinitely," Goyo answered with his crackling bitter laugh. "How long did Gandhi hold out? Sixty days?"

"You will not survive thirty days."

"My dear friend, do not look so worried. Just bring me a little water. I will make that concession. Not eating can be rather pleasant, but thirst is another matter. The lips become dry. The tongue swells. The throat begins to feel like a dried-up *culo*. If I must suffer for my freedom, I will do it in comfort. I am what you might call a hedonistic martyr."

I brought him some water from the breakfast table. "Ah, like cool wine," he said. "I can feel it going to my head."

"Goyo, a piece of *bolillo* to dip in the wine?"

"Please, do not tempt me. You are too big in the chest and too overweight to play a convincing serpent. I feel as pure as Adam and Eve before the apple. I shall spend the morning composing a poem to describe my sensation."

He was pleased at the look of concern on my face.

"If you want to help me you will make it very clear to Licenciado Alvarez that not another morsel of food will pass my lips until I receive written assurance of my safe passage. I believe in my destiny. I have read my fortune in the stars. It is not the destiny of Gregorio Solano to die on a narrow cot in a stale-smelling dormitory in the attic of the embassy of a third-rate banana republic."

Half an hour later Alvarez came down the aisle with his folders under his arm like an old rural medicine merchant selling much and caring little.

The wrong Gamboa got his licks in. I admired his stamina. He was too stupid to surrender. The Jews of concentration camp Germany surrendered because their minds told them they had no choice against hob-nail boots and gas chambers: to take a single flour-faced Aryan racist with them made no sense. So the intelligent sheep forsake the opportunity to drag a Nazi underling with them into the faceless void of genocide. But old man Gamboa still had the humanity to scream, "I tell you—why will you not listen—you have the wrong Gamboa!"

Licenciado Alvarez, the admirable bureaucrat, knew his business. He shrugged. He nodded. He pretended to listen. He pretended to smile. "Sí—sí. I will look into it. Next week perhaps I will have some good news for you. *Próximamente usted podrá salir.*"

Over the shoulders of his solicitors I caught his busy, practiced eyes.

"Sí, Señor Presidente," he called. "Your wife is in good hands, but for you, as yet there is little news—"

"Not me," I called. "Solano. A very serious problem." And then I raised my voice. "Hunger strike!"

The words could not have struck our chargé d'affaires more sharply if I had flung them in the form of stones. He stopped his shuffling of manila folders and elbowed his way out of the group pressing around him.

"Señor Moreno Suárez, are you threatening me, are you threatening to go on a *hunger strike*?"

"Not me. Gregorio Solano."

The Licenciado took a tighter grip on his portable files as if to strengthen himself for the ordeal. Then he looked in the direction of Goyo's cot. Goyo was giving a perfect imitation of a martyr, lying back weakly with his eyes half shut! Gandhi in the days when his frail self-deprived figure was tormenting the British Empire.

Alvarez hovered over the cot. Goyo looked up at him with his funny eyes that were always partly closed because they were so slanted and the overlid so fleshy, so that his face had the look of a fawn and yet something of the look of a frog.

"Buenas noches, Your Excellency the Ambassador."

Goyo spoke in a dry, pathetic voice. I could sense him smiling behind his mask of hunger and duplicity.

"It is noon, not nighttime, and I am Licenciado Alvarez, not the Ambassador. Now what is this about a hunger strike?"

Goyo nodded solemnly. These were his first enjoyable moments since he had been forced into sanctuary. "I throw myself on the conscience of my fellow-poets and all my Latin comrades of the mind and heart."

Alvarez made a face. "Señor Solano, I assure you, you are in-
flicting suffering on yourself for nothing. We handle each case
impartially and efficiently. First we register you as a qualified political asylee. Then we press the Bello government for your safe
passage. Hunger strikes have no effect, either on us or on Bello's
ministers. Surely you realize that?"

"I want this crisis broadcast to the outside world," Goyo said.
"The whole lot of us could rot in here and the world will have forgotten we ever existed. I am doing this not only for myself but for
all the rebel spirits being persecuted in this"—he stared up at the
faded ceiling—"putrid blue limbo."

Alvarez pressed his lips together. "Señor Solano, I urge you to get
out of that bed and come down for your meals. Let me assure you
again, your case will be processed just as rapidly whether or not
you choose to inflict this ordeal on yourself . . ."

"Ordeal?" Goyo laughed. "For you it may be an ordeal. For me
it is a celestial fiesta. I feel lighter than the angels. I float on golden
butterfly wings. Tell me, my good Licenciado, are those my own
lines or do I borrow them from Gabriela?"

Alvarez glared at his armful of manila folders. "For me it is not
an ordeal, it is an—"

"Inconvenience! For you, all of us thrown into those folders
under your arms are inconveniences. Well, Gregorio Solano is much
too big an ego to be satisfied being anyone's inconvenience, particu-
larly a petit-bourgeois bureaucrat who is anti-simpático to poetry.
So, Gregorio Solano chooses to become your ordeal. Do I make myself clear, Licenciado?"

Alvarez glanced at me, as if to enlist me in his cause. But I did
not return the look.

"Señor Solano, it is my explanation that is clear and that you
refuse to understand."

"Your explanation," Goyo was enjoying himself immensely, "is
a direct quote from the handbook of every chargé d'affaires too
lazy to do his own thinking. I will speak directly to the Ambassador."

"The Ambassador has returned home for the christening of his
granddaughter."

"Lord, these petty domestic interruptions," Goyo said. "Then send him a cable. Tell him this is more important. The impending death of a poet laureate."

"Please," Alvarez insisted. "Hunger strikes interfere with my work. And if that is interfered with it means less cases can be processed."

"Cases?" Goyo said. "These are people—not cases. And they should be freed—not processed."

"Exactly," Alvarez said. "Simply a question of semantics. We mean the same thing."

"But we do not feel the same thing."

"Maybe yes, maybe no," Alvarez said as he straightened up, gripping his folders. "Now if you will let me get on with my work."

"Of course I will let you get on with your work," Goyo said. *"Próximamente ustedes podrán salir.* Just be sure and send the cable. I want it in the papers. Broadcast on the radio. One of the great voices of our age will die if he is not saved by the conscience of the Pan American world. Cross out Pan American. By the entire civilized world."

"I will make a thorough report on your case," Licenciado Alvarez said. "And I will look in on you again tomorrow."

He turned away, ready to face with his professional smile the *when? when? when*'s that pressed him for definitive answers that did not exist.

"Goyo, maybe this time Alvarez is right," I said. "At least let him send you a cup of hot soup. After all, you are taking a little water. The soup will be no more than hot water colored pale green."

"No thank you, I am very content. I am flying like a rabbit with wings of a flamingo."

"You must live, Goyo. Not only for yourself. If we lose you we lose our only candidate for the Nobel Prize."

"If they would give me a beautiful virgin fifteen-year-old Swedish boy, I might be interested," Goyo said with that laughing self-mockery. "But have no fears, love, I intend to live. I do not fast to die but to live. I can hardly wait for the clamor on the short-wave radio when they hear of this challenge Gregorio Solano throws in the face of the Bello regime. No, I want none of your green pea soup. I will live longer without it. Oh Justo, I am feeling so glorious. As if I am on the road to something mysterious and marvelous. You know, dear one, my whole life has been devoted to the principle of trying everything. I adore marijuana. I have chewed the peyote buttons and smoked opium. So why should I not try fasting? The feeling is not so different from taking the magic mushrooms. Did I ever tell you about that? It was an isolated village high in the mountains of the Mocaños."

Goyo closed his eyes.

"It was like climbing to the rooftop of the world, Justo, misty, and wild orchids growing everywhere. When I came into the long thatched hut to meet the *bruja* who was to conduct the ceremony, it was dark. There were mattresses on the floor and against the adobe wall. One candle was burning. The *bruja* looked sixty or seventy years old. A brown face with a thousand wrinkles. With her was a ragged little boy, her grandchild. The God of the Mountain is fond of children. This one was the most beautiful I had ever seen. This one was Marcelo."

Now Goyo seemed unaware of my presence. His eyes, half closed, no longer stared at the faded blue ceiling but at his magic mountain where he was ready to raise to his lips the sacred mushroom. Time past and time present had become twin tributaries flowing into the Oriental river of timelessness running neither forward nor backward but inward into the *tierra incógnita* that can only be discovered by the inner, inner eye.

"I felt like an empty receptacle waiting for the *bruja* to fill me with the spirit of the sacred mushroom. She passed them through the smoke of the *copal* on the brazier in front of her and chanted prayers in her native language. Then she spread six pair in front of me, the traditional portion, and told me to eat them very slowly, every bit, including the stems. The fresh-looking *hongos* were tasty and slightly sweet but the smaller, dried ones were bitter. When I had finished, she blew out the brown beeswax candle. Silence. Oh, Justo dear, I will never forget that sweet silence. Soon I heard whispering and then a faint humming, and then a distant chanting as though it were coming from a cave in the mountain. The *bruja* was calling on her God to speak to her through the power of the divine mushroom. She would sway back and forth, break off her chanting, mutter a Mocaño prayer, clap her hands in rhythm and go on chanting again.

"At first a cold, numb feeling set in at the back of my neck. Then I no longer could feel my fingers. My feet were coming off. I know it sounds frightening, but I was screaming with laughter. Everything was funny . . . and then my dear Justo, everything was beautiful. First it was geometric patterns. Then they were filled in with color. Then I saw architecture. Classic architecture. It was like seeing Athens, ancient Rome, a classic Mayan city. And then I saw fireworks in the sky—but what fireworks—like brilliant abstractions by Miró—only not on any canvas—just shimmering in the air, beautiful little curlicues and shining bronze question marks. I was floating in the air over the city. I felt like a huge colorful balloon-of-a-head with lots of tentacles, floating in the air. So did Marcelo. We were floating through the air like sanctified balloons—no, not through the air, through the firmament, the heavens, through golden clouds and glittering bronze needles in the form of question marks, and it was such joy, so funny that our throats were almost bursting with laughter. There was no floor. We were weightless like the astronauts. I said to Marcelo, 'Here, we must tie our shoelaces together, so we do not lose each other in the sky.' But we were rolling around so much that we could not find our laces. And then we remembered that we had no legs, no feet—so how could we have shoes! Oh Justo, how we roared with laughter. 'We will tie our tentacles together,' we said. We were like two Portuguese-men-of-war with those blue-veined tentacles trailing from the jellyfish body in all directions."

Goyo laughed. It was a sound from the mouth of the cave where the God of the *bruja* lived.

"Oh Lord, it is so funny!" His voice sounded far away now. No longer here in this dormitory talking to me, he was back in the thatched hut in the mountaintop world of the Mocaños. "We can't tie our tentacles together. Maybe our testicles but not our tentacles!" The echo of his laughter laughed and laughed. He rolled until it seemed he would slip off the side of the cot. Firmly I pushed him back. He grabbed for my hand.

"Give me your tentacle! How can I tie us together if you won't give me your tentacle?"

I let him hold on to my hand.

As if from a hollow sound box, the voice went on. "Our tentacles are shoelaces. So if we tie our shoelaces together we cannot be separated. Unless we take off our shoes!" Again laughter possessed him. "We tumble in space tied together like astronauts. The *bruja* has married us with a shoelace. Oh look, look, she is calling to us. From a golden throne. Just behind the archway. A thousand steps leading up through the stars. She is reaching out to us, beckoning to us. She is waiting for us beyond the arch."

Goyo squeezed my hand, squeezing and releasing feverishly. "Come, Marcelo my love, our priestess summons us. Come, come! Are you coming?"

"Here I am, Goyo," I said.

He drew his hand away. "I know that voice. A throat full of lead. Reality. Heavy chains of reality. You cannot fool the Experience. You cannot cheat the Experience! Let go of me. I will go alone, all the way to the top. I snip the ball and chain of reality as if it were a shoelace. I fly! *Volare . . . o o o o . . .* Oh God, it is so beautiful. I have no feet but I float upward along the stairway." He stretched his arm forward. He sang croakingly in English, "Take my hand, I'm a stranger in Paradise." The laughter rose out of his stomach. "Every time Marcelo laughs I laugh. Only I can hear him laughing before he begins to laugh and that makes me laugh and we roll on the floor in the sky laughing together."

He opened his eyes and looked at me, anxiously. "Where am I?" He dropped his hand on my arm. "Justo, where am I?"

"Safe in sanctuary," I said. "In the dormitory."

"Please, leaden-voice, ball-and-chain," he said with that peevish arrogance I had heard him use on overly inquisitive visitors when he was Queen-Bee of the artistic hive of our city. "I am not asking where my body is. I mean the mind free of appendages like bodies weighing it down."

"At the top of the stairway. The arch. The *bruja*. The golden throne."

He drew his arm back, slipped it under the blanket and then

squirmed deeper into his bed like a challenged caterpillar retreating into its cocoon.

"I feel cold. I am afraid I am going to fall from the top of the staircase. My legs and arms are back again. I am afraid to go through the archway. If I do, all the way to the throne, I will never come down again. I feel cold—afraid . . ."

I put my arm around Goyo to support him. Reading an outdated issue of *La Verdad* in the next cot, Rubén Silva twisted his death-head in our direction and cleared his throat in a froglike grunt of disgust. "Screw you socialist fairies."

I ignored him. I was going to lose my *macho* reputation through my attentions to Goyo. Well, screw *you*, you Zamora-loving opportunist.

"Goyo, Goyo," I spoke firmly with my face close to his. "You are right here, safe in bed, see, feel, you are not falling anywhere."

He fluttered his eyes and rolled his head from side to side along my arm. "Yes, yes, I know where I am. I was afraid to go through the archway. You see, between that final step at the top of the stairway and her throne there was a space—too wide to leap. Unless I could catch the hand of the *bruja* like the high flyers in the circus."

He pressed his head back against my arm. "Ah, you have a good, strong arm, Justo." He gave a little moan of wearied pleasure. The Death-head glanced up from his paper in disgust again. Goyo seemed oblivious to everything except the *bruja* and me—or was I Marcelo?

"But at least from the top of that stairway I had the most fantastic view. I was staring into the heaven above, no *beyond* our conventional image of heaven. It was as if—as if the universe had split—and instead of just vast sky with stars and planets and moons —the sky we are accustomed to think of as beautiful, I suddenly was able to sail through it. Not me a body, but my eyes, my spirit, the me stripped of Me— Oh Justo my dearest, even if I am the greatest poet in a land of poets I can never tell you. There were stars of a thousand delicate colors, only they were not stars but musical notes and they were dancing and I could *hear* them. Oh, but so much more beautiful than words. Because much more than the sight and the sound was the feeling, Justo, no—realization. I was free of myself and free of time and I could look all around me and gaze in all directions. Only they were not directions exactly but great streaming eras of time. I could look into the past, back into thousands of years, eons, and into the present and the musical notes streaming around me in brilliant colors were truths I could see like bright lights on a cold night. And the future—there it was, like a gleaming shore and I was in harmony with it, with all of it and flowing with it. Justo, it was so strange, so beautiful, so perfect. I could see myself standing on that top step. But another part of me *was* the musical notes that were dancing and singing and shining and changing patterns like a kaleidoscope. Oh Justo—you have never tried this magic mushroom?"

"No—"

"You miss so much in life. People are only pretending to be alive if they do not taste everything."

"You sound more like your own self. You must be feeling better."

"I feel more like my conscious self. Which is not necessarily better."

"Let me ask Momentito to bring you a piece of bread. One little piece of bread will not compromise you."

"Thank you, Justo *cariño*. But I do not want a little piece of anything from Momentito." He giggled wanly.

"Goyo, you are hopeless."

"To the end of time I will be whirling on the second floor of the Devil's department store." Goyo laughed. "You think I am bestial? Merely honest."

It startled me. There was self-righteousness in my attitude toward Goyo Solano. And yet was I not on my way to the *eighth* level, reserved for hypocrites whose robes are brightly decorated on the outside but lined with the heavy lead of dissembling on the inside?

"Goyo, I admire you, I want to save you. One piece of bread will hardly compromise your hunger."

"Your arm around me is food enough," Goyo said. *"Volare—oh —o . . ."* He laughed; hollow, satanic, cosmic laughter. "Everything is so funny. With our giant egos, we are such little specks in the universe. Even the great Gregorio Solano is only a tiny speck in the universal kaleidoscope."

Goyo's half-closed eyes fell shut and he sighed contentedly. "We must try it together, Justo dear. You will see the colors. You will fly along on colors like a magic carpet! And from the top of the golden stairway you may even catch a glimpse of the golden beauty of the cosmos."

He stretched out his arms as if he were executing a free-falling dive from a plane. He raised and lowered his arms gracefully as the wings of a bird controls its glide. "*Volare* . . ." He was drifting off. His arms slowly sank to his sides. I felt his forehead. Warm but not feverish. The bangs looked grotesque now, the two faded colors damp and clinging to his skin. His hand with its long, tapering fingers was turned palm up and I held his wrist. I did not know how to count a pulse, but it reassured me to feel it beating.

18

When I awakened next morning my first thought was to look after Goyo. Selfishly—one of the frightening aspects of sanctuary, it did not tend to make us more compassionate but more self-centered—it was a momentary tonic to have something outside myself to think about, outside myself and Adriana. For Adriana and I were constantly together now, not only mated each evening in the privacy of my cot but in the privacy of my secret thoughts by day.

"Goyo. Buenos días, compañero. *Cómo te va?*"

The skin-tone of his face had lost an element of liveliness. And his gray-green hair was matted. He had not sat up to use his comb and brush from the meager supply of toilet articles in the cigar box. But his spirit was still flying.

"All night the most wonderful dreams. I am dozing in a little blue chapel. Even the angels are painted blue. There is candlelight on the altar. When the candles burn down a little altar boy comes in to replace them. In one hand he carries a lighted taper for the candles and in the other a fat iguana hanging from a string. In the voice of an angel he asks me if I am hungry. His mother will roast the iguana for me. I tell him, 'No, I am on a hunger strike.' He dangles the iguana in front of my face to tempt me. Then he laughs and disappears. Ding dong ding dong dong the chimes are soft and far away."

"Goyo," I said, "our breakfast here is the next best thing to a hunger strike. Please let me bring you some. Think of it this way: who else in this tunnel has the creative power to describe the experience? To write the epic poem on diplomatic asylum?"

"It was five o'clock in the afternoon," Goyo intoned in his nasal, mocking voice. "It was five o'clock by all the farts. The valet of El Gordo massaged his balls. At five o'clock in the afternoon . . ."

He lay his head back against the pillow and laughed, not the cosmic laughter of the mushroom journey but the brittle, bitchy laugh that was so familiar. "Oh yes, I must write the great, epic poem of this monastic urinal." He laughed again and began to choke.

"I'll bring you some water."

"Yes, love, my lips are a little dry. But mind you—nothing more. I shall eat my first epicurean meal only when I am safely deposited in Mexico City."

I caught up to El Gordo being helped along by Búfalo and Jesusito. He was limping badly, unable to place any weight on his left foot despite the pills which he seemed to have in endless supply.

Búfalo looked around in dumb surprise. We lived strictly according to the rules in sanctuary, rules we had come to acknowledge as a means of living together in an uneasy but functional *pax sanctuaris*. The occasional fistfight that broke out in the dormitory or in the courtyard was much the same as the breakdown of law and order on the outside: one of us suddenly cracking and refusing to abide by the rules. So it seemed to Búfalo that I was doing now. It was my privilege to disturb General Romano only after he had enjoyed his toilet for twenty minutes of privacy.

"What are you doing, *hijo*?"

"I need to slip in ahead of you to get water for Solano."

"—your mother! Screw Solano."

This was the first time we had ever talked together at the bathroom door. A breach of protocol. Now our arrangement was shattered even more unexpectedly. El Gordo spoke up, his voice surprisingly high-pitched for a man of his bullfrog belly and heavy jowls, and what he said was even more surprising.

"Búfalo, let him go ahead if he wants to. After all, no sense in letting the poet die for one little glass of water."

"*Muy amable,*" I said. "Gregorio Solano thanks you."

"At his service," replied El Gordo, and stood aside on his painful, gouty leg to let me pass.

"While you're at it, you might as well take a piss for yourself," he added. "And then give me thirty minutes. I need extra time to get ready this morning."

The sly bastard. So that was why he could afford to be so magnanimous. It was the Day of Matrimony. The color of envy is not the green of the forest and the sugarcane that inspired our Green Revolution. It is the bitter green spot you find when you clean out the intestines of a fish. The green spot of bile.

Goyo. My mission was Goyo, to save Goyo Solano from his own romanticism. I filled two paper cups with water and brushed past my benefactors without saying a word. Pushed deep into a hole of silence was my envy of El Gordo's going to Adriana on what should have been my matrimonial day.

At Goyo's bedside, I found that Alvarez had preceded me. With him was Momentito, holding a breakfast tray. It was the kind of feast the diplomatic staff were enjoying every morning and that we asylees no longer dared to dream about: orange juice, papaya with limes, soft scrambled eggs, fresh *bolillos*, fragrant brown honey and a pot of what smelled like genuine coffee.

"Señor Solano," Alvarez was saying. "Please. I insist. You must eat. Look at this delicious breakfast I have brought for you."

Goyo shrugged. "I haven't the slightest interest in breaking my fast. I feel very content. Give your delicious breakfast to one of the poor wretches you are slowly starving to death."

Alvarez ran his tongue nervously over his lips and shook his head in self-pity. Why must these inconveniences always occur when the Ambassador was away?

"Your Excellency," the flustered chargé d'affaires appealed to me, "you are his good friend. Perhaps you can persuade him—if he will give up this—this futile gesture of—defiance, I can assure him that—"

"Tell me, Alvarez."

I spoke sharply, my voice an echo of my dimly remembered role as civilian judge of the High Court under Zamora, and of my early days as Provisional President of the revolutionary Republic when I spoke with confidence if not with authority. "What have you done—specifically—about Señor Solano's protest? Have you cabled or telephoned the Ambassador? Have you released any news of the hunger strike to the outside press? Have you forwarded Solano's petition to the Organization of American States? Or to the Association of Pan American Writers? After all, these were Señor Solano's specific requests. He enjoys a distinguished reputation all through Latin America. He is right to believe his hunger strike would attract sympathetic attention from Washington to Tierra del Fuego. He is not a prisoner here, he is a diplomatic guest of your government. If it is your personal decision to bury his petition you are denying him his individual right to protest his condition."

"Bravo! Bravo!" Goyo Solano said.

Alvarez pressed his lips together and looked crossly at Momentito, waiting resignedly in his white serving jacket. "Set it down there," he said pointing to my cot within arm's length of Solano's. "In case he changes his mind." Then Alvarez tried to cope with me, in the patient voice of the parent lecturing an unruly child.

"Señor Moreno, I am well aware of my obligations. I have included a full report of this situation in my memorandum to the Ambassador. After all it is not up to me—the policy decisions, the releases to the press."

"You never really answer a direct question, do you, Licenciado Alvarez?"

"I will answer you this, Señor," Alvarez said. "I have no idea how our Ambassador will handle this problem. But it would not surprise me if he chooses not to air it in public. He sees a good deal of the First Colonel, as you know. It is the duty of our Ambassador to remain on friendly terms with Colonel Bello. That is how he is able to maintain such a good working relationship with the regime.

My Ambasador knows his man well. Angel Bello can be as stubborn as an Indian. If you challenge him or threaten through some overt act, as Señor Solano does with his hunger strike, it could have precisely the opposite effect."

"But you can't tell me Angel doesn't care about the artists and the intellectuals. After all, two-thirds of them are already sympathetic toward him. They admire him for being our only leader who year after year has the *huevos* to pull Uncle Sam's beard."

Alvarez smiled guardedly and remained silent.

"I think you know my Angel as well as your brilliant Ambassador," I said. "Angel needs those intellectuals. He wants to make allies of them all over Latin America. That's why he stages these cultural conferences, why he courts Sartre and Simone de Beauvoir and is so anxious to convince them that he is their existentialist man. Hear me Alvarez, if Solano—" I hesitated to say it in front of Goyo—"if he dies here it becomes a front-page story."

Alvarez sighed. "All I can tell you is—we will do everything possible. But I would urge the Señor again to abandon this extreme measure."

"I don't agree. This whole miserable story deserves to be told. Sanctuary is supposed to be a temporary haven. You are breaking Pan American law to keep us herded in here like this. You too are guilty, Alvarez."

"How am I guilty? One insignificant official? Only the government of the country from which you defected can issue the order to pass you or your poet through. What more can we do than to keep you alive, and to hope—?"

"*Hope.* You can protest to Angel's government. He values your country's recognition. As a spokesman for the embassy, you could have considerable influence. But you never seem to use it."

"Your Excellency," Alvarez insisted, "I am just a functionary here. When the Ambassador returns, I suggest you discuss these matters with him." And then, with a disapproving glance at Goyo he could not resist adding, "You even have my permission to starve to death—as long as you do me the favor of postponing your superheroics until the Ambassador is back at his post."

He bowed stiffly, with that meaningless, "At your service, gentlemen," and turned away from us, moving swiftly down the aisle to avoid "the wrong Gamboa" and the rest of his tormentors.

Goyo shook his head slowly. "Nothing. He has done nothing. I saw headlines, 'Gregorio Solano On Hunger Strike!' I saw picket lines around Angel's embassies, university students in Mexico City —Rio—La Paz—walking out of their classrooms, reading my poems at the flagpole. I saw Angel himself hurrying here to the embassy to confer with the Ambassador before everything got out of hand. I saw myself being whisked to the plane—a hero to intellectual freedom." Goyo rubbed at his forehead, at the frayed green fringe. "Oh God, Justo, I am so depressed. I worry so much about my poor Marcelo. By this time I am sure those disgusting policemen have raped him nine different ways. Pigs! If we could only do away with the police, nine-tenths of our crimes would be eliminated. Justo, I am so-oo depressed. I feel so weak. I feel I am drifting away. That *pendejo* of a bureaucrat does not care if I die. All I am is a little inconvenience in his report. Maybe he will not get his promotion because Gregorio Solano refuses to accept his bribe of a breakfast. What a bloodless cockroach is *homo sapiens bureaucratis*." He closed his eyes and seemed to be slipping softly into sleep.

I shook him gently by the elbow. "Goyo, if the hunger strike is not going to work, if Alvarez refuses to publicize it, then what is the use—you might as well give in—eat, live."

Goyo answered me without opening his eyes. "Never fear, Justo dear, I am feeling fine. I am not ready to try my wings on yet. I'll just doze for a little while. Let me intimidate Alvarez a day or so longer. They say even a stone finally begins to bleed if you squeeze your hand around it long enough."

"It will be your blood on that stone."

"Go," Goyo ordered. "I prefer to be alone right now. Leave me to my visions. Go, Justo, play your silly window game with the Dulcinella of asylum. Weep no more for Goyo. I give you my solemn word not to die before you return."

He sank into his pillow and pulled the worn blanket up to his chin. Color was draining from his face and his hair looked like city snow covered by a thin, cracking layer of green paint.

"Goyo, hold on. If I have to strangle Alvarez I am going to get a cable through to the Ambassador."

If Goyo heard me he gave no sign. There was a faint smile on his lips and then he was moving them slowly as if in a silent prayer.

I drummed on the bathroom door and shouted for El Gordo to appear, always putting more feeling into it on the Day of Matrimony. This time the sting was sharp and I could taste the blood. I felt an urge to retaliate, but the unwritten law forewarned me that this would only lead to a stronger blow from Búfalo, which I would have to avenge. There would be an unequal but vicious fight. El Indio would try to separate us. Others would crowd in. Minutes later it would be a free-for-all. It had happened before.

So I stepped back, ready to drown my frustration in rum as Paco had done. El Gordo appeared wearing a heavy gold chain from which hung a cluster of religious medals, a fine cotton shirt elegantly embroidered in white silken thread, freshly pressed white sharkskin slacks and one white suede shoe. That was encouraging. The gout was spreading. And gout is not merely limited to the foot. It spreads up the leg, the knee, the thigh. It was heartening to think that all the gold in his money belt could not cure it.

Just the same, with the assistance of his retainers, El Gordo was able to depart for his rendezvous. Restless all morning, I could not drift to the dormer because that perfumed monster was in there with her. During the afternoon meal I felt no hunger pangs. I seemed as indifferent to food—if you could call our asylum pap food—as did enfeebled Goyo. I walked around the courtyard in a kind of daze. An *hour* they said. And that white-silken swine still had not returned. El Gordo and his special privileges. A fog had settled over us. There was a mist like fine rain. Soon it would be the rainy season again. Not only had I lost track of hours, weeks, months, but finally of seasons. I was groping through a long tunnel, one of those interminable transportation tubes running under a wide river, with the lights turned off. The only light, the only face at the far end was Adriana's.

"Hey, how you doing, keed? Haven't talked to you in a coupla days."

I mumbled something about having been preoccupied with Goyo.

"Never knew him very well," Johnie said. "He was always too snobbish to invite me to those parties. Or maybe he thought a real man would feel out of place, eh?" He gave a short, self-righteous laugh. "But I sure hope he doesn't croak. I tell you, that First Colonel has about as much respect for Human Rights as a pig for a fingerbowl. Hey, if there's anything I can do to help you with Goyo . . ."

"Thank you thank you—" I tried to turn away as a *manso* bull turns from the point of the picador. But Johnie had a way of drifting along with you shoulder to shoulder. No wonder he had proved such an effective gossip columnist.

"By the by, have you heard from the little woman?"

I frowned at him and shook my head. This was a familiar Latin game, practiced by the regulars at the popular drinking hangouts where frozen daiquiris and spicy gossip are swilled happily together. It is called "placing banderillas." Under the guise of solicitude they sink their pointed barbs through your skin and into your tender flesh. A husband who is being cuckolded, practically in public, will be asked with elaborate concern if his charming wife is enjoying her visit to some swank sea resort known for the seductive attractions of its lean, bronze beach boys.

Johnie's riposte was a similar barb in the opposite flank. In fact he was so bold as to glance mischievously toward that beckoning dormer window as he asked his innocent question.

"Well, I suppose that is one cure for the gout," Johnie nodded toward the window. "Nothing like the rub of that sweet little brush to help you forget your pains."

Johnie's eyes scanned the enclosure. The homely little maid Reencarnación was carrying a bowl emptied of *arroz con frijoles* back to the pantry steps. "I am making myself so horny I may have to take a bite out of that bony little peach." He gave me an exaggerated wink. "Well, don't stand too long. You might catch cold. My respects to the *esposita* when you write her. The Day of Matrimony is a tough bone for us *solitos,* eh Justo? See you later, alligator."

I did not bother to watch Johnie Valdez bantam-cock his way through the barnyard. I lingered beneath the window a few moments and then went forward to intercept Momentito who was carrying away the last of the clay serving bowls. "Would you ask Licenciado Alvarez to come to the dormitory as soon as possible? Tell him it is an emergency."

"Licenciado Alvarez is at the Foreign Office, Señor. I would not expect him back before six or seven in the evening."

"Please tell him I am waiting for him."

"Very well, Señor."

Momentito had that perfect balance of servility and pride of the old servant class for which changing political systems held no meaning. In lieu of "politics" he had Tradition and Manners. I felt he respected me, not because I had risen to prominence as a professional ally of Angel Bello, but because, out of my past experience I treated him with that combination of authority and kindness that he had been accustomed to and now often found wanting in his thankless job as valet and majordomo to a hundred disgruntled asylees.

When I returned to the dormitory, most of the inmates were still down in the yard. But El Gordo was back in his double cot. He must have come in while we were eating. He was sleeping peacefully. I fought back an adolescent temptation to go over and kick him in his bad foot.

El Indio was lying in his cot, which was neither long enough nor wide enough to contain him. He missed fresh air and was usually the last man up the fire escape at the end of the afternoon promenade.

"Indio, are you all right?"

He nodded.

"There is nothing wrong?"

He shook his head.

"I am surprised to see you here when you could still be outside."

"I think," he said.

Goyo was awake when I came to his cot. His eyes were open. But they had lost their darting vivacity. The tray was still on my cot but the dishes were empty. The eggs were a yellow smear on the plate, there were crumbs left of the bacon and the *bolillos*, and the bowl of brown honey had been licked clean.

"Goyo?"

"Mmm?"

"Have you eaten this?"

"No. The hungry crows came. I could see them perched on the edge of my cot."

"Can I bring you anything?"

After a moment Goyo said, "Yes." Then he began to close his eyes again. I sat on the edge of his cot and patted his arm.

"Goyo?"

"You can bring me a mirror. I have no idea what I look like any more. Like a carnival witch, I suppose."

I went down the aisle in search of a mirror. A few of the asilados had small ones fastened to the wall above their cots. One of them was our most recent arrival, Hector Loyaza, the Communist wheel-horse who had played parliamentary parlor games with Zamora until the eve of the Angelista victory when the Central Committee had swung over in a burst of Marxian rhetoric. His Party and Angel's Little Green Angels had merged in a shotgun marriage and Hector had been riding high for a while as Director of Agricultural Reform. But he was an old Stalinoid hand who packed the land-reform jobs with party hacks and even relatives. The original guerrilla fighters were short on ideology. But they fought back, and Angel—cleverly positioned between his original comrades-in-arms and the Moscow doctrinaires—suddenly turned on Hector and denounced him as "sectarian," "dogmatic," "guilty of left-wing infantilism" and finally of that most extreme of mortal sins, "counter-revolutionary oppor-tunism." Hector Loyaza was ugly but extremely dapper. He was undoubtedly guilty of all the political crimes Angel had abused him for, but it is also probable that Angel resented Hector's well-tailored suits, his bourgeois haircut and his careful grooming. Hector Loyaza resembled less a revolutionary than a middle-class Communist mayor of a prosperous Italian city like Florence or Milan. And for that reason he had a mirror on his wall. Not a picture of Lenin, or of the current Kremlinistas or of Ho Chi Minh but a mirror in which he could part his thinning hair and study the ends of his narrow mous-tache.

He and I had not talked in several years: I despised the strait-jacket Left as much as I did the oligarchy of the Zamoras and Ro-manos. He had sent hundreds of innocent revolutionaries to jail—or worse—for opposing the iron broom with which he tried to sweep the Agriculture Department free of non-Communists. But Goyo was asking for a mirror.

"Please," I said, "Gregorio Solano is asking this favor. To borrow your mirror for a few moments."

"Of course, of course," Loyaza said, immediately obliging, jiggling the mirror loose from the wall. The glass was a small one, about the size of one's hand and a diagonal crack ran from one corner to the other. He handed it to me with a slight, non-Communist bow. "At your service. My good wishes to Señor Solano. Politically he is what we would call 'irresponsible.' But I happen to admire his poetry very much."

I thanked Loyaza and hurried back to Goyo, thinking, it takes the whisper of death to unite extremes of Right and Left. Touched by the frail fate of Goyo Solano, the fleshy cheeks of El Gordo and the lined cheeks of simian-faced Hector Loyaza reflected a faint glow of human emotion.

Goyo was sitting up in bed when I returned, his knees drawn up in front of him. "I am afraid to see myself," he said. He reached for the mirror.

He held it in front of him and stared at his image in the cracked glass for at least ten seconds. "Oh my God," he said finally, "my poor face. And my hair. It would frighten the scarecrows. I had forgotten how gray it was. Oh Justo"—he handed me the mirror—"take it away. I used to adore looking at myself. My face always fascinated me. And my hair—always bright orange or gold like the sun or grasshopper green. And now gray—gray—what a sad porridge of a poet I have become."

Goyo was so upset by the ghost in the mirror that it seemed to revive him. It had the effect of a handler's blowing on the beak of a bantam sorely wounded in the cock pit. He became more animated, more talkative in his desperation.

"Goyo, maybe you would prefer to cut off the green. At least it would all be uniform."

Goyo covered his hair with his hands as if to protect it. Then he nodded reluctantly. "Maybe so . . . You do it for me, Justo dear."

Again I went down the aisle, this time to Jesusito's place beside El Gordo's double cot. El Gordo dozed peacefully. I kept my mind

fastened to Goyo Solano. Jesusito was sitting on the edge of the cot
darning one of El Gordo's socks. I had seen him use a pair of scissors
to cut El Gordo's hair and trim his toenails. The shy shadow of his
master reached into his sewing basket and offered me the scissors
with alacrity.

I took Goyo's towel, draped it around his shoulders and slowly
clipped away at the green fringe that had been for such a long time
his trademark. When I had finished, the effect was even more dramatic than I had anticipated. Shorn of his green covering, Goyo
became a gray-haired old man. Snow had fallen. This year would
never see green again. The strange Lorca poem flashed in my mind—
"Green how much I love you *green . . . green* flesh, *green* hair . . .
green boughs, *green* wind . . . *green* how much I love you *green . . ."*

"Goyo?"

He shook his head. "Take the mirror away. I do not want to see
it. No. I do not want to see it." Was he unconsciously quoting
Lorca?

I took the mirror back to Hector Loyaza who was lying on his
cot reading nothing more subversive than a paperback murder mystery. I thanked him and he smiled. "Any time. You see I still believe
in the basic doctrine. From each according to his ability to each
according to his needs."

I nodded and was able to laugh. "If only society were as simple as
this dormitory."

"I believe it is," Hector Loyaza said. "The laws of society are
simple. It is only the people who are murky and complex and get
in their way."

No wonder Hector Loyaza could remain an unquestioning Party
member for thirty-five years. It was easier to follow every tortuous
twist of the party line and to call *that* the historical dialectic than
to follow the instinctive turnings and twistings of the people themselves who are actually living and making that history.

When I returned to Goyo's bedside he seemed to have dozed off
again. He stirred when I sat on my cot beside him. "What is happening? . . . it is taking so long . . . so long . . ."

"Goyo, Alvarez has been at the Foreign Office this afternoon, working on your case. I will question him severely when he reports back to us."

Goyo nodded. "Good. Good. Bureaucrats. You must beat on them—harder than burros."

"Don't worry—I will. But Goyo—if you have sent your letter—if Angel's foreign officers have been told what you are doing—if the Ambassador is aware—your hunger strike has served its purpose. If action isn't forthcoming, you can start another strike. After all Gandhi did it not once but over and over again. I will help you, I promise. But meanwhile, please, let me bring you a bowl of the evening soup."

Goyo shook his gray head. His skin looked paler without the green bangs across his forehead. Like a doused candle the glow had gone out of the face which had begun to look waxen and sallow.

"Just another glass of water," he said. "My mouth is very dry. But I am over the worst of it now. I can coast on this way for days and days . . ."

I went quickly to the bathroom for Goyo's glass of water. Two inmates were perched on their thrones. Another was shaving. Two more were in the shower half hidden in steam. I hurried back to Goyo. He touched the water to his lips and wanted only a few drops.

"There should be mass meetings," Goyo mumbled. "At all our great universities where my poems are read—Mexico—Rio—Buenos Aires—La Paz . . . I do not understand . . ."

At that moment I realized I had to do something spectacular. There was no longer time for formal petitions. On a much larger stage, Angel Bello must have felt the same sudden sense of urgency when he decided not to wait for the proper revolutionary conditions to present themselves but to grab history roughly by the neck and shove it forward, ready or not. In place of sound revolutionary theory and careful organization, he gambled on personal flair, derring-do, *machismo*.

In this spirit I pulled the sheet out of my bedding and spread it on my cot. Then I picked up my razor from the few possessions on the ledge beside my bed and removed the blade. I shut my eyes, pressed my lips together, gritted my teeth and screwed my face into an anticipated grimace of pain. Then I slashed at my left wrist. I looked. It had worked. Blood was spurting from the central vein.

There was no pain. But the sight of it made me queasy. Quickly I touched my right forefinger to my left wrist and began to print in large letters on the sheet "!SOLANO—" I had to dip the improvised pen in the red ink many times before the bloody message was completed: "HUNGER STRIKE!"

As soon as I hung the sheet out over the windowsill, Johnie Valdez popped over to see what I was up to. "My God, what is this, suicide?" I asked him to take my pillowcase, tear it in strips and tie my wrist. He did so, chattering away at what a heartless fiend Angel Bello was to drive outstanding men like Goyo and me to these terrible extremes. My wrist was throbbing but felt secure. It had not been as difficult as I thought; only the anticipation had hurt me. Afterward there came a sense of exhilaration. The sign looked out on the side of the embassy grounds where visitors and employees could see it easily. Beyond the wall Angel's security guards already could be seen talking to each other and pointing at the offensive sheet. One of them ran around to the front of the building, no doubt to inform the embassy receptionist of this crude affront to the dignity of the People's Republic.

I told Goyo what was happening. At least his self-denial would not be altogether in vain. Word would now reach Angel quickly. And if Bertie Alvarez had not passed the news on to the outside world, passersby would see the emblazoned sheet and speed the word along. Maybe Dr. Levy, our Garbo, would flash the news from his radio station. If he was still alive and functioning.

Goyo was delighted. He even wanted to rise from his cot for the first time in days to see his name in great red letters.

"No, you must conserve your strength," I said.

"It will give me strength," he insisted. I helped him to the window. He did not walk easily. But he laughed when he saw the homemade sign.

"Justo, what a brilliant idea. My name in your blood. No one has ever done that for me before. What a loving friend. Are you all right?"

I waved my bandaged wrist with bravura. "As you see, I was stingy with the words. Like a cablegram where you can only afford the barest minimum."

"It is perfect," he said. "Justo, I could kiss you. Now it will buzz

through the city. My supporters will chant under Angel's window—
Freedom for our Poet Laureate! The cry will be taken up in every
capital! And Justo, once I am free I will take up your cause. I will
write a ringing protest exposing this whole shameful violation of
diplomatic asylum. 'A passport to nowhere.' "

"Get back to bed, Goyo. If you are going to do all those things
you have got to save your strength."

Momentarily cheered, Goyo climbed back into his cot.

A moment later Alvarez appeared, striding furiously up the aisle,
followed almost at a trot by Momentito.

"What is going on here?" he demanded. "Señor Moreno"—he
had caught sight of my bandaged wrist—"I am shocked at you."
He ordered Momentito to go to the window and remove the offending
banner. "All this sensational agitation! Isn't my job difficult enough
without your causing these unnecessary complications?" He took
the sheet from Momentito, rolled it into a careless ball and threw it
back at the old house-servant. "Burn it."

Then he turned to us again. "Do you know what I have been doing all afternoon? Pleading the Solano case at the Immigration Office. They have promised to consider it. There is a good chance that
Solano will be the first one passed through after the Bishop, who
should be leaving us any day now."

"You mean the hunger strike is working?"

"Rubbish!" Alvarez fumed. "I said no such thing."

"At least it got you off your *nalgas.*"

"Moreno Suárez, let me tell you something. When you first came
in here I admired you—I thought you were a gentleman. You were
the last person I expected to break the asylum rules, surely not to
engage in a public act of protest—something you are both guilty of
at the moment. A hunger strike is illegal here. Public protest cannot be countenanced. Otherwise this dormitory would reek of politics and agitation."

"Abandon your souls and your politics, all ye who enter here," I
said.

"Your souls, no. But your politics, assuredly yes," Licenciado
Alvarez said. "That is why I urge you, no I order you, Señor Solano, to give up this childish hunger strike. And you, Señor ex-

Presidente, for you to help him with written agitation—that is shameless, disgusting. You should be especially careful. Your case is still extremely borderline. They are pressing us very hard to allow you to be extradited—returned to the jurisdiction of their High Court of Justice to try you on charges of espionage. It is only our concern for your personal liberty that prevents it. But if they should make too strong a case, if the other two involved should confess that you were the third member of their intelligence ring, it would not be so easy for us to hold out. So I think it would be in your best interest not to provoke us."

"Let me understand something, my benefactor. That letter Goyo sent out to the Association of Pan American Writers. He asked them to release it to the press. So far we have heard nothing. Is it possible that you have taken it upon yourself to censor it, under this new ruling of 'public protest'?"

"All letters are deposited at our mail room," Licenciado Alvarez said, as if by rote. "Then they go out through the regular mail system. If there is postal censorship, we are not responsible. Once it leaves our hands—"

"You were not able to send it out by diplomatic pouch?"

"Absolutely not, our diplomatic pouch is for official business only. Even my personal mail must go through the regular postal system."

"In other words Solano's condition may still be a secret to the outside world?"

"Señor, as I told you this morning, it was included in my report to the Ambassador. When His Excellency chooses to act, you will hear of it."

Goyo had been listening with his fleshy eyelids half closed, a giant lizard in that reptilian state that seems neither awake nor asleep.

"But since we have heard nothing for days, and since this distinguished man is in danger of death, I must insist on sending a cable directly to the Ambassador."

"That is not protocol," said Alvarez. "In the absence of the Ambassador, his deputy, Señor Pineda, is Chief of Mission. You would have to address your appeal through me to Señor Pineda who in turn would decide whether or not to cable the Ambassador."

"Damn your red tape. This man is dying!"

"Moreno Suárez, speaking for this embassy, we will not permit him to die. Hunger strikes are strictly against regulations." He wagged his finger at Goyo's apparently sleeping face. "I warn you, Solano, if you fail to eat what we send you for *cena* tonight, you will force me to take emergency measures."

He executed something very much like an about-face and almost ran down the aisle, to keep the asilados from intercepting him.

Goyo began to chuckle. "Oh God he is so funny. If I die it is against regulations. Justo my dear, you realize he is totally mad. The closer you tie yourself to rules, the more you believe in them—as if these little petty regulations came down from on high like the Ten Commandments—the more sane you seem, the madder you are. Maybe we all go a little mad in here. But our chargé d'affaires is totally insane." He laughed his nasal, nasty laugh. "Even if my fellow-poets do not rise up to save me—it will be worth it just to upset his precious routine, to become his supreme inconvenience."

He lay back and rolled his head on the pillow in uncontrolled laughter. I thought of him up there in the remote Indian mountain crying with laughter at sights and sensations that, under normal circumstances, would have paralyzed him with terror.

From the common room that evening I carried back to Goyo a bowl of the tepid pea soup. But he shook his head and whispered, "No, no, no—I say *no*."

"But you drink water. This is only luke-warm water."

He shook his head weakly. "I am content. I wait—for safe passage." He seemed to be dozing off more and more now. He was not in pain. He was many days beyond pain. He lay in a trance like an Indian holy man. Sometimes he would mutter. Sometimes he would smile and nod. His head would bob and then he would catch himself and his eyes would open wide and he would become his conscious self for a minute or two.

"The short-wave? Is there any news on the short-wave?"

"Try a few spoonfuls of the soup. It is cold now. No different from the water."

"Please. Do not corrupt me. The incorruptible Gregorio. I feel so clean. I sail the sky like a small white feather."

Alvarez was back again, agitated and businesslike. Behind him Momentito and another embassy *mozo* carried a large folding screen. At Bertie's instructions they set it up around Goyo's cot. "So the other asylees will not become too disturbed," he explained.

"Is this the best you can do? Is it not possible to remove him to a private room?" I asked.

"The only one available, not being used by some of the ladies, is the Bishop's."

"Well? Isn't the Bishop a good Christian? It seems to me he's done precious little in here for his children."

"The Bishop is suffering from bleeding ulcers," Licenciado Alvarez said. "That is why we are trying to get him out of the country as an emergency case."

"I bleed with the Bishop. But even so, perhaps he would—"

"Please," Alvarez said with his expression of long suffering. "When you were President of your country, I was doing my job here in the embassy. I was in no position to advise you as to how to do your job. Now our positions are reversed, so to speak. My job is to administer to the asylum. Your job is—to endure. After all, it is no fault of ours that you are in this predicament. We did not ask you to join the Revolution. Or to defect from it. That is your business. But please do not try to tell us how to run our business."

"At least you admit it is a business."

"You people are impossible," Alvarez said in exasperation. "First you come running to us to save your precious skins and then you complain about everything. Sometimes I'd like to see you all lined up against Angel's *paredón* and good riddance."

"Licenciado, I think your bias is beginning to show."

Alvarez glared at me. "Stay close to your friend. We will attend to him in a few minutes."

He turned away muttering, *"Cochinos*—pigs! All of them!" With Momentito trotting after him, he stormed down the aisle. Inside the high folding screen with Goyo, I could not see him but I could imagine the scene as I heard him shout, "Get away from me! This is not my visiting hour! Go to sleep, Gamboa! No more questions! All of you go to sleep!"

Goyo cackled. "Oh God, everything is so funny. The world seems very funny tonight, *cariño.*"

I raised the water to his lips again.

"I wish I could send for my coffin," he said. "I always sleep much better in my coffin."

Then he drifted off again. I sat there by his side, half dozing, as his lassitude was infectious. I had no idea how long I had been dozing when I heard a bustle in the aisle and peered around the screen to see Alvarez approaching with Doctora Julia. Behind them was Momentito, carrying a contraption I recognized as the mechanism for intravenous feeding.

Alvarez put his finger to his lips to signal that we should not awaken Goyo. He stepped aside to allow Doctora Julia to enter the enclosure with her medical kit. We nodded to each other and she stooped to examine Goyo. While Momentito was setting up the contraption, I stood in the aisle outside the screen with Alvarez.

"You see, Señor Presidente," he said, "we are going to pull him through. And that will give us time to work out his safe passage. If he gives his word that he will not involve himself in any political activities once he is freed, I really believe we can arrange it."

"The only time he ever indulged in political activities was in favor of Angel's overthrow of Zamora," I said. "He is a man without *política*. With deep feelings, but no politics, not as you and I think about politics."

"Rest assured, we will do everything we can in his behalf," Alvarez said. There was genius in his ability to avoid responding to what was said to him. Just as we had been "premature-antifascists" in the mid-Thirties, he was a premature Orwellian-man of the middle Sixties.

In a few minutes Doctora Julia turned to us.

"He has no fever. His heartbeat is regular but weak. I have no idea how much weight he has lost, although I would guess seven or eight kilos. There is the first suggestion of edema, air pockets under the skin which begin to fill with liquid. Nothing too serious so far if we can restore his metabolic balance with glucose."

She knelt beside Goyo and reached into her case to prepare a hypodermic.

"What are you giving him?"

"Sodium pentothal," Julia told me. "This will put him to sleep before we connect the tube."

"No!" Goyo stirred. "You are not going to put me to sleep. Get away. Leave me alone. This is a hunger strike!"

Julia looked up at me. "Justo. Alvarez. Hold him down."

"No," Goyo said, turning away from her. "Take the needle away. You are not going to put me to sleep! This belongs to me. Have you no respect?"

I hesitated. Had we the right to save him by force? It seemed a betrayal of his faith. Still, I could not let him die.

"Justo, do you hear me? Hold him down!" Julia's voice cut through my doubts. In spite of Goyo's protesting and wrenching from side to side, I found myself allied with Alvarez in holding his shoulders firmly to his cot while Momentito held his legs from thrashing. Julia gripped his left arm and in a few seconds of tense stillness thumbed the needle in. There was a momentary reaction against it and then it was startling to see how quickly the chemical took effect, frightening to know how vulnerable we are. Almost instantly the unequal battle was over. He sagged. His fleshy, nervous eyelids shut. He breathed deeply. Peace—no matter how involuntary. Sleep had been administered.

Working rapidly, Doctora Julia taped a splint to his inner elbow close to the vein into which she inserted the end of the tube that ran from the cylinder hanging near his shoulder. She watched him for almost a full minute and then put the stethoscope and other tools of her trade back into her leather work-bag.

"He should grow stronger during the night. Check him every few hours to see if the feeder is working. If anything goes wrong, Alvarez says to call Momentito. He will summon me."

Alvarez nodded, pleased with himself. "The first time a woman has ever been admitted to the men's wing. In the humanitarian spirit of His Excellency the Ambassador."

Also in the self-serving spirit of the chargé d'affaires afraid to lose an inmate in His Excellency's absence.

"Thank you for calling me a woman," Julia said with a gray smile, "but I come here as a doctor. And as an admirer of Señor Solano."

I walked down the aisle with this rebel-aristocrat who carried with her an Old-Testament determination to endure.

As we approached the double cot of El Gordo, Alvarez hurried up behind us. "Doctora Bécquer, I know you are not officially on duty in this Embassy, but as long as you have so kindly volunteered to treat Señor Solano, you might also volunteer to treat General Romano. We supply him with colchicine but his gout has spread from his foot to his right knee. He says it is very swollen and painful."

The Doctora looked at him coldly. "Romano can afford the best doctors in the city."

"But his own doctors are in Miami," Alvarez said. "And the ones who are left are afraid to come here—they might fall out of favor with Colonel Bello."

"I am just an asylee like the rest," said the Doctora. "A moment ago I was guilty of practicing without a license. I am in your country, not ours."

"That is true. But his pain is very great, and you—"

"Alvarez, I would not trust myself to touch that man." It was spoken as a flat statement without the slightest suggestion of emotion.

Apparently Alvarez did not know the story. Both her older and younger brothers had been doctors who ran a clinic together. Unlike their sister, they had not been involved in the underground against Zamora. But from time to time, students who had been tortured or shot by the Tigers of Romano would come to the clinic. Her brothers cared for them as patients without asking questions. One day the Tigers came and dragged them out of their houses on the clinic grounds in front of their wives and children. Next morning the mutilated corpses were found on the doorstep.

At the door I asked Julia if Goyo would survive. "I think so," she said. "But bear in mind, a hunger strike is quite different from involuntary hunger and malnutrition. Different psychological and emotional factors affect the patient. A man feeding on his own body for energy can live for a month or—lose all ambition, even the desire to live. Then there are the complications, the strain, the possibility of heart attack. Gregorio's own eccentricity, his extreme moods could be a factor. I do not make empty promises like our chargé d'affaires, but I would like to save him."

Then with a hand on the door, she said, in her same matter-of-fact tone, "Have you heard from Marta?"

I stared at her. Marta, Marta, a name from the past, sealed up with Clarita in an attic of my mind. I knew they were there and I worried and wondered about them and yet they no longer seemed real to me. They were my loved ones but more like the half-real, departed shadows who look back on their lives from the village cemetery in a play I had seen long ago.

I shook my head, no, there was still no news from them.

"Strange," Julia said. "Marta had promised to write to me as well. I would like to know about Clarita. Knowing Marta—I imagine her letters come to a dead end in the censor's office. Discretion has never been one of her virtues."

"Julia, how is your own case going?"

The Doctora shrugged. "I do not even ask. I keep busy. I take care of my patients. I more or less govern the dormitory, hear the complaints, settle the disputes. My philosophy is still—live as usefully as you can. What happens, happens."

Licenciado Alvarez was holding the door open for her, urging her to go. "Doctora—if you please."

"And Garbo?" I asked.

There were some who believed that Julia and the underground leader had worked closely together only as conspirators. Others were convinced they were long-time lovers.

She shrugged. "Some say he is broadcasting again. But I do not hear him on the short-wave. If del Campo had him, the official station would be boasting about it. *Quién sabe?* I go from day to day."

"Until tomorrow, Doctora Julia." I kissed her hand. "Go well."
"You also. And be careful."

The door closed behind her. I wondered what she meant by that
parting word—*cuidado*. In our underground it had been said that
Doctora Julia did not need a secret radio system like Garbo. She had
developed her own radar. She could sense where the Tigers were going to pounce, smell the Romano informer who had infiltrated our
ranks. A single word of warning from the Doctora was never to be
disregarded.

Passing the domino players and their incessant argument, I returned to the high folding screen that now set Goyo's cot off from
the rest. He was sleeping peacefully, the cylinder of glucose silently
feeding into his vein. But his skin had taken on the dry, dead look
of parchment, drawn so tightly over his cheek bones that it seemed
it might split.

At the end of the room a radio voice caught my attention. The
volume grew louder. Half a dozen asylees gathered around the cot
of Johnie Valdez, whose short-wave set was balanced on a suitcase
that served as his end table. The listeners were talking excitedly. I
hurried to join them. On the side of Johnie's cot, tense and erect,
stood El Indio. He was staring at the set as if he were hearing superhuman voices.

"Fantastic!" Johnie filled me in. "The Arawaks have gone on the
warpath, killed the manager of their state farm and announced they
are taking back their land. They've disappeared into the sierras behind the farm. Boy oh boy, the Zamoristas never had been able to
get their hands on them when they were holed up in there. The
Arawaks know every rock by name! Can you see Angel's face? These
aren't the brainwashed kids. These are the real campesinos fighting
back."

"Ssst! I want to hear." The deep voice of El Indio turned Johnie
off. According to the official Voice of the Revolution, Arawak
farmers, "a group of petit-bourgeois counter-revolutionaries," had
mutinied against the People's servants who had been guiding their
agricultural development on a state farm in the province of Ocampo.
The criminal uprising had been put down by the alert local militia,
although it was admitted that a few of the bandits may have escaped

to their old haunts in the recesses of the sierra. This small, anti-social band would be flushed out and brought to justice within the next forty-eight hours.

I studied El Indio's face. Except for its dark concentration, it seemed to reflect no emotion. Around him was the buzzing of instant predictions and oaths of surprise. But as he stood there with his arms folded on his powerful chest, the voices seemed to break against him like waves thrown back by an insurmountable black boulder that rises from the sea.

"I want to hear," he said again.

But now the news broadcaster was repeating the approved version of the day's events in faultless English.

"Try the V.O.A." I said.

Johnie moved the dial a fraction of a point and there was the confident voice of Washington, rendering one of its dull basic-English history lessons on how the Dutch happened to establish the city of New York. It was followed by routine news—Negro riots in several northern cities. Another abortive attempt to find a U.N. formula for peace in the Middle East. Missiles that would be able to reach Mars and probe the mystery of Venus. The suicide of a glamorous Hollywood film star who had just turned thirty-one. An encouraging rise in the Wall Street market . . .

And then came our turn. "Taking up the old cry of Land and Liberty that carried them into battle first against the Spaniards and then against army dictatorships supporting powerful landholders, the Arawaks have risen in a dramatic rebellion against their state farm officials. Reports monitored in Miami indicate that the freedom-loving Arawaks drove back government security troops that attempted to encircle them. Well armed and determined to reestablish control of the land of their forefathers, the Arawaks, once led by the Maceo-like Captain Sandungo who fought at the side of Angel Bello, have established rebel headquarters in the rugged hills behind the state farm and are urging other campesinos to rise up and join them in a battle for their land to which they believe they have an indisputable right and for which they fought Zamora and Romano. So the Bello dictatorship is called to account by the very campesinos who were Angel's first allies in the jungle of Ocampo.

Further bulletins will be issued as they are relayed from our monitors in Miami."

The news was followed by a Frank Sinatra medley. Four or five of us surrounded El Indio. "Does this come as a surprise?" "Do you think it's a protest at your being forced into asylum?" "How long can your people hold out in the hills?" Johnie Valdez asked directly, "Indio, I suppose it must be a funny feeling for you to listen to all this without being able to do anything about it?"

El Indio silenced us with a noncommittal stare and walked to the window. He stood there for a long time and the intensity of his silence warned us not to approach him.

When I went back to look at Goyo he was still sleeping, the glucose solution feeding sweetly into his vein. The folding screen was arranged so that from the pillow of my cot I could look in on him. I lay on my back planning to stay awake, glancing in at him every twenty minutes or so. But finally, to the rhythm of his steady breathing, I must have fallen asleep.

20

I was awakened by the sound of Goyo's voice. Switching on the flashlight Alvarez had given me, I could not be sure whether Goyo was awake or talking in his sleep with his eyes open. The effects of the drug had worn off and he was wrenching himself from unconsciousness. His eyes were dilated and he seemed to be straining against invisible cords that bound him to the cot.

"Beloved countrymen! My dear public! I come before you! Only the Poet-President speaks to you as . . . as comrades with a small c!"

With my arm around his waist I propped Goyo up to a half-sitting position but he did not seem to be aware of me. His eyes were shining. He used his hands in feeble imitation of energetic gestures.

"Only the Poet can save you from the Demagogues! Only the Poet preaches the true religion—the hunger gnawing in us to become more . . . human . . . How to become human, more and more human until at last we are human beings! Only the Poet, the Poet-President . . . can lead you there, my friends, and so . . . my dear ones, I accept! I come back from the tomb because you . . . you honor me with your call to this high office. Not a dictator, not a *Jefe,* not a Colonel. A Poet. I say, no more Commissars. No more firing squads. No more secret police. No more central committees. Instead of propaganda I give you poetry. Instead of hate I give you love. Instead of iron rules I give you golden rules. Do unto others. It has never been tried."

His face was damp now, as if he were walking through a fine mist.

"Goyo, Goyo, wake up—look at me!"

It was the way my father had died. Growing weaker day by day, on the last night he had begun quoting his Martí, reciting his private devotion hour after hour as a Dominican priest might say his Office. Until his breath weakened in the final minutes it had been as audible as when he used to recite to us before our frugal but festive Sunday lunch. "Instead of the Mass, we do poetry," he liked to say with a piously agnostic smile. And so my dedicated schoolteacher father had died, "saying" his Martí, as others die with Hail Mary's on their breath.

"Goyo, do you hear me? Wake up!"

Goyo turned his head toward me. As if I had flipped a switch, he seemed to snap into the present again.

"Oh—Justo—I was dreaming—about you. Only I was the President. Remember I said we needed a Poet-President? Who is not ashamed of love, Justo? Angel was a Poet. When he was a student. When he was hiding with the peasants. But when you take power you put away your dreams. You measure it all by . . . how much of this? How many of those? You become . . . a pragmatist. Production and purge trials. Only the Poet, Justo, working with the heart, can show us the inner meaning, cut through the jungle of chaos into the plain where everything is green with hope. When? When? A thousand years, ten thousand years is such a little while. Unthinkable to the tyrant. But for the Poet . . . like a single creative day in his life. Only a Poet-President, Justo, has the wisdom to . . . to free his mind of facts—see his destiny as a solution to the anxiety—bewilderment—the hatred and death that we still confuse with life . . . scientists, statesmen, technicians—what do they know of humanity? Those realists who can only cope with what they see. To become . . . human, we must deal not with the little tip of the iceberg above the surface, but with the enormous mass of unseen experience that supports the tiny visible tip. That is it, Justo! The statesman-politician sees only the little tip of the pinnacle and makes the great practical mistake of thinking that is all there is. But the Poet's intuition is clearer than all the scientific machinery. He does not need sonar and radar. He sees the spirit of man evolving, evolving . . . Five thousand years, ten thousand . . . whenever it is that man is able to get rid of his selfish, bestial nature and become human, achieve humanity . . . the Poet-President who went on ahead to blaze the trail will be there waiting for him."

Goyo shook his head slowly and chuckled to himself without parting his lips. "That is what I was dreaming, Justo, that you and I were one person—the one Poet-President, whose eyes are in his heart. We see it, Justo, we see it, the green valley of love still hidden by mountains of mistrust and destruction. Only the Poets, Justo, can see through the mountains."

As he raised his hands to symbolize the mountains standing between man and his humanity, he felt the tug of the tube inserted into his forearm. Now he was sharply awake, no longer the ecstatic poet-prophet but the patient punctured by reality.

"What is this?" He pulled against it. He looked up and saw the cylinder still half full of its life-giving formula. "No, no, take it away —away! I don't want it."

"Goyo, we want you to live."

Goyo tried to wrench his arm away. I held him down.

"No!" He glared up at me. "You compromise me. My honor. My hunger strike belongs to me! Nobody can end it for me. Nobody!"

"But Goyo, if you would only hold out ten more days—two weeks —I really believe they intend to let you—"

"No! I say No, Alvarez!"

The strength of his arm was surprising. I had thought he would be too weak to fight off my hold on him. He raised his left arm and pulled it away from the tube. The tape stretched but held. With his right hand he ripped at the adhesive but the strips were thick and they had been tightly wrapped around his arm and the splint. I tried to hold him down but he kicked at me. I put my arm across his chest and he bit me hard. I cried out and rubbed the place he had bitten.

"Quiet, I am sleeping." The voice of Rubén Silva from the next cot down.

"While you sleep, he could be dying."

"And good riddance," came the voice beyond the screen.

Goyo was pulling the attached tube to his face, gnawing at it with his mouth. Before I could stop him he had pulled it free. The tube dangled to the floor. Blood was on his arm where the connecting needle had been ripped from his open vein.

"Goyo—you're mad!"

"No—true to myself. If my fellow-poets, if my public, if the world does not hear me—I want to die!"

"No, lie down, let me call—"

"You betrayed me. You let them set up this ugly—"

He swung his left arm out against Doctora Julia's contraption sending the whole thing crashing against the screen. The cylinder with its glucose solution fell heavily to the floor and smashed. There were cries of protest from inmates trying to sleep. In my pajamas I ran down the aisle.

"What's all the racket?" Johnie's voice.

"Stay with him. I have to get help."

"Hokey dokey."

Johnie was getting out of bed as I ran to the common room. But the door to the outside corridor was locked. I had thought that in this emergency Alvarez would have left it open. How did he expect me to call Momentito for help? I had to run back for the key that I kept hidden in my mattress. I poked my head around the screen. Goyo's eyes looked glazed. But he recognized me. "Keep away, gusano," he said. "I despise you."

I ran back down the aisle. Johnie was still on his cot. "How's the poet?" he asked. "Find out for yourself," I said and kept on going.

I unlocked the door, stealthily. The key must remain my secret.

Then I hurried down the steps to the third floor and through a narrow hallway to the small room where Momentito slept. I could hear him obediently muttering *"Momentito, momentito,"* as he came to the door in an old-fashioned nightshirt. He said he would awaken Señora Lorona to call the Doctora. I took the stairs back to the attic level two at a time. Johnie was waiting near my cot.

"He was howling like a cat. I think he's in pain. I tried to go to him but he insulted me," Johnie said. "For a poet he knows some real *picante* language. Maybe the sailors gave him a few lessons, eh Justo?"

The sound of prolonged moaning came from behind the screen. Then a sharp scream. Johnie shook his head. "First he recites poetry, then he screams. I think he is loco—your poet pal."

Goyo was tightly clasping his wounded arm, rocking slowly back and forth in pain and moaning, "Ay . . . ! A-aaaa-y!" Then he seemed to lapse into a stupor again, his head turned into his pillow. His lips were reciting a poem:

> *"Como el toro he nacido para el luto*
> Like the bull I was born for mourning
> and grief, like the bull I am marked
> by infernal brand on my side
> and as a man by a seed in my groin."

It was not one of his own but a poem he wished he had written. I had heard him recite it before, on the stage of his jewel-box theater:

> "Like the bull I find my immeasurable heart
>   too small
> And with a face enamored of a kiss
> Like the bull I fight for your love.
> Like the bull I grow with punishment
> I have my heart bathed in courage
> And feel at my neck a strong west wind
> Like the bull I follow and pursue you
> And you leave my desire on a sword
> Deceived like the bull, like the bull."

Incredibly he went on. His eyes were large and bright but did not see. Or perhaps they saw beyond—beyond the faded black screen, the narrow cot, the smashed feeding apparatus, the cracked ceiling. Goyo's lips could not stop reciting. On those sensuous, almost feminine lips danced the ghost of a hundred flamboyant performances. A thousand poems burned in the brain of Gregorio Solano.

When he paused he cried out in pain. The black-and-blue mark around the tear in his forearm was spreading. "Ay! Ay! Christ help me! It feels like . . . Ay-eee torture!"

He bit down hard on his teeth and ground them together. The sound was unnerving.

> "Loving, cruel and hungry bull
> use my heart for a pasture, for tragic grass
> if this bitter business pleases you.
> A love of the world torments me
> as it does you.
> And over that world spills the blood of
>   my heart
> Dressed for the grave."

He finished in a grimace of pain and screamed again. Then he opened his eyes suddenly. "Justo, Justo help me!" I knelt down in confusion to comfort him. There was movement and voices outside the screen and then Doctora Julia was there with Momentito. The old servant began to clean up the mess of the toppled intravenous contraption while the Doctora bent over Goyo.

"Can we get another I.V.?" I asked.

She shook her head. "I don't know. Certainly not until morning. When a patient has his own ideas as to what to do with his life, he is the ultimate specialist on his case. We can help him to live but we cannot insist. We cannot play God."

As she spoke she reached into her medical kit. With a piece of white gauze she fitted the needle into a syringe and dipped it into one of her row of small bottles. "When you do what he did," she said, "the pain can be unbearable. This will make him more comfortable."

But Goyo fought her off. He was afraid she would leave him unconscious again. We could have held him down once more but Doctora Julia chose not to force him. She put away the syringe and offered him some pills instead. "These will dull the pain," she said. "Codeine. I will leave more here on the shelf."

"Codeine. That sounds better," Goyo said. "If you find any sacred mushrooms—" He laughed in pain.

"Take them now." She reached for the glass of water that Momentito had brought and held it to Goyo's lips.

Goyo swallowed the pills. "Thank you, my *bruja*."

"Now let me see what you've done to your arm." He winced as she reached for it. "I won't pull at the tape," she said. "But let me cut through it, just where it is loose, so I can apply an antiseptic. No use getting it infected."

With a slender scissors she quickly cut through the gap between the adhesive and his skin, where the tube had been. Goyo shut his eyes and turned away while she dressed it.

When she had finished she shut her bag. "I will come back in the morning. But if you need me before that—"

Goyo was cradling his arm again and nodding vaguely, his eyes still shut. I followed Julia into the aisle.

"He is in a state of extreme hypertension," she said. "But in a few hours—"

"Julia, there is nothing more we can do?"

She gave a shrug of resignation. "We have no injection for the will to live."

"He waits for the conscience of the world to rescue him."

Doctora Julia's expression did not change. "Which is almost the same thing as waiting for death." She shuddered and pulled the cord of her night robe tighter. "Forgive me. When I feel this tired, I should talk only with my instruments and my little bottles." There was a pause. "Good night, Justo. Or rather, good morning. Take care of yourself."

I watched her go down the aisle toward the exit, an erect figure in an old robe, carrying her worn medical bag.

Too restless for sleep I paused at the dormer window and stared out through the darkness separating me from Adriana. The crisis of the hunger strike had drawn a temporary curtain between us. But I had bitten into that apple and the worm of lust seldom ceased its twisting in my mind. Down the aisle I noticed that El Indio was not in his cot. I went into the common room but it was empty.

At what point did Bolívar lose his faith? If Martí had not stopped that bullet, what would have been his reaction to the Americanization of his revolution? This should have been an ideal time to further my notes on *The Making of the Dictator*. I tried, but I could not keep my mind on it. Too many sounds. Too many bodies. At least I could write to Marta. Again I began, but the night sounds, and now a noisy argument over a stolen comb, made concentration impossible. In sanctuary there was no ideal time, only restlessness, distraction and fits of discouragement that pointed toward madness.

I stopped at the bathroom. The shower was running full force. Vapor from the hot water had transformed the room into a stationary cloud. But from somewhere in the cloud a deep voice chanted or prayed. I stared through the mist until I recognized the naked, sweating figure of El Indio. He was drinking a dark liquid from a jelly-glass and chanting in his native Arawak. He would take a few sips, as priests with a ritual wine, and then he would chant again. In his enormous right hand he held the glass and with his left thumb he squeezed blood from his forefinger into the glass of what must have been hot water darkened with his own bleeding.

"Indio?"

He did not answer.

I raised my voice through the steam: "Indio!"

He heard me this time. He came back to my world. His eyes were hating me now. "What do you want?"

"What are you doing?"

"If I tell you, you will betray me."

"Why? Why? I am your friend."

"A *blanco* is never my friend." He raised the potion to his lips again.

"That is insane."

"I speak the tongue of the Arawak. We are not insane. Now leave me. Soon I go into battle."

"Indio—"

"It is you who are insane," he said. "I have been watching. In my province we kill old men who go insane. To put them out of their suffering." He made a threatening gesture toward me with the glass that held the dark liquid.

I had heard of this drink they call *paoli-paoli,* the ceremonial "wine" of braves whipping themselves into a frenzy of courage. And with El Indio's tribe there had been a strange historical coincidence: when nearly all the Indians had been worked or beaten to death, the Yorubas had been dragged across the seas to replace them. There were runaways who took refuge in remote jungle villages like El Indio's. There they found that many of their customs and even their gods seemed to overlap. When his tribe offered them the *paoli-paoli,* the blacks rejoiced that they had found their brothers, for this elixir under a different name on a distant continent was so similar to their own. Together they had gone into battle.

"Indio," I called to him through the steam. "You are not a savage. You are Sandungo, the leader of the Arawaks."

He drank again from the glass of hot water blood. Then he turned off the boiling shower. The shower nozzle dripped slowly. It was quiet, like a sultry countryside after the torrential rain of tropical summer.

Huge, naked, black, glistening, he advanced on me. "Why you think I drink the *paoli-paoli?*"

I wanted to escape. I backed toward the door but El Indio followed. "I drink the *paoli* because I am Indian. You *blancos* can pick your own politics. See my skin." He hit his chest fiercely. "My politics cry out from my skin."

"Yes," I said. "Yes, I understand."

"I do not need your 'understand.' " His tone was guttural sarcasm. He took another step toward me. My back was against the door. He was much taller and bigger, and black. How profound is the fear of the best-intentioned white when confronted with a giant and hostile black.

"I will get what I want," he roared. "Even if it is only death. At least it will come when I choose it. I, El Indio Sandungo. You will not push it on me."

If I had the power I would have given him the gift of life, of freedom. But with the understandable madness of the *chingadas,* he had come up to the scratch line, the line of battle, and there, instead of the enemy he had found only a would-be friend. And just as white men's eyes were blind with centuries of arrogance, his eyes were blind with centuries of pain, inverted pride and the hunger for revenge now intensified by *paoli.*

"We will not go back to the bad time before the Revolution. Not go back to four months in the cane fields to sweat for the *latifundistas* and eight months of the dead season to stare at the empty bellies of our babies. We will not go back to the *bohíos* with mud floors, and roofs of palm fronds that fly away in the autumn *huracanes*. We will keep the school and the medicine and the good things the Revolution brings to my people. But our tongue is thirsty for freedom! We want our own farms. Our own Revolution. Freedom! You never give us our freedom!"

As he called out again that word "freedom" he hurled the empty glass against the wall.

Then he turned. "You *políticos blancos!*" I thought he might try to strangle me since there was no one else available. "You—!"

"Do not call me *you*. I am not 'you blancos.' I am not 'you commissars.' I am not 'you' anything. I am me. I feel. I think. For myself. *Me.*"

"*Blanco!*" El Indio shouted. "I will kill you."

With my hand behind my back I reached for the doorknob and managed to escape. Then inexplicably I heard him laughing behind the door. At this moment he was insane, out of control, vicious. But right.

By my cot I heard a voice. It came from inside the folding screen. I looked in and saw Goyo hugging his pillow. "Oh, Marcelo, my baby, my sweet baby. Love me, love me, my Marcelito. Like the moon between the palm trees. Love me, Marcelo, open your sweet young lips, take me into your mouth of honey, suck me my own Marcelo Luna between the palm trees."

His skin was like white paper, fragile as onion skin. I could feel him longing to live, living to die, begging for the final thrust of life, the ultimate connection. "Marcelo, Marcelito, my love, my life. Your sweet lips. Your mouth full of wonders."

He reached out for me until his arm was behind my leg pressing me toward him. "Come to me, my sweet love."

I drew away. "No, Goyo, no—I am not your Marcelo."

He made a slight whimpering sound. I sat on my cot wondering what I could do. There seemed to be only one reassurance he wanted now.

"Come to me, precious one. Hold my hand. Feel how cold it is."

He stretched his left arm out, the one injured when he had ripped the suture from the incision in his vein. The arm looked long and naked and painfully thin. His hand groped for me and I reached out. His fingers welcomed the touch and closed around mine with extraordinary force.

"Ah yes, yes, come to me, my precious."

He drew me toward him. I wanted to wrench my hand away but his need for this human connection was so much greater than mine for escape. It seemed an act of petty cruelty to deprive him of my hand. He drew me still closer. "Oh my sweet little friend. How long it has been! I have been dying for you. Literally dying." He turned toward me and his other hand went around the back of my head. At first gently and then more insistently he pressed my face toward him. It was dark. I was not Marcelo. But in this moment someone had to be. I tried to bury my aversion, and to think only of his need. I thought of Xavier going to the victims of the plague and sucking the yellow pus from their wounds because he loved them. I did not love Goyo as he wanted me to, but I responded to his hunger, his naked human need to manifest his love. "Marcelo, my Marcelito," he moaned with his eyes closed. Then he began to sense the hesitation, the unspoken reluctance.

"Marcelo? No, you are not Marcelo." His eyes opened slowly. "You are . . . Justo . . . my friend . . . my loving friend . . .

"But no," he said, his voice a little stronger now. "You do not want to. So, go. Back to your women." Already the color in his cheeks showed signs of the embalmer's perfection. He inhaled slowly, his mouth barely open: an effort to smile. "But thank you, Justo my dear, I thank you."

Lying back on my cot, the closing lines of the poem Goyo had been reciting rang like a desolate bell across the lake.

> Learn, flowers, from me, what parts we play
> From dawn to dusk. Last noon the boast
> And marvel of the fields, today
> I am not even my own ghost . . .

But, as the great Góngora has written, we play at many parts. In Goyo's last moments I had been ready to play an unaccustomed one in the *Allegory of the Brevity of Human Things*. I was not even my own ghost. With blood rushing to my head and my mind clearing, I rose from my cot again and looked down at Goyo Solano. And then I realized that he would never write another line, caress his precious Marcelo Luna, strain against the invisible cords, or breathe again.

With his hair gray and his skin drained of color, he looked like a stone effigy of the vivacious green-haired eccentric who had come to sanctuary. I drew the sheet over his head, a reflex imitation of something I had seen in movies perhaps. Lifeless faces are simply not supposed to lie around exposed to the public. But perhaps there is a reason. Perhaps it is what García Lorca was feeling when he wrote that farewell for his lamented Ignacio. *I do not want to see it! No, I do not want to see it!* There was no need for Goyo to lie in state with his hair restored to the color of grass and pink roses slipped into the cold wax of his skin. He would live on in the staunchest of his verses, and in the memory of a score of poets who had been too far away to heed the SOS of his heartbeats.

In a shock of efficiency I hurried downstairs to pass the news to Momentito. Ten minutes later the dormitory was bright with activity. Alvarez had been summoned. Doctora Julia confirmed with her stethoscope what I had known the moment following Goyo's final ecstasy when his golden stairway suddenly faded into the black of the mind gone dead.

Under the supervision of Licenciado Alvarez, two night guards from the main floor removed the remains of Goyo on a stretcher. Behind them Momentito carried out the thin mattress on which Goyo had cried out against his final loneliness. Alvarez took out his frustration at Goyo's breach of asylum etiquette by snapping irritable orders at the guards. They were carrying the stretcher too low. They were not moving down the aisle fast enough. Momentito, hardly big enough to carry the threadbare mattress by himself, was warned not to drag it on the floor. "Higher. Faster. Do as I tell you. Stupid burros we get for servants these days!"

And to the curious who formed a line along the aisle and asked legitimate questions as he passed, he snarled, "Stand back! Out of the way! None of your business where he's to be buried. A service?

We will see. Perhaps an announcement tomorrow. Now back, back, no more questions, you crowd around like a lot of silly geese!"

From outside the building came the sound of automatic rifle fire. Asylees rushed to the windows. The guards paused in the aisle with their burden. "Go on, go on, get that cadaver out of here!" From the windows inmates were shouting, "They're shooting! The militia outside the wall. They've got lights on! Someone must be trying to climb in!"

I ran to the bathroom. El Indio was not there. I ran back and looked over the confusion of the long room. No sign of El Indio. On the shelf above his cot the few personal effects he had were gone. I tried to look over the shoulder of others crowding at the window. The rapid fire of the automatics splattered over the embassy wall. El Indio had not lost his touch. These special conditions of Goyo's removal: the outer door momentarily left open, the embassy guards drawn away from their posts. I could imagine El Indio's thundering laughter at Alvarez' confusion. With the searchlights and the rifles of Bello militiamen it did not seem possible that anyone could scale that high wall and survive their fire. Still the shooting persisted. If they had cut down El Indio quickly, this one-man battle should have been over. Looking into the glare of the arc lights, we could see militiamen crouching and firing. "It must be students trying to run the gantlet and take asylum," someone said. "What bastards they are, shooting down innocent kids!"

Alvarez was pushing to the window with them, trying to see for himself. In his agitation, he had forgotten his authority. Then a prolonged burst of machine-gun bullets struck along the top of our window. Everybody dropped to the floor. That was an old trick of the security militia. In the confusion of a battle at the wall it was sometimes possible to pick off an asylee or two. I found myself close to Alvarez on the floor. "Why does everything have to happen at once?" he said. "I'd better get downstairs. If any of those damned penniless students are trying to get in, I will turn them right over to Angel's—" Then he had a second thought. "Wait a moment! How do we know they are trying to get in? It could be someone trying to get *out*! That does not happen often, but—" He glanced around nervously. Outside the shots were continuing but less frequently now.

"Señor Presidente—look around. You do not notice anyone missing?"

I pretended to look carefully around the room. "I do not notice."

Alvarez nodded unhappily. "I must go down and find out what is happening. Meanwhile, maybe you can check for me."

"It is your job to administer the asylum. It is my job to endure. I believe I am quoting you correctly, Alvarez?"

Alvarez permitted himself a moment of anger. "The more I try to do for you the less you appreciate it. All of you. Typical. There will be a roll call in fifteen minutes. I order everyone to stay away from the windows and turn off the lights."

Switching off our own lights made little difference because the militia were still playing their powerful arcs on the embassy wall and their great beams spilled into our window. I tried to see what was happening beyond the boundaries of our sanctuary. El Indio? Could he be lying out there with his chest shredded with machine-gun bullets and the blood that had beat so strongly in him wasting itself in the street? Or was he still the same black panther who had managed to escape the traps set for him on the fringes of the jungle by the frustrated army of Zamora? I could see him moving by night and hiding by day until he had come home to his native Ocampo and, knowing some secret jungle passage, slipping through the ring of soldiers that surrounded his Arawaks. I could hear him laughing as he led his people once again into midnight skirmishes in his endless quest for the elusive grail—Land and Liberty.

In the early-morning hours, after the roll call had revealed his absence, after Licenciado Alvarez had hurried off to write his apopleptic report on this latest assault on diplomatic authority, when the dormitory had finally settled down from the long night's adventures, I lay in my solitary cot and thought about Goyo. I would miss the poet with the green hair and the satyr eyes and the soft mouth and the hard little mind, miss the intellectual games—tackling everything from Bolívar to bullfighting, from Marcelo to Marxism, with his strong opinions on every conceivable subject and his outrageous outspokenness. "I despise all politicians, left, right and center," he had said one evening. "Including me?" I had asked in jest. He had flared his rebellious unicorn smile and said, "I mind you less. Because you are only an amateur politician." The more I thought about Goyo Solano the more the eccentricities, the vanity, the pretensions, the collection of pornographic wood carvings, the petty jealousies and gossip, the virulent homosexuality, seemed minor subtractions to the sum of his virtues. The flaws he accentuated might have been his way of disguising his sanctity. I had a strange thought. What if he were Christ returned to us in the form of a green-haired effete homosexual so that we would not fall on our knees too easily, so that we would have to cut through our undergrowth of prejudices to the true measure of the man? And if not Goyo why not his physical opposite El Indio, sent to redeem us with his black skin and the fearful swing of his machete? Or what if Christ were both of them, the sun and the moon of a single, eternal night?

I pressed my hands against my temples as if literally to hold my brains together. Think of the basic functions of life. Think of eating, think of breathing, think of fucking Adriana until we roll off the bed together without losing a precious stroke and squeeze out the last seeds of ecstasy there on the floor.

And so at last I fell asleep, full of mourning, awe, worship and sin, a man bent by circumstances like a crudely hammered nail.

In my dream her tawny inner thighs were making room for me and her Nefertiti eyes were beginning to close with anticipated pleasures. We trembled as we waited for that first delicate touch of outer want to inner need. "Oh Adriana my sweet *cuera*—," I cried out.

A big hand smashing against the side of my face jarred me from my fantasy.

Búfalo loomed over me in the darkness. *"Tu puta madre!"* From his double cot El Gordo was leaning on one elbow to watch the performance. "That will teach you to talk filth about the Señora. A man of your position!"

My position, I thought to myself. Was there anything more humiliating than my position? I wondered if Búfalo knew what I had been doing when he struck me. I felt trapped and guilty.

"Stay away from that window," his gravel voice commanded. "Stay away from the lady of Romano. That is an order from the General."

I rose from my cot.

"In here there are no Generals. Or Presidents. Only asilados."

"You keep the Señora out of your dreams or they will be the last you ever have."

From the cot of the cantankerous Rubén Silva came a "Shhh! *Por Dios!* Fight it out in the morning! A man never gets any sleep in this madhouse!"

Búfalo uttered a reflexive curse, glared a final warning and went back to his post. I lay on my bed listening to the rain on the attic roof, consumed with the idea of putting horns on El Gordo. But how? When? Where? Instead of the sentimental Cupid, an evil *banderillero* had embedded those question marks deep into my skin. It was not blood that spurted forth around their vicious little hooks but transparent beads of sweat flowing from the opened vein of lust.

In the morning my waking thought was to devise some ingenious plan of consummation. I would pass up breakfast so that I could communicate with her across the frustrating space between our wings. I had envisioned myself as the only one to remain behind. What I had not foreseen was that El Gordo would stay in bed because of his painful foot. He lay there reading another historical novel of southern gringo plantation life, *The Vixen*. Had he known its author was an American Negro he might not have enjoyed it so publicly. In his days of power he had hunted black rebels in the province of Ocampo with a special relish. Now he lay back against his pile of pillows indulging in the bulky romance and ignoring me.

I paced near the dormer window, hesitating to approach it and yet determined to find a way. With my mind still focused on the where and how, I wandered around the common room until breakfast was over.

Johnie called me to listen to the news and I lingered to see if there were reports of El Indio. But there was no mention of him. There were statistics on the inroads being made in rural illiteracy by young volunteer teachers which were probably reliable and other figures on the rise of rice production that sounded inventive. The program ended with the repeated theme of Goyo's still fashionable "Angelitos Verdes." I went back to the common room, ignored the noisy domino players and glanced through an old sports magazine. There was a full-page rotogravure picture of some señorita's understandably celebrated posterior. I stared at it and thought of holding my hands around the full amber cheeks of the lady in the window. That insistent muscle began to harden again, a large live rat biting into my thigh. I had to choke it, tame it back to quiescence. But how? When? Where?

I went back to my cot, took some writing paper and a stubby pencil from my cigar-box shelf and wrote down the first words that boiled out of my mind. "Bewitching image! I know not how or when or where. I only know *must*. Send me a sign that you share my passion and Eros will find a way. Your impatient—J"

When I looked up El Gordo was watching me. But it may have been only in my mind. His eyes looked past me and then returned to his romantic novel. I folded my note in half, and then in half again, and once again and hid the small square in my pocket. I could feel it burning against my skin like dry ice.

When we were let out for our afternoon *frijoles*, I avoided the serving table and walked impatiently around the courtyard. Everyone I saw was appraised as a possible bearer of my note. By this time I had sealed it into a small envelope I had found in the common room. I glanced at Cookie Gamboa. She would accept it willingly enough. But she would also file it open to enjoy the scandal. Then too, there was her basement liaison with El Gordo. Although he was no longer well enough to enjoy her behind the rocks of the fish bowl, she could easily find some way of telling him. Reencarnación, poor little thing, I could not trust her either. Doctora Julia? I would be ashamed because of Marta. I studied the faces of a dozen others. I didn't know them well enough to speculate on whether or not they would betray me. Then I saw the Señora Lorona waddling among her charges. This huge stuffed duck of a woman, I thought, was stupid and kind. By nature she seemed neither suspicious nor self-serving. In the fat folds of her face her eyes were almost hidden but what you could see of them radiated a motherly warmth and an easy-going default of any wish to reason why.

"Señora Lorona," I said, "as you know, General Romano is indisposed—"

"Yes, yes, I know, the poor gentleman." Her loving nature would have welcomed the fatal caress of a rattlesnake.

"—So he asked me if I would give you this for his Señora."

I produced the small envelope. "He said it was—er—confidential. And urgent."

Her row of good-natured chins nodded in understanding.

"Of course, of course. I will bring it to her immediately. *Pobrecito.*"

"Thank you, Señora," I said. "And since it is a confidential message, we would appreciate it if you did not mention it to anyone."

I had never been an intriguer in the game of adultery but I was learning under pressure.

"I shall deliver it in person," Señora Lorona assured me.

"Speaking for the General, I thank you."

Discreetly, she dropped my small note into the enormous folds of her bosom where I hoped it would not disappear like a pebble in a deep well. I looked around for anyone who might have seen me. I had tried to use her as a bulky shield between myself and the inmates filling their plates at the serving table. But Johnie Valdez was watching us inquisitively. That ferret with his gossip-column curiosity would be wondering what possible business I could have with her.

I sat with Johnie while he picked at his wretched beans. "I was asking Señora Lorona if she had heard from Doctora Julia as to what they had done with Goyo, whether there would be a funeral. I thought we might have a service here in the courtyard."

Goyo would forgive me. He would understand how closely connected are death and desire.

"I hear Bertie says 'nothing doing.' Doesn't want to make too much of the Solano affair. Afraid it might be catching. Or that Angel gets wind of it and thinks the embassy is making heroes of mere fugitives from revolutionary justice."

Although I knew it by heart, I listened to his diatribe until it was time for the ladies to lead the way up the fire escape. I watched Señora Lorona plodding her way up with my note tucked into her corset. Her patient climb looked no different from the same perspiring ascent she had made hundreds of times before. But as she reached the top landing a sense of panic tightened in my throat. I felt like the Spanish explorers going forth into *tierra incógnita*. They would not turn back but they knew that each step forward brought them closer both to terrible danger and exquisite reward.

When I returned to the dormitory I could feel my nerves twitching under my skin. I could not read. I could not sit still. I could not hold normal conversation. I was sensitive to Búfalo's sullen observation. Still I could not resist turning to the window to see if she was waiting for me. She was not. Had my note driven her away? Was it merely an idle flirtation to brighten her hours of imprisonment and speed the wearisome months of waiting? Had I leaped to a foolish and perhaps fatal conclusion? If she were only dallying with me, would she turn my impulsive note over to El Gordo who in turn would pass it on to his executioner? Yes, now I wished I could retrieve it. What a schoolboy of an idiot! And yet, to think of her as merely a chronic coquette who enjoyed leading men on as the matador capes the bull to the pic—no, I could not believe it. The loving messages signaled from window to window! I had to believe her. The nerves were twitching in my eyelids. I believed her. I had no alternative. Except to hang myself in the shower like poor Miguelito Flores.

Dusk was closing in again when Johnie called me over. There was unexpected news about Goyo. Not on the local station or the V.O.A. From Mexico. Obligingly he turned up the volume: after a

stormy session, the Association of Pan American Writers had peti-
tioned Angel Bello to save the life of Gregorio Solano by issuing
safe passage. The wording was sympathetic toward the Bello Revolution. "We Latin writers recognize its value for the cause of
freedom from North American domination. At the same time we
urge Angel as a champion of the new revolutionary spirit in the
Western Hemisphere to allow a preeminent poet like Solano his
freedom to go into exile if he so chooses." It was a clever document.
It permitted our left-wing intellectuals to voice their loyalty to
Angel while at the same time not abandoning their colleague Solano.
There were a few abstentions from Communist poets who refused
to lend their names to any petition that would detract from Angel's
luster as Pan America's most celebrated revolutionary. Still, the
list of names of those underwriting the petition was impressive.
Goyo would have been pleased.

"Too late. Always too late!"

"What's the matter with you, keed?" Johnie asked. "You're as
jumpy as a tomcat with his balls in a ringer."

"I'm sick of hearing people's voices," I said. "Awake and asleep,
people's voices. Your voice, my voice, saying the same damned
things over and over. Your stupid jokes. Loyaza's Communist plati-
tudes. Gamboa's long-playing record. Bertie's bureaucratic drivel.
I have got to get out of here!"

"Take it easy there, pal. You gotta hold on. Down boy! Hokey
dokey?"

"I hate your god damned hokey dokey. I told you I am sick—I am
sick of the sound of the human voice!"

I turned away from him and walked into the common room. It
would be safer there, away from the temptation of the window, away
from the eyes of El Gordo and Búfalo.

I waited for night before I quietly left my cot. But her window
was dark. More and more it seemed as if she were hiding, as if my
indiscretion had terrified her into breaking off our liaison. In despair
I returned to twisting and turning on my cot, so driven by the need
for her now that I feared I would surely cry out her name once

more in my sleep. Many times that night Búfalo's threats invaded my dreams. In a half-waking nightmare he tore the member from my body as it stood there pulsing for his master's wife.

In the morning El Gordo remained on his bed. Evidently he could no longer rise even for short periods. Now the pressures would be greater on everyone: on Angel to pass him through to Miami for proper medical treatment, on His Excellency Don Ernesto to rid his embassy of an invalid, on El Gordo himself to raise the ante so as not to prolong his suffering. So this creeping gout was a threat to my plans. Any moment I might expect Alvarez to burst in with the news of El Gordo's safe passage. Any moment Adriana would be taken from me. My nerves were trembling, threatening me with collapse.

When I found the bathroom door locked and realized that my place had been usurped by Búfalo and Jesusito, I pounded harder than Paco O'Higgins ever had. This was no longer token protest. We had to lead an ordered existence here. There was no other way to survive. Búfalo was transgressing our rules. He was allowed first privileges only as an appendage of El Gordo. But if the master was not with them I was not going to defer to his gorilla. I slammed my fist at the door, not just to knock but to smash through it. I used every foul name I could remember from masters like Paco. In a few moments I could hear the inside latch sliding and Búfalo filled the doorway. He was wearing a soiled blue terry-cloth robe. I grabbed at the front of it and pulled him forward. He swung at me with a curse that roared out of his chest. If we had been far enough apart he would have hurt me, but still holding on to the fold of his robe I was too close to him, inside the arc of his heavy arms flailing at me. I hung onto him as hard as I could and put one leg behind him. I pressed my head and chest forward and as he leaned backward he tripped over my leg and we both fell heavily to the floor of the corridor. Fortunately I was on top. His robe fell open in the fall and when I saw the huge exposed ham of his shoulder I butted my head against it and sunk my teeth in. He let out a hoarse animal howl and butted his head up at me. Like a battering ram it smashed into my nose and I saw white flashes of pain and my nose felt soft and wet. Búfalo was trying to roll over on top of me so he could smash his head into my face from a better angle and I was terrified that one more butt of his head would cave in the bones of my face. I would have given up if he had understood the civilized tactics of surrender. But he would batter or choke out my life if I relaxed for a second. I held on as he began to roll over on top of me, and when he tried to drive the top of his head into my face, I twisted my head as far out of danger as possible and he slammed his forehead with all his might into the metal rim of a cot. I had no idea we had thrashed so close to it. He howled in pain and rage. There was a bloody crease slanting down the middle of his forehead and across the top of his nose. It looked as if the flesh had been torn to the bone and blood leaked down both sides of his flattened nose.

He let go his grip and so did I and in that moment we were pried apart. I was on my feet and Johnie Valdez was dabbing my bloody nose with his handkerchief. Most of the asilados had crowded around. Johnie guided me off while Jesusito led Búfalo away. It seemed as if Búfalo temporarily had been blinded by the collision. I had done nothing except hang on for desperate life. But Johnie and others patted me on the back and called me a hero and I was so relieved to have escaped this lightly that I was ready to believe them.

In the bathroom I had won through our David-Goliath struggle, I quickly sponged off my face. The nosebleed was superficial. The bone felt tender but not broken. When I reappeared in the corridor Momentito and an embassy guard were there. The old valet led Búfalo off to the first-aid room to have his face treated. It was a gory mess and he seemed utterly sobered by his injuries. As a prize-fighter he had had a tendency to quit at the sight of his own blood. Bloodletting excited him until it became his own.

When everyone went in to breakfast I stayed behind again in hope of receiving that signal from Adriana. A long afternoon and night had passed and already we were halfway through the morning. The dormitory was empty except for El Gordo propped up against his pillows waiting for Jesusito to bring him breakfast. He was clearly disregarding my presence. With Búfalo out of my way, I went boldly to the dormer and looked out. The rainy season was coming early this year. The courtyard looked drab and desolate. And Adriana's shade was drawn.

I heard footsteps down the aisle behind me. It was Bertie Alvarez. "Good morning," he said. "I hear you had a little scuffle this morning. Strictly against our regulations, Moreno Suárez. I thought surely you would be our model citizen here. What is happening to you? If this keeps up we may have to put you in the security block."

To soften this threat he put a smile at the end of it. The security block was a locked corridor maintained by the embassy marines with a single barred cell for the offenders.

"Is that what you have come for, to lecture me?"

"I have a letter."

At last, at last! As he reached in his pocket he said, "And more good news. The Bishop is leaving tomorrow. His private room will be free. I cannot move you into it without the Ambassador's authority but as soon as he returns—"

"Yes, yes. Excellent. Thank you." The room. My note. Everything might be coming together.

"From the diplomatic pouch," he said, handing me the envelope.

Immediately I recognized the handwriting of Marta. I mumbled *thank you*, my mind vibrating between the vanished Adriana and the letter in my hand. Alvarez said he would let me know about the Bishop's room. I nodded. He bowed and departed. I sank down on my cot and cracked through a thick seal of wax to loosen the flap. Unusual formality for Marta . . . But the moment I unfolded the letter, her personality burst out at me:

Justo, my fat bear, how are you? I have written you through the regular mail but in Miami they tell me these probably do not reach you.
That *pendejo* of a censor must have some collection! You know how I
am. I try to be discreet. But *cursi* things about all those *pendejos* are
bound to slip through.

Oh but this time I did something very clever. I went into the Bank of
America to cash a check and who should I see at the assistant manager's
desk but Madame de San Martín. She was taking thick rolls of bills out
of a large purse and the manager was counting them and listing them
for her. Without a doubt our money. The fat *mordidas* from us asilados.
The greedy whore. We have heard lots of rumors about this here in this
cursi capital of rumor-mongering—that the Ambassador's wife flies to
Miami every two weeks with her *contrabando*—that they may have a
million dollars salted away here from their big traffic in the misery
business, as we once called it.

She seemed embarrassed for me to find her there. I stalled by going
to a nearby desk and asking another assistant a lot of questions about
loans and then I conveniently got up to leave at the same time she did.
She remembered me of course from the diplomatic dinners and was
very polite and asked if she could give me a lift. I accepted and on the
way I asked her a great favor—whether I could send you a personal
letter through the diplomatic pouch. She said she would do even better
than that. She was flying back to the embassy in two days time and
would take the letter on her person. I will bring it to her tomorrow, at
the Consulate's, with the heavy seal which I hope you have just broken.
I will tell her I have sealed it this way because it is so highly personal
and because we have heard that underlings in the embassy have been
known to open letters to asylees and do their own prying and censoring.
Madame de San Martín will obviously try to do everything she can to
make me forget those stacks of bills at the bank!!!

So, Justo dear, I have made her the messenger of a letter accusing her of being a she-wolf who grows fat and rich on the suffer-
ings of others. When I think of her and the Ambassador with his
noble pleas for humanity, I say piss in the milk of both their mothers!

Of course if that *sinvergüenza* Alvarez should crack the seal, well,
things cannot be much worse than they are right now, can they, *cariño*?
Now—for the news. First of all, Clarita is well. The abortion was easy.
Fortunately, with all the refugee doctors they have good men here. And
psychologically and emotionally, well I could be wrong but she does not
seem as wounded by the whole thing as we would expect. Oh maybe she
is a little tougher now, a little more realistic, but she is still very much
a happy teen-ager, headstrong and impossible but not scarred for life.
Maybe we old elephants romanticize about sex. The fall from virtue still
seems a terrible plunge to us. But these kids no longer think of it as
virtue and they take it in stride. I have a friend here who is terribly

upset because her daughter has taken a *male* roommate at college. She says they don't even claim to love each other. It is simply a more *efficient* way to live. "Marta, what is this generation coming to!" she cries. "Maybe to their senses!" I tell her and she becomes furious. Anyway I have taught Clarita about the pill. She has made many friends here and although she does miss home she seems happier than you would believe. Sixteen-year-olds are really selfish little beasts, whether overprotected or suddenly exposed to oversexed toads like your dear friend Paco. In short, Clarita is fine!

As for Miami, I enjoy the sunshine and daily gossip with my friends, but the place is a swamp of refugee politics that disgusts me. There is a center called the Unified Movement for National Liberation and Social Justice. You know how our people are, always better at thinking up grandiose titles for organizations than at getting them organized. If the Unified Movement is any criterion, Angel Bello will be there for life. The rich old guard Zamoristas are excluded but of course their spies are busy. Nearly all the rest sit around at café headquarters drinking their espressos and denouncing each other. Everybody accuses everybody else of working for the CIA—'working for the Company' they call it. Can you picture 10,000 *chinches* running around in circles reporting on each other—and the self-important busy-bodies of the CIA solemnly recording all the spite and wishful thinking and convincing themselves that they're undermining Angel? What they're really doing is corrupting our people, welfare disguised as political intrigue, they're absolutely brilliant at not being able to understand that the only possible anti-Bello revolution would have to be completely independent of Uncle Sammy's Company Store. In short they've done an excellent job of compromising the few good people left around here.

As you can imagine, I get a big reception as they look on you as a martyr and maybe the one person honest and reasonable and strongly enough identified with the original Revolution to unite all the idiot splinter groups into one effective Resistance movement.

Of course you know me, Justo, I say *tu madre* to all these parties. I say *basta* to politics. One day you and I will get to some quiet place and you can write and I will invent some juicy gossip to relieve the monotony and we will live happily ever after. *Cuando?*

                                                                    Your devoted Marta.

I read the letter several times. I could hear her voice, see her lively gestures. I believed what she said about Clarita. A different style from ours but our daughter was all right, she had come through it. Maybe Marta's toughness was in her all the time but had not proved itself until need called it to the surface.

I thought of that refugee *centro* teeming with conflicting parties,

ideas, slogans, leaders and would-be leaders. And of the farce that
I could unite them into a meaningful force for social justice. How
could I unify contentious ideologies when I could no longer unify
my own? And not just my ideologies, my emotions. One part of me
was plunged into guilt by that letter. But another was more selfish,
more driven, more primitive. I loved Marta, but her letter was not
going to cheat me of Adriana. Yes, that is what they were trying to
do, all of them. Marta, El Gordo, Alvarez, Johnie Valdez, the Ambassador, all of them!

I was sitting on the cot in a kind of daze, in that nether world
that Goyo had described, as if I had consumed his mushrooms and
their hallucinatory images were beginning to possess me.

I looked across at her window and waited. With all my pent-up
energy I concentrated on what I wanted her to do. Moments later
the window shade slowly rose. Like Duse revealed at curtain-rise
Adriana was centered in the window. How exquisite she looked! In
her right hand she was holding my note. Her other hand was at her
breast holding together an ivory lace shawl that flowed from her
shoulders. Oh God, to leap the space from window to window! She
touched the note to her lips and blew the kiss across it. Then, without taking her eyes from me, she softly caressed it with her cheek.
For a few moments we looked at each other, savoring the intrigue.
Then she pulled the shade down again. Why? To dress, to sleep
again, to caress herself? To taunt me? Desire was rabid and would
not let me rest.

I flung myself on my cot and ran my fingers over the letter from
Marta as if to reread it by touch. But I quickly folded it and buried
it in the pages of Martí. Now that Adriana had given her consent I
had no emotion, no mind for anything but to find the scheme that
would bring us together.

The Bishop's room was the answer. But how to get her there? And
if she chanced it, how to keep the bees in this hive of an embassy
from finding out?

Out in the yard, under an overcast sky, eating sparingly of our
beans and rice, I was joined by Johnie Valdez.

"Well, I see you finally got a letter from the old lady."

"How did you know that?"

"You were sitting on your cot reading it when I came back to the dormitory. Who else would write you such a long one?" He tapped his temple with a knowing grin. "Am I right or am I right?"

I nodded, annoyed, but trying to be pleasant. "You watch human beings, Johnie, the way some people watch birds. Only I am not so sure your motives are as pure. Even here without a column—the Walter Winchell of the world of *frijoles*."

Johnie seemed to take it as a compliment. "Don't forget, when you're raised in an orphanage like the Niños de Valdez, you have a thousand little brothers and sisters. You can't help watching them, you get more and more curious. It becomes second nature, no?"

I picked at my rice. If not the Bishop's room . . . there had to be a way.

Johnie snapped his fingers in front of my face.

"So, what is the latest news in Miami?"

I tried to bring my mind back from Adriana.

"Just you wait, Señor Presidente," he was saying. "We might even put you back in office again."

"No, thank you."

"Are you kidding? Then who would you pick as the leader of the opposition?"

I shrugged. "Who knows. Maybe Angel."

"Holy cow, Justo. Now you're beginning to talk cuckoo. I'm serious about this and you make jokes."

"Jokes? I—" I had to put my mind together. Maybe this kind of concentration could still save me from my obsession. "I—only half-joke. Give me a minute, Johnie, let me think this out. The opposition —it will be split twenty ways, as usual. The CIA will be backing the right wing. The real hope will be the students, the young *rebeldes*. But if the extremists push them too far they'll be divided, undermined. So, in all that confusion, maybe I would back Angel—even knowing his faults. Yes, our people still seem to need heroes, rallying points, *macho* leaders. If—if only we could get him to lead by persuasion instead of force. That's what I tried to do and—maybe I don't make much sense, defecting and still half-supporting him, but—"

Johnie stared at me. "In other words, you are changing your mind?"

"No, I defected from the authoritarian Angel. But I still prefer him to the Zamoras."

"You do? I am amazed. How can you choose one tyrant over another?"

"Zamora was a tyrant of greed backed by American business. Angel is a tyrant of hope, a true revolutionist being used by the Communists. But using them, too."

"Fantastic! After all, you have lost your freedom because of Angel, not Zamora."

"This time," I said. "But if I had to choose I would rather sacrifice my freedom for Angel—"

"Wow! You must have been smoking grass in the yard! If Miami could hear you now!"

It wasn't grass. It was like flexing an old muscle.

"I love freedom, but if I have to lose it I would rather lose it to the tyranny of the future than to the tyranny of the past. At least the one that looks forward has more hope of softening—"

"Well, I will go down the line fighting Angel," Johnie said. "Everyday, yeh and twice on Sunday because I was raised a good Catholic."

I was relieved when Momentito called us together for the climb up the fire escape. I suppose I had been crystallizing a new approach to my relationship to the Bello regime for a long time although I had not been thinking about it consciously. Idly I wondered if captivity was softening my brain or sharpening my insight.

I had only been back in the dormitory a few minutes when Momentito came to tell me that the Bishop would like to see me in his room. A private farewell. He would be leaving in the morning.

I was eager to see the room again. I remembered it from my farewell visit with Marta that seemed so long ago, but now I would reappraise it for another purpose. I told Momentito I would go with him at once. He seemed pleased. As Catholics, the men of our country were mostly backsliders but Momentito belonged to a generation and caste far more pious. He took it as a sign of respect that I was so ready to accept the Bishop's invitation.

At the Bishop's door, Momentito said that Alvarez would call for me in twenty minutes. Then he knocked respectfully. When the Bishop appeared, Momentito murmured, "Your Holiness, at your service," and backed away in awe.

"Come in, come in, my dear Moreno Suárez," the Bishop said. He was wearing his black cassock with an ornate cross hanging almost to his waist. He bowed me to the one easy chair and seated himself on a straight-backed one turned away from his desk.

Then he leaned forward to offer me a cigarette from a thin gold case.

He was a fat man who moved with the elegance of a thin man. He spoke with a Castilian lisp. His manners were polished but there was something democratic about him, as if he had been lowborn but well trained in the ways of the aristocracy.

I waved away the cigarette. "No thank you, I only smoke cigars. Or I should say, I used to."

He took a cigarette himself and lit it from a gold lighter that matched the case. That was the trouble with the Church, they always have their hands on gold. At the same time I was savoring the room, the wide bed with its carved headboard, the ornate armoire with its full-length mirror. Adriana was resting against the headboard, watching her undulating body in the glass. The ideal room if only we could find our way to it.

The Bishop wanted to talk man to man, heart to heart, soul to soul and I—that imposing silver-and-ebony crucifix on the wall over the headboard—would he take it with him?

"I must apologize for not visiting with you earlier," he was saying. "Usually I am not such a recluse. But my ulcer has been giving me great pain. Rather an embarrassing affliction for a religious who is supposed to enjoy inner peace. And yet, we are men. That is our difficulty. A good priest cannot be less than a man. But if he is not more, if he cannot rise above his human limitations—" He gave a deep, expressive shrug and inhaled his cigarette.

I looked at the small private altar set up in the far corner. A delicate Christ-figure carved from olive wood stared down at us. The altar was flanked by slender silver candlesticks and a narrow vase held white blossoms. I was wondering if the altar would be dismantled when he left, and if not, would its presence disturb Adriana? I didn't know how deep her Catholicism ran and I remembered years ago making love to a pious Catholic lady unable to commit adultery until the crucifix over the bed had been removed.

"—meditation, self-appraisal, in fact reappraisal of our Church," the voice of the Bishop called me back. "I ask myself, who comes to our Church? To answer truthfully, mostly ladies. In the country perhaps a few of the old campesinos. We are not a part of the whole life of the people. And then I must also ask myself, yes, and who are our priests? Eight out of ten are Spanish. I love my Spain but I must admit that the Spanish Church is the most narrow of them all. A new wind is blowing but we do not open the windows to let it in. Instead of Spanish priests whose minds are still in the middle ages we need young priests with close ties to the people here. And so, my dear Moreno Suárez, it is time that I move on. When the winds began to blow I could feel them but I was not ready to take full advantage of them. My own mind was still too cluttered with conventional attitudes. With the traditions of the Church. I forgot that one of our noblest traditions is the ability to recognize social change."

I nodded. "Not recognize—enhance it, Excellency. More priests like Carmelo Torres. Modern Martís."

There was a time when I would have welcomed this talk. But now I was too conscious of the thick wool rug by the side of the bed, the perfumed votive candles on the end tables, the door to the private bathroom. What luxury. I would be lying on the bed waiting impatiently for Adriana to appear with that long ivory lace shawl around her shoulders.

"When I go to Mexico I will not live in the city," the Bishop continued. "I will go to a small *ranchero* outside of Cuernavaca where I can talk to the ragged followers of Zapata. All over the Latin world we have lost the manpower of the Church and we can only reclaim it by going to the poor and identifying ourselves with them as Pope John had begun to do. Carmelo Torres may have gone too far— actually joining the guerrillas. But we do need priests whose hearts reach out to our Indians who cannot hold a dance or set foot off the *latifundio* without the permission of the landlord. What kind of Catholics, my friend, are those feudal lords who still hold the power of life and death over their serfs? And what kind of Catholics are those human beasts of burden? Now when I pray, I ask for the insight and the courage I did not have in sufficiency to reach the hearts of the people in my Bishopry as Angel Bello reached them. For let us not delude ourselves, he reached them and he moved them as our Church was unable to do because it was so inextricably bound up with the feudal system."

As he tapped his cigarette into the ashtray, I became aware of the elegant sapphire ring on his finger. I wondered, when he turned his Church upside down and his spirituality inside out, would he also divest himself of his gold accouterments and his precious stones?

"And now, I must write some farewell letters and pack—the few things they allow me to take with me. I hope you will soon follow me out of this bureaucratic limbo." He rose. He did not quite offer me his ring to kiss. But somehow the gesture was suggested in that moment between us. "I hope you will come to see me in Mexico. In the solitude of my small ranch I shall be working on specific programs to free our people from their bondage on the plantations and in our unspeakable slums."

"Yes, yes," I said. "Success to your programs, Your Holiness."

"Until we see each other again, go with God," the Bishop said.

We both felt better. I had appraised the room and the Bishop had appeased his conscience.

Waiting for me in the corridor was Alvarez who had just returned from a conversation with Elena Concepción. She had come to the embassy for a personal visit with the Ambassador, and she hoped to see me alone for a few minutes, if I were willing.

"This would be a very special privilege," Alvarez emphasized. "The Ambassador has asked me to arrange it in my private office, if you wish me to. Of course as a certified asylee you are under no obligation to meet with any representative of the territorial state either officially or unofficially. In fact it is our sworn duty to protect you from such intercession. The decision is up to you."

Elena Concepción! The sound of her name stirred emotions long forgotten: yes, I said, yes, I would see her. The more I thought about it the more curious I became. After all this time why would she seek me out? Angel never did anything without a revolutionary purpose, even if that purpose changed from day to day. And Elena never did anything contrary to Angel's purpose. Unless—unless? I had been out of touch for such a long time now. Perhaps even the ruthful Elena Concepción had become disillusioned. Ready to follow us into sanctuary. No, I was dreaming. Elena would follow her knight to the bitter or glorious end.

How early would I be able to see her? As soon as she had concluded her visit with the Ambassador, Alvarez would come back for me.

"And about this room of the Bishop's, Alvarez? Will it be possible to move down here when he leaves tomorrow?"

"There is a complication," Alvarez said. "We may have to assign it to General Romano because his affliction is becoming so serious. The Señora de Romano could move in with him to help attend to him. Then Doctora Julia would be able to have the Señora's room. She has been doing a great deal of medical work among the women and needs some privacy."

"But Alvarez, only this morning you told me—"

"Nothing has been decided yet. I will have to discuss it with his Excellency Don Ernesto when he has time for me. It may take another few days."

Another few days, I thought, or another few pesos? The old *mordida* game of playing one against the other. As I passed through the dormitory I kept my eyes on the floor. I sat on my cot in a sweat of anxiety and waited to be summoned for my rendezvous with Elena Concepción.

23

Elena was already there, seated in a black leather chair near the desk when Alvarez led me into his office. She rose and shook my hand rather formally, her gray woolen dress and jacket reinforcing my instant impression that she had aged. Her hair was tucked into a bun, without the style she had shown in earlier days. How attractive and spirited she had seemed when last we saw her at the beach house in her black riding attire, sharp-brimmed Andalusian hat and ruffled shirt. Now the effect was that of no longer caring how she looked—no, not quite that—more practical, businesslike, grave.

Her handshake was firm, a grasp that said "Soldier first, woman second." Joan of Arc might have removed the glove of her sword hand and shaken hands like that.

For a moment or two there was an awkward pause as we sat silently appraising each other.

"Well, I must say this is a surprise. A pleasant surprise," I said. "How have you been, Elenita?"

"As usual, very busy." Her face softened in a worn smile. "Angel has more to do than ever before. Nothing seems to work if he does not attend to it himself. He goes flying all over the country day and night. The more I follow Angel, dear Justo, the more amazing I find him. You may not agree but I have a feeling that history will see him as, well, what Bolívar was to his time, Angel will be to ours."

"Yes, yes, perhaps," I said, not only to be polite. The mind of Bolívar was finer but when the smoke of battle blew away perhaps the force of Angel Bello would prove more persuasive. I was still of two minds, that glorious if fatal flaw of democratic socialists. But I was in no mood for a philosophical appraisal of the Bello regime—it all seemed idle speculation, a wearisome and pointless luxury. I thought only of myself and what I most wanted. Elena Concepción was my remaining link with the Revolution and she might hold the key to the forbidden door.

"I did not come here only to sing the praises of Angel," Elena was saying. "Even though I believe he is the one man who can make this Revolution work. And it is working, Justo, for the simple reason that the people trust Angel. Whatever he decides is right—they love him. It is as simple as that."

"Yes," I agreed, "it is amazing how he holds the country together. But—if he should die—a downdraft, as he flies too low over the mountains one night—that is always the trouble with one-man governments—even the best of them, Elena. And I am willing to concede that Angel's may be one of those. A benevolent dictatorship in which the Man, the Party, the Revolution, the People are all wrapped up in one heroic package. I am for it, in many ways I am for it, only God help us if the One True Leader explodes into dust. And meanwhile, God help those who get in his way."

At my suggestion that Angel might not be as immortal as he appeared, Elena had crossed herself. "I believe that Angel will live to be ninety-nine," she insisted. "He has already died a thousand deaths and survived through a thousand miracles. Even now he has many enemies, but see how he walks through the crowds unafraid. Although he denies God, God watches over him. I am a very timid person, but when I am at his side I am not afraid either. That is the most important thing about Angel, Justo, not all those political theories you worry about."

"Perhaps you are right." I found it surprisingly easy to bow to her evangelism. "In our world there has never been such a force for change—not since Bolívar. I do not deny his greatness, Elena. His wisdom sometimes, but not his effectiveness."

"And he admires you also, Justo—and misses you. You would be surprised. He is more forgiving than you realize. I have never heard him speak unkindly about you."

She looked straight into my eyes, in that ingratiating way she had, her eyes so open that they insisted on being trusted.

A dear girl, Elena. But she would not visit me without Angel's permission. Whatever he's after, I must turn it to advantage.

"Elena, tell me. There is something specific you came here to tell me?"

"Justo, you know that one of Angel's strongest qualities is his intuition. Well, somehow he has got it into his head that you may have begun to have second thoughts about your defection."

"I did not defect. I was hounded, virtually arrested."

"Well, whatever. Angel has heard that you may regret your present position. Enough to—"

"Has heard?"

"—with his mind. His intuition. Is it true, Justo? That you have begun to have second thoughts?"

What game were they playing with me now? I must not think of Elena as an old friend but as an agent of Angel's Intelligence. What service could I provide for them? And if I should agree to it, what price could I extract? Was it possible that Angel wanted me to return to his government? Was some spectacular change of political direction in the wind? Or was he preparing himself to grant my safe passage on the theory that my political will was broken and I no longer constituted any threat? In that case, Elena might have been sent ahead to check my state of mind. More than at any moment in my life I needed to think clearly. And that was impossible with my mind clouded with lust.

"The truth is, Elena, I am tired. I am no longer political. Whether I come back to Angel or go to Mexico—no importa. At heart I am a scholar, a teacher. No more Parties for me. No more programs. All colors look black in the dark, and that is how I feel, in darkness. I cannot see white or red or green any more. I just want to be left in peace. Wherever I am, in peace."

She sighed and reached out as if to take my hand, then apparently thought better of it.

"We are not so different, Justo. I don't care a fig about Moscow or Peking. In the long run I still do not think they will decide what is done here. This is still Angel's Revolution, no matter how many times he calls on Marx and Lenin. I never read them. I just read Angel's face. That is all the Revolution I need to follow. I have faith that he will come back to the humanistic Revolution you supported. Because that is the true, inner Angel. The rest is just—expediency."

"You may be right. I hope you are."

"And if the government should decide to do a great favor for you, you would promise not to let yourself be drawn into any political action against the Revolution?"

I looked at her steadily. "Anyone can make a promise today and forget it tomorrow. But you know me. Is that not better than a promise? I did not wish to be President of the Revolution, Elena, any more than I wish to be President of the Anti-Revolution. Is that enough?"

"Only Angel can answer that. Ambassador de San Martín is giving a diplomatic dinner for him this evening. I've come early to see that everything is in order. Perhaps you would like to talk to Angel himself. I could bring him here while the guests are having after-dinner coffee. Together you may come to some agreement. If there are—certain things you want—you may be able to scrub each other's backs."

"Perhaps. It's been a long time. In sanctuary you—"

"Begin to starve. For everything."

I stared at her. What did she mean? What could she know?

"In sanctuary it is mostly the boredom," I replied. "Like prison, only worse. Without safe passage we are trapped up there like dying tomcats."

Elena rose. "I understand. I sympathize, Justo. And so will Angel, believe me."

There was a knock on the door. Alvarez. Had he been listening? His interruption seemed almost too opportune.

Elena leaned over and kissed me gracefully on both cheeks.

"I must go. Angel is flying back from Ocampo where he dedicated a new secondary school this afternoon."

"Isn't there a peasant rebellion in Ocampo? The Arawaks?"

Elena shook her head loyally. "You must not believe what you hear on the Voice of America. The campesinos always mob Angel

when he goes to their villages. I wish you could see it with your
own eyes, Justo. Well, after tonight, maybe you will. Maybe you
will come back to us. In any case it is good to see you again, Justo
dear. Go well. *Adiós*."

Long after darkness had administered its temporary opium to my
cell-mates, I could find no comfort in my narrow cot. Again and
again I reviewed my conversation with Elena. What she had said.
What I had said. What she had not said. A flash. My turn for
intuition. She had not mentioned Marta. Not asked how Marta
was, or if I had heard from her. Strange, unnatural, unless—she
knew—about Adriana—and did not want to embarrass me. But
what could she know? And what gave Angel his "intuition" that I
was changing my mind, that I was reassessing my opinion of the
regime? With whom had I discussed this? In whom had I planted
the seed of my possible turn of mind?

When it struck me, it came like a hurricane, uprooting trees in
my mind and tearing down fences. Of course. Marta would have detected this human booby trap long before. There had to be a spy
reporting back to Juan del Campo and the successors to El Gordo's
Tigers. Of course!

Duplicity came hard to me. As part of the anti-Zamora underground I had had to be suspiciously selective in whom to confide.
The conspiratorial life was a necessary evil of our time. But it had
rubbed against my nature. Some men, like Garbo, reveled in it. It
was their way of life. It must also be true of second-rate intriguers
like Johnie.

Carried forward in a frenzy, but without knowing what I was
going to do, I went up the aisle until I leaned over his cot. In the
darkness I could sense that normally frenetic body now dormant
like an unplugged wire. His legs were drawn up and his head pulled
into the folds of his blanket.

"Johnie."

He stirred. "Mmm, yeh?"

"Johnie Valdez."

"Yeh? Yeh? Oh . . . Justo? What—what can I do you for?"

"You already did me for, Johnie. You make me sick."

"Hey, Justo, down boy! You been having nightmares or something?"

"You are the nightmare. Nothing but a lousy plant. An informer. A *chivato* bleating your weekly reports to the secret police."

"No, no, Justo, please, you are dreaming."

"Chivato!" I raised my voice. "Spying on me. Only with you did
I discuss anything about Angel. But Elena Concepción has heard
it. How? From you. From you!"

Johnie was sitting up now, fending off what he feared might be
a physical attack. "Justo, stop, you and I are together!" The dormitory had become aroused, at first with only the usual Shhh's and rude
comments about disturbers of sleep. But when in answer to the
shouted question, "What in the name of Christ is going on?" I said
I had caught a *chivato*, the atmosphere changed. Zamora's *chivatos*
had sent thousands to the torture chambers. It was the *chivatos* who
were literally torn apart or rushed to the wall in the first days of the
Angelista regime when the victor appropriated the methods of
the vanquished and the persecuted became the persecutors.

Our lights had been turned off for the night. Some with candles
and a few with flashlights moved forward until they formed a circle
pressing in on Johnie. "You're sure he's a spy? Johnie?" He was
sitting up with his back against the wall and his arms clasped tightly
around his knees. "Who needs a fucking *chivato* in here?" His eyes
darted from candle to candle. "String him up in the bathroom!"

Some began laying hands on him. Johnie pressed himself against
the wall. "No, no, I am no *chivato*, I am innocent!"

Búfalo lumbered across the aisle to join the attack.

"*Hijo de puta*, it was you who asked my General about anonymous accounts in Jamaica!"

"No, no. Búfalo, please I am inno—"

"Angel thinks he's got money hidden there," Búfalo cut him off. "That's why they won't let us out, *hijo!* And you were trying to—"

"In the name of the Holy Virgin—" Johnie cried out.

"—in the milk of the Holy Virgin!"

Búfalo closed his huge hands around Johnie's neck, "There is only one way to get the truth out of you, you whore. Choke it out!"

Johnie was gagging and at the same time making a desperate effort to twist his head and bite Búfalo's fingers. "Pull him off!" I shouted, "help me pull him off!" Many hands joined mine in prying Búfalo loose. Johnie was gasping and rubbing his neck.

"Now listen to me, all of you." I called out through a wave of nausea that swept over me, sickness at their bestiality. "I made the accusation. But why did we overthrow Zamora and the Tigers if not to get rid of cruelty?" I had to raise my voice louder to be heard. "No matter what I think of Johnie, he must have a hearing instead of being rushed to the wall. Give him a trial!"

Except for the handful of Zamoristas, the asilados welcomed the idea. A trial. A fair trial. Better than a fight at the bathroom door to break the monotony. Even my cantankerous old cot-neighbor Rubén Silva warmed to the trial. He had come down the aisle in his long nightshirt. "Why don't you be the judge, Señor Socialist President? After all, you were so fair in the Bello case that you let the bastard go."

"I'd do it again!"

"Even if the result is to throw you into this dungeon of an attic?"

"That has nothing to do with it. A principle was involved!"

"Moreno Suárez," the Death-head said, now lowering his voice with an attempt at dignity, "you are obviously a lunatic. Which is one good reason why you should serve as judge of this lunatic trial."

"No, I disqualify myself—since I press the charges."

"Ah, such democratic purity," the Death-head said, "from the man who helped the man who transformed our country into a Communist prison."

"Stick to the trial," I said. "I accuse Johnie Valdez as a plant in this sanctuary for the Bello regime. I will prosecute the case and also take the stand as a material witness."

"Then I will defend him," Silva said. "When he wrote for my magazine I knew him as a liar, a blackmailer and an habitual padder of expense accounts—in other words a fairly typical *capitalino* newspaperman. But a paid informer for Angel Bello—I challenge you to prove it."

A judge was chosen who had organized a group of lawyers to demand that Zamora restore our Constitution. He had been jailed for his zeal. When Angel freed all the political prisoners, this man, Licenciado Mora, had become a Deputy Minister of Justice. But the vulgarity and brutality of the mass trials had prompted him to resign and to circulate a petition of lawyers against the one-day show trials and instant executions. Then he had dropped out of sight until granted asylum here a few weeks ago. Yes, I agreed, Licenciado Mora was the ideal man for the job. Since he had not been involved for long in the day-to-day struggles of sanctuary life, he might lend some objectivity to these highly charged proceedings.

For the jury, I suggested that everyone in the dormitory write down twelve names. The twelve with the most votes would weigh the case. Licenciado Mora, a grave, gray-haired man with thick glasses who had spent his first days quietly playing dominoes or reading, suggested twenty-four jurors, whom Rubén Silva and I could cross-examine, each having the right of six dismissals.

Most were for plunging into the trial immediately. A kind of midnight diversion. But Mora thought otherwise. "My friends, the hour is late. I suggest tomorrow morning in the common room after breakfast. That will give the defendant a reasonable amount of time to consult with his counsel. It will also provide the prosecution more time to present his charges in an orderly manner. And in addition, a trial by candlelight strikes the court as rather melodramatic."

I asked Johnie if this was agreeable to him. His voice came in a whisper. "Yes. My President. Hokey dokey."

I wondered out loud if the Zamoristas among us who had brutally murdered our Constitution should be entitled to take part in this democratic experiment. "I would vote that they be disqualified."

This led to an angry rebuttal from El Gordo. He had heard enough nonsense since he had been cooped up with me here. It was the lousy Communists who should be disqualified and no matter what my reasons for taking sanctuary he still considered me a dirty Red. "So is Mora, and you Moscow agents aren't going to set up subversive political machinery in my dormitory. If this worm is an informer then Búfalo and I will take care of him like real *machos*, not like you Communist fairies."

"You don't mean *machos*, you mean fascists," I shouted back, and the expedient political truce that had kept us in delicate balance so long had broken down at last.

"I am no fascist, I am a patriot," El Gordo was shouting. "And another thing, you keep your eyes away from my wife or this won't be a trial, it will be a pig-sticking."

The coarse laughter and loud voices were interrupted by the opening of the door. The lights came on and Licenciado Alvarez was in our midst.

"What is going on here, gentlemen? The Ambassador can hear you at his dinner party. What is all this shouting about a trial?"

I told him about Johnie and our plans to deal with him in a civilized manner. Alvarez shook his head at us like a disapproving proctor with wayward boarders.

"You should know better, Moreno Suárez. I should not have to remind you that once you take refuge here you are in our country. Only a body under *our* jurisdiction can decide whether any asylee has broken *our* rules of asylum. What you should do, if you wish to make charges, is to present a petition through me to the Ambassador. Only the Ambassador can resolve your questions. Do I make myself clear?"

He turned to Johnie, who still held himself in fear against the wall. "Señor Valdez, tomorrow morning I will bring you down for preliminary questioning. Then I will make my report to His Excellency Don Ernesto. Meanwhile"—Alvarez raised his voice—"if any asylee dares to lay a hand on this man he will be turned over to our security marines. Remember, by the same right that we have certified you for political asylum, we can also rescind that privilege." A hush fell on the dormitory. One could almost smell the fear of being

dragged to the front gates of the embassy compound and pushed out
into the hands of the waiting militia.

Alvarez turned back to me. "It seems you are becoming our
principal troublemaker, Moreno Suárez. I think I will take you along
with me and let you see the inside of one of our security cells. Will
you come along peacefully? Or shall I summon our marine guards?"

"Peacefully, by all means. I am a man of peace."

"Who constantly involves himself in violent arguments," Alvarez
observed.

"You are describing the condition of modern man, my friend."

"Enough, no more discussion, you have already interrupted my
evening long enough. Now come along."

"All right, let me get my toothbrush and—"

"You won't need them. If you are not back for morning toilette,
Momentito will bring you what you need. Vámonos."

I glanced back at Johnie. It was disquieting to see a human being
so transformed by fear. Jaunty Johnie with his "What can I do
you for?"

He spoke to me in a hoarse whisper. "Take it easy, keed. And
Justo—I am innocent. I swear it on my sainted mother."

I wanted to say, "Your sainted mother was a whore" but now I
could not. "All right, Johnie, we will see what we will see. Adiós."

"Abyssinia." I must say this for him: Johnie tried to smile.

Outside the common-room door, Bertie Alvarez immediately confided in me. "Colonel Bello has come. He's dining with the Ambassador and he would like to see you privately before he leaves."

"And for that you threaten me with marine guards!"

"Calm yourself, my friend. You are getting too nervous."

"Calm myself? In this madhouse?"

"It is only a madhouse to the mad, Señor."

He smiled in his superior fashion. I could feel rage rising in me,
but I realized if ever there was a time to "calm myself," it was now.

On the second floor, Alvarez led me down the hall to a side wing
I had never seen before. A uniformed marine was on duty at a desk
in front of a barred door. Alvarez ordered him to unlock the door
and then bowed me into a narrow corridor. Another marine was on
duty inside. There were two small empty cells. The guard unlocked

the door of the first one and I was ushered in. There was a cot attached to the wall, and a small wooden chair. The walls were dark brown stucco.

"You are not being punished," Alvarez reassured me. "It would arouse too much curiosity if your bed-mates upstairs thought you were coming down to meet the Colonel. This way they are content to think that I am putting you in solitary for the night."

"What do you mean, *think*? You are."

"The cell door will be left unlocked. This is only for your own convenience. To the guards it will seem as if we had to isolate you from your fellow-asylees because you have changed your mind and now want to return to the fold."

"Is that what Johnie told them?"

Alvarez shrugged expressively. "If I say 'yes' or 'no' what does it matter? All that matters now is that you and Colonel Bello will talk together. What happens then is up to you."

I studied him. He was such a well-oiled little cog in the terrible machinery of sanctuary. He stepped back from the door and shut the bars in my face.

"Remember, you are not a prisoner. Try to rest, relax. If you need anything, call the guard. I will be back for you as soon as possible."

I paced for a while and then I lay on the cot and simply waited. Or rather, I tried simply to wait. It was impossible to sleep. Or was I already sleeping and dreaming? To be lying in a cell, a small cubic cut into nowhere's land waiting to talk with an inspired madman I had been so sure I would never meet again. And all the while Adriana was with me in sensual insistence. On the cot, several inches too short for me, I could feel her elegant breasts brushing across my face and teasing me with their nipples. The centers were large and erect, so real that they no longer seemed symbols of fantasy—I could feel them. Goyo's words flashed like warning lights in the darkness: *Oh, so you think I am mad, my dear one? But obsessions are also madness. Obsession is . . . madness.* How could I exorcise it except by heading directly into the eye of the hurricane, by quelling and killing it as the planes of the hurricane fighters will one day put an end to tempest by pouring their chemicals into its vortex? Yes, into the vortex and through the vortex to sanity again.

I caught her and it was no longer a game but a battle, the unceasing battle of life in love with death and through that intermingled double-death to life again.

Adriana, Aphrodite in Sanctuary, open yourself to me, ah yes, yes . . . yes.

We were rocking together in the warm depth of the tropical sea when I heard a voice from the shore, "Moreno Suárez, Moreno Suárez, are you awake? Colonel Bello is on his way up from the drawing room. Come along. I will show you the way."

25

In his office Alvarez said, "The Colonel should be here in a few minutes. Help yourself." Left alone with a bottle of Rémy Martin and two brandy snifters on a silver tray, I poured some cognac. It seemed very strong and burned into my nostrils. I had not held such a glass for a long time. The cognac made me sad. I savored it nostalgically, the fumes carrying me back to my book-lined den, to Dolores and her litter scattered in confusion, to the old servants I had abandoned. Their names, at the low tide of memory—Don Pepe, yes, and María Magdalena. I felt tears in my eyes for the house at Papagayos, the children, pets, birds, the flowering trees. I felt old and tired. I was trembling inside. I had to escape. Out of here. To Adriana.

The door opened and Angel bounded into the room. No announcement. No Little Green Angels carelessly swinging their automatics. The First Colonel alone. It was a formal dinner but he was still wearing his dirt-brown guerrilla uniform. Only he did look somewhat changed, more civilized, his hair cut, his beard trimmed. He had aged, or matured, the lines spreading from his eyes and around his mouth seemed deeper.

But his energy filled the room as it always had, and his warmth, when he wanted it to. He was holding a glass he had brought from the library below and puffing on a zeppelin of a cigar. He put them both down with a shout of animal delight at seeing me again. He embraced me and pounded me on the back.

"*Hola!* So how goes it, compañero? You know I miss you, you old *leoncito!*"

From the inside pocket of his tunic he handed me one of his cigars, and as soon as I had bitten off the end, held his against it to give me a light. Not in a single gesture or tone of voice did he reflect the man who had charged me with espionage, shouted denunciations and threats, and denied me safe passage. I found myself drawn to him. The greatest actor in the world could not simulate this spontaneous display of affection.

"Well Justo, what do you think of our Revolution now?" he began, as if continuing a congenial discussion from the night before. In fact this deep-rooted optimism, this contagious enthusiasm was an overpowering political force. His most important decisions could prove to be fiascos, but Angel Bello had the amazing capacity for transforming material defeats into moral victories. If the rice and coffee crops had disastrous seasons on the state farms, if industrialization became a tragic farce of mismanagement and miscalculation, it did not prove that Angel and his Revolution were wrong but only that they had to struggle more heroically against the enemies in their midst, the bourgeois-minded farmers and the formula-ridden bureaucrats. This super-confidence convinced the people that here was a leader who could do no wrong. Bolívar had been flawed or humanized by self-doubt. Bello went rolling along like a laughing river. It was a frightening but magnetic quality.

Characteristically, he would ask a question and answer it himself:

"Why are we riding higher than ever? We are riding higher than ever because the gringos thought their blockade would stop us—so we trade with everybody else, not just the Communists, but England, France, Canada, the entire world!"

I sipped my brandy, waiting to discover where this was leading. He gave the impression of a haphazard, compulsive talker, but

there was always a method to his long-windedness. The room filled
with the smoke of our cigars.

"And you cry-babies think the Communist Party will swallow
me up?" He laughed. "So what happens? I swallow them up. First
your companion upstairs, Comrade Loyaza. Now I am putting four
of the old-time Party chiefs on trial. That will give the Kremlin
something to chew on."

I leaned forward. "An honest trial, Angel?"

Angel nodded vigorously. "Fairer than the ones we used to get
from those fat-bellied Zamora judges! Anyway, the point is, I may
call myself a Marxist but no International tells me what to do. I am
not even sending a delegation to the Communist Congress in War-
saw. And we are shipping the last of the Soviet soldiers back to
Moscow this week. So you see, Justo old cock, maybe you jump to
conclusions too fast. Maybe now, as an honest nationalist, you
change your mind and come back to us, eh?"

"Is that what you came to ask me?"

Angel drained his glass as if he were thirsty and the cognac was
water.

"Actually I came to do you a very special favor."

"Safe passage?"

"Call it—a variation. Look, amigo, I hear you have been growing
very *macho* here in the dormitory. You have found a *mango de
manila* that you would like to eat for breakfast, eh Justo? You old
leoncito! And maybe for lunch and dinner and a midnight supper,
eh? Eh?" He leaned forward and slapped me energetically just above
my knee, so hard that I felt a sting of pain. Then he leaned back in
his chair and indulged himself in loud laughter, his own best
audience. His big hand sponged his whole face, wiping away the
tears of enjoyment.

"There is no lust like an old lust, is there Justo?"

He filled my brandy glass. He was deliberately creating an inti-
macy between us, like a college roommate confiding vicarious passions. I could feel Adriana on my skin. The smell of her rose from
the glass. Fearing vertigo, I forced myself to rise and take a few
steps, in search of reason. But there was only one cure for my
madness—Adriana.

"Well, now—" The sound of his hands clapping together helped

me hear him more clearly. "—what shall we do about it?" Angel
was enjoying himself. "What would you say to a beautiful villa on
Lago Escondido? If you agree, I have arranged for you and the lady
to be driven there after midnight. You will have the villa to yourselves."

To ourselves. Before I could say anything, his voice went on as-
saulting me, persuading me from all corners of the room.

"A man has only so many dreams in his life, Justo, only so many
passions. God is very stingy when he hands them out. So when you
have one in your hand, or almost in your hand, you seize it, Justo,
if you are a man, if you are a real *macho* like the *macho* giants we
grow in our country, then you seize it, *compañero*, you lay your
mango down in the sweetest way you know and you fuck her like a
bull." His head went back and he laughed again. "I'll let you in on a
little secret, Justo. She wants it as much as you do."

Adriana, the fumes of the brandy, the villa to ourselves, all whir-
ring in my head, like the last fevered moments of a dream that
prompts awakening.

"Why, Angel? Why do you offer me this?"

But he was talking again: "And then when you feel like a new
man, when you have showered and dressed with new clothes we will
provide for you, not these rags you have on now, then we will take
your lady back to the embassy. That fascist *cabrón* will never know
she has been away on her little holiday." Angel's voice came to me
through the cigar smoke like the hypnotic words of Goyo's *bruja*.
"You will be on your way to the television station. Elenita herself will
interview you. And you can tell your people what you now believe,
that you have changed your mind, that you regret the unfortunate
words you spoke to the English journalist and that you salute the
Revolution as the first great victory in the inevitable struggle between
American imperialism and our people."

"And then? Angel, what happens to me then?"

Angel shrugged good-naturedly. "Then you are free. You can
come back to the government service. A government with Communist elements, to be sure, but without their running it for Moscow's benefit. Or, you may move on to Miami or Mexico City or

Tibet. As long as you promise not to join any of the exile groups trying to overthrow me for the CIA. Of course if you break your promise I will have to break the story of the Señora Romano affair. But meanwhile—we are a happy-go-lucky people. We love music and dancing and making love. Those East German commissars aren't going to knock that out of us, are they, Justo? So let us look on the happy side, eh? The Revolution is willing to drop the charges of espionage against you, and to grant you safe passage if you want it. Have your feast with the beautiful Señora, admit the truth about the Revolution, and you have my word, you are a free man."

Then he was on his feet. "It is time to return to the diplomats in their fancy clothes. The Ambassador thinks he can charm me into calling off our guerrilla activities in his country. He says he wants to bring us back into the great Pan-American family. But he is only a bourgeois humanitarian who loves to talk about the Rights of Man while he piles up money in the foreign banks." He embraced me in his bear hug and pounded me on the back. "Now, go well. Enjoy yourself. Make her cry!"

Over his shoulder he called, "Go well, *leoncito*," and when he closed the door behind him he left a vacuum.

I drank more brandy and puffed my cigar and waited. I have no idea how long as time had become scrambled in my head like a message I could not decode. I thought the cognac might clear my brain but it had the effect of clearing one section and beclouding another.

The door opened. Alvarez. "Everything is arranged," he said. "A limousine will take you where you are going as soon as the last of the dinner guests leave. You may wait here if you wish."

"No, I would like to pack—things—books . . ."

"I will take you to the door and wait."

I entered the darkened dormitory and felt under my pillow for my Martí, notes on 'The Dictator,' my one clean shirt. I threw them quickly with my toilet articles into the suede satchel Alejandro Castillo had loaned me at his home in the Lomas a thousand years ago. Then I went to the bathroom to shave so I would look fresh and clean when I came to Adriana. As I studied my face in the mirror I heard a groan. I swung around and pulled aside the shower curtain. A man was lying face down. The shower floor was stained red around his head. I knelt and turned him over. Where Johnie's eyes had been were now small pools of blood. And then I saw through a haze of onrushing nausea an eyeball that had been thumbed out of its socket and was lying on his cheek still attached to its bloody ganglia. The eye that had winked at me nervously— "Abyssinia." It was the eyeball of Johnie Valdez that would do no more snooping and peeping and spying. It throbbed slightly, like a bloody oyster that had been pried out of its shell but that had not been separated from its nerve center.

I turned away to keep from fainting, moving with muscles that had gone soft and quivery. I staggered out and groped to the door where I told Alvarez. He ordered me to go back to his office and wait there until I was summoned.

EPILOGUE

EPILOGUE

1

When Alvarez came for me at last it was late and my hourglass, the cognac bottle, was almost empty. "All right," he said, "ready to move out." It had the snap of a military order and I felt more like a member of a reconnaissance patrol than of a passionate assignation.

I gathered my few belongings and followed Alvarez down the corridor to the marble steps that led to the grand gold-carpeted stairway curving down to the main floor. Then I was back in the pillared, rococo entrance hall through which we had passed on our way into sanctuary.

Now I followed Alvarez out the same side door through which our ebullient Alejandro Castillo had shepherded us after we had traveled like dead lovers sealed in the baggage compartment of his Mercedes. In the driveway a black limousine was waiting. Alvarez held the door open and nodded. There were no false *abrazos*, no farewells. I climbed into the deep back seat of the hearselike vehicle and the door closed behind me. It was dark and the side blinds were drawn.

"Good evening," a man's voice said. I peered through the darkness. I recognized the voice, and the trim silhouette of Tony Cruz, the young assistant in my days of eminence.

I had expected to find Adriana at my side, not this compact watchdog. With his small aquiline nose and neat moustache he looked more like a boulevardier than a revolutionary. In the front seat next to the driver slouched a bodyguard in loose militia uniform. The car was moving forward through the embassy gates. It was not happening to me but to someone else whom I was watching from the dormitory window. I was the watcher and the watched. I had fainted twice before in my life and now as I leaned back against the upholstered seat I felt as I had when the white circles of the pinwheel gradually slow down until you begin to realize what has happened but not yet where you are. I must have glanced in alarm at Tony Cruz because he said, "Relax. You have nothing to fear from us. You will find everything is going to be—very nice."

Then he offered me a cigarette. I shook my head. "Excuse me," he said. "Of course you smoke cigars. I should have brought some. But you will find a full humidor at the villa."

He lit a cigarette for himself, leaning back and crossing his legs in perfect self-containment.

After that there was only silence between us as the limousine drove on through the night. My mind was not leaping ahead to the prospect of Adriana, as I would have expected. It was still coming out of its white circles of the pinwheel. The limousine was only the black hallucination of escape from the dormitory where I was dreaming of Tony Cruz as a nightmare angel of vengeance hovering over my cot. Who would be fool enough to leave the sanctuary only to deliver himself back into the hands of Tony Cruz and the security police?

The limousine seemed to be moving very fast now, as if it were following open highway. The sound of the spinning tires was not so much monotonous as mysterious. Were they leading me to the boudoir or to the wall? The pinwheel circles were floating from my mind like smoke rings toward an open window. "Do you mind if I roll down the window?" I asked Tony Cruz. "The car is at your disposal," he said. "First lever on your left." I touched the small electric switch and the window lowered rapidly. The cool night air rushed in, abrasive and refreshing against my face. I shut my eyes, not to sleep but to think more clearly. Or rather, to begin to think clearly. Think clearly again. I did not know where I was or where I was going. Nor did I understand now why I was going. The black limousine was my destiny racing along an unseen highway. It did not seem like my doing. Surely I had not come to sanctuary to involve myself in bizarre adventure. No, I had come in search of freedom, not an erotic rendezvous but human liberty, the only dignified solution for man. It was easier to think with the wind in my face. I felt as if my mind, mucked and scummed in the stench of the dormitory, was being washed by the wind of the open country. I thought of the wounded deer that throbbed in the verses of Martí, the wounded deer fleeing to the mountain, symbol of his anxiety and sacrifice. I thought of Martí, dying in the purity of his convictions. When had I stopped turning to him for solace? When had I given up my study of martyrs and dictators? When had I begun to seek surcease instead of salvation? When had I chosen to lower myself to crawl to lesser gods and goddesses? Blow, blow, nightwind, fumigate my mind, air out my soul. Let me breathe again. Let me breathe free.

The limousine was no longer speeding. The road was bumpier, and winding. We had turned off the highway. We drove on this way for what seemed like another half-hour. Finally we came to a stop. A gate was opening. We drove on, another few minutes, along a gravel driveway. Then we stopped again, and the chauffeur and the bodyguard got out. The door was opened for me. In the moonlight I saw a stately two-story country villa with a wide balcony overlooking a broad lawn surrounded by tropical gardens. My mind flashed with memory of this place. I had been here before, in the Zamora days. It had been Garbo's country retreat, where we had held many meetings before a *chivato* informed the Tigers of Romano as to what was going on here.

Garbo back in the fold? Was I being taken to a confrontation with him? Or did this mean that he was indeed in captivity and that his villa had been confiscated by the Revolution for its own clandestine meetings? With a sense of foreboding I accompanied Tony Cruz to the entrance. He rang and a male servant came to the door. I remembered the hallway, airy, beautifully tiled, with some of Garbo's collection of modern paintings on the wall.

Tony Cruz said, "Good evening, Vicente. This is the Señor you were expecting."

"Ah yes, welcome, at your service," the quiet major-domo bowed. "I will show you to your rooms."

Tony Cruz turned to me. "You will find everything in order. The villa is at your disposal. We will return for you tomorrow in the early afternoon. Your appearance on television is scheduled for fifteen hundred hours. To be featured on 'News—1700.' "

Five o'clock in the afternoon.

The wind blew away the deceptive cloth/At five in the afternoon.

"Meanwhile, if there is anything you wish, do not hesitate to call on Vicente. Until tomorrow—" and he was gone. As I followed the servant up the stairs, I could hear the door of the limousine slamming shut and the hearse driving off into the night.

Climbing toward the first landing in the wake of the noncommittal servant who carried my small bag, I felt awkward, foolish, out of place. I followed him up the tiled stairway to the second floor, passing a small den with its corner fireplace and red leather furniture, where I had once conferred with Garbo, Doctora Julia and Elena Concepción in our underground days. It was unnerving and unromantic to wonder where Garbo had gone and why Angel had chosen his villa for my rendezvous.

The major-domo led me to a high-ceilinged bedroom with an enormous canopied four-poster bed with a headboard inset with miniature mirrors in gold frames. The colors of the room were bright tropical pinks, leaf greens and marine blues. There was a native painting that caught the colors of the sun. Vicente, like a well-trained bellboy at a grand hotel, showed me the bathroom which was built on three levels and tiled in various shades of blue with exotic motifs that had been copied from the Etruscans. A waterfall controlled by a switch fell from the first level down a mosaic-tiled stairway to the Roman bath below. Sprays and showers seemed to come from everywhere, depending on which button one pushed. The bidet was a swan and it too was blue but so much paler than the rest that it seemed white. These must have been improvements of El Gordo's, before Garbo reclaimed his villa after the Revolution. It was a caricature of the kind of luxurious bathroom one might imagine for serving and intensifying erotic experience. Disoriented, I could not escape the sense of schoolboy's-first-visit-to-the-golden-brothel. Nor the confusing sense of having been spirited to Garbo's country hideaway to carry out some obscure mission I no longer understood.

The soft-spoken servant was informing me that the Señora was already in her connecting suite and that he would announce my arrival as soon as I had had time to refresh myself. He handed me a deep blue tie-silk robe and a pair of slippers.

I nodded but the figure standing here answering to my name was only representing me, as someone in a dream who resembles you and yet manages to be a subconscious variation, at least half a stranger.

I turned to the French windows that opened onto the long balcony. The fabric of the robe was gossamer on my skin. From the balcony I could see the lake lying still and yet alive in the moonlight. There were fruit trees, mango and banana and guava and in the far corner a sturdy stand of bamboo. The air was scented with jasmine and from the woods came a loud, rhythmic call that sounded like tree frogs. I looked up at the close three-quarter moon and felt no exhilaration, no sense of excitement or anticipation, only a dull, what am I doing here on this balcony under that remote reflection of the sun?

I heard a sound behind me and turned back into the room to see Adriana. She was wearing a long cyclamen quilted robe and her abundant hair was soft and flowing. I was aware of the strong bone structure and the large eyes that had made her beauty so celebrated.

How long had it been since I had been this close to her? Fifteen years, for fleeting moments at balls and social gatherings? Staring up at her in her tower room at the Papagayos or in the window across the patio separating the dormitory wings, I had seen a distant vision of the face that glowed in my mind. Now in a room alone with her for the first time, I saw her skin was not the smooth olive warmth that I had imagined but was covered with a careful make-up meant to conceal but actually suggesting the erosion of age.

"*Mi amor*," she said. Her smile furrowed the smooth mask she wore for a face. She stretched her arms out to me. I hesitated. Then I moved forward and embraced her. "At last," she said, "at last." Her cheek pressed against my face and I felt I might suffocate in French perfume.

I tried to make some sound of reciprocation, but I have always been an incompetent liar. I took her hand and said something about ringing for champagne. Had she seen the balcony? We went out together. She breathed deeply and theatrically of the night-blooming jasmine. "It is so exciting, *mi amor*. We will drink our champagne and think of the joys the evening will bring us." With her tongue she made a complete circle of her mouth, a very large mouth with a great deal of lipstick on it.

To be a true instrument of passion one must be totally clear or totally disordered and I had maneuvered myself into limbo. She raised her mouth to me and put her hand to the back of my head. I tasted her lipstick. She parted her lips and I could feel her tongue searching my mouth. In my fantasies of the dormitory, the first touch of her tongue had carried me to a frenzy of pleasure. I closed my eyes and tried to accept the gift. I could hear the call of the tree frogs, noisy and demanding. And the jasmine from the garden gave off the sweet odor of a third-rate bordello.

"*Mi amor, mi amor,*" she was saying. "How perfect everything is. I've waited so long." How many times I had imagined her speaking to me in that throaty voice that suited her so well.

The elderly servant with eyes that asked no questions brought the champagne, the silver ice bucket and goblets, and retired without a sound. I poured the wine, we touched glasses and she stared at me over the rim of her glass with her great, artist-model eyes. As she raised her face to receive my kiss, I put my lips to her mouth briefly. In courtesan fashion she labored to make more of it than was there. I sipped the champagne feeling clod-heavy and ready for ridicule.

"Ah Justo," she whispered and ran her hands down over her robed body, asking mine to follow. I tried. But I was an understudy for the overage lover in one of those Spanish plays that tour the provinces, not up in the lines and with gestures mechanical. Still she moaned and shut her eyes as if I were the most tactile of Don Juans. And she said, in a tone that seemed the perfect instrument for confiding desire, "Let me tell you my secret. Ever since Carlos sent me that jewel box—of course you know what was in it—I would have nothing more to do with him."

"But when he goes to see you?"

"I lie there like a stone."

She had found the punishment to fit the crime. So every time he had returned to the dormitory like the cat who swallowed the fat canary, it was a stage performance for the envious eyes who could not see the lining of humiliation.

I should have been laughing out loud at my victory, but I felt only tight apprehension as she went on in that marvelous voice. "So I come to you almost like a virgin again, Justo." She pushed against me boldly. "Another secret. The day your wife was able to leave, I thought to myself, 'Now he will begin to grow lonely, and restless, and this—this will be searching for a new home.' So I went to the window and began to trap you." She paused for a lovely, selfish smile. "I was always able to have any man who appealed to me."

"Why me, Adriana?"

"Mmm," she murmured, "I've had this desire for a long time. And maybe I love you a little bit extra because my husband hates you so much." Her laugh was beguiling. "But how many reasons does a woman need?"

I began to move my hand away but she would not let it. In spite of an impulse to escape, I made my fingers free the buttons down the front of her robe. I felt her neck, her shoulders. She was still a handsome woman. I urged myself on. If only I could recreate the fantasies that had delighted and tortured me, perhaps I could fulfill this obligation.

She rubbed her hand against my cheek and then she rose. "Turn out the lights, in a moment I will be back, *mi vida.*"

I switched off the lights and the glow of the moon filtered softly through the balcony doors. There were frogs and crickets and the distant cry of owls, but nothing in the tropical night could appeal to me now, as once the fragrance and the birds who came alive in the night had delighted my senses at the Papagayos. I wanted only to be back there with my honest blustery Marta.

I even wished I were back in the dormitory, with my dignity of the early days in the sanctuary, waiting and hoping in good faith for safe passage.

The wind blew mockingly through the upright cluster of bamboo. . . . fool . . . a stronger man would have stood up to prison or asylum life and not lost his grip on his mind, like an airborne balloon that pulls loose its string. But you, poor fool, let it float out through that dormer. There was no Mona Lisa in the window. There was only your refusal to think and work and remain true to yourself. At that moment I so loathed myself that I wanted to lean over the balcony and let the overweight bulk of me drop to the ground. Blot out the past and crush the future. End the comedy. But I thought no, in height it is only one story and a half. I will not die a tragic death. I will fall into a hibiscus bush and fracture my little toe. It is no accident that the one great hero of our literature is Don Quixote. We romancers are never more in character than when we reach the heights of our self-delusion and confuse it with the call to glory and conquest. God help me I was just another demented Quixote making passionate love to elusive moonbeams.

I was mad. I had gone mad. I had done a few sane things in that dormitory, even at the end trying to put Johnie on trial, trying to act the responsible citizen, all the while careening into irresponsibility. Goyo, Johnie, even El Indio in his frenzy of the *paoli,* had recognized the sickness in my eyes and called it by its proper name.

At the bed Adriana drew off her gown and there she was at last, the ultimate distortion of my fantasy. Her large breasts no longer stood high and taunting. Like most abundant bosoms they had fallen until now they hung like the water bags one drapes over the front of an auto on a long drive through the desert. I sat down on the bed and she came to me. Her hand rested on my shoulder and then moved down my chest, making me conscious of my potbelly. Even on the starvation diet of asylum I had not lost that unnecessary flesh. Her fingers moved along my inner thigh until they came to rest. To my discomfort and shame it hung useless in her hand. Her fingers played with a practiced motion, but it felt nothing but its own wretched nakedness.

"You are too excited," Adriana said. "You have waited too long. Lie back."

It reminded me of the patient professional with the straw-yellow hair and the dark patch below who had gentled me through the first of these ceremonies in my first year at the Naval Academy. I lay back and closed my eyes, reaching down to touch her long hair. She took it soft into her mouth, pausing to stroke and tease. *"Mi vida, mi vida, mi gran amor,"* she moaned, and then her knowing mouth went back to its work and in spite of myself it was responding, slowly taking the form she required. When she thought it was ready she ran her tongue from the base to the tip, studied it with satisfaction and brought her body up to mine.

"Now, now, take me, my stallion!"

I mounted her dutifully but the artificial little fire was already extinguished. She made a guttural sound, this time of disgust. I rolled over on my back and told her I was sorry.

"*Pobrecito,*" she said and she lifted it sympathetically, or mockingly, and let it fall back on my thigh like a dead sparrow. Damn my Quixote soul, and the cock who crows grandly because it is mad and then falls from the fence to the floor of the barnyard in limp humiliation. I had had to create my own temptress in order to stage my disenchantment and my punishment.

But why punish this poor lady further? I rose from the bed. I felt completely sane now, lost, disarmed and insignificant but sane as Quixote on his deathbed, freed at last of his illusions and resigned to his epitaph: There are no birds this year in the nests of yesteryear.

"Señora, get dressed," I said. "I am sorry. This is—no reflection on your charms. No, no please do not take it as such. I feel humiliated enough for the two of us. I—it had nothing to do with you. Looking back I—another person—living another life. So—it is time for both of us to—. Then—I wish you good luck. Go back to torturing your husband. And forgive me for seducing you into this—this fiasco."

"I wonder if you will forgive me?" she said, and she was smiling as she began to pull the gown on over her head.

"You?"

"I was lying when I said I singled you out because I was so attracted to you."

"But then—why—?"

"Men only think of my beauty. But I came up from very low to very high. I know many beautiful girls who are still fifty-peso *putas.* The difference is in the mind." She stretched and rose theatrically as if there were a spotlight on her and she was acknowledging applause. "I see you alone and I think how much Angel wants to get his hands on you—you and my General are the ones he wants most —so a clever idea flies into my head: I will make an arrangement with Angel. I will lead you on—promise to meet you here and if you fall into the trap, Carlos and I will receive our safe passage. Without having to give up all of our money."

"I see. You do have a fascinating mind. And when you get to Miami?"

She shrugged.

"You plan to stay with El Gordo?"

"I have little choice. He will still have his Tigers with him. A lot of them are waiting for him there, and if I leave him I leave millions of dollars. Maybe he will die of the gout. It seems to be getting much worse."

"And I thought that El Gordo was the monster. I should have known that monsters only mate with other monsters. Like crocodiles."

"Thank you," she said. "I am sorry, really sorry that we could not have enjoyed this. After we both went to so much trouble. Ah well, c'est la vie! And now I leave you—and your little friend—to whatever awaits you."

I stared at her for the last time, the love of my dormitory life, and then I put my robe on again and went back onto the balcony. The tree frogs were laughing at me. They had a right to. Their sense of self-preservation was stronger than mine. They were not free, they were bound by the demands of their own nature but they did not indulge in fantasy. Tree frogs, so far as I knew, did not condemn other tree frogs to prison because of their political differences. Nor did they surrender themselves to illusion.

2

I remained on the balcony, pacing or leaning against the railing and looking out over the garden until the moonlight haze began to blend into the first morning light. Finally I went back to bed and fell into an exhausted, perspired sleep. An insistent knocking at the door awakened me. I had no idea what time it was but the sun was beating in from the balcony. I went to the door and found Tony Cruz waiting for me.

"Good morning," he said. "We should be leaving for the television station in an hour. There will be a private office there where you and Señorita Elena can work out your statement. I will be waiting for you downstairs."

In the bathroom I glanced at the mosaic Roman bath that seemed a bizarre throwback to some earlier reincarnation. I stared at myself in the mirror and wondered if there had been any connection between my self-deception regarding the physical perfection of Adriana and my self-deception in accepting Angel as the apostle of revolutionary perfection. Both had begun in the same period of Zamora domination and underground romanticism. I shaved slowly, my hand trembling and my mind in disarray. It did not seem just that I must now play out my side of a bargain in which fate had made a mockery of what for one blind period in time I had thought to be a passion worthy of any sacrifice.

Half an hour later I came downstairs and a sweet-faced young maid served me a breakfast of eggs and bacon, hot rolls and real coffee but I could not eat. Too many hungry days of stale sanctuary breakfast had left me out of practice. And this morning in particular my stomach was tight with fear and indecision.

I was ready to make a retraction but not in the debased style of Moscow. The only kind of retraction I could make would endear me neither to Angel nor to the squabbling counter-revolutionaries nor to the smattering of true revolutionaries in exile. An honest reassessment, a reevaluation that would satisfy no Party in the world. In a world of oligarchies, rubber-stamp central committees and loudspeaker politics, I was a groping party of one.

I forced down the rich black coffee half and half with warm country milk. To retract. Not to retract. To speak not the over-simplification but the complex truth. Was that possible on television in the land of Bello—or any other land on either side of the Berlin Wall or the Bamboo Curtain? In time. Maybe in time. It was still too early in the march of man, still a time when people wanted to hear only what they already believed, shouted in the simplistic slogans of television commercials and propaganda.

By the limousine with Tony Cruz stood a young militiaman with a round, pockmarked face that smiled easily. When the militiaman opened the car door for us I heard a hearty *"Hola,* how goes it, compañero?" in that vibrant, self-confident voice that could only be Angel's. Elena Concepción moved over and I found myself sitting between them. Elena had a notebook on her lap and in his weathered hands Angel held a thick report, with scribbled notes in the margin which he had been dictating to her.

"So, you big lion, the mango always looks better at the top of the tree, eh?"

I glanced at Elena who had murmured a greeting and then kept her eyes focused on her notebook. I could feel her thinking of Marta and my guilt was so strong I wished I could disappear into the upholstery.

Long ago Angel had declared a war on silence. If he wasn't talking, people around him were, and filling in the interstices there was always music, Spanish trumpets, guitars, bongos. Now he switched on the radio and music came at us in stereo bombardment. He took two long cigars from his pocket, handed me one and lit it for me.

"Well, all I can say is, I'm sorry, Justo old goat. But we did our part. You know the old saying that the gringos stole from us—you can lead a donkey to a burro but you can't make him—"

"Angel!" Elena said softly without looking up.

Angel laughed like an incorrigible child who enjoys his spankings.

"Angel!" He mimicked her very well, her propriety, her protectiveness, her love.

"You're right, you're right, it is no laughing matter, is it, old friend? I think I can guess the reason for the fiasco. No matter what those *huevos* try to tell you, she's a fascist. And lying down with a fascist is like going out to one of the sows in the barnyard." His laughter drowned out the music. "It's even worse. Sows are useful to the people. Well, I suppose fascists are too, if you use them for fertilizer.

"Put that down," he gestured to Elena. "At last we have found something useful for the Zamoristas. Use them for fertilizer. Or would that poison our fruit and vegetables, Elenita? So that is why you would not eat our queen of the mangos, Justo my boy? It would give you political ptomaine!"

There was no answer. I could not enter the game and I could not blame him for playing it. I felt like the ball caught in the *cesta,* about to be hurled the length of the jai alai court and smashed against the wall.

"Justo, I wish you could have been with us this morning. We flew over to breakfast with the kids on Los Gatos." That was the island just this side of Las Barricudas, where Zamora and the new millionaires had built vacation villas leading down to their private docks and their steamer-sized yachts. "You should see what they're doing there, twenty-year-old professors teaching the fifteen-year-olds, young girls, who would have been whores for the tourists, getting up at dawn to do their work chores before attending classes all day, and then at night meetings on what more they can do to build a new society. It's these teen-agers who are going to make our Revolution, Justo, a new generation that isn't poisoned by money, who work for the fun of sharing, a better motive than profit! You should see them for yourself, how they organize themselves for the common good, how they volunteer— You know what Los Gatos used to be, an is-land of greed and pleasure for the idle rich. Now it's a paradise for children, a working paradise. It might restore your faith."

The car was filling with cigar smoke. Elena waved it patiently away from her face.

"Angel," I said when his voice finally came to rest for a moment like a giant butterfly, "I have not lost my faith. I see your youth brigades, full of fervor and good works. But I also see the vigilante committees who report them for negative remarks, the ostracism of those who don't wish to volunteer, the constant indoctrination . . ."

Angel shook his head and talked across me to Elena. "Señor Yes—But. Every time he opens his mouth a little *mosca* of a But flies out." His laughter shook the ash from his cigar and it dropped on the lapel of his rumpled tunic. "I am Comrade Yes. I say Yes we are making our Revolution. Yes we are giving our people the rich-est life they ever had. Yes our form of Communism is the fullest and freest in the world."

"If only I could be that sure."

"Señor Yes—But."

I was aware of the spring sunshine, of yellow-green rice fields, of thatched roof huts sheltering scrawny chickens and naked brown children shaded by guava and banana trees behind cactus fences that had begun to grow again.

"Justo? You are not very talkative."

"I am enjoying the view. A long time since I've seen the rice country."

"Stop the car and ask those good people," Angel insisted. "Go out and ask them if they are not happier now than they were before."

"That is not the whole question."

"What is the whole question, Señor Yes—But?"

"You would not understand, Angel. With your youth camps and your volunteer labor to make up for the bureaucratic inefficiencies and your mystique of the new man, a new man who still has to be spied on by vigilantes, you would not understand."

"That is where you are wrong, my friend. The Revolution understands everything. Even you. That is why it is giving you a second chance to confess your errors and come back to us. After all, no matter what happened or did not happen, we made a bargain. We lived up to our part. Soon it will be your turn. Are you ready?"

"I—simply do not know."

"But my dear old comrade, you realize that you must know by the time you reach the television station."

"Angel, if you would give me time to explain my position—"

"How long should it take to make a retraction? A simple retraction?"

"Why must everything be simple? Why can't we take all the people into our confidence? They aren't fools. If you ran for election, honestly ran, I think you would win. The very fact that you gave them a chance might bring you a landslide."

"Of course I'd win. Who would vote against me except some bourgeois imperialists and some leftover *gusanos?* So why go to all the trouble of holding elections?"

"So others can be heard, Angel! Other points of view. Let the people grow up to it. If they choose Communism, fine. But—"

"Look, old man, we made a bargain. If the lady was not everything you—"

"The lady is the least of my *desilusión*." I laughed, actually laughed for a moment. It was a good sound in my own ears. "If she had been all the enchantresses in one, I would still be asking you—now that I've come to my senses—begging you to let me do this my way."

Angel studied me quietly, faintly amused.

"And what would you say, comrade, exactly what is it that you are so anxious to say to our people?"

"I would say many positive things about the Revolution. I would make it very clear that I am not a counterrevolutionist."

"Que bueno! If you have changed your mind, that is all we ask."

"But—" I had to weigh my words carefully. Despite Angel's smile and relaxed attitude, they could be my last. "—I have to be true to myself. Don't you see? It is all I have left. I would also have to say that—quite the opposite of a counterrevolutionist—I am a re-revolutionist."

Angel glanced at the noncommittal Elena and then looked at me skeptically. "We are not familiar with that category."

"Of course not. It is not in the catechism. I mean every revolution needs a fresh revolution to keep it honest. The American. The Russian. The Chinese . . . Otherwise it's Thermidor. They freeze. Become fixed. And whether in the name of Capitalism or Communism, repression is reactionary."

Angel shook his head. "You are an incorrigible—professor. The rector of our University, a Party member to boot, had to be exiled to a minor diplomatic post in Europe for saying half of what you are saying. And you expect me to let you go on our television network and—"

"Why not? You think the students are going to storm the television station? Chances are, they will laugh me off as an old-fashioned liberal. But why not take the chance? I'll attack the Yankees and their stupid boycott. They should recognize us since we co-exist whether they like it or not. But I will have to add that I am a die-hard freedomist who believes our people—all people have a right to decide their own fate. And they can only do that if censorship is lifted, if political prisons are emptied, if—"

"What do you think, Elena, should we let him broadcast an open invitation to betray the Revolution?"

Trained sounding board that she was, Elena gave off only vibrations and silence.

"Not betray it, renew it," I said. "Give it back its humanity. I tell you, millions of doubters in the third world, still afraid of neo-Stalinists, will join you in the fight against reaction, the struggle for national liberation. I will give two cheers for you and all you have accomplished. But Angel, I must save that third cheer for socialism without repression. That's where the new wind is blowing. Why shouldn't you put that wind at your back instead of turning into it?"

Angel sucked on his cigar and then puffed a cloud of smoke around it. "You seem to be finding your voice in your old age. I think you talk a lot of bourgeois horseshit but—go ahead! I am in a good mood this morning. Those kids on Los Gatos will be taking over from us sooner or later anyway. So go on television and have your say. I think you are right: the Revolution will survive it. The Revolution will know how to handle—"

At that moment our car came to a screeching, swerving halt. We all rose and leaned forward to see why the militiaman-chauffeur had slammed on the brakes. In the middle of the road was an enormous red sow who could not have been more pregnant or sound asleep. Rice farmers were running from their fields with their cotton work pants pulled above the knees and their mud-caked legs gleaming with paddy water; their women and children from the thatched huts and yards, cluttered but vivid with flowers and fruit trees, came running too. As they neared the car Angel swung the door open and stepped out onto the road. Elena and Tony followed him out and so did I. If I were a prisoner I certainly did not feel like one, more like an old friend returned to the fold.

"A fine place to leave a pig!" Angel was saying in response to excited greetings. "Do you realize every pig is valuable to the Revolution? And a beauty like this one who is about to drop her litter! Shame on you, comrade!"

"I do not know what is the matter with her, Angel," said an old man with very few teeth. "She always liked to sleep in the middle of the road. Even when she was a little one."

The children were shouting "Angel! Angel!" and jumping up on him, one small boy managing to climb up to his shoulders as if he were a fruit tree.

"Well, come on, we all have work to do, let's push the old girl off the road!" Angel leaned down over the sow, laughing and shoving her vigorously from the rear. Villagers joined in, but she resisted them stubbornly. "Now all together, push!" Angel led them. It took a few minutes but finally they managed to get the reluctant sow to her feet and the children were able to drive her off the road.

"What is the name of your village?" Angel asked.

"Santa María de las Flores," said the old man.

"Such a big name for a little place." Angel wiped the sweat from his forehead with his sleeve. "It looks very pretty. How is your rice production, old one?"

"This year will be at least fifteen percent better than last year."

It seemed as if Angel had taught even the lowest of the peasants the fine art of statistics.

"*Que bueno!* And can everyone read?"

"All but the very young and the very old," said the toothless farmer. "My son has been teaching me."

"Now that is what I like to hear! We are grateful to your pig for introducing us to Santa María de las Flores."

"Thank you, my *Jefe,*" said the old man.

"I am not your *Jefe.* When I stepped out of the car you called me Angel. I like that better. In our army we are all privates together."

"Yes, yes, thank you," said the old peasant blinking in the sun, confused by so much familiarity on the part of someone so clearly his superior. "Er—*Jef*—Angel, may we ask you something for our village?"

"Of course. Why not? Speak to me, comrade."

"Well, understand we are not complaining, our life is so much better now. Except for certain things like—not enough sugar. So we have sent our deputy José Luis Aragón to the capital to present our case and now it is already two weeks and—"

Angel beckoned Elena. "Put this down in your notebook, Elenita. Santa María de las Flores Deputy José Luis Aragón—sugar."

While Elena was dutifully recording this, Angel was assuring them, "Okay, little comrades, I will look into it. As soon as I get back to my office I will look for your deputy."

Everybody thanked him and tried to touch him. The old man invited him into his shack to have rice cakes and coffee and he seemed about to accept when Elena patted his elbow. "Angel, the television broadcast. It has been scheduled for three o'clock. If we do not leave immediately—"

"All right, all right!" Angel shouted good-naturedly, for the benefit of the villagers. He always had thrived on these contacts with "the people." He was their father, big brother and loving son. "She is my alarm clock," he laughed at Elena. He kissed a ragged moon-faced little girl who reached up to put her arms around his neck. He kissed, shook hands, patted shoulders, talking all the time as the group love affair moved toward the incongruous limousine.

"Now—that is your real democracy," said Angel, exhilarated, as we finally settled back on the rear seat. "Do they have to vote? They vote with their abrazos. The trouble with you is you are too mental, Justo. You want to count all the votes in your mind. I am feeling for a whole new, happier ambience that comes from the senses." He winked at me and said in unexpected Americanese that sounded more like Johnie Valdez than Angel Bello and that he had probably picked up from some Harlem delegate to one of his revolutionary conferences, "Can you deeg it, ba-bee?"

Still not wasting a moment, he resumed his dictation to Elena Concepción. The spirited music beat on. I leaned back against the upholstery and wondered if he would make good on his promise to send more sugar back to the little village. Chances are he would pass the mission on to an aide who would lose it in the mass of statistics cluttering his desk. But maybe it did not matter. Meanwhile he had left those villagers with hope. And that seemed to be the principal commodity of the Bello Revolution. After a little while I closed my eyes and tried to concentrate on what I would say in what would be either my reintroduction to our national life or my last farewell.

3

Inside the television studio Angel disappeared and Elena excused herself to go to the makeup room. "Please do not think me vain," she apologized. "But when that television camera comes too close it can be cruel."

"Our makeup man might attend to you also," Tony Cruz suggested. I shook my head. "At least powder your forehead. It will absorb the—"

I felt cold and alone. I was aware of the perspiration above my eyebrows. My entire body felt wet and clammy. "No—no, thank you. They do not expect me to look like Gable. If I move them at all it will be with what I have inside my head, not on the outside."

"As you wish. I will take you to the waiting room."

It was a narrow room with a row of wooden chairs and a window opening on a small sound stage. On the other side of the glass two television cameras were focused on El Indio.

"So you caught him," I said.

"No, a friendly agreement. Angel worked it all out with him. Sandungo is announcing his renewed support of the Revolution."

Tony Cruz went over to the old television set in the corner and switched it on, but nothing happened. "It seems to be disconnected."

"*No importa.* I can imagine what he is saying. Has Angel really reversed his decision and given them back their land?"

"Angel learned from the campesinos themselves that the state farm policy was being enforced too rigidly," Tony said evenly. "The fault of the old-line Communists who are going on trial. For certain people in certain areas self-operated cooperatives are more efficient."

El Indio had never allowed himself the luxury, the distraction of political theory. With a single-mindedness some call monomania he thought of nothing but his people and their land. While I, unlike him and Angel, still wandered in a maze of multiple choices, torn by appealing opposites that sent me swinging back toward middle-view.

"—so you see, we are not quite so inflexible as you may have thought," Tony concluded.

There was something about this sudden flexibility that seemed smugly orthodox and stung me to retaliate: "You know what I most admire about Angel? Nothing is ever his fault. He is in charge of everything, he approves administrators, he approves policies, but when they fail they are always the fault of some agrarian bureaucrat or some old-line Communist. And when the people are abused they go around muttering, 'If only Angel knew—' as if he were not the root cause of their protest. It is a system based on mystique, on a god—"

"You are more stubborn than El Indio," Tony interrupted. "Even this peasant leader is willing to admit his mistakes . . ."

"In return for his land! But you know my main concern, freedom to breathe, freedom to dissent. I could accept your faith, Tony. It could be our salvation. If only you could free yourself of the dogma. And the demagogy."

"Old man, it works," Tony said sharply. "And when Angel is ready to—"

"But meanwhile we live with political prisons. Are yours any better than Zamora's? The truth is they're the same ones, the fortresses, the dungeons, the Isla, the same old dice cage simply turned upside down. You boast of the glories of the Revolution by pointing out the number of old Communists being put on trial. I am waiting for the time when people, whether Party members or free spirits, are no longer arrested, put on trial and convicted in twenty-four hours."

"Our tribunals are composed of trustworthy revolutionaries," Tony said, less gently now. "If a case required more than twenty-four hours you may be sure they would ask for more time."

"The Pan-American Commission on Human Rights is not so sure."

"Screw the Commission on Human Rights."

"You have."

His stare was hostile and yet not without pity. "Is that what you intend to say on television?"

"Angel told me to speak my piece."

"So speak it, old man. Spit it out. It will be interesting to hear."

A few minutes after El Indio had done his turn, Tony led me to the recording stage. A young technician showed me to my chair and looped a small microphone around my neck. A few moments later I was joined by Elena who looked handsome in her makeup, more like her old high-styled personality at the Papagayos.

"I will give you a brief introduction," she said professionally. "And then you will be on your own. If you seem to be lagging I will come in with a question. You may talk as long as you wish. *Buena suerte.*"

I glanced up nervously toward the control booth and saw Tony Cruz taking a seat beside Angel. Angel looked relaxed, raising his hand as if to send me an encouraging salute.

The technicians fussed around me. The red eye of the television camera fixed me with its noncommittal stare. I was asked to speak a few lines so they could get my voice level.

I said, "Hello hello do you hear me?"

"Can you speak up just a little?" said a mechanical voice from the control room.

I cleared my throat, which felt tight and dry. Elena poured me a glass of water and I swallowed it slowly. I could feel the perspiration beading on my forehead again. Angel had told me to speak my mind but who could forecast his weathervane personality? "This is Justo Moreno Suárez getting ready to say one two three four . . ."

"Perfecto!" said the loudspeaker.

"All right, this is sound and picture," said the director. "When the stage manager points at you, begin, Elena."

The stage manager held up his hand dramatically and when it fell, Elena said:

"Good evening, comrades. With me in the studio tonight is Justo Moreno Suárez. As you know he resigned from the presidency, thereby giving aid and comfort to the enemies of our great Revolution. Now he returns voluntarily to tell you with complete candor how he feels about the old regime and the new society cast in the image of Angel Bello." She turned to me with an engaging but now practiced smile. "Señor Moreno, is it true that if you had it to do all over again you would support Angel against Zamora?"

I took a deep breath like a high-jumper trying a height he has never cleared. "Let there be no doubt as to how I feel about Zamora and all the American puppets. I know the fable of the shark and the sardines. I do not need any lessons on what Wall Street and its American marines did to Nicaragua—they deboned that sardine—or to Cuba or Haiti or Panama or Guatemala or the Dominican Republic, or to Mexico until Cárdenas cut off their oil. So I would back any nationalist movement against any Yankee colonialism. Compare Angel to Zamora and the American leeches who kept him in power and I say, Viva Angel, at least that sick chapter is over. That virus will never infect our people again."

Elena looked pleased. "Thank you, Justo Moreno, you speak as an honest man not afraid to admit his mistakes. And I understand that you also approve of many of the policies that Angel is introducing?"

"Yes, I freely acknowledge that. Any fair-minded person would see tremendous improvements. I see the schools, the illiteracy program, I see the hospitals, I see a new generation willing to sacrifice selfish comforts for social progress. I see the campesinos developing a pride they never knew before. I see a small nation that has never known anything but the colonial yoke at last beginning to taste its independence. Even a sense of hemispheric destiny."

I glanced up at Angel who was nodding and smiling, and at Tony Cruz who was waiting to hear what I might say next.

"And so I say Viva to the end of gringo domination. And Viva the clearing of the slums, the building of the schools, the expulsion of the sugar profiteers—"

"Justo Moreno Suárez," Elena spoke as if on cue, "our people, our country, our Revolution thank you for this courageous statement."

"But wait, I am not finished." I drank quickly from the water glass. "I have told Angel I could give two cheers for his Revolution. And I have done so. But I reserve the final cheer for restoration of intellectual freedom. If only Belloism with all its accomplishments, its removal of the old garbage, could itself be moved forward through a fresh rebellion! Can't there be total welfare without totalitarianism? I say Yes if we respect our individual selves and do not bury them in mass sacrifice to human gods."

Elena's discomfiture was overt now; she was drawing away as if to disengage herself from my heresy.

"So I say to the new social conscience, *Sí!* To the block vigilante squad, *No!* To the new ideal of voluntary service to revolutionary society, *Sí!* To compulsory labor in the fields disguised as voluntary, *No!* To mass education of our peasant children, *Sí!* To their indoctrination as depersonalized cogs in a Youth Machine, *No!* To the release of new creative energies, *Sí!* To their censorship and repression by state orthodoxy, *No!"*

I paused to glance at Angel again. He still seemed perfectly composed. Perhaps I was breaking through. But the face of Tony Cruz suggested otherwise. And Elena had become a frieze of disaffiliation. I knew I should stop but my visions carried me on.

"Ladies and gentlemen, I call on my North American friends to lift their shortsighted blockade and to recognize us as a living, breathing, proudly functioning people. And I call on Angel and my friends here at home to recognize us dissenters as living, breathing, responsible citizens too. I say liberalize our Communism. Take it out of its straitjacket. I call for a new society based on liberated individuals voluntarily joined together in modern revolution. Angel represents a heady but primitive step along that road. I remain a revolutionist still hopefully in search of the human revolution. Viva Angel! Viva the Revolution! And beyond them Viva the revolution that says with Camus, 'If absolute truth belongs to anyone in this world it certainly does not belong to the man or party that claims to possess it.' " I looked up at the control booth for a long moment. "Thank you, my comrades, and good night."

The end of my talk was greeted with silence. But I did not feel crushed by the lack of response. Had I expected applause? At least for this moment I was no longer Don Quixote but his master Cervantes, stronger and more free in his Algerian prison than when ransomed home to authoritarian Spain.

Angel had disappeared from the control booth. Tony Cruz was looking down at me. I watched him move toward the side exit and when I turned back Elena was quickly closing the stage door behind her. Even the technicians had disappeared. The silence made a rushing sound. Then I heard shoe leather approaching smartly and Tony Cruz was there.

"Moreno Suárez, you will come with me."

We were on the main highway from the capital driving south, toward the beach at Papagayos. When we reached a key intersection, Tony Cruz looked up from a report he was reading, gave an order and we turned onto a road I had not traveled before.

"I find it interesting," I said, "that the political credo none of you want to hear now is the same one that Angel defended so fervently and that you all once applauded with such gusto."

Tony continued making notes on his report.

"I still believe that credo is the only way for a clean revolution. I would bet anything on it. Everything!"

"You have," Tony said.

We drove on for another hour. The land became marshy and covered with mangrove trees. I saw some white egrets flying. A great blue heron was wading in a shallow canal along the road. We were approaching the sea. When we reached the small fishing village and pocket-sized port of Mariano, I knew where we were going. Isla de Las Barricudas. On the modest *malecón* the limousine drew up in front of a rotted dock and Tony Cruz and the smiling militiaman escorted me to a government launch. It was a thirty-minute ride skimming across the blue-green bay. The island had been and was meant to be a tourist paradise. It rose proudly out of the sea. There were white beaches and coconut palms and the water was famous for its clarity.

Tony and his militiaman led me to the receiving officer. I was fingerprinted and asked to fill out a questionnaire. When it came to Political Affiliation—I wrote: Former President of the First People's Republic. I was issued not really a prison uniform but a loose white muslin pajama suit like the traditional apparel of the campesinos. Only it had a number stenciled over the breast pocket.

Tony spoke to me. "You may have heard that prisoners never return from Las Barricudas. That is not entirely true. Under exceptional conditions—" He paused. "In any event, your case will be reviewed by Angel and his Minister of Justice—"

"Juan del Campo?"

"Juanito is now your fellow-prisoner here on the Isla," Tony said. "He was tried and found to be a traitor. Loyal to Moscow."

"Where did *he* go wrong?"

"He was one of the group who made the mistake of pushing the state farm policy too far. Slavish imitation of the Russians. We are nationalist Communists who put our country first. Our own International."

Not the Fourth, I thought. By now it must have been the Fifth, the Sixth, the Seventh . . . Once long ago I had sung "The International shall be the human race." But which International? The human race was a mechanical rabbit chased by a brace of yelping whippets with different numbers on their backs.

A guard in a dirty uniform took me to my cell. It was neither small nor large, just bare, with a cot, a corner latrine and a barred window. I looked out at a sandy courtyard. A dozen prisoners, six on each side, were playing soccer under the hot sun. The game would not have been more fiercely fought if it had been for international honors. The ball was kicked hard down the field and a short, burly, hairy-chested man blocked it neatly, ran forward from his goal and gave it a tremendous sail up the field. I recognized Gorilla Ortiz, the famous old goalie of our national selection. His kick was intercepted by a slight, sandy-haired man in soiled white shorts that hung to his knees. He began to work the ball down the field in excellent style. His legs looked too thin for him to run on them so swiftly. I stared at him. It was Claude Lewison, a long way from the rooftop-bar of the Press Club. My mind floated back—where would the two of us be now if only he had not insisted on that third double daiquiri?

No more of that. The destiny of any single man cannot balance on the rim of a cocktail glass.

I watched the game until Lewison's side scored. With a perfectly played head shot, he had passed the ball to a forward who had kicked an angled goal past the expert blockage of Gorilla Ortiz. Claude Lewison, his tattered T-shirt and baggy shorts soaked in sweat, had hugged his teammates with passion, like the joyous old Cambridge-man he was. He had been a graceful, slender, urbane man in his early thirties when I saw him last. Now he looked so thin and narrow-chested and hollow-cheeked that he seemed not to be of any age, like the human creatures one remembers from pictures of Devil's Island. Except that he was cheerful, unmistakably cheerful.

The window of my cell was about twelve feet above the level of the field. As he passed, I called to him. He looked up, and called back, "Moreno Suárez. Greetings!"

I nodded. "I wish we could talk."

He smiled amiably like a passerby one might pause to greet on Berkeley Square. "And why not? I'll drop in on you after I've had a wash. Sorry they caught you but—they're awfully good at that sort of thing you know." He strolled off with his arm around a fellow-player.

I was still staring out at the sea beyond the far wall of the yard when the guard Celestino brought Lewison to my cell. I was surprised that they would let us visit this way. "Oh, they are not a bad lot really," he said casually. "I've been in worse jails—in Turkey one time. Rat-infested and the guards were all monsters who enjoyed our discomfort. These are all rather nice chaps. Good-natured and easygoing. And luckily my embassy keeps me in pesos to improve their disposition. They won't hurt you unless they have specific orders."

"How long have you been here?"

"Since shortly after I saw you."

"Can't your government get you out? Surely they know you are innocent of espionage."

"On the contrary, old boy, they know I am guilty."

"Guilty! What have they done to you?"

"Oh come now, you don't believe that old brainwashing business? Bloody old-fashioned rubbish."

"But—how could you be guilty?"

"Very simple. Because I was working for British Intelligence. My cover is blown now so why bother to hide it any longer? I wasn't trying to overthrow the state like the silly-ass CIA but I was giving Garbo money to help finance his new underground. And of course passing on information about it to my superiors in London."

"Are you joking with me? They haven't tortured you?"

"Nonsense. They treat us rather well, considering the shortages. One of these days maybe we'll catch one of their chaps and I'll be exchanged. Meanwhile I read and play soccer and make the best of it."

"It can't be—Angel was right? I can't believe it. An actual liaison between you and Garbo?"

"Oh come off it, old boy. You are as guilty as the rest of us. Why play the innocent with me? You know they caught you dead to rights. Why would you go on the telly and beat your chest about the evils of Zamora and his Wall Street friends and the wonders of Angel and his Revolution of Boy Scouts? I would have done the same thing if I had the chance. Anything to escape the ruddy wall, eh, comrade?"

"Then you heard about the broadcast?"

"Heard about it? The Comandante kept us all in the mess hall after lunch and showed it to us on the tube. Quite a show. Everybody whistled when Angel's lady came on at the end and thanked you for having the courage to admit your change of heart and urge support for the Revolution."

"At the end? That was only the first half. In the second half—"

"There was no second half, dear boy."

"But what I said on the other side—about censorship, block committees, absolutism . . . ?"

"Not on our telly, old chap. It ended just as I tell you, with Missy Elena righteously thanking you for your contribution to the cause, then Over and Out."

I saw he was telling the truth. So that was why Angel had been having such a good time in that control booth. I was careful to say no more. Was Lewison here to report on me and thereby shorten his own period of confinement? He chattered on about prison routine. But when the guard came to take him back to his own cell and he bade me a cheery farewell I stared after him, no longer sure of anything. Waiting for Celestino to return with the writing materials I had requested, I watched the sun's slow plunge, like a fireball, into the waiting sea. I leaned my head against the bars and tried to picture where Marta was this very moment. Marta. Marta.

Later I picked up a pencil and began to write. *Now that I am here waiting, I try to remember . . .*

POSTSCRIPT

At least I have accomplished something in this tunnel of time. I have put it down as I remembered it. Now if I can smuggle out this manuscript others will learn of the mockery of Article V.

Once again there are footsteps approaching in the corridor. One more night to wonder at their meaning. A threatened invasion could convince Angel that the time has come to send me to the wall. Or are they coming to invite me back to that unpredictable Revolution? I could be a peace offering to Tío Sam with whom Angel was ready to make an accommodation. Or—has there been a counter-revolution over which they hoped I would throw the mantle of legitimacy?

Of the outside world we know only what the Comandante wishes us to know so we are left with elusive shadows, imagined events. Anything seems possible. Angel the student democrat has become a Communist god. In his final frustration Bolívar had been driven to repudiate his lifelong political faith and become a dictator. In his next seasonal reincarnation, Angel could become once more the apostle of social justice tempered with mercy. Bolívar had said in his dying breath that he and Jesus and Don Quixote were idiots three. What shall I say if they take me trembling to the wall and ask me to embrace once more our necessary but culpable, our treacherous but inspirational Revolution?

Long live Angel. May he yet commit himself to that final idiocy—forever to seek the unobtainable—liberty and justice for all. The village idiot and the dictator, each makes strange sounds and thinks he is a god. Long live the final idiocy, the final rebellion! I see a socialism without bars, a revolution without firing squads, a brotherhood of men who have forgotten, in some future century, how to despise and torture and destroy each other . . .

Thus at the wall would speak Justo Moreno Suárez, who failed. Failed to speak when words still might have been a factor. Failed to act when action was still a possibility. The making of a dictator . . . indecision apathy default. Into the vacuum storm the *caudillos*, the strongmen, the *Gran Chingones* of the Right or of the Left. It is the well-intentioned passivists who make dictators, human weakness feeding inhuman strength. Maybe that is what has drawn me to Angel all these years. Still rejecting his excesses, I am drawn to him as the tack to the magnet.

My quest is over. I am the making of a dictator. I and all the self-righteous to-be-or-not-to-be's who wait and when we take our stand take it too late. For Hamlets and pliant peasants and the student phalanx, Angel is necessity. Thus confesses Justo Moreno Suárez, who waits.

The footsteps are closer now. The men who play God come closer. Whether I will join them or defy them I do not know. I can neither deify our Revolution nor deny it. I only know that we must make our Revolution and break it and remake it, to the end of our days. The footsteps come down the corridor like summer thunder. And toward that thunder I lean my ear forward to catch the first or last flutter of hope.

Los Angeles
Bellagio
Mexico City
San Juan

June, 1969

ABOUT THE AUTHOR

BUDD SCHULBERG, noted author, film writer, and teacher, was born in New York City, raised in Hollywood, and graduated from Dartmouth College with honors in Sociology. Mr. Schulberg is best known for his novels, *What Makes Sammy Run?*, *The Harder They Fall*, *The Disenchanted*, and his award-winning screenplay, *On the Waterfront*. His novel on the same subject won a Christopher Award. *Sanctuary V* is the author's first novel with a Latin background in more than ten years.

Mr. Schulberg, founder of the Watts Writers Workshop and editor of *From the Ashes*, is also known for his short stories, articles, and essays, which have appeared in *Esquire, The Saturday Review, The New Yorker, Playboy, Harper's,* and other national magazines. Currently he is writing "The Schulberg Report" for the Newsday Syndicate, succeeding his friend John Steinbeck, and is involved with Elia Kazan on a film with a Puerto Rican background. He also has another novel "in the notebook stage." He is known for an unusually wide range of interests, from boxing to Mexican archaeology to the Black arts movement to Hollywood history and critical commentary. He is married to actress Geraldine Brooks and divides his time between Los Angeles and Mexico City.